"Laura Lee Guhrke is always
a delight to read."
Christina Dodd

∽ ◦◦ ∽

Supremely sensible Emmaline Dove wishes to
share her etiquette expertise with London's readers, and as secretary to Viscount Marlowe, Emma
knows she's in the perfect position to make her
dream come true. Marlowe might be a rake with a
preference for can-can dancers and an aversion to
matrimony, but he is also the city's leading publisher, and Emma is convinced he's her best
chance to see her work in print . . . until she discovers the lying scoundrel has been rejecting her
manuscripts without ever reading a single page!

As a publisher, Harry finds reading etiquette
books akin to slow, painful torture. Besides, he
can't believe his proper secretary has the passion
to write anything worth reading. Then she has
the nerve to call him a liar, and even resigns
without notice, leaving his business in an uproar
and his honor in question! Harry decides it's time
to teach Miss Dove a few things that aren't
proper. But when he kisses her, he discovers that
his former secretary has more passion and fire
than he'd ever imagined, for one luscious taste of
her lips only leaves him hungry for more . . .

By Laura Lee Guhrke

AND THEN HE KISSED HER
SHE'S NO PRINCESS
THE MARRIAGE BED
HIS EVERY KISS
GUILTY PLEASURES

*If You've Enjoyed This Book,
Be Sure to Read These Other*
AVON ROMANTIC TREASURES

AUTUMN IN SCOTLAND *by Karen Ranney*
A DUKE OF HER OWN *by Lorraine Heath*
HOW TO SEDUCE A DUKE *by Kathryn Caskie*
SURRENDER TO A SCOUNDREL *by Julianne MacLean*
TWO WEEKS WITH A STRANGER *by Debra Mullins*

Coming Soon

CLAIMING THE COURTESAN *by Anna Campbell*

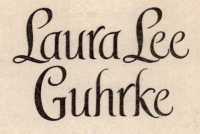

Laura Lee Guhrke

And Then He Kissed Her

An Avon Romantic Treasure

AVON BOOKS

An Imprint of HarperCollinsPublishers

This is a work of fiction. Names, characters, places, and incidents are products of the author's imagination or are used fictitiously and are not to be construed as real. Any resemblance to actual events, locales, organizations, or persons, living or dead, is entirely coincidental.

AVON BOOKS
An Imprint of HarperCollins*Publishers*
10 East 53rd Street
New York, New York 10022-5299

Copyright © 2007 by Laura Lee Guhrke
ISBN: 978-0-06-114360-1
ISBN-10: 0-06-114360-X
www.avonromance.com

First Avon Books paperback printing: March 2007

Avon Trademark Reg. U.S. Pat. Off. and in Other Countries, Marca Registrada, Hecho en U.S.A.
HarperCollins® is a registered trademark of HarperCollins Publishers.

Printed in the U.S.A.

10 9 8 7 6 5 4 3 2 1

For my critique partners,
Rachel Gibson and Candis Terry.
Without your support and encouragement,
I could never have written this book.
I'm more grateful than I can say.
Thank you.

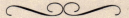

Chapter 1

Working for a handsome man is fraught with difficulties. To those girl-bachelors so employed, I recommend an unflappable temperament, an unbreakable heart, and plenty of handkerchiefs.

Mrs. Bartleby
Advice to Girl-Bachelors, 1893

"Why?" The exotic, raven-haired creature in tangerine silk started to cry. "Why has he done this to me?"

Miss Emmaline Dove did not venture a reply to that question. Practical, as always, she saved her breath and pulled out a handkerchief. She handed it to the woman on the other side of the desk without a word.

Juliette Bordeaux, the now-former mistress of Emma's employer, Viscount Marlowe, snatched

1

the offered square of cambric. "Six blissful months we have had together, and when I receive from his footman the pretty little box, I am happy. But then I find a letter with the present, a letter which ends our amour. *Mon Dieu!* He thinks with jewels to soften the blow that shatters my heart! How cruel he is!" She bent her head and sobbed with an abandonment that was wholly French and somewhat theatrical. "Oh, Harry!"

Emma shifted uncomfortably in her chair and cast a glance at the ormolu clock on her desk. Half past six. Marlowe could return any minute, and she wanted to speak with him about her new manuscript before he went on to his sister's birthday party.

She was fairly certain he'd be back to his offices yet this evening. The present she had purchased for Lady Phoebe on his behalf was still here, wrapped and waiting. Unless he had forgotten the evening's festivities altogether, which she had to admit was not an unheard-of possibility, he had to fetch the gift from here before going home.

This was her best chance to speak with him, she knew, for he was leaving on the morrow for a week at his estate in Berkshire. With no meetings to be rushing off to and no deals to negotiate, and with his family remaining in town, he would have leisure time at Marlowe Park. Emma hoped the serene atmosphere of the country would put him in a more relaxed frame of mind and enable him to see her work in a more favorable light than he had in the past. It was worth a try anyway.

Emma's gaze moved to the typewriting machine on her credenza and the tidy stack of manuscript pages beside it. Her own birthday was only eight days from now, and if Marlowe agreed to publish her writing at last, what a wonderful birthday present that would be.

Suddenly, a vague disquiet stole over her, something so at odds with the delicious sense of anticipation she'd been savoring a moment before that Emma was startled. It was a feeling hard to define, but there was dissatisfaction in it, and a sense of restlessness.

She tried to dismiss it. Perhaps she was just afraid of another rejection. After all, Marlowe had rejected her four previous literary efforts. He felt etiquette books were unprofitable, but Emma knew that was because the advice offered in most of them was hopelessly old-fashioned, not at all in keeping with this modern age. In light of that, she had worked especially hard with her newest manuscript to create something fresh and current. If she could just explain to Marlowe why this new book would have popular appeal, he might be more receptive to it, especially if he was then able to read it with no distractions in the relaxed atmosphere of the country.

Miss Bordeaux, however, showed no sign of departing. Emma studied the distraught woman on the other side of the desk, trying to find a polite way of getting her out the door. If Marlowe's former mistress was still here when he returned, the pair would no doubt have a row, any conversation Emma wished to have with her employer about her book would be impossible, and a golden opportunity would be lost.

Some might have deemed her inattention and lack of sympathy toward the woman opposite to be coldhearted. But that was not really so. As Marlowe's secretary for five years now, she had seen the viscount's mistresses come and go, and she had learned long ago that love had little to do with such arrangements. Miss Bordeaux was a cancan dancer in a music hall who accepted money from gentlemen in exchange for her favors. She could hardly expect love to result from such an illicit liaison.

But perhaps, Emma reflected, these observations were unfair. His lordship did have a potent effect upon many members of the female sex. Some of his appeal, no doubt, was due to the fact that he was one of Britain's rarest commodities: an eligible peer with money. But there was more to it than that. Whenever Harrison Robert Marlowe entered a room where women were present, there was always an inordinate amount of fluttering, hair-patting, and sighing.

Resting her elbow on the desk and her cheek in her hand, Emma considered her employer with thoughtful detachment as Miss Bordeaux continued to weep over him with dramatic fervor.

He was handsome. A woman would have to be blind not to notice that. His eyes, a most extraordinary shade of deep blue, were all the more striking because of his dark brown hair.

He was a well-proportioned man, too, very tall, with fine, wide shoulders. He had wit and a boyish sort of charm, the latter trait enhanced by what could only be described as a devastating smile.

Emma imagined that smile without feeling any increase in the pace of her pulse, but she hadn't always been immune. There had been a time early in her employment with the viscount when she had felt that fluttering, feminine thrill at the sight of his smile. In the beginning, she had even patted her hair and sighed a time or two. But she'd realized early on that nothing honorable could come of such hopes. Aside from their difference in station, Marlowe was a thorough scapegrace, whose only associations with women were of the most dishonorable sort. As his secretary, she regarded his reprobate private life as none of her business, but as a virtuous woman, she had ridded herself of any romantic notions about him long ago.

Any other female with sense ought to be able to see the flaws in his character as clearly as she did. He had divorced his wife for adultery and desertion, a scandalous proceeding that had taken five years to obtain and had shocked all of society. His family felt the social stigma of it to this very day. Whether his wife's infidelity had brought about his contempt for marriage or had only served to make that contempt obvious was anyone's guess, but those who read Marlowe Publishing's weekly periodical, *The Bachelor's Guide*, knew from the viscount's editorial page that he approved of matrimony as much as he approved of slavery—pronouncing the former merely a manifestation of the latter.

His past actions and cynical views should have impelled women to regard him as a poor prospect for future happiness and steer clear, but strange as it seemed to practical Emma, the opposite was true. His well-known vow never to wed a second time only seemed to enhance his attraction and make him an irresistible challenge. There were many women of all classes who dreamt of being the one to capture Marlowe's unyielding heart. Emma was far too sensible to be among them. Rakes had never held any charm for her.

She studied the crying woman opposite, thought of Marlowe's beguiling smile, and her conscience began to smite her. Not all women were possessed of good sense. Perhaps the dancer had been foolish enough to fall in love with him and had hoped for his love in return. Perhaps his abandonment had hurt her deeply. Emma's experience with affairs of the heart was not extensive—she'd had only one to her credit a decade earlier—but she still remembered how painful heartbreak could be.

She opened a drawer of her desk and pulled out a cardboard box of pink and white stripes. "This entire business must be very distressing for you," she murmured as she lifted the lid off the box. "Will you have some chocolates? I find them most comforting in situations such as this."

The woman across from her did not seem to regard the offered candy as a kindness. She lifted her head, sniffed, and eyed the box with disdain. "I do not eat chocolates," she said and blotted her rouged cheeks with the handkerchief. "They ruin the figure." She paused, giving Emma a critical glance across the desk. "Although you should certainly eat more of them, *chérie*, for you could do with the padding. Not that it matters," she added at once. "A spinster does not worry about her figure, *n'est-ce pas?*"

Emma stiffened. *Spinster.* That stung.

Her strange, restless discontent returned, stronger this time, and she realized the cause was her impending birthday.

She put the chocolates away and tried to adopt a philosophical attitude. Turning thirty was just something that happened. To everyone. It was a fact, one she could do nothing about. Granted, thirty sounded rather . . . old . . . but it was just a birthday. Nothing to make one upset.

As for her figure, it wasn't as if her shape had *anything* to do with her unmarried state. She gave Miss Bordeaux's jutting bosom a resentful glance and tried to tell herself a French cancan dancer's opinion didn't matter anyway.

"So you are Miss Dove." The Frenchwoman studied her with an intensity that was quite rude. "His secretary."

Those words were spoken in an assessing, calculated sort of way that put Emma on guard. Readying herself for more thoughtlessly cruel remarks, she replied, "I am Miss Dove, yes."

The dancer laughed, but to Emma's ears there was no humor in it. "Marlowe would have a woman for a secretary. It is so like him. Tell me, does he keep you in a flat, or in a house?"

Emma bristled. This was not the first time others had cast aspersions upon her character. She was employed by a man in a man's position, and her employer's reputation with women was a notorious one. But none of that meant she had to allow reprehensible assumptions about her virtue to go unchallenged. "You are mistaken. I am not—"

"It does not matter." Miss Bordeaux gave a dismissive wave of her hand. "Now that I have seen you, I know you are no threat to me. Marlowe does not like flat-chested women."

Emma made a smothered sound of outrage. She wanted to offer a cutting reply, but she knew that would be foolish. There was always the possibility that the dancer and Lord Marlowe would reconcile, and she could not afford to risk her position for the momentary satisfaction of losing her temper. Though it galled her, she held her tongue, just as she had done so many times in her life before.

Besides, she acknowledged to herself with wry chagrin, her anger was hardly of a virtuous kind. It was the dancer's dismissal of her as too old and too thin to compete for a man's affection that had gotten under her skin, not the assumption that she was a kept woman.

"*Non,*" Miss Bordeaux continued, interrupting Emma's train of thought, "it is not you for whom Marlowe has abandoned me." She leaned forward, and her black eyes narrowed. "Who is she?"

Putting aside the rather petty desire to fabricate a *small-bosomed* mistress for her employer, Emma said primly, "That is his lordship's business, mademoiselle, not mine."

"It does not matter, for I shall learn her identity in time." Miss Bordeaux cast aside the damp, wadded-up handkerchief, and her tear-stained face took on a hard expression that made her seem older—by ten years, at least, Emma decided. Not that she would ever stoop to being catty.

"Miss Dove," the dancer went on, "since you are Lord Marlowe's secretary, you may give him a message from me." She opened her reticule and pulled out a dazzling chain of yellow topaz and diamonds set in gold. "Tell him this pitiful excuse for a necklace is an insufferable insult, and I will not stand it!" She flung the string of jewels on the desk with contempt. "I shall not be bought off with such a paltry thing as this!"

Emma had gone on an exhaustive shopping expedition the week before, not an uncommon occurrence, for Marlowe was hopeless when it came to the choosing of gifts and remembering the occasions on which to give them, and she had long ago taken over that task on his behalf. Not only had she found Lady Phoebe's birthday present, she had also purchased the necklace Miss Bordeaux found so unappealing.

Though she didn't mind buying presents for

his family, she had always regarded finding gifts for Marlowe to give his various mistresses one of the more distasteful tasks of her job. She was certain it could not be a proper thing for her to be doing. Aunt Lydia, were she still alive to see it, would have been appalled, for she had instilled within her niece the most scrupulous attention to proper behavior. Nonetheless, Emma felt a bit miffed at the dancer's condemnation of her judgment. She had put a great deal of thought into the purchase, spending nearly an hour at the jeweler's on Bond Street, though in all fairness, she had wasted some of that time lingering over the lovely emeralds and indulging in a bit of wishful thinking.

She had finally chosen a necklace for the dancer she felt was just right. It was expensive enough, yet not too expensive—it was meant to be a parting gift, after all. It was also big enough and gaudy enough for others to admire through opera glasses at the opera, and eminently salable should the woman ever need funds. Emma had thought that important, deeming the job of mistress a precarious one at best.

Miss Bordeaux did not seem to agree with her judgment in such matters. "Topaz?" she cried. "Topaz is all I am worth to him? This necklace is a trinket, a *bagatelle*, a mere nothing!"

This particular trinket would have kept Emma in funds for a dozen years, but it was clear Miss Bordeaux was not so thrifty.

"He casts Juliette aside like a worn boot, believing a necklace of topaz sent by a servant will pacify her? *Non!*" Miss Bordeaux jumped to her feet.

Breathing hard, her dark eyes glittering with tears of fury, she leaned over the desk. "This pathetic offering is nothing to me!"

These theatrics only served to make Emma all the more impassive. "I shall convey your message to the viscount," she said without emotion, "and I shall inform him that you have returned his gift." Hoping this uncomfortable scene was now at an end, she moved her hand to pick up the necklace from the desk.

Miss Bordeaux was quicker than she, snatching back the string of jewels before Emma's hand had even touched it. "Return it? *Non!* Unthinkable. Did I say so? How could I return a gift, however trivial, from the man I love? The man who has been my dear companion? The man to whom I have given all my affection?" She clasped the necklace to her bosom. "Though he has broken my heart, I love him still, and I have no choice but to accept my fate and suffer."

Emma heartily wished the temperamental dancer would go do her suffering somewhere else.

Miss Bordeaux sank back down in the chair. She once again began to sob. "He has abandoned me," she moaned. "I am unloved. I am alone. Like you."

Resentment flared inside Emma, not toward the dancer, but instead toward Marlowe, for it was he who had put her in this impossible position. A secretary, even a female one, did not have to bear the tantrums of her employer's mistresses, surely.

Emma reminded herself that the viscount paid her a very generous salary, just as much as he would have paid a man. It was far more than she could have expected, as a mere woman, to receive from any other employer. She ought to be grateful, but she did not feel grateful. She felt decidedly cross.

What was the matter with her today? Resenting Marlowe for having horrid mistresses and rejecting four of her books, resenting the world because she could not afford emeralds, resenting the fact that all the chocolates in the world could not increase the size of her bosom, resenting fate because she was no longer young and had never been beautiful. Absurd, all of it.

Thirty is not old.

For a woman of her situation in life, she was very fortunate. An unmarried woman of staunch morals with no family had few options. Unlike the poor girls who slaved away in match factories or shops, her duties were both challenging and interesting, often enabling her to exercise her intelligence and her ingenuity. Most important of all, she wanted to be a published writer, and her employer was a publisher, making him her best hope to someday see her books in print.

As her own literary creation, Mrs. Bartleby, would have said, a woman of true gentility endures what she must, and does it gracefully.

With a resigned sigh, Emma handed Miss Bordeaux another handkerchief.

Harry was late. This was a rare occurrence nowadays, but not because Harry had ever been a punctual sort of person. In fact, he was known to be the most absentminded man alive about times and dates and other such things, but he was also fortunate enough to possess the most efficient secretary in London. Usually Miss Dove kept Harry's schedule running with the precision of the British rails, but today was an exception.

Not that Miss Dove could be blamed in any way. Harry had encountered the Earl of Barringer outside Lloyd's this afternoon and had taken that opportunity to once again bring up the topic of purchasing Barringer's *Social Gazette*. Harry knew the earl was in Queer Street at present, his financial situation perilous. Despite that, Barringer was reluctant to sell because he considered his own publication far superior to any of Harry's less high-minded ones and considered himself far superior to Harry. He had also opposed Harry's divorce proceeding in the House of Lords, orating at tiresome length about the sanctity of marriage.

Despite their mutual animosity, the two men had managed to be civil long enough to spend the afternoon discussing a possible sale. In the end, however, they had been unable to come to terms.

Harry loved making deals and making money.

Business was child's play to him, exhilarating, fun, and far more profitable than his title and estate, neither of which could earn a peer a shilling nowadays. The challenge of trying to persuade Barringer to sell him the *Gazette* for less than the exorbitant hundred thousand pounds he was demanding had put all other matters out of Harry's mind. If the earl hadn't ended their meeting by announcing his intent to attend the opera that evening, Harry might have forgotten all about Phoebe's twenty-first birthday, and the fat would have been in the fire.

He was out of the hansom cab before it had even rolled to a complete stop outside the offices of Marlowe Publishing, Limited. "Wait here," he instructed the driver over his shoulder as he headed for the entrance door of the darkened building. He reached in his pocket to retrieve his key, then unlocked the door and went inside. He ran for the nearest set of stairs, familiarity guiding his way in the dark, and he took the steps two at a time.

As he approached the top, Harry could see that the gaslights were on in his suite of offices, and he could hear the rapid, staccato rhythm of a typewriting machine.

Miss Dove was still here, a fact which Harry did not find remarkable in the least. He had come to understand long ago that outside the walls of this building, Miss Dove had no life.

She stopped her work and looked up as he entered the room. Anyone else in his employ would have been surprised to see him here at this hour, but nothing ever seemed to surprise his placid secretary. She didn't even raise an eyebrow. "My lord," she greeted and stood up.

"Miss Dove," he answered as he strode into the room. "Did those contracts for the purchase of Halliday Paper arrive?"

"No, sir."

Having expected an affirmative answer, Harry paused beside her desk. "Why not?"

"I telephoned Mr. Halliday's solicitors, Ledbetter & Ghent, to inquire. Apparently there was a bit of a muddle."

"Muddle?" He raised an eyebrow at her. "Was this muddle your doing, Miss Dove? Wonder of wonders."

She looked a bit affronted. "No, sir."

He should have known better than to even ask. Miss Dove was never muddled. "Of course not. Forgive me. What happened?"

"Mr. Ledbetter would not say, but I was assured the contracts will be delivered here one week from tomorrow. I can read them for errors over that weekend to be sure all is in order, and you will be able to sign them Monday following. You and your family are attending the Earl of Rathbourne's water party on that day, but it will be a simple matter for you to come here first. Shall I pencil that into your appointment book, my lord?"

She held out her hand. Harry pulled out the small leather volume and handed it to her. After writing the reminder in his book, she handed it back. "Once you've signed the contracts," she went on, "a boy from Ledbetter & Ghent can pick them up, and you will arrive at Adelphi Pier in plenty of time to board Lord Rathbourne's yacht." She picked up a handful of papers. "Here are your other messages."

"You are the soul of efficiency, Miss Dove," he murmured as he accepted the offered slips of paper.

"Thank you, sir." She took a deep breath and gestured to a stack of paper beside her type-writing machine. "I have written a new manu-script. If you have just a moment—"

"I don't, I'm afraid," he was relieved to inform her. He started toward his office, skimming through his messages as he went. "I'm supposed to be at the opera tonight, you know, and I'm already late. Grandmama will cheerfully shoot me with a pistol if I make them miss the opening act, especially on Phoebe's birthday. What is this?"

He stopped at the doorway into his office, staring at the note that was now on top of the stack in his hand. "Juliette was here? Whatever for?"

His secretary, having written the details of Juliette's visit on the paper at which he was now staring, made no answer to that, correctly as-suming his question was rhetorical.

"Hmm," he murmured as he read. "Dis-pleased with her gift, was she?"

"I am truly sorry, sir. I thought a topaz neck-lace with diamonds would be suitable, but it seems she did not agree."

"I don't have time for the details, and I don't

give a damn if she liked the blasted thing or not." He crumpled the message in his fist and tossed it to the floor. Juliette could wrap her greedy little hands around some other man's jewels—and his gemstones, too—from now on. The only females whose opinions he cared about were in his own family.

"Ring up my house, Miss Dove, and tell my mother I won't have time to fetch them from Hanover Square. Have them take the carriage and meet me at Covent Garden."

"I already telephoned, my lord." She circled her desk, picked up the message he had tossed aside and put it tidily into her wastepaper basket, then sat back down. "I inquired if you had arrived home, for you had not returned here to pick up Lady Phoebe's gift, and I thought you might have been delayed. I was informed by your butler that your mother, grandmother, and sisters had already departed for Covent Garden without you."

"Gave me up for lost, did they?"

Ever tactful, Miss Dove did not answer that. She resumed her typing, and Harry went into his private office, a once sparse affair Miss Dove had redecorated a couple of years ago, and though he approved her taste, he wasn't ever in his office long enough to appreciate her efforts. As Harry well knew, money wasn't made sitting behind a desk, even if that desk was made of exquisitely carved mahogany.

He tossed his remaining messages onto his chair, then walked through a connecting door into his dressing room. Because his London residence was across town, his valet and his secretary saw that this room always contained several suits and plenty of fresh shirts. He poured water from the pitcher on the washstand into the basin and soaped a shaving brush.

Within fifteen minutes, he had shaved, exchanged his striped wool suit for a black evening one, and fastened his cuffs with heavy silver cufflinks. After turning up his shirt collar, he looped a black silk Napoleon around his neck, tucked his watch into the pocket of his waistcoat, slipped on a pair of white gloves, picked up a black top hat, and headed out the door.

Miss Dove stopped typing and looked up as he paused beside her desk. "Phoebe's present?" he asked her.

"In your pocket, sir."

He set down his hat and patted the pockets of his suit jacket. Feeling a bump in one of them, he pulled out an absurdly tiny box wrapped in pale yellow tissue paper and tied with a bow of thin lavender silk. A cream-colored card no bigger than the box dangled from one end of the ribbon. "What did I get her, in heaven's name? A petit four?"

"A Limoges box. Your sister collects them, I understand. This one dates from about 1740. It has angels on it, rather fitting, if I might be so bold as to venture an opinion. Angelface is your pet name for your youngest sister, is it not?"

The things Miss Dove knew never ceased to amaze him.

"Inside the box is a sapphire ring," she added.

He frowned with a vague sense of uneasiness. "Don't I usually get her a pearl or something?"

"She completed her add-a-pearl necklace last year. In any case, Lady Phoebe is now twenty-one, old enough for other jewels. I felt a half-carat sapphire ring set in platinum was just right."

"I have no doubt of it."

Miss Dove picked up a quill, dipped it in her inkwell, and handed it to him. "Might I suggest you sign the card, sir?"

He eyed the cream-colored square of paper with doubt. "Good thing my name is only five letters long." He pulled off one glove and scrawled his name as best he could in the small space.

He handed Miss Dove her quill, remembered to blow on the ink to dry it, then tucked the box back in his pocket. He put his glove back on, picked up his hat, and started to turn away, but her voice stopped him.

"My lord, your tie."

"Hell!" Once again dropping his hat, he lifted his hands to his neck and formed his Napoleon into a bow. "How's that?"

She shook her head. "Crooked, I'm afraid."

With an impatient sigh, he tugged at the ends and began again.

"Sir, about my new manuscript," she said as his gloved fingers fumbled with his necktie. "I was hoping you would consent to read it and—"

"Confound this thing!" Harry gave up and gestured his secretary to her feet. "Miss Dove, if you please."

She rose and circled her desk. "About my new manuscript," she said again as she began to repair the mangled mess he'd made of his tie, "it's different from the others."

Harry felt a smothering need to get away. Even the opera was preferable to Miss Dove's etiquette books. Unfortunately, she still had hold of his tie. "Different in what way?" he asked, manfully forcing himself to remain where he was.

"It is still a book of correct conduct, but it speaks directly to women such as myself. That is, to girl-bachelors."

Oh, God. Not only etiquette, but also girl-bachelors. Harry suppressed a groan.

"Yes," she went on, working to free the knot in his tie. "It is a . . . a sort of . . . girl-bachelor's guide to life, along the same lines as your *Bachelor's Guide*, you understand, but for women. How to find a respectable flat at a reasonable rent. How to eat well on four guineas a month. That sort of thing."

Harry glanced between the upraised arms of the woman in front of him, eying her slender frame with doubt. In his opinion, Miss Dove needed to increase her budget for food by a guinea or two. Perhaps he should raise her salary and order her to spend the increase on pastries.

As for her manuscript, well, Harry would rather go to the dentist and have teeth drawn than read a guide to life for plain spinsters in shirtwaists who lived in respectable flats. He had no doubt other people felt the same. And that was the problem.

He published books and newspapers to make money, not to teach people how to behave. "Miss Dove, we have discussed this before," he reminded her. "Etiquette books are not profitable enough to be worth the bother. There are so many nowadays, it's difficult for any particular one to stand out."

She nodded. "That is why I took quite a modern approach with this manuscript. Given the success of *The Bachelor's Guide*, and taking into consideration your views that women ought to be allowed to work in any profession for which they are qualified, I hope you will see the appeal of my idea. Girl-bachelors are a growing segment of our British population. The statistics . . ."

Harry felt a headache coming on as she trotted out the number of girl-bachelors currently living in London. He didn't care about statistics. He cared about his instincts, and his instincts told him that no matter what approach Miss Dove took with her manuscripts, she would never be able to write anything that would stand out, for she was so innocuous in reality. A bit like her name, really. With her brown hair, hazel eyes, and dulcet voice, Miss Dove was soft agreement personified.

He had originally hired her on a whim, tickled by the chance to prove his theory that

LAURA LEE GUHRKE

women were fully capable of earning their keep, just as most men were forced to do. She had gone beyond all his expectations. She was exemplary at her job, far superior to any male secretary he'd ever had. She was never late, never sick, and always efficient.

Most important, she had that quality so often attributed to females and yet so often absent in their character: Miss Dove was compliant. Hers not to reason why. If Harry had ordered her to get on a ship, go to Kenya, and bring him back a one-pound sack of coffee beans, she would have glided out of his office and headed to Thomas Cook & Son to book passage.

While convenient for his own life, Miss Dove's compliancy made her seem a bit unreal, not like any flesh-and-blood woman Harry had ever known. Having an interfering mother, an even more interfering grandmother, three interfering and woefully disobedient sisters, as well as a personal weakness for tempestuous lovers, including—alas—his former wife, Harry's lifetime of experience with the fair sex told him that real women were anything but compliant.

It was Miss Dove's lack of passion, he supposed, more than her unremarkable looks, which made employing her so uncomplicated. An enticing, defiant female secretary, now, that would have been an impossible situation, much more fun but very short-lived. No, as secretaries went, he preferred Miss Dove, and from the beginning he had vowed never to entertain amorous notions about her. It was fortunate she'd always made that resolution so easy to keep.

"There," she said and stepped back, bringing Harry's observations about her to an end. She studied him for a moment, then gave a nod. "I hope you will find that satisfactory, sir."

Harry didn't bother to verify her handiwork in a mirror. He had no doubt whatsoever that his tie was now a perfect bow, and probably the one most fashionable for gentlemen at the moment.

"Miss Dove, you are a treasure." He folded his collar down, picked up his hat, and once again started for the door. "I don't know what I should do without you."

"About my new book," she began, her words impelling him to walk toward the door at an even faster pace. "Will you—"

"Have it delivered to my house before I leave tomorrow morning," he said quickly, cutting her off before she could cite him any more statistics about girl-bachelors. "I'll have a look at it while I'm in the country."

"Thank you, my lord."

Harry departed with profound relief. Too bad he couldn't avoid the opera as easily as he avoided Miss Dove's manuscripts.

Chapter 2

Sisters are the very devil. When they are children, they torture and torment you. When they are grown, they try to find you a wife, which amounts to the same thing.

Lord Marlowe
The Bachelor's Guide, 1893

"Lord Dillmouth and his daughters have arrived in town. Their cousins, the Abernathy girls, came with them."

With those words from his sister Diana, Harry knew what was coming next. He signaled to the waiter hovering nearby for more wine, knowing he would need it. "What a thrilling piece of news. Shall I print it in one of my papers?"

"Mama and I saw them at intermission tonight." The eldest of his three sisters, six years younger than himself, Diana was beautiful and clever. She was also amazingly single-minded. Undaunted by his lack of enthusiasm for the subject she had introduced, Diana ceased discussion of it only long enough to tuck a loose tendril of her dark brown hair behind her ear and take a sip of her wine, then she carried on. "They were looking so well. Lady Florence, especially. She is an acknowledged beauty."

"I daresay she is," he agreed at once. "Odd how her brains are less admired."

"Juliette Bordeaux being a prime example of how much you value feminine intellect," Diana shot back at once.

Harry decided not to mention he'd broken with Juliette. It would only encourage the hope he'd remarry. "She's a keener mind than Lady Florence," he said instead. "Although that's not saying much, I grant you."

His youngest sister spoke up. "Why do you associate with that woman?" Phoebe asked, her adorable cherub face scrunching up with genuine puzzlement.

Harry didn't enlighten her, for the appeal of voluptuous cancan dancers was hardly a subject that a gentleman discussed with his sisters.

His mother seemed to share his opinion on the topic. "Phoebe, that will be enough," Louisa said, trying to sound firm and authoritative, but his mother, alas, was as firm as a custard. Which was why, Harry felt sure, he had three impossible sisters.

"After all," Louisa added obscurely, "we are dining at the Savoy."

His middle sister, Vivian, began to laugh. "What does that have to do with it, Mama?" She glanced around the luxurious private dining room in which they were seated. "These red walls, crystal chandeliers, and gold brocade draperies seem lavish enough for a music hall dancer."

"Vivian!" Antonia, his grandmother, cast a disapproving glance around the table. "We shall not discuss that Bordeaux woman any further," she ordered, her ponderous voice far more impressive than his mother's dithery accents. "It upsets my digestion."

Because she was close on eighty, Grandmama's commands and her digestion were both regarded with respect. The subject of Juliette was dropped, much to Harry's satisfaction. Too bad they couldn't also leave off speculations about his nonexistent future wife, a subject of unceasing fascination for the women in his family, especially his sisters.

"Lady Florence is a bit thick, Di," Vivian said, reverting to the subject Diana had introduced, agreeing with Harry's assessment on the intelligence of the younger Dillmouth girl. "Surely we can do better."

"My preferences mean nothing, I know," he said, donning an air of humble deference to the wisdom of his sisters' matchmaking abilities, "but the idea of marrying Florence Dillmouth makes me shudder."

"The idea of marrying anyone makes you shudder," Diana said wryly. "That's the problem."

"That, Di, is not a problem. It's a blessing. Phoebe, pass the ham."

Phoebe complied with his request. "What about Florence's sister, Melanie?" she suggested as Harry helped himself to ham. "Melanie's all right. She's nice without being humbug. I rather like her."

"Excellent," he said around a mouthful of ham. "Then why don't you marry her?"

"Harrison, don't talk with your mouth full," Antonia ordered as if he were a boy of seven instead of a mature man of thirty-six. "And girls, stop trying to find your brother's next wife. It only makes him more determined not to find her himself. It's understandable, I suppose," she added grudgingly, "that he would be chary of remarrying after that unspeakable American."

That unspeakable American was his grandmother's only way of referring to his former wife. Not that he minded the phrase. He preferred not to speak of Consuelo, either.

"One bad experience shouldn't deter you from marrying again," Phoebe told him.

"The voice of knowledge," he said, trying to deflect from the unpleasant subject at hand by teasing her.

"We just want you to be happy."

"I know, Angelface, and I adore you for it." He leaned over and bussed her cheek with an affectionate kiss. "But marrying again would never make me happy. Trust me on that."

"How tactless of you to speak this way, Harry, with my wedding only ten months away." Diana's amused voice once again entered the conversation. "Unlike you, I am quite thrilled to be making a second venture into matrimony. Edmund is the most wonderful man I have ever known."

Diana's first marriage had been an unfortunate one, and though her husband had caused her terrible pain with his blatant infidelities, he'd had the good sense to die in a railway accident. Despite the misery she had endured, Diana had never lost her utter faith that love and marriage went hand in hand. Six years after her first husband's death, she was about to make a second match. Perhaps this time her faith would be justified. For her sake, Harry hoped so, but that didn't mean he intended to follow her example.

"You're a romantic, Diana. Always were."

"And my fiancé? Edmund's past experience with marriage was just like yours, you know. He fell in love with one of those Americans, too, and married her. His divorce was every bit as difficult and painful, but unlike you, he wasn't made cynical by it."

Cynical? Pain shimmered through his chest, a faint echo of what he'd felt the night he'd finally accepted the truth about his wife and their future. The night she'd left him and he'd abandoned any notions of love everlasting that had managed to survive the four hellish years of their life together. "I am not cynical," he said, lying through his teeth. "I simply see no reason to get married a second time."

"No reason?" His grandmother looked up from her meal to stare at him in shocked disapproval. "What about an heir to the estate?"

"I have an heir. Cousin Gerald."

Antonia made a sound of contempt.

"But Grandmama, he wants the job, anticipates it most eagerly, in fact. Every time he visits Marlowe Park, he counts the silver, asks about the drains, and spends hours interviewing my steward. I should hate to see such exemplary self-education go to waste."

Antonia, a bit like the Queen in many ways, was not amused. "Stop talking nonsense, Harrison. You always do that when you wish to avoid an unpleasant subject. You are a viscount. It is your first and only duty to marry well and have sons."

Grandmama was well behind the times. She simply could not accept that the landed aristocracy were a stone-broke lot nowadays. Harry had seen the way the wind was blowing years ago. The one thing he could thank Consuelo for was her father, and the valuable lesson old Mr. Estravados had taught him. It was captains of industry, he'd told Harry, not aristocrats, who would wield the money and power in the future. Harry had taken those words to heart, and it had paid off handsomely these past fourteen years. Having entailed estates and sons to inherit them wasn't the crucial thing it used to be.

But his mother just had to offer her opinion on the matter. "Harry, you must marry and have sons. Of course you must. Time is going by. Why, you're thirty-six now, and in a few more years, it'll be too late. You'll be forty, and we all know what happens to men around that time, poor dears."

Harry choked on his wine.

Louisa didn't seem to notice. "You must find a wife immediately."

He told himself his mother didn't know what she was talking about. "Why should I go to the trouble of finding a wife, Mama, when my sisters are exerting such strenuous efforts to find one on my behalf?"

"What happens to men at forty?" Phoebe wanted to know.

"Never mind," Diana told her, and before Phoebe could ask any more questions, she once again returned the conversation to the Dillmouth girls. "You know, Phoebe, I believe you're right. Lady Melanie would be a better choice. Some would say she's on the shelf a bit at twenty-eight, and she isn't as pretty as Florence, but she does have black hair, and Harry has such a decided preference for women with hair of that particular shade. Melanie is also the more intelligent of the two sisters."

"Intelligent?" Harry gave a long-suffering sigh. "Melanie Dillmouth can't carry on a conversation. She's so tongue-tied, I wonder how any of you can form an opinion of her intelligence."

"She's tongue-tied around *you*," Diana told him. "It's understandable, I suppose, given her feelings, though I'm not sure those feelings make her a good wife for you or not."

"What are you talking about?"

His eldest sister groaned. "Oh, Harry! Sometimes you are the densest of creatures."

"No doubt," he agreed at once. "I am a man, after all. But what is it about me that causes Melanie Dillmouth's tongue to cease functioning?"

"She's in love with you, of course!"

"What?" Harry was astonished. "Don't be silly."

"She is," Diana insisted. "She always has been. Ever since you saved her cat."

He paused in his supper to take a glance around the table, and his lack of memory about the event in question must have shown in his face. His inquiring glance was answered with four sighs of exasperation and one aggravated elderly harrumph, all of which slid off his back like water off a duck. Surrounded as he was by females, with his father dead nearly twenty years now, and without a single brother to help even the odds, he had learned long ago it was impossible to live up to feminine expectations. "You're mad, Di," he said and resumed eating. "I'd never save a cat. I loathe cats."

"I can't believe you don't remember," Diana chided him. "That summer when the Dillmouth girls stayed with us at Marlowe Park. You were just out of Cambridge. Melanie's cat got caught in a rat trap and you got it out."

A vague memory surfaced. "For heaven's sake, that was ages ago. Fifteen years, at least."

"She's never forgotten it," Diana told him. "She cried when you married Consuelo."

"If I'd known what I was in for, I'd have cried, too."

None of them seemed to find that amusing. Harry wondered how his family could ever think the image of Melanie Dillmouth crying over him would spark any romantic interest on his part. The only desire that pity for a woman inspired in a man was the desire to run away.

"What about Elizabeth Darbury?" Phoebe suggested. "She's got black hair."

"Good breeders in that family." Antonia gave a nod of approval. "The Darburys always have at least two sons in every generation."

"Lizzie Darbury won't do," Vivian said. "She never understands Harry's jokes. She just stares at him as if he's a bit touched in the head and doesn't laugh."

"And that's important," Louisa said. "Men do hate it when we don't find them amusing. Especially Harry. It quite upsets him."

"It does not upset me. And I don't know why my sisters are so determined to choose a wife for me."

"Because you are so bad at it," Vivian said at once, eliciting a round of nods from the other women at the table.

Unable to refute that very valid point, and too kindhearted to remind them that Diana's first marriage choice hadn't been any better than his own had been, Harry decided silence might discourage his sisters. Three seconds told him that strategy was seriously flawed.

"There's Mary Netherfield," Vivian said. "She's a stylish way about her. Always so perfectly turned out."

From Vivian, who adored clothes and paid attention to every feminine fashion, that was the highest of compliments.

Phoebe negated Lady Mary with a shake of her head. "She hasn't a prayer. She's blond and blue-eyed. And she's the steady, sensible kind."

"Yes, but that's just the sort of wife he needs." Vivian made a vague gesture in his direction. "He's so erratic, he needs a steady, sensible girl."

"But Harry hates that type."

What Harry hated was how they discussed him if he weren't even in the room. "This is a pointless conversation," he told them, becoming irritated. "I am never getting married again. How many times do I have to say it?"

"Oh, Harry," his mother wailed, looking at him with profound disappointment, "you are so hopeless when it comes to anything important."

As if the money he earned, money that kept all of them clothed in Worth gowns, entertained at the opera, and dining in a private dining room at the Savoy, wasn't important. But he knew it would have been futile to point out to Louisa where the money came from. With his mother, logic was useless, especially about money matters. He'd tried to explain stock shares to her once. It had given them both a headache.

"You must get married and have sons," she went on. "Decent cottages are so difficult to find nowadays."

What cottages had to do with having a son was beyond him, but there, that was Louisa all over. Saying things he couldn't follow was second nature to her.

It was Phoebe who correctly interpreted his puzzled look. "Gerald would never let us live at Marlowe Park if you died and he became the viscount," she explained. "Since it's entailed, we'd have to go let a house somewhere."

"Ah." Enlightened, Harry did not point out that the million or so pounds sitting in Lloyd's earning interest was more than enough security for his family's future. Instead, he pretended to think the matter over. "I suppose you could always move to America after I'm gone. They've plenty of cottages there. Village called Newport has some nice little places."

His mother never knew when he was teasing. "Well, this is a fine state of things," she said, her voice quavering. "What ever shall we do if you die without an heir?"

Somehow, Harry found his own demise a far more distressing thing to contemplate than his lack of a son, but obviously he was the only one who saw the matter in that light.

Diana gave a little cough. "As I mentioned before, the Dillmouths brought their Abernathy cousins with them, Nan and Felicity. And I thought—"

"Enough!" Harry dropped his knife and fork onto his plate with a clatter, at the end of his tether. "Will all of you stop this? No woman on

earth will inspire me to make a second attempt
at matrimony. I shall never marry again. Ever! Is
that clear?"

In the wake of his outburst, the five women
he loved more than anything else in the world
stared at him like a litter of wounded kittens.
He hated it when they did that.

He pushed back his plate, and since everyone
else had also finished eating, he gestured to the
waiter to begin clearing the table. "I don't know
why we're discussing me anyway," he said. "It's
Phoebe's birthday. I think it's time for her to open
her presents. Speaking of which . . ."

He reached into his pocket and pulled out the
tiny, tissue-wrapped package. He presented it to
his baby sister with a flourish. "There you are,
Angelface. Happy birthday."

She looked up at him, and her blue eyes were
shining. "It's a Limoges box, isn't it? It must be.
It's so small, it can't be anything else. Am I
right?"

"Open it and see."

She untied the ribbon and pulled off the wrapping paper. When she opened the paperboard
box and saw what was inside, she began to laugh.
"It has the faces of angels painted on it."

"So it is Limoges?" Vivian craned her neck,
trying to have a look.

"It is. Look." Phoebe held it up so the others
could see.

Miss Dove's description came back to him, and
he leaned over his youngest sister's shoulder. "I

say, those boxes open, don't they?" he asked in pretended innocence.

Phoebe fell for the ploy. "Yes, they do," she said and demonstrated by pulling back the small, hinged lid. "See how they—Oh, my!"

She tumbled the ring into her palm. "A sapphire! Look, everyone, it's a sapphire." Setting aside the Limoges box, she held up the ring only long enough for everyone to get a glimpse, then she slipped it on the finger of her right hand. It fit perfectly. Of course. Miss Dove, heaven bless her, would never let it be otherwise.

"You're twenty-one now," he said, "and sapphires seem right. Go with your eyes, you know. Like it?"

"Like it?" Phoebe turned to wrap her arms around his neck. "I love it," she declared and gave him a smacking kiss on the cheek. "It's perfect! And the Limoges box is perfect. You give us the best presents always!"

"That's all right, then," he said and pressed a kiss to her forehead.

Her mother, her grandmother, and Vivian gathered around Phoebe to admire her present, but Diana did not join them. Instead, she remained where she was and leaned closer to Harry. "That Miss Dove is amazing," she whispered. "She always finds us the perfect gifts."

"I don't know what you're talking about."

"Don't worry, dear brother. I'm the only one who's figured out your secret, and I won't tell."

"You're a brick, Di."

"Well, you may not say that after I confess what I've done."

He turned to look at her.

She told him.

"What?" His roar silenced the room, and the four other women looked at him in alarm. Diana grimaced at the expression on his face.

"I was carried away by a spirit of compassion," she explained and bit her lip, trying and failing to look contrite.

"Compassion, my eye!"

"Heavens," his mother spoke up, "whatever is the matter?"

It was Diana who answered. "I told him about the invitation."

"Oh, dear." Louisa frowned with concern, studying him for a moment. "He doesn't like it, does he?"

"How could you think I would?" Harry demanded, his voice rising.

"Well, it's done now," Diana said.

Louisa's face brightened at those words. "Yes, and it was the right thing to do, after all."

"Right thing?"

"Harry, darling, don't shout. Those poor girls came to London with only crotchety old Dillmouth to watch over them. I mean, really! Awful to bring them for the season without a proper chaperone. What was he thinking?"

"No." Harry shook his head. "I refuse to allow it."

He might have been talking to the wind.

"All I can say is that losing his dear wife all

those years ago has finally unhinged his mind," Louisa went on. "Heavens, those poor girls wouldn't have been able to go about at all. So dull for them." She looked at him with a queer sort of defiance. "I still say Diana did the right thing."

The idea of having four additional women living in his house for the next six weeks, all of whom were his sisters' notion of marriage prospects for him, filled Harry with dismay. He thought of the weeping Lady Melanie, and his dismay deepened into dread. "Get a gun," he muttered. "Put me out of my misery now."

"What is all this about?" Antonia demanded. "Explain yourself, Diana."

"Mama and I saw Dillmouth, his daughters, and their two Abernathy cousins during the intermission when we were at the opera. They have no chaperone but Dillmouth, and once I understood their situation, I issued an invitation for all four girls to come to us for a six-week visit. It never occurred to me that Harry would mind."

"The hell it didn't." Harry scowled at her.

"I issued the invitation in front of Dillmouth," she went on serenely, "and he accepted for them. I cannot retract it now."

"I should say not!" Antonia frowned at the very idea. "That would be abominably rude."

Harry groaned, knowing he was trapped. Though Dillmouth was severely in debt, he was a marquess, well above Harry in rank, and very powerful in the House. He was not the sort to forget a snub. With his sisters' social prospects severely curtailed by his divorce, they could not afford to snub a man like Dillmouth. He didn't know whether to throttle Diana or go pound his head into a wall.

"It's settled, then. They come in a week, just in time for your return from Berkshire." Diana smiled at him. "By the way, Harry, you have never met Lady Felicity. Beautiful girl."

He looked at his eldest sister, saw the little smile playing at the corners of her mouth, and he realized she'd had Felicity Abernathy in mind all along.

"She is lovely, isn't she?" Vivian chimed in. "She has black hair, if I remember. And dark eyes. That sort of coloring makes jewel tones so stunning on her."

"She's hot-tempered, though," Phoebe cautioned, but even in profile, Harry could see the smile she was trying to hide. "Latin blood in that side of the family, so they say."

Sisters were the very devil. They knew all a man's weaknesses. Harry wondered if he could go off and lease a cottage in America.

During the week that followed, Emma did not dwell much upon her impending birthday, but the night before it arrived, she dreamt of silk. Rich and shimmery silk taffeta, made up in a sumptuous ball gown that rustled when she moved and had those enormous puffy sleeves so fashionable just now. Green silk, it was, with a figured design of blue and green beads on the skirt that shimmered in the light from the chandeliers overhead.

Chandeliers? Yes, she was at a ball, and a waltz was being played. She was dancing with a man. Odd how she couldn't see his face—that was a blur—but he was making her laugh, and she liked that. Suddenly there was a fan in her hand, a lavish, exotic fan of peacock feathers. She opened it and gave the man a flirtatious glance over the top, delighting in the feel of the feathers tickling her nose.

Emma woke up to find Mr. Pigeon's face inches from hers, his long cat whiskers brushing her nose. He gave a loud meow of greeting, and this abrupt change of scene made her close her eyes, but when she opened them again, there was no mistaking the orange tabby curled up beside her on the pillow.

She'd been dreaming, she realized. And such an absurd dream when all was said and done. Why, silk taffeta was outrageously expensive! And how on earth could one waltz with a man and wave that enormous fan about at the same time? Still, she couldn't help feeling a wistful little pang that the beautiful gown and handsome man were not real.

The fan, though . . . the fan was a different matter. It was real. Such a lovely thing, with its long feathers, carved ivory handle, and blue silk tassel. She'd seen it in that little curiosity shop on Regent Street, the same shop where she'd found Lady Phoebe's Limoges box. It was the sort of shop where sham lapis beads for three pence a strand sat beside bejeweled Charles I snuffboxes worth hundreds of pounds, just the sort of shop that would possess a fan like that. A fan that cost two guineas, she reminded herself. An outrageous price for such a frivolous thing.

Emma turned onto her back and stared up at the ceiling, her gaze moving beyond the butter-yellow walls of her flat on Little Russell Street to the far-flung outposts of the Empire. She thought of the stories of the *Arabian Nights* and places with names like Ceylon and Kashmir, where the air was full of spices and the sound of sitars, where there were marketplaces filled with thick Persian carpets and colorful China silks. Looking at that fan through the dusty glass of a display case in a Regent Street antique shop had made her feel, just for a moment, as beautiful and exotic as Scheherazade. Emma gave a dreamy sigh.

Mr. Pigeon nuzzled her ear, purring loudly, and she gave up on fantasies of being Scheherazade. Instead, she gave the animal an affectionate rub with the side of her face, liking the feel of his soft fur against her cheek. Then she sat up, pushing aside the counterpane.

The cat made a protesting meow as she got out of bed. "I know, I know," she said in reply, "but I have to go to work." She gave him a glance of mock sternness over her shoulder as she padded across the wood floor in her bare feet. "I cannot laze about napping all day like some."

Unimpressed, Mr. Pigeon yawned and settled himself more comfortably on her pillow. As always, Emma allowed him to remain there while she went about her morning routine, leaving the making of the bed until the very last thing.

She poured water from the white stoneware pitcher into the bowl and reached for the jar of Pears' Soap. After washing, she dressed in a crisp white shirtwaist, dark blue skirt, and her black leather high-button shoes, then drew back the curtains.

After sitting down in front of the washstand, she unraveled the long braid of her hair and picked up her hairbrush.

In the mirror, Emma watched the brush move through her waist-length hair, and the sight of its mother-of-pearl back was always a bittersweet reminder of her aunt. One hundred strokes to make it shine, Aunt Lydia had told her from the time she was fifteen. Papa, had he been alive by that time to hear his sister-in-law's advice, would have deemed such time in front of a mirror sinfully vain.

Perhaps it was vain, but Emma did like her hair this way. Most of the time it just looked brown, rather the color of bread crust. But loose like this, a little wavy from the braid, with the sunlight shining on it through the window, the color seemed coppery red, not humdrum brown.

That green silk dress, she thought, would have been lovely. Ah, well.

Emma twisted her hair into a chignon at the back of her head, pinned it, and added a pair of pewter combs to be doubly sure the heavy knot would stay in place all day. Satisfied, she started to stand up, then stopped, remembering.

Today was her birthday.

Sinking back down, she stared at her reflection in the mirror. She was thirty.

She told herself she didn't look as old as that. She told herself the freckles across her nose and cheekbones, freckles no amount of lemon juice could ever remove, made her seem younger. Ordinary hazel eyes in a long, oval face stared back at her, eyes surrounded by lashes that weren't dark enough to matter and bracketed by tiny lines that hadn't been there a year ago. She lifted her hand and traced her fingertips over the three faint parallel grooves across her forehead.

Discontent returned again to plague her, and Emma jerked her hand down. Any more of this mooning about, and she'd be late. She got up and left the bedroom. Since it was already past eight o'clock she'd missed breakfast in the dining room downstairs, but if she was quick about it, she'd have time to make herself a cup of tea before catching an omnibus to work.

After drawing back the curtains of her parlor, she heated water from the pitcher on her tiny stove-lamp and nibbled on shortbread as she waited for it to boil. She made her tea, and as it steeped, the scent of jasmine and orange peel wafted up to her nostrils.

Ceylon. Kashmir. Green silk. Scheherazade.

Absurd, she scoffed, to pay two guineas for a peacock fan, even on her birthday. More than half a week's wages for something she would never have the opportunity to use? Ridiculous.

But she thought about that fan all the way to work.

Chapter 3

A true lady always behaves with restraint. She is cheerful, understanding, and sensible. She does not give way to displays of emotion, lose her temper, or make a scene.

Mrs. Lydia Worthington's advice
to her niece, 1880

Newspapers were not only a significant part of Harry's livelihood, they had other uses as well, refuge being the most important this morning.

It was terribly rude, he supposed, to hold up a newspaper as a wall between oneself and one's houseguests, but he didn't care. There were limits to what a man could endure, and with four additional women at his breakfast table, women his sisters considered marriage prospects for him, a

man had to hide somewhere. The morning after
his return from Berkshire, Harry chose to hide
behind a copy of Barringer's *Social Gazette*.

Fortunately, breakfast in his household was a
casual affair of warming dishes on the sideboard
and everyone helping themselves at their leisure.
Even though it was becoming more acceptable to
conduct the first meal of the day in this manner,
his household had been doing it this way for
years. His mother had long ago given up any
hope he would keep to a regular household routine. Today, the casual atmosphere enabled Harry
to both ignore his guests and get work done at
the same time.

It was really no wonder the *Gazette* and its
owner were in financial trouble, he thought as he
munched on a slice of bacon. For such staid, dull
stuff as this, one might just as well read the *Times*.

A single feminine voice rose just enough to be
heard above the rest. "What is your opinion,
Lord Marlowe?"

The room fell silent, and Harry pulled down
the newspaper just far enough to meet the melting dark gaze of Lady Felicity. She was beautiful, no denying it, but then, Diana knew his
tastes well enough. If Felicity were not a young
lady, his interest might be sparked, but young
ladies were dangerous creatures. They expected
marriage.

He gave her a polite smile. "My apologies, but
I was not paying attention to the conversation."
He rustled the *Gazette*. "I am engaged in a most
important task at present."

"An important task?" She gestured to the paper in his hands. "Is the day's news so important, then?"

"To Harry it is," Vivian told her, laughing. "He's always reading the papers of his competitors."

"Though not usually at breakfast," his grandmother pointed out, her voice heavy with disapproval which Harry chose to ignore.

He took another look at Felicity over the top of the *Gazette*. "You see, Lady Felicity," he explained, "reading the newspapers of my competitors is crucial to my financial success. Staying one step ahead and that sort of thing. I am a man of business, and I enjoy it."

"Enjoy it?" Felicity began to laugh. "You tease me, Lord Marlowe."

"Indeed, I do not. I enjoy it far more than my estate. Collecting land rents is a bore. And very unprofitable. I prefer business."

She knew she'd made a blunder, and she attempted to smooth it over. "You prefer your business affairs to your estate? How . . ." She paused, floundering for a moment. "How very modern."

Harry saw Diana wince, and he lifted his newspaper again, grinning. So she'd thought Lady Felicity the perfect wife for him? He was really going to enjoy ragging Di about this later. "Yes, well, I am a very modern sort of fellow," he murmured in his best self-deprecating fashion.

Ignoring his grandmother's sound of exasperation, he glanced at the clock on the mantel and gave an exclamation of mock surprise. "Half past nine already?" He folded the paper and stood up, doing his best to look apologetic. "Forgive me, ladies, but I must go earn my living."

"Don't be late this evening, dear," his mother said as he gathered the stack of newspapers and the morning post the butler had placed beside his plate. "We're having music after dinner. Nan is going to sing for us."

He gave the musically inclined Lady Nan a smile. "How lovely, Mama. I shall do my best, but I'm afraid I can't promise something won't come up to detain me." He bowed and was out the door before Louisa could reply. Giving a deep sigh of relief, he walked from the dining room to the foyer.

"My carriage, Jackson," he instructed, "and fetch me when it arrives. I'll be in my study."

"Very good, my lord." The butler signaled for a footman, and Harry crossed the foyer to his study, where he promptly dropped the *Social Gazette* into the wastepaper basket. He'd read as much of its pompous self-importance as he could stomach for one morning. First thing he'd do when he bought the thing was liven it up. And he was determined to buy it. He was convinced if he gave it a more modern slant, he could make it profitable. And its location, a four-story brick building right across from his own offices, was perfect for expansion. Of course, scoring over Barringer had a sweet satisfaction all its own. Sooner or later, the earl would have to give in. It was only a matter of time.

He opened his dispatch case, intending to

place the newspapers of his other competitors inside so that he could read them on the way to his offices, but he paused at the sight of a stack of manuscript pages tied with twine.

Miss Dove's new book.

He'd promised to look the thing over while in Berkshire, but upon his arrival there, he'd promptly forgotten all about it, deeming fishing a far more amusing pastime than anything written by Miss Dove. It would take about ten minutes for his driver to bring his carriage around front from the mews. That, he knew from previous experience with Miss Dove's manuscripts, was about nine and one-half minutes more than he needed to keep his promise and verify what he already suspected.

He pulled the manuscript out of his dispatch case, sat down at his desk, and untied the twine. Then he curled his fingers under a section of the stack and opened it to a random page.

The tiniest flat, possessed of not a single ray of afternoon sunlight to brighten it, can be transformed into a most inviting nest at very little cost, if the girl-bachelor employs her innate good sense and ingenuity. And, of course, if she knows where to shop.

Harry closed the manuscript. Dull as a scullery maid's dishrag, just as he'd known it would be. Poor Miss Dove just couldn't seem to understand that nobody wanted to read this sort of piffle.

He tied up the twine, put the manuscript back

in his case, and pulled out his appointment book, which had been delivered to his doorstep yesterday in anticipation of his return, with all his engagements listed in his secretary's perfect copperplate script.

He grimaced at the first notation. A meeting with his book editors. That monthly conference was always such a delight. Harry thought about giving it a miss altogether—after all, he did own the company. But if he wasn't there to keep them in line, his editors would run amok, deciding to publish God only knows what. It didn't bear thinking about. When Jackson announced his carriage was out front, Harry accepted his hat, resigned himself to the inevitable, and went to his offices. Because of his hasty departure from the breakfast table, he arrived at his offices on Bouverie Street well ahead of his meeting.

Miss Dove stood up when he came in. "Good morning, sir," she greeted him. "You are early today."

"Shocking, I know," he said. "Domestic difficulties, Miss Dove."

"I am sorry to hear that. There are several good agencies, if your housekeeper or butler is short of domestic staff. I can—"

"Not that sort of domestic difficulty. This particular problem won't be solved by an agency, I fear, unless you can find one that will locate husbands for all my sisters and get them out of my house." He paused, as if considering the matter. "My mother, too, now that I think on it. She could be married off. A Scottish peer, for choice. Scotland's a long way from here, two days' train, at least."

"Overnight, if one takes the express." Miss Dove always accepted everything he said at face value and responded accordingly, a fact which had long ago forced Harry to conclude his secretary had no sense of humor.

"I believe there are one or two agencies that facilitate the finding of a spouse," she went on doubtfully, "but I would not have thought your sisters needed assistance of that sort. And isn't your eldest sister already affianced to Lord Rathbourne?"

Smiling, he leaned a bit closer to her over the desk. "I was having you on, Miss Dove."

"Oh." Her expression did not change. "I see," she said in the tone of one who clearly didn't.

Harry gave it up. Teasing his secretary was pointless, for she never understood it. In any case, he was only trying to stave off the bad news he had to give her as long as possible.

Taking a deep breath, he set his leather dispatch case on her desk, unfastened the buckle, and opened it. "I looked at your new book," he said as he pulled out her manuscript, "but I'm afraid this one still has the same problem as the others. For one particular etiquette book to make a profit, it has to be fresh and different, it has to stand out."

"Yes, sir." Her lips pressed together in disappointment, and she ducked her head to hide it. "I understand, but I had hoped—"

"Yes, I know," he cut her off, wanting this

over as quickly as possible. He held out the twine-tied stack of paper. "I'm sorry."

She stared at it for a moment, then took it from his hand and put it in a drawer of her desk. "Would you like your coffee now?"

"Yes, thank you."

She duly brought his coffee, just the way he liked it, strong, hot, and with no milk or sugar. After that, he dictated some correspondence to her until the editors came upstairs for their meeting with him. Three hours later, he ushered the other two men out into the corridor, acting genial even as he wondered in exasperation why editors could never seem to grasp the financial considerations of publishing. They unerringly passed up the salable book for the book of literary brilliance, a trait that always left Harry baffled at the end of each monthly meeting. If a book didn't have mass appeal, he didn't care how beautiful its metaphors or how subtle its literary allusions or how profound its theme, he wasn't going to publish it.

As he came back into his own suite of offices, he found his secretary putting on her hat.

"Going now, Miss Dove?"

"Yes, sir."

He ducked his head to peer beneath the wide straw brim of her bonnet. "No hard feelings, I hope?" he asked, looking into her face.

"Of course not," she answered with a bright, forced sort of cheerfulness. "I comprehend your reasons for rejecting my work, but I shall not be discouraged."

He didn't have the heart to tell her not to bother. "That's the spirit. Persistence pays off, so they say."

"I intend to regard this as just one more no out of the way," she went on as she put on her gloves. "Getting all the no's out of the way will eventually lead to a yes, as Mrs. Bartleby says."

"Who?"

She paused, looking at him in puzzlement. "Mrs. Bartleby," she repeated, her tone conveying that he was supposed to know the name.

He frowned, trying to remember if he'd ever heard of any woman named Bartleby. After a moment, he shook his head. "Sorry, Miss Dove, but I don't know her."

"But—" She broke off and stared at him, her hazel eyes wide and her lips parted, her puzzlement replaced by what seemed to be utter astonishment.

The expression on her face was so at odds with her usually cool, unruffled demeanor that he was startled. "Miss Dove, are you all right?"

"You don't know who Mrs. Bartleby is." She said it in the strangest way, as if trying to accept something impossible. Harry began to feel uneasy.

"Should I know of her?" He gave her a smile. "You must refresh my memory, for I cannot recall ever hearing of any such person. One of my competitors publish a book by her I don't know about?"

"No." She swallowed hard and gazed past him, still as a statue.

Harry's uneasiness deepened into worry. Was she going to faint? He couldn't imagine Miss Dove fainting, but there was a first time for everything. "You're white as chalk. Are you ill?"

"No." She shook her head, coming out of her daze. She seemed to regain her usual poise, almost making him wonder if he had imagined that shocked, frozen look. "Thank you for your opinion about my manuscript," she said. "Since today is Saturday, and it is now well past noon, I shall be on my way, if there is nothing else?"

She didn't wait for an answer, but started for the door.

"Miss Dove?" he called after her.

She halted. Her head turned slightly back over her shoulder, but she did not quite look at him. "Yes, sir?"

"Who is Mrs. Bartleby?"

It was several seconds before she answered. "No one important," she said and departed, closing the door behind her.

He frowned, staring at the closed door, still uneasy. No doubt she was disappointed, but what some woman named Bartleby had to do with it, he couldn't fathom.

With a shake of his head, Harry dismissed the strange conversation from his mind. It always hurt Miss Dove's feelings when he rejected her work, but she'd get over it. She always did.

He'd never read her books. Emma repeated that fact over and over as she strode up Chancery Lane, but she still could not seem to take it in. He had not read a single one of her books.

It occurred to her that she might be mistaken, but even as that thought crossed her mind, she knew it wasn't possible. If Marlowe had read her work, he'd have known Mrs. Bartleby was Emma's pseudonym and the fictional author of all her manuscripts. Heavens, the woman's name was typed right on the title page. How could he miss it? And there were references to the late Mr. Bartleby sprinkled throughout the text. No, there could be no mistake.

All her time, all her hard work, all her duties for him loyally fulfilled, and he couldn't even be bothered to read the title page?

Emma's shock gave way to rage, a deep, burning fire in her belly. Never had she felt so close to violence. All this time, all these years, he'd only been pretending to consider her work. It was all a lie.

She wanted to confront him. She should have, but at first she'd been too stunned. Standing there by her desk, looking at his face, realizing the horrible truth, she'd been numb. Only now, long after she'd left the building, had the fog of numbness disintegrated, and now it was too late.

No, it wasn't. She halted at the corner of High Holborn, turned on her heel, and headed back toward Bouverie Street. She would do it. She would confront him, fling his lie in his face, tell him just what she thought of his duplicity.

The moment she imagined such a scene, Emma knew how stupid it would be. He'd sack her. Any employer would, for impertinence like that.

It wasn't worth it. Emma stopped again, this time earning herself an indignant exclamation from a young man walking behind her. Out of breath, she stood there on the sidewalk as the young man walked around her, and she knew she couldn't confront Marlowe. No matter how momentarily satisfying such an action might be, she couldn't afford to sacrifice her job for it.

Thwarted by her own common sense, Emma clenched her hand into a fist and ground it into the palm of her other hand with a sound of frustration. She was angry, by heaven, and she wanted an outlet for her feelings. She wanted to scream, to cry, to throw things, but that was out of the question. She was in a public thoroughfare, surrounded by people, and a lady never gave way to her emotions in front of others.

She'd go home. Emma turned back around and retraced her steps to the corner. At home, she could throw things, cry, and scream to her heart's content. Except, of course, that she'd throw something she loved and break it, and she'd regret that later. And her landlady would hear the noise and think some lunatic had gotten into the building. She might even send for the police. What a horrible thought.

Given no other way to vent her frustration, Emma took several deep breaths and settled for walking. She strode along High Holborn, her boot heels drumming on the pavements like the rhythm of a fast and furious engine.

She'd resign, she decided. First thing Monday, she'd walk in, announce her resignation in a

quiet, dignified fashion, give the proper fortnight's notice, and swallow down her anger long
enough to request a letter of recommendation.
That was the sensible thing to do.

No, it isn't, an inner voice cautioned. Resigning
wasn't sensible. She earned seven pounds and six
a month. Where on earth could she earn that sort
of money working for someone else? Men like
Marlowe, who felt a female secretary should be
paid the same as her male counterpart, were rarer
than unicorns. She had a snug, comfortable flat
in a very respectable neighborhood, the security
of a post that would be hers for a long time to
come, and an ever-growing nest egg sitting in
the bank earning three and one-half percent per
annum, her protection against the ravages of
poverty when she was too old to work.

Emma stopped again and turned to lean back
against the wrought-iron railing that surrounded
the Royal Music Hall. She sighed. There were
times, like now, when being sensible was a terribly aggravating thing to be. She stood there for
some minutes, not knowing what to do, dither-
ing in a way that would have made her stern
military father quite cross.

One shouldn't be sensible all the time. Surely
there were times when she ought to be able to
give in to reckless impulse, be carried away by
the spontaneity of the moment, but she could
never seem to manage it. Oh, how she wished
she could.

She straightened away from the railing and
stepped forward to the curb, preparing to hail

the first passing omnibus. For once in her life, she was not going to be sensible. She was going to go to Mayfair and buy that peacock fan, and she wasn't going to care how much it cost. Every woman ought to feel beautiful and exotic on her birthday.

The little bell above the door of Dobbs's Antiques and Curiosities jangled as Emma entered the shop, but Mr. Dobbs didn't even notice. He was hovering with anxious solicitude near a group of young ladies gathered around the counter in the center of the room.

Emma froze by the door. One of the ladies, a pretty girl with blond hair in a dress of rose-pink swiss, was holding that peacock fan. Her fan.

The girl waved it at one of her companions. "Will this suit for Wallingford's ball, do you think?" she asked, laughing as she playfully curtsied.

Everything within Emma cried out in protest. She took a step forward, then stopped. Short of ripping the fan out of the younger woman's hand, there was nothing she could do. She could only watch and wait.

Like beautiful butterflies, these girls, as they floated around the room in their pretty pastel morning dresses, each playing with the peacock fan in turn, while Emma hovered by the door, fingers crossed behind her back, hoping against hope they would put it down and depart. She listened as they talked gaily of their upcoming ball, their various suitors, and the fullness of their dance cards.

"So, should I buy it or not?" the blonde finally asked, raising her voice a bit to be heard above the chattering of her companions. At once it was agreed by all that peacock feathers would be the perfect thing to set off the blonde's ball gown of turquoise silk.

With a sinking feeling of misery in her tummy, Emma watched the girl pay for her purchase. She knew her feelings were all out of proportion to the situation, and she tried to be reconciled to the loss. It was just a fan, she told herself, and that young lady surely had more reason to own it than she ever would. Even had she bought it, Emma didn't know what she would have done with the thing. Hang it on the wall, she supposed, where it would only collect dust.

It's the springtime of that girl's life, Emma reminded herself. A time when a peacock fan was of some use to a young lady, a time of parties and dancing and romance, a time of hopes and dreams and plans for the future—a future that was exciting and fun and full of possibilities.

Her own springtime had passed by years ago, if it had ever existed at all.

Emma's mind flashed back over the past dozen years. She thought of herself at eighteen, nineteen, twenty—of being desperately in love and hoping Mr. Parker felt the same, waiting for a declaration of love and a proposal of marriage that had never come, watching him marry someone else.

Then dear Aunt Lydia had gotten sick. Emma thought of the five years she'd spent caring for her, waiting and hoping so desperately that the old woman would get better, and then watching the casket as it was lowered into the ground.

And now there was Lord Marlowe, who had no intention of publishing any of her books, who hadn't even read them. Five years of hope and hard work, slaving over a typewriting machine every night, had come to naught.

Such was the pattern of her life. She had spent her entire youth waiting and hoping for things that never happened. Now she was thirty.

The young ladies were coming toward the door. Emma stepped aside and turned, watching that absurd, extravagant peacock fan go out the door with its new owner, and something cracked inside of her.

Too late, she realized. She'd spent so many years putting off what she wanted until it was too late.

With that thought, all the emotions she'd been holding back since leaving the publishing house surged up within her like floodwaters rising. She pressed her gloved fist over her mouth, trying to maintain her composure, but it was a futile attempt. Like water breaking a dam, all her outrage and all her despair came flooding out. Much to her mortification and horror, Emma started to cry.

Chapter 4

Men wonder why women cannot behave in a rational fashion. What they fail to understand is that we do.

Mrs. Bartleby's Essays on Domestic Life, 1892

In regard to his family, Harry considered himself a tolerant man, but by God, there were limits. Four days of his sisters lauding the talents and charms of their houseguests at every opportunity, and Harry's tolerance was gone. Melanie's woeful hero worship, Nan's mediocre singing, Felicity's marriage-minded eyes, and Florence's inane conversation were threatening to destroy not only his good humor, but his sanity as well.

By Monday morning, when he was informed their houseguests would be accompanying them aboard Rathbourne's yacht, where he would be trapped in their company for an entire day and evening with no place to hide, Harry knew something had to be done. But he didn't know what.

He couldn't send the silly girls packing back to Dillmouth. His mother would cry, a dreadful prospect. His sisters would simply set about finding a fresh lot of potential marriage partners for him, which was even worse. Their social standing would dip yet another notch, for Dillmouth would do Harry some sort of injury for the slight to his daughters and nieces. In short, the whole thing would become a sorry mess, and Harry tried to avoid those whenever possible.

Unfortunately, sorry messes did not always avoid Harry. When he stopped by his offices to sign those Halliday contracts before departing for Rathbourne's water party, his plans went awry, his day went to hell, and Harry found himself in a very sorry mess indeed.

It all started with Mr. Tremayne. In charge of the newspaper side of things, Tremayne was a rubicund, cheery soul, able to handle almost any crisis with ease. Not today. He was at the front doors of the building when Harry came in, and the look on his face indicated something was very wrong.

"God, Tremayne, what's happened? You look the picture of misery."

"I don't have Miss Dove's operations schedule for today."

"She didn't send it down yet?" Harry asked in some surprise as he crossed the foyer, passed the newsrooms where clerks were busily typing away, and started up the stairs.

The other man followed him. "Miss Dove is not here."

"What?" Harry paused with one foot on the stair and pulled out his watch. "That's impossible. It's half-past ten. Miss Dove's about somewhere. She has to be."

"Mr. Marsden—he sits at the front desk, sir, you know . . ." Tremayne paused to indicate Marsden's desk at the other end of the foyer by the front doors. "He says Miss Dove has not arrived yet today."

"He probably missed her coming in, that's all." Unworried, Harry tucked his watch back into his waistcoat pocket and resumed walking up the stairs.

"Yes, sir," Tremayne replied, as he followed Harry up to the third floor. "I thought so as well. I sent my clerk to investigate, but when Carter went upstairs, he observed that Miss Dove's bonnet and umbrella were not on the coat-tree by your office doors. We conducted a search, and she is nowhere within the building. Perhaps she is ill."

"Miss Dove is never ill. That's a scientific fact, Tremayne, much like gravity and sunrises."

"She's never late, either, sir. Yet she is not here, and I do not have a schedule."

The two men entered Harry's office suite and paused beside Miss Dove's desk. Harry observed that the desktop was devoid of anything save the inkstand and blotter which sat precisely in the center of the polished oak surface. Her type-writing machine was still cloaked in its leather cover. The hat rack was empty.

"You see, my lord?" Tremayne spread his arms wide. "It doesn't look as if she's been here at all."

"Well, have Marsden ring her up and find out why she isn't in."

"I don't believe Miss Dove has a telephone," the other man said doubtfully. "If she does, Marsden wouldn't know what number to give the exchange." He paused, then gave a cough. "Sir, what shall we do? I have to have that schedule."

Before Harry could address the problem, the door opened and Mr. Finch, in charge of the book division, entered the room. "My lord, Mr. Tremayne," he greeted the other two men, then glanced at the desk behind them. "Miss Dove on an errand?"

"My secretary is not here yet this morning, Mr. Finch," Harry told him.

The other man looked surprised, a feeling Harry understood quite well at this moment. "My lord, Miss Dove is always here first thing."

"Not today, it seems. I suppose you need something as well?"

"Yes, sir. I'm in need of the book schedule for next year. Miss Dove brings it up to date every month. She's so good at making certain the authors meet their deadlines, you know."

"Do you really need—"

The door opened, interrupting Harry's question, and Mr. Marsden came in. "There is a clerk from Ledbetter & Ghent downstairs, my lord. He says he is here to pick up some signed contracts?"

"Hell!" Harry cast another look at his secretary's desk, but there were no papers lying about. Miss Dove was supposed to have read those contracts over the weekend and have them ready for his signature this morning. "Wait here," he told the other men and went into his office. Sure enough, the contracts were there, sitting in a neat pile in the center of his desk. An envelope, addressed to him in Miss Dove's handwriting, lay atop them.

Relieved to find those crucial contracts, Harry shoved the envelope aside and flipped through the pages of the legal documents to those lines requiring his signature. He signed them, then went back to the outer office. Dropping one copy on Miss Dove's desk for her to docket it, he handed the other to Marsden. "Give that to Ledbetter's clerk," he ordered and returned his attention to the other two men.

Tremayne spoke first. "My lord, I have to get the five evening editions assembled and ready to print by three o'clock. I can't do it without that schedule."

Harry rubbed a hand over his face, trying to think of a solution. "It might be in her desk somewhere. Go through the drawers and see if you can find it."

"What about my book list?" Finch asked. "If any author is going to be late completing a book, which they always *are*, you know, I need to know about it."

"Yes, yes, but do you really need to know today? Can't this wait?"

Finch began a long, involved explanation as to why waiting was not possible. In the midst of it, the door opened again, and in came Diana. "Harry, we have been waiting in the carriage forever. What on earth is taking you so long?"

"It's not here," Tremayne said, shutting the bottom drawer of Miss Dove's desk. "I've looked in every drawer and pigeonhole."

"My lord," Finch said, "I am supposed to meet with the book publishing staff in a quarter of an hour."

"Harry," Diana said, "Edmund's yacht is to set sail at eleven o'clock. If you don't hurry, we're going to miss the party."

"Sir, I need Miss Dove's schedule." Tremayne rose from the desk. "Without it, I can't—"

"Enough," he interrupted the flood of voices and turned his attention first to Tremayne. "There was a time when we managed to get our newspapers out in a timely manner without Miss Dove. I'm sure we can do so without her daily schedule. Go back down to the newsrooms and find a way to get those evening editions out on time, and I don't care how you do it." He turned his attention to the other man. "Mr. Finch, you don't have to have the updated book schedule today, so go back down and postpone your meeting. And one of you find someone to locate Miss Dove."

As the two men departed, his sister spoke. "Miss Dove is missing?"

"So it would seem."

"How very odd. It's so unlike her, isn't it? I hope nothing untoward has happened. She left no word she would not be working today?"

"No. At least—" Harry broke off, remembering the letter on his desk. "Perhaps she did."

He returned to his office. Leaning over his desk, he picked up the envelope and broke the wax seal, then scanned the lines of the note Miss Dove had left for him. Its message was clear, concise, and completely unbelievable.

"What on earth?" Harry read the missive again, but there was no misunderstanding the message contained in the five lines typed on the sheet. Her neat signature was penned in ink at the bottom.

"What is it?"

He looked up to find Diana standing in the doorway. "She resigned," he said, unable to believe it even as he said it. "Miss Dove resigned."

"She did? Let me see." Diana crossed the room, took the letter, and read it. Then she looked at him, and to Harry's irritation, she was smiling. "You seem shocked, dear brother."

"Of course I'm shocked. Should I not be?"

"Well, Harry, not to be critical, but I wouldn't want to work for you."

"Miss Dove never complained."

"Yet she was unhappy enough to resign."

"What does her happiness have to do with anything? I don't pay her to be happy." He snatched the letter back. "She came here originally to apply for a post as a typist. In giving Miss Dove the position as my secretary, I did her a great favor. I hired a woman, and a woman with no experience in secretarial duties, at that. I pay her a salary far greater than she could ever expect to receive anywhere else. She can be happy on her own time."

"You only hired her to prove a point in the House," Diana reminded him. "Remember? You were suggesting how society might solve the problem of surplus women by promoting that radical idea of yours that my sex be allowed to earn our way in the world so men don't have to marry us and take care of us. So absurd."

"It is not absurd. It's a sound idea, with—"

"And why?" she went on, ignoring him. "All because you are cynical about the institution of marriage."

"I am not cynical!" he shot back before remembering there was just no arguing with Diana about this topic. He returned to the matter at hand. "The point is that I gave Miss Dove an opportunity no one else would have given her. I picked her at random out of a host of applicants. And after five satisfactory years, she up and resigns. With no reason, no warning, no notice." Harry began to feel quite nettled. "How could she do this to me after all I've done for her? Where is her loyalty?"

"I don't see why this is such a problem for you. Get another secretary. You should easily be able to find one. Ring up an agency or something."

"I have no intention of finding another secretary. I am quite satisfied with the one I have."

"Had," his sister corrected. "She resigned."

"I refuse to accept her resignation, and when I find her, I'm going to tell her so. She's not allowed to leave me."

"Bullying her? Oh, yes, that's sure to bring her back straightaway."

Harry glared at his sister's smiling face. "Do you have a better suggestion?"

"Since I can't imagine any woman with sense working for you in the first place, I've little advice to offer. But you might start by determining why she resigned. There must be a reason to make her do so without giving notice."

"A reason?" That took Harry aback. He paused, considering the matter. "I did reject her new manuscript."

"You've done that before, haven't you?"

"Yes, but this time she seemed to take it particularly hard. I'll wait a day or two, then I'll go see her. That should give her enough time to get over her hurt feelings."

"If that's her reason for resigning."

Harry paid no attention. He was following out his own train of thought. "She's a sensible sort of person," he reasoned, tapping the letter against his palm as he spoke. "Not at all prone to irrational, spur-of-the-moment decisions such as this. Two days should give her enough time to realize she made a mistake. She'll probably be relieved I've come to offer her back her post. She'll be grateful for the chance to rectify her mistake."

"Grateful?"

"I'll tell her there's no hard feelings, offer her a raise, and that should settle things."

Diana burst into merry laughter. Turning away, she started for the door.

"What is so amusing?" he demanded.

"Let me know how well your plan succeeds, will you?" She reached for the door handle. "I take it you're not coming to Edmund's water party?" Without waiting for an answer, Diana departed, closing the door behind her.

Emma told herself not to be nervous. She kept her hands folded firmly on top of the stack of Mrs. Bartleby manuscripts in her lap, tried not to fidget in her chair, and refused to think about the fact that her entire future could hang on what happened today.

This was not the safe thing to do. It was not the sensible thing to do. But she was over being safe and sensible.

Two days ago in that little shop on Regent Street, she had fallen apart. After spending the night of her thirtieth birthday hugging her pillow and crying on Mr. Pigeon's furry shoulder, she had put herself back together. By Sunday morning, she'd known just what she had to do. After church services and some serious prayers for divine assistance, she had gone to the publishing house, typed her letter of resignation, and put it on Marlowe's desk.

It was wrong, she knew, not to have given the proper fortnight's notice, but fourteen days would have given her too much time to think things over, too much time to talk herself out of her decision and let Marlowe talk her into staying. Now it was Monday, he had the letter, and there was no going back.

This was the dawn of a new day, and a new Emma Dove. Never again was she going to sit by while life went on around her. Never again was she going to wait for fate to hand her what she wanted. From now on, she was going to reach out and grab her dreams and not let go.

She had never been more scared in her life.

"Miss Dove?"

She looked up. The clerk she had spoken with upon her arrival was standing by the stairs, waiting for her. "Follow me."

Emma rose to her feet, trying to quell the jittery quivers in her tummy. One arm wrapped around her manuscripts, she followed the clerk up the stairs and into a reception room, where another man, clearly a secretary, was seated behind a desk. The clerk departed, and the secretary stood up. He gestured to an open doorway behind his desk. "You may go in, miss."

She stared at the doorway for a moment, then took a deep breath and stepped past the secretary into a large office every bit as expensively furnished as Marlowe's, though perhaps it was a bit too overcrowded to be a truly efficient place to work.

"Miss Dove?" A tall, exceptionally handsome man came around his desk and walked toward her, smiling. "It is a pleasure to meet you at last."

"At last, sir?" She watched in astonishment as he bent over her hand and kissed it.

"Everyone around Fleet Street knows of Marlowe's extraordinary female secretary. I've heard a great deal about you, Miss Dove," he added, retaining her hand in his, "and all of it has been complimentary."

Emma was growing more astonished by the moment. "I wish I could say the same," she murmured, "but though I have heard a great deal about you from Lord Marlowe, sir, none of it has been complimentary."

Lord Barringer threw back his head and laughed. "Of that, I have no doubt."

Chapter 5

When it comes to women, a gentleman must learn to expect the unexpected. It's what so often happens.

Lord Marlowe
The Bachelor's Guide, 1893

Miss Dove's lodgings were in Holborn, where blocks of flats formed a respectable neighborhood along Little Russell Street. Harry paused in front of number 32, a tidy brick building with lace curtains. A small, handpainted sign in the window declared that a parlor flat was available to be let, but only to women of good character. A pair of potted red geraniums flanked a freshly painted door of dark green. The door's brass knocker and handle gleamed in the late afternoon sunlight.

Just the sort of place where a paragon like Miss

Dove would live, he thought as he entered the building. The foyer seemed a bit dark after the brightness outside, but the pleasant scent of lemon soap told him the inside was as pristine as the outside. As his eyes adjusted to the dim interior, he could see that to his left was a parlor. To his right, a staircase with a wrought-iron railing curved upward, forming a sort of alcove where there was a large oak desk. Behind it, on the staircase wall, numbered cubicles held messages and letters for the tenants.

No landlady or servant seemed to be about, but Harry needed no assistance. He confirmed the number of Miss Dove's flat from the cubicles on the wall, then ascended the steps to the fourth floor and emerged onto a landing where the doors to flats 11 and 12 stood opposite each other and another set of stairs led to the roof.

Behind number 12, he heard the familiar rhythmic tap of a typewriting machine. When he knocked, the typing stopped, and a few moments later the door opened.

"Lord Marlowe?" She seemed surprised to see him, though why she should be surprised, he had no idea. She must have known the impact her sudden departure would have. Even if she didn't appreciate the havoc that had ensued after her departure, Harry certainly did. Throughout the day, members of his staff had come to him in a constant stream, clamoring for schedules and reports and all sorts of other things Miss Dove usually provided for them, things Harry didn't even know existed but which his staff couldn't seem to function without. He'd intended to wait a couple of days before coming to see her, but after only eight hours, it had become clear waiting wasn't going to work. He needed her back at her desk first thing tomorrow, or his staff would likely mutiny.

He doffed his hat and bowed. "Miss Dove."

"What are you doing here?" She glanced at the watch pinned to her starched white shirtwaist. "It is now half-past six. Did Lord Rathbourne's yachting party end early?"

"I didn't go." He held up her letter. "My secretary resigned. Because of that, my offices are now in utter chaos, the evening editions were late getting out, and I missed the boat, so to speak."

"I am sorry to hear that."

She didn't look sorry. She looked . . . damn it all, she looked pleased. There seemed to be a tiny curve to one corner of her mouth, indicating she was actually taking pleasure in his difficulties. Harry thought of the hellish day he and his staff had experienced, and he could not share her amusement.

"I can see you find our distress at your absence gratifying, Miss Dove."

"Not at all." A polite, perfunctory response, and also a lie. She was pleased as punch.

"If you're not gratified, you should be," he told her as he tucked the letter back in the breast pocket of his jacket. "All the other members of my staff were running around like panicked rabbits without you."

"But not you, I am sure."

"I was too astonished to panic. Your resignation was most unexpected."

"Was it?" That glimmer of satisfaction in her expression vanished, and a queer sort of hardness took its place.

"Yes." He gestured to the interior of her flat. "Might I have a moment with you to discuss it?"

"It's a straightforward resignation. What is there to discuss?"

"After five years, does not courtesy allow at least a conversation on the topic?"

She hesitated, and her lack of enthusiasm was not an encouraging sign. He might have been precipitate, he might not have given her enough time to think over the consequences of her action, but it could not be helped.

"Did anyone see you come up?" she asked, glancing past him. "My landlady? A servant?"

"No." He remembered the sign in the window, and the implications of her question dawned on him, but the impression his visit might leave on an overly inquisitive landlady or her servants or any of the women who lived here didn't concern him half as much as losing his secretary. "No one saw me, Miss Dove. But if I linger out here in the corridor, someone eventually will."

She opened the door wider to let him in. "Very well. You may come in for a few moments, but when you leave, please try not to let anyone see you. I do not wish anyone to think . . . think things."

The parlor of her flat surprised him, for it was

unlike any he'd ever seen. It was unconventional, to say the least, with a hint of the exotic about it. Brass incense pots decorated the mantel, a copper boiler pot held coal, a big round basket overflowed with colorful pillows, and a Turkish carpet covered the floor. There were two over-stuffed settees of cream-colored velvet, and between them a round leather ottoman which, oddly enough, seemed to act as a tea table, for reposing upon it was an enameled tea set.

Bronze chintz draperies bracketed a pair of windows that lit the room with afternoon sun. Between those windows stood a glass-fronted bookcase lined with volumes and a dark walnut cabinet with an inordinate number of drawers and compartments. At the far end of the room, an elaborately carved oak door led into another part of the flat. Beside it, a French window led to the fire escape and a drop-leaf table held a type-writing machine. The parlor was separated from a small alcove by a painted wooden screen. Though the flat was small, the effect was one of almost sumptuous comfort, not at all the sort of living quarters he would have imagined for the no-nonsense Miss Dove.

Something brushed his leg and he looked down to find an enormous cat at his feet. Too chubby to walk between his ankles, it twined around him, rubbing its body against his legs, no doubt depositing quantities of orange cat hair all over his gray wool trousers.

Harry eyed it with dismay. "You have a cat."

"That's Mr. Pigeon." She sat down on one of

the settees and gestured for him to sit opposite her.

The moment he sat down and put aside his hat, the animal jumped into his lap. Rather amazed that such a huge cat could jump anywhere, he watched as it curled up in his lap and began to purr with gusto.

"He likes you," Miss Dove said, sounding surprised.

"Yes," Harry answered with an unhappy sigh. He had long ago accepted the fact that cats adored him. The reason, of course, was because both God and cats had the same perverse sense of humor. When the animal buried its claws in his thigh and began to knead with happy abandon, he set his jaw and bore it. "Mr. Pigeon? Rather fitting for you to choose that name, Miss Dove. Both birds, you know."

"Oh, that isn't why I named him Mr. Pigeon. It's because he stalks the pigeons on the roof. Always has, even when he was a tiny kitten. Whenever he catches one, he brings it down the fire escape for me."

"How sweet." What bloodthirsty creatures cats were, really. He tried to adopt a jovial attitude. "Eats quite a few of those pigeons, too, by the look of him."

"Are you saying my cat is fat?"

"Not at all," he lied and decided a change of subject was in order. "Miss Dove," he said, pushing the terror of the rooftop pigeons off his lap as gently as possible, "I have come to offer the olive branch, as it were. I know you must be upset by my rejection of your manuscript, but you know I have to be true to my instincts in matters of this kind."

"Of course."

"I cannot publish what I do not believe will make a profit." He smiled gently. "I would be a sad man of business indeed, if I made such unwise decisions."

"Certainly."

There was a long silence, and Harry began to feel as if he were pushing a boulder uphill, but he persevered. "I appreciate that you are upset in your feelings and perhaps discouraged by my response to your writing, but surely that does not warrant resigning your post."

"Amazing that you possess such an intimate knowledge of my feelings."

Harry decided to change tactics. "What will you do now? Where will you go? Respectable employment, particularly for women, is not easy to come by nowadays." He gestured to their surroundings. "It is certain no other employer in London will pay you enough to afford you a parlor flat like this one."

"My lord—"

"But even should you find another post at a wage that does not force you to move, what if you are unhappy with your next situation? Or your employer does not treat you well?" He put on an air of gentlemanly concern. "The world can be a hard place for a woman alone, Miss Dove. What will happen to you? Without me, your future is very uncertain, you know."

"How kind you are to be so concerned about my future." The inflection of sarcasm in her voice was becoming more pronounced.

"I am concerned for both of us if you do not come back," he replied. "And I am concerned for my staff. They value you as much as I."

She smiled at him. "There is no need for you or anyone else at Marlowe Publishing to worry about me or my future. You see, I have already secured a new position."

Harry sat up straighter on the settee. "What? Already?"

"Yes. I am now working for Lord Barringer."

"Barringer?" He was appalled. "That pompous, self-righteous hypocrite?"

Her smile widened into what he could only describe as a smug, satisfied grin. "The very one."

He shook his head, knowing full well what she said was impossible. "Barringer hired himself a female secretary? I don't believe it."

"He did not engage me to be his secretary. He is going to publish my writing."

Harry began to laugh. He couldn't help it, the idea was so absurd.

Miss Dove, of course, did not appreciate the humor as much as he did. She stopped smiling, her eyes narrowed, and he smothered his laughter at once. "Forgive me. I fear you have misinterpreted the reason for my amusement, Miss Dove. It stems from the irony of the situation."

"Irony?"

"Yes. I can see I must explain Barringer to

you. Though he is an earl and displays the pretense of being a gentleman, he is not. For all the high-minded airs he puts on, he is notoriously immoral in his private life. Barringer publishing etiquette books is like the devil giving a morality lecture."

No hint of a smile, no appreciation of the irony crossed her face. "Your private life being such an excellent moral example, there would be no such irony if you published etiquette books?" She gave him no chance to reply to that. "In any case, Lord Barringer is not publishing my work as a book. I shall be writing a column for his weekly periodical, the *Social Gazette*. And though matters of etiquette will be of paramount importance in my dialogue, it is not the only topic I shall be discussing."

Before she had even finished, Harry had already figured out what Barringer was up to. "He's hired you to thumb his nose at me, of course. He loathes me, and knowing how much I depend upon you, he is enjoying the notion of stealing you away from me. A column allows him to flaunt his victory on a weekly basis."

"I don't suppose it's possible his decision has nothing to do with you? That he has decided to publish my writing because it's good?"

"Barringer wouldn't know good writing if it bit him. He went to Oxford."

She did not find that amusing. "The fact that you belittle Barringer's ability to appreciate good writing does not surprise me. But I am baffled by how you can denigrate my writing as not being good when you haven't even read it!"

Harry had the feeling he was digging himself deeper into a hole with every moment, but he wasn't going to lie to her about her work in order to extricate himself. "I read enough of it to know I wasn't interested in publishing it."

She rose to her feet, implying their conversation was at an end. "Then it shouldn't bother you in the least that Lord Barringer chooses to do so."

"That is not what bothers me." He also stood up. "What bothers me is losing my secretary, a secretary who had no experience, no references, not even a letter of character when she first came to me, but to whom I gave the chance to prove her abilities."

She gave an indignant huff. "How generous of you."

"Damned right it was generous. Who else would have hired you? Who else would have paid you the same wage as a man? Who else would have given a mere secretary yearly bonuses at Christmas and Saturday afternoons free? No one. Barringer wouldn't, that's certain."

"And in exchange for your so-called generosity, I have fulfilled my duties in exemplary fashion for five years! You've nothing in my conduct with which to find fault."

"Nothing? You up and resign, having given no indication you were dissatisfied with your position, having told me nothing of your discontent.

You accept employment with my fiercest competitor, a man who despises me and would love nothing better than to worm confidential information out of my former secretary."

"No one worms anything out of me, I can assure you!"

"And," he went on, paying no heed to her words, "you commit this disloyalty without even having the good manners and sense of *etiquette* to give the customary fortnight's notice of your departure."

For the first time, Miss Dove had the grace to look a bit ashamed of herself. As well she should. "I regret that circumstances forbade my giving notice." She turned and walked away. "I can only say," she added over her shoulder as she paused by a window, "that my actions were dictated by the certain knowledge you will have no trouble replacing me."

"Replace you? Woman, have you not yet comprehended why I'm here? Haven't I made it plain enough? I don't want to replace you. I want you to give up this notion of writing silly etiquette stuff for Barringer and come back to work for me where you belong."

"What I write is not silly!" She whirled around, and her chin came up. The sun glinted off her hair. "Since you are speaking plainly, so shall I. What I write is important and useful, and I will not allow you to disparage it. As for where I belong, I have decided that it isn't working for you! And who could blame me? I have been a loyal, reliable employee, doing everything required of me and more, but in return I have been rewarded with nothing but more work."

"And generous pay," he shot back.

She ignored that. "You have piled task after task upon me, yet you have never spared a moment to discuss my writing, you have taken advantage of me at every opportunity, even going so far as to require me to buy the gifts you give your mistresses!"

"I asked it. I never required it. And if it was such an objectionable part of your duties, you should have said so."

"You have never appreciated me nor any of the many things I've done for you and for Marlowe Publishing," she went on as if he hadn't spoken. "All you have done is take me for granted. Well, I have had enough!"

Harry's frustration faded into bafflement as she unleashed this torrent of criticism upon him. Never before had she shown a shred of anger, or any other emotion, for that matter. This was not the Miss Dove he knew. This was not the compliant secretary who had been gliding in and out of his line of vision half a dozen times a day for five years now, who followed his instructions and obeyed his orders with cheerful acceptance, no questions and no complaints. This was certainly not the Miss Dove who always behaved with efficiency, exactitude, and propriety. This was someone else altogether, someone he did not recognize.

He studied her, and something about the way she stood in the shaft of sunlight through the window caught his attention. "Miss Dove," he said in surprise, "you have red hair."

"What?" She blinked. "I beg your pardon?"

"Your hair is red. I never realized that before. I always thought it was brown, but it's not. In the sunlight it turns red."

She frowned at him, looking thoroughly vexed. "I know the color of my hair, thank you. What on earth has that to do with anything?"

Somehow, he'd managed to offend her yet again. "No need to get touchy about it," he assured her. "Some people don't like their red hair, I know, but you needn't worry. Yours isn't a violent sort of red. It looks brown, but when you stand in the sun, it goes all coppery and shimmery. It's . . ." He paused, feeling as if he'd just discovered something rather extraordinary. "It's very pretty."

She was not pleased by the compliment. She actually seemed insulted. "Oh!" she cried, hands balling into fists at her sides, "you are the most manipulative man I have ever known! And the most insincere."

"Insincere? What, you don't believe me?"

"Of course I don't! It's too convenient a compliment to be a true opinion. Besides, you only like women with black hair."

She saw his surprise and gave him a look of triumph in return. "Hah! You see? I know you, Lord Marlowe. The five years I've been in your employ have given me a complete understanding of your character. I know you like the back of my hand, so trying to get around me with compliments is useless. You dole out flattery as if you are handing out candy to children. It's all meant to charm, or to soothe, or to get what you want, or to help you wriggle out of unpleasant situations. Why others fall prey to such tactics, particularly women, is beyond my comprehension, but I am not such a fool as that."

Red hair, and a temper, too, he thought, amazed. He hadn't known she possessed either. "I have never thought you a fool."

" 'You're a treasure, Miss Dove,' " she quoted him with scorn. " 'I don't know what I'd do without you, Miss Dove.' Do you really think such innocuous flattery ever made me feel valued or important? It didn't," she said, answering her own question before he could do so. "But now you want me to come back, so you're using flattery as a tactic, as if a compliment about my hair ought to impress me enough for that!"

Impressing her hadn't even occurred to him. It was true that in his private life he happened to have a certain susceptibility to women with black tresses, but that didn't make his comment about Miss Dove's hair insincere. It nettled him that she thought so.

Harry opened his mouth to set her straight, but she didn't give him the chance. She sucked in a deep breath and went on. "Besides, you've lied to me before, so why should I believe anything you have to say?"

He stiffened at those words. He was not a liar, and no one had ever dared accuse him of being one. "I do not lie, Miss Dove. Despite your assessment of me and my motives, I do not give false compliments, only ones I genuinely believe. I concede to being manipulative—I doubt I could succeed in business if I were not so—but I do not lie."

"Equivocate, then. Is that a better way of putting it? You didn't even know Mrs. Bartleby was my pen name, and it's right on the title page of every manuscript I've ever given you!"

"Is that what this is all about?" Now he knew the identity of Mrs. Bartleby, but at the moment, having his curiosity satisfied on that point was hardly gratifying. "Good God, I don't read your title pages. Why should I? When you hand me a manuscript, I know perfectly well who wrote it."

"Title pages aside, if you had actually read my work, you would still have known who Mrs. Bartleby is. You led me to believe you have read my manuscripts, but you have not!"

This was becoming ridiculous. "I told you, I have read enough of your work to form an opinion. That's all any publisher does. Unless it sparks his interest, he doesn't read it all. If we read everything we receive all the way through, we should never get any work done. And having been employed by a publisher five years now, opening all the unsolicited writing I and my editors receive, you ought to know that."

"What I know is that you will never publish any of my writing because you cannot look at it objectively. You are too closed-minded."

"I am not closed-minded!"

"I have finally come to accept that flaw of your character," she continued with blithe disregard for his denial, "and I have taken my writing else-where, to someone who respects my work. Some-one who respects me."

"Respect?" The implication that he did not have respect for her was an insult to his charac-ter that made Harry truly angry. "If you think Barringer has a shred of respect for you or your writing, you are deceiving yourself. To be blunt, you're not of his class, and Barringer is one of those pompous asses that abound in this world who care about distinctions of that sort. He's a snob and a hypocrite."

"He had some equally flattering things to say about you."

"I'll wager he did."

"Things which my own observations of you over the years only served to confirm."

"What observations? You claim a full under-standing of my nature, but if that were true, there would be nothing that blatherskite Barrin-ger could say about me with which you would agree. You believe you know me? Obviously, you do not know me at all, Miss Dove."

"And if you think I will come back into your employ only to tolerate more of your denigra-tion of my work as silly, you do not know me, my lord!"

Harry stared at her, noting the flush of out-rage in her cheeks, the red glints in her hair, and the clenched fists at her sides, and his own anger faded as quickly as it had come.

Five years of having her in his employ, with each of them assuming those passing years had given them a thorough knowledge of the other's character. She thought him insincere and a liar and God only knows what else. He thought her cool, dispassionate, compliant, and—truth be told—somewhat inhuman. Both of them, it seemed, had been wrong.

"I want you to leave."

Interrupted in the midst of these realizations, Harry didn't quite catch her words. "I beg your pardon?"

She stalked over to him and stuck her chin up looking him square in the eye. "I said, leave."

What else about her had he missed? He studied her face, not as if it was the one he saw nearly every day, but instead, as if they had never met before.

Her eyes were hazel. He already knew that, but what he hadn't known until now was that the gold flecks in them seemed to snap like sparks when she was angry. Until now, he hadn't really noticed the freckles sprinkled over her nose and upper cheeks like so much pixy dust, or that there was a faint, star-shaped scar on her cheekbone. Until now he hadn't realized that her brown lashes were light at the ends, as if the tips had been dipped in gold.

"Are you hard of hearing?" She brought her hands up between them and pushed with all her might. When he didn't comply, she pushed him again. "I said, go away!"

He outweighed her by a good five or six stone, at least, so all her shoving didn't move him an inch. He continued to look at her in this new way, seeing her as he'd never seen her before. To his surprise, he found himself enjoying the view. She was not a beautiful woman, but right now, with rosy color in her cheeks and those sparks in her eyes, she was a sight any man would appreciate. Miss Dove was very human indeed.

Seeing that her attempts to force him out were useless, she stopped. "Depart this instant, Lord Marlowe," she ordered. "If you don't, I shall fetch the police. They have a station at the corner."

Knowing she would be unmoved by any more words about how much he valued her, he decided it was time to negotiate. "I'll increase your wages. Say to ten pounds a month?"

"No!" She pushed him again, and this time he allowed it, knowing he would gain nothing by doing otherwise.

"Twenty," he said. That was exorbitant pay for a secretary, but he could afford the expense.

"No."

"Thirty. And I'll give you all of Saturdays off, not just afternoons."

"No, no, no!" With each refusal, she pushed him closer to the door. "This is not about days off. It's not about money."

"What is it about, then?" he asked as she paused by the settees and grabbed his hat. "Your hurt feelings?"

"No." She slammed the hat on his head with one hand as she continued to propel him backward with the other. "This is about me and what I want. I want to be a writer, not work for you."

"I am not accepting your resignation."

"You have to accept it."

He took off his hat and held it to his heart. "What will it take to get you back?"

She made a sound of thorough exasperation through her teeth. "Do you never give up?"

"Not when I want something. I'm rather obstinate that way. Since you claim to know me so well, you should know that."

"Then we have something in common, my lord, for I, too, am very obstinate."

He had to tell her the truth about Barringer. It was only right. "I beg you to be sensible. As my secretary, your future is secure, while this venture with Barringer is doomed to fail. He's facing—"

"I don't want a secure future," she interrupted, "and I shall not reconsider! I've had enough of being sensible to last a lifetime. And I don't believe I will fail. There are a great many people who are concerned with good manners, though you are obviously not one of them."

"You do not understand the circumstances under which Barringer has offered to publish your work. I'm not surprised that he didn't enlighten you, but you need to know—"

"He's not you. That's the only thing I need to know." She stepped sideways and opened the door. After a quick glance in both directions, she looked at him and waited.

When he did not move to depart, she gave an aggravated sigh and returned to stand in front of him. She flattened her hands against his chest, crushing his hat, and began pushing him out into the corridor. "I shall finally be a published writer, which is what I have always wanted to be. Barringer will make pots of money and score off you, just as you say he wants to do. Our venture will be a raging success." She came to a stop on the threshold, breathing hard from the exertion of getting him out the door. "But the best part of all is that I shall never have to buy another gift for one of your horrid mistresses!"

She started to shut the door, then stopped. "And Mr. Pigeon is not fat!" With that parting shot, she shut the door in his face.

He stared at the closed door, unable to quite believe what had just happened. He was supposed to have come here as the benevolent employer, giving his misguided secretary another chance. She was supposed to have regretted her impetuous decision. She was supposed to have thought things over, and upon such reflection, come to her senses. She was supposed to be back at her desk tomorrow morning. Instead, he'd had a door slammed in his face, and his compliant, sensible, efficient secretary was now working for the loathsome Lord Barringer.

Harry rubbed a hand over his eyes and began to wonder if, like Alice, he had just stepped through a looking glass into a world where everything was upside down and topsy-turvy and nothing was what it seemed.

One thing, however, was very clear. Miss Dove was unaware of Barringer's financial situation and had no idea that her fate was to be back in Harry's employ in very short order. Barringer was good at putting up a show of prosperity, but Harry knew the earl was being pressed by creditors at every turn. He would soon be forced to sell the *Gazette*, and when Harry bought it, his plans to make the newspaper more entertaining did not include an etiquette column.

He'd tried to tell her all this, but she had refused to listen. Twice she had interrupted his attempts to explain. She had also insulted his manners, accused him of lacking respect for her, and called him a liar. Such behavior, damn it all, couldn't be acceptable in anybody's etiquette book.

Harry decided not to make any further attempts to enlighten her. Let her find out the truth about her new employer for herself. When she did, he'd be there, happy to offer her back her former post and willing to let bygones be bygones.

Harry reshaped his flattened hat, put it on his head, and started down the stairs. Perhaps this entire episode was for the best. Perhaps Miss Dove would finally see that etiquette books weren't worth writing and they weren't worth publishing. People didn't want to read about how to behave. They wanted to read about how other people were misbehaving.

She didn't know it yet, but within a few weeks, Miss Dove would be back at her desk. He just had to hire a temporary replacement for her and exercise a little patience. How hard could that be?

Chapter 6

❦

It is not the fairness of the price which matters. It is how much one is willing to pay.

Mrs. Bartleby
All Things London
The *Social Gazette*, 1893

If Harry had any doubts about the demise of Miss Dove's literary career, the following Saturday's edition of the *Social Gazette* assuaged them. He shifted the folded-back newspaper from his right to his left hand, continuing to read her debut column as his valet, Cummings, assisted him into his jacket.

His curiosity satisfied by the first two paragraphs, Harry dropped the newspaper onto the silver tray held by his butler. "Thank you, Jackson. Take it back downstairs and put it with the others in the dining room. I shall be down directly."

"Very good, my lord." The butler withdrew, and Harry turned around, lifting his chin so that Cummings could do up his tie. The proper way to give a luncheon party was just the sort of stuff he'd expected Miss Dove to put in a column, and he could see little help there for the sinking fortunes of Lord Barringer. He and the earl ought to be able to come to an agreement on an acceptable price for the newspaper quite soon. A fortnight, Harry judged as he went downstairs. A month at most.

"Go to Chelsea for table linens?" his mother's voice was saying as he entered the dining room. "I don't believe it. Good morning, dear."

"Morning, Mama." He kissed Louisa's cheek. "Good morning, ladies." He bowed to them, noticing in amusement that Lady Felicity seemed to have developed a passionate interest in newspapers, for she held one in her hand this morning.

"You are in good spirits today, Harry," Diana commented as he walked to the sideboard.

"Should I not be?" he asked, helping himself to kidneys, bacon, and toast.

"You weren't a few days ago," his eldest sister reminded him. "Yet today you seem quite reconciled to the loss of your secretary."

His grandmother spoke before he could reply. "Harrison, I cannot believe Miss Dove has left your employ." She shook her head with a heavy sigh. "You shall never be on time for anything again, I fear."

"Do not distress yourself, Grandmama. I have not lost Miss Dove." He took his place at the head of the table. "She is temporarily absent, that's all."

"Only you would refer to a resignation as a temporary absence," Vivian said, laughing. "You are forever an optimist, Harry."

"Why Chelsea?" Louisa asked, reverting to the topic they'd been discussing when he entered the room. "Does she favor a particular shop there?"

Felicity lifted the folded-back newspaper in her hand, skimmed it for a moment, then nodded. She cleared her throat and began reading aloud to the others at the table. " 'If one is in need of fine table linens, Maxwell's of Chelsea is an excellent place to acquire them. Their Irish linen is of an unsurpassed quality, and those of a frugal nature may be assured that Maxwell's is most reasonable.' "

"Let me see." Louisa stuck her pair of gold-framed pince-nez on her nose and took the paper from Felicity's outstretched hand. "Hmm . . . she says that for decorating the tables at a luncheon party, ivory linen or white are equally acceptable."

Harry stopped eating. "Are you reading the *Social Gazette*?"

"Yes, dear," Louisa answered without looking up. "Some woman named Bartleby. Felicity wanted to see which newspaper had so captured your interest that you had Jackson fetch it specially from your plate this morning, though

I wouldn't have thought you interested in luncheon parties and where one ought to buy linens. Hmm . . . she favors orchids as a centerpiece, which would be lovely—unscented, of course . . . hmm . . . place card holders that have the shape of pink flamingos? How charming."

Charming was not how Harry would have described it. Downright absurd, he'd have said.

"Origami, she calls it," his mother went on, "a tradition from the island of Nippon. 'Using origami,'" Louisa quoted, "'paper is folded into the shape of animals or flowers, and provides the hostess with an infinite variety of unusual decorations suitable for any party. At the conclusion of the event, the hostess may choose to give one of the origami decorations to each guest as a parting gift.'"

"What a unique idea," Vivian commented, "and very clever."

This elicited nods and murmurs of agreement from all the ladies at the table, and Harry felt a glimmer of uneasiness in his gut. "Surely you're not taking this woman seriously?" he asked.

"Giving a luncheon party, or any other sort of party, for that matter, is a very serious business, dear." His mother unfolded the newspaper and turned the page, looking for the remainder of Miss Dove's column. "One party, properly given, can make a hostess the shining light of the season."

"Somehow," Harry said, "I doubt pink paper flamingos would have much influence upon a hostess's social status."

"Oh, but things like that can be very important, Lord Marlowe," Lady Felicity informed him. "Because my father is a widower, I act as his hostess, and I can assure you that giving a party requires a great deal of thought and attention. I'm certain Melanie, who acts as hostess for her own widowed father, would agree with me. Clever ideas such as this woman describes can be most helpful in making a social event successful."

Melanie, who still seemed to have no ability to speak when he was in the room, could only confirm this with a nod.

"Girls, listen to this." Louisa leaned forward in her chair, eager to impart more of Mrs. Bartleby's wisdom. "She says there is a stationer's directly across the street from this draper's shop in Chelsea that supplies beautiful colored papers suitable for this origami business. They can provide instruction on how to make the flamingos, or one can have them made to order in quantity. She gives this stationer's her soundest recommendation."

"Oh, does she?" Antonia sniffed and took a sip of her tea. "And who is this Mrs. Bartleby, that her recommendation means so very much?"

Harry could have enlightened them, but he had no intention of doing so. If his sisters discovered the Bartleby woman was Miss Dove, they'd rag him endlessly for rejecting her oh-so-clever ideas and for losing her to Barringer. Even though it was only a temporary situation, they'd never let him live it down. Wisely, he kept his mouth closed.

"What are her connections?" Antonia went on. "Who are her people? I know of no prominent family in Britain with the surname of Bartleby."

"Perhaps she is American," Phoebe suggested.

"Oh, American," Antonia said with an emphasis on the second word that made her opinion of both the fictional Mrs. Bartleby and the possible country of her origin quite clear.

"She couldn't be American," Vivian said, gesturing with her piece of toast to the newspaper held by her mother. "An American wouldn't know the best places in London to shop for linens and stationery, would she?"

"Regardless of who she is, one thing is obvious," Diana put in. "We shall be making a shopping expedition to Chelsea today."

"Go to Chelsea?" Harry looked at her askance. "Because some woman you don't even know tells you to go there?"

"No," Diana answered at once. "We are going in the hope of finding beautiful table linens."

"And so that we may learn to make pink flamingos!" Lady Florence said, laughing. She looked at Harry. "Will you accompany us, Lord Marlowe?"

He'd rather jump off a cliff. "Alas, Lady Florence," he said, feigning polite regret, "but I cannot. I have matters of business to attend to. If you will forgive me?"

With that, he rose to his feet, gathered his newspapers and his morning post, and gave the ladies at the table a bow of farewell. Deep in discussion of pink flamingo place-card holders, shopping expeditions to Chelsea, and the possible bona fides of Mrs. Bartleby, they didn't even notice his departure.

During the two months that followed, Harry's uneasiness at the breakfast table proved far more accurate than his long-held opinions about Miss Dove's writing. By the time sixty days had passed, everyone seemed to be talking of her and praising her clever ideas, much to Harry's amazement and chagrin.

He had always known Miss Dove was an intelligent woman, but even he hadn't known the vast scope of her knowledge. She seemed to be a walking, talking *Encyclopedia Britannica*.

Mrs. Bartleby knew everything about everything, it seemed. She knew how to get ink stains out of silk, the appropriate way for a young lady to refuse a marriage proposal from a widower, which restaurants were respectable establishments where ladies might dine after the theater—accompanied, of course!—and which bakeries could be counted upon for the freshest tea cakes.

She assured girl-bachelors that it was perfectly acceptable to walk with a young man along a public street in the afternoon unaccompanied, provided their acquaintance had been of at least several years' duration, the woman was on her way home from her job, and she was certain of the young man's respectability and good character. Ladies, it seemed, had less freedom than girl-bachelors, for they were required to have their chaperones present at all times until the age of thirty.

Mrs. Bartleby did not neglect the male sex in her weekly dialogue. She knew where a gentleman might find the best-made, most comfortable boots. She knew which tobacconists carried the finest cigars, which the gentlemen would, of course, have the consideration to smoke *outside*. She staunchly defended detachable shirt collars and cuffs as sensible devices for unmarried professional men, but abhorred cuff protectors and dickeys as inventions unworthy of even the poorest clerk.

The words "Mrs. Bartleby says . . ." were repeated in so many conversations, Harry felt if he heard them one more time, he was going to go mad.

In addition to this unexpected and rather nauseating development, Harry had been unable to find a satisfactory replacement for Miss Dove. The day after their altercation at her flat, he had rung up an agency, and since then, a series of secretaries had come and gone from Harry's offices. Time and again he had been promised someone with vast secretarial experience, but there was always something wrong. One took dictation with all the speed of a turtle, another could not get it through his head that Harry preferred coffee to tea with no milk or sugar, another couldn't keep track of appointments.

The latter flaw was the most inconvenient of all, for Harry had somehow mislaid his appointment book. With Miss Dove, the loss would not have been a problem, for she had always managed to know where he needed to be and when, but in this regard, her successors were hopeless.

The most recent one, a chap named Quinn, Harry deemed the worst of the lot. He had the irritating habit of hanging his head like a whipped puppy every time a mistake was pointed out to him. Still, explaining the same procedures to a new face every other day had grown wearisome for him and the others on his staff, and Harry had reluctantly accepted Quinn as a temporary replacement. But as the days of May went by and Mrs. Bartleby's popularity continued to rise, Harry began to fear he was saddled with Quinn, or someone equally irritating, for a long time to come.

As if all that weren't bad enough, the females in his own household had found their shopping expedition to Chelsea and the subsequent advice of Mrs. Bartleby so gratifying that they insisted upon reading her column aloud to each other at breakfast every Saturday morning. They were now planning their lives around whatever new information Miss Dove's fictional counterpart chose to hand out and spending Harry's money on whatever she advised them to buy.

"Diana, today's column might have been written for you." Louisa rustled the newspaper in her hands. "Today Mrs. Bartleby discusses the giving of wedding breakfasts."

This news was greeted with exclamations of delight by every female at the table. Harry, who was contemplating a ban on reading newspapers at breakfast with the excuse that it was rude, stared glumly into his plate of eggs and bacon and wondered if he should start eating at his club on Saturdays.

"'Stand-up and sit-down breakfasts are equally fashionable this year,'" his mother read, "'although each requires a menu particular to its design.' Hmm . . . no hot entrées during a stand-up breakfast, of course. Crab puffs and pâté de foie gras to start, a chilled tomato soup served in teacups to be sipped. That way guests needn't bother with spoons as they mill about the room— what a sensible idea! And so clever!"

Harry couldn't help rolling his eyes, but the women didn't seem to notice.

"'In addition to the customary cold meats and game,'" his mother went on, "'a hearty salad is always a welcome addition. A chicken salad, for example, with almonds and mayonnaise, is most delicious when served on tiny croissants as finger sandwiches.'"

This suggestion was met with a torrent of praise, though what was so exciting about chicken sandwiches Harry couldn't fathom.

Jackson appeared beside him with the morning post. Harry pushed aside his plate and sorted through his letters, pausing on one with Lord Barringer's coronet.

He opened it, and the information it contained was so appalling, he had to read it twice to be sure he wasn't having a bad dream. Circulation had doubled at the *Social Gazette* during the past two months, Barringer informed him with obvious relish. As a result, advertising revenues had also increased significantly, and the earl was raising his asking price for the newspaper to one hundred fifty thousand pounds. Barringer was in desperate need of ready money, and time should have made him more willing to lower his asking price. Instead, he was raising it. And why? Because of paper animals and soup served in teacups.

"Harry, dear, don't grind your teeth," Louisa admonished him, then peered over her pince-nez at her eldest daughter. "Diana, Mrs. Bartleby's menu is an excellent one, don't you think? Most suitable for your own wedding breakfast."

Harry could take no more. "Absolutely not!" he snapped and stood up. "I am not going to sip cold tomato soup out of a teacup, Mama, not even for Diana!"

With his opinion on that now perfectly clear, Harry tossed his serviette into his plate, thrust Barringer's letter into his pocket, and departed from the table, leaving nine astonished women staring after him.

Since he didn't know what his appointments were and neither, it seemed, did his secretary, Harry decided to go to his club. A gentleman's club was sacrosanct, the last bastion of sensible men who didn't give a damn about wedding breakfast menus and which young men the girl-bachelors walked out with in the afternoon.

Upon his arrival at Brooks's, he found two of

his closest acquaintances were also there, seated at a table in one corner. He crossed the room toward them.

Lord Weston was the first to see him. "By all that's wonderful," he cried, standing up to give Harry a hearty clap on the shoulder, "glad you're here, Marlowe. We're having a bit of a dispute, and you've arrived just in time to settle it."

"Indeed?" Harry greeted the other man at the table, Sir Philip Knighton, then pulled out a chair. "What are the two of you arguing about this time?"

"I say the four-in-hand tie is still perfectly acceptable, but Sir Philip says it is now *comme il faut.*"

"I'm not the one saying so, Weston," Sir Philip protested. "The Bartleby woman was quite emphatic about it in her column last week. The four-in-hand is out."

"That tears it!" Harry jumped to his feet so violently he knocked over his chair. "Damn it all, can't a man even go to his club anymore?"

All the gentlemen around him, including his companions, stared at him in astonishment. Harry drew a deep breath. "Forgive me," he said with a bow, "but I must go. I just remembered that I have an important engagement."

He left his club and called for his carriage, but when it came, he waved it away. Instead, he took a long walk.

He went over everything he could recall of Miss Dove's manuscripts—which wasn't much, for he hadn't read much. And what he had read had so failed to capture his interest that he could only remember a few things. Something about how a girl-bachelor could decorate her flat. Stuff about how to give an Afternoon-at-Home. The proper way for a lady to ride in the park. Just thinking about these topics, and he was already bored to distraction. So what was making her a success? He just didn't see it.

That, he realized with dismay, was the crux of the problem.

Though he could not see the appeal of Miss Dove's writing, other people did. Somehow, in the space of two months, her Mrs. Bartleby character had become a sensation. How could he have been so wrong about her appeal to the reading public?

Her accusation came back to slap him in the face. *You are too closed-minded.*

Was that true? He had always prided himself on being open to opportunities. Had he somehow become closed-minded without even realizing it? He thought of his editors, of all the manuscripts they had recommended over the years that he had rejected. How many more Mrs. Bartlebys were in the rubbish heap? There was no way to know.

He had always trusted his instincts, and they had never failed to tell him the truth. His success as a publisher had always come from his ability to know what people wanted to read and providing it for them at just the right time.

Was he losing that ability? Were his instincts deserting him? Self-doubt, something he seldom had cause to feel, whispered through his mind. Were the qualities that had made him Britain's most successful publisher deserting him?

He paused at Hyde Park Corner, where a boy in a cap stood amid stacks of newspapers. Three of his own were there, along with the *London Times* and the *Social Gazette*. Harry bought a copy of the latter, found himself an empty bench in the park, and sat down. He read every word of today's *All Things London*, by Mrs. Honoria Bartleby.

When he had finished, he knew all about the giving of wedding breakfasts, but he still felt no more enlightened as to why she'd caught the public's fancy than he had before. On the other hand, he knew his private opinion of her work no longer mattered.

Harry sat back on the bench and considered the situation as objectively as he could. Publishing was a cutthroat business, always shifting and changing. He could not afford to become closed-minded. Some of his most profitable ventures over the years had sprung from unexpected events that he turned into opportunities. Perhaps this was such a moment. Harry began to get an idea, and his innate optimism began to return.

After about an hour, he stood up, knowing there was only one thing to do. He'd meet with Barringer and accept the terms of sale the earl had outlined. He had to do it now. The way things were going, if he delayed, Miss Dove's success would cost him another fifty thousand pounds.

* * *

Emma loved her new life. She loved spending her afternoons exploring London shops in search of information to share with her readers. She loved exercising her ingenuity, inventing ways to transform the commonplace into the unusual, so that even the most frugal matrons could arrange elegant meals for their families and even the busiest girl-bachelors could make their flats comfortable and cozy. She loved writing, and she loved seeing her compositions in print. She loved Mrs. Bartleby, because every morning when she sat down to work, when she typed the advice of that fictional character, she could hear dear Aunt Lydia's voice again. It was almost as if Auntie were sitting beside her, helping her along, sharing her newfound success.

And she was successful, surprisingly so.

Despite her former employer's rejections of her work, Emma had always felt that her particular knowledge and experience could be of use to others. But she was astonished by the extent of her popularity and the speed at which her success occurred. Within a month, she had become the talk of the town every Saturday morning, and when she asked for an increase in her wages, Barringer granted it, enabling her to stop dipping into her savings so that she could live comfortably on her writing income alone.

Within two months, she was receiving stacks of letters, so many that she couldn't answer them all in a timely fashion. Sometimes she heard the name of Mrs. Bartleby while standing

with others on a street corner waiting for an
omnibus or while waiting her turn in a grocer's
shop. All this notoriety gave her a thrill, rather,
although if the letter she received or the opinion
she overheard was negative, she felt depressed
for hours and was compelled to eat far too many
chocolates.

Despite the occasional minor bout of depression over criticism and the resulting bilious at-
tack, she had never been more content. What
she was doing now was far more useful than
making sure one erratic, thoughtless man got to
his appointments on time. It was certainly more
gratifying than buying his presents for him.

On the other hand, her new job was not an
easy one. She had to accustom herself to writing
under a deadline, and that was hard. She had to
be painstaking in her research and judicious
with her advice. She was also required by Lord
Barringer to keep her identity as Mrs. Bartleby a
secret, and that was hardest of all, for she was by
nature a person of scrupulous honesty. However,
as Barringer pointed out, secrecy whetted public
curiosity, and that could only assist in her success. Even more important, she was dispensing
advice under the guise of a matron, and her
credibility would be hurt if it was discovered
that she was unmarried. After all, no one wanted
advice from a spinster, which was why she had
adopted a pseudonym in the first place.

While she appreciated the reasons for the sub-
terfuge, she didn't understand how it would be
possible to maintain it. Marlowe knew the truth

and had every reason to reveal it publicly, but when she had pointed out this fact to Barringer, the earl had given her a strange little smile and assured her that Marlowe would be the last person in the world to give the secret away.

Though baffled by how the earl could be certain of Marlowe's discretion, she had agreed to keep mum, and it was soon understood by all who knew her that she had left the employ of Lord Marlowe and had accepted a post as secretary to the now-famous Mrs. Bartleby. Emma felt a bit guilty about the deceit, but whenever she thought of Marlowe's opinion that what she wrote was silly, her guilt was easy to vanquish.

With each week that passed, Emma found it a bit easier to play her part. On Sunday afternoons when she took tea with the other girl bachelors in the lodging house, she became quite adept at fielding their questions about the beloved etiquette writer without telling any outright lies. And Sunday afternoon tea had its rewards. Sitting in Mrs. Morris's genteel parlor, with its faded, cabbage-rose wallpaper, potted ferns, and plum-colored mahogany furnishings, Emma listened to her friends discuss her latest column and saw first hand the results of her influence. Emma found Sunday afternoons most gratifying.

"Mr. Jones proposed."

There was a delicate clinking of porcelain cups being set on saucers, followed by five exclamations of surprise as the women already enjoying their tea looked toward the doorway where Miss Beatrice Cole, always the last to appear for Sunday tea nowadays, had just entered the room.

"Oh, my dear Beatrice!" Mrs. Morris set her cup on the tea table beside her and turned toward the younger woman. "This is a happy day indeed."

Beatrice took her usual place in a wingback chair of somewhat worn brocade stripe. Her face glowed with satisfaction, partly due to true love, no doubt, and partly due to the triumph of securing that item so rare in a girl bachelor's life: a young man with prospects.

"To think it was all due to Mrs. Bartleby." Beatrice hastened to pull off her gloves and show everyone her ring of engagement, a silver filigree band. "If it hadn't been for her, my fate would probably be to die an old maid."

Miss Prudence Bosworth and Miss Maria Martingale both winced at that, but they expressed their congratulations in the true spirit of friendship and tried to hide their understandable envy.

Mrs. Morris and Mrs. Inkberry set aside their tea and exclaimed over the ring with a happiness untarnished by any less savory feelings. Unlike their unmarried companions, they had no cause to worry about the security of their future. Mrs. Morris, a widow, had inherited the lodging house upon her husband's death and did very well on her own. Mrs. Inkberry's husband owned a bookshop near Fleet Street, and though the couple did have to live in the cramped quarters above the shop, their home was cozy, the shop was prosperous, and they'd managed to raise four daughters quite comfortably. Though Emma was firmly on the shelf at thirty and had rather given up on the notion of matrimony, she was not immune to the green-eyed monster. Nonetheless, the envy she felt upon hearing Beatrice's news was nothing in comparison to her satisfaction at the part she had played in securing her friend's present happiness.

"Beatrice, you must explain," Mrs. Inkberry said and took a sip of her tea. "How is it that you give Mrs. Bartleby the credit for your engagement?"

"That's right, you've been away at Yorkshire, so you don't know how it all came about." Beatrice accepted a cup of tea from Mrs. Morris and reached for a crumpet from the tray on the central tea table. "You know of Mrs. Bartleby, of course."

Mrs. Inkberry nodded. "Of course! I've been trying to read her column whenever possible, but it's much harder to get the *Social Gazette* in Yorkshire."

"Well," Beatrice continued, "Mr. Jones has been asking for ages if he could walk with me on my way home from the shop, but Mrs. Morris advised me it wouldn't be proper for us to walk together, both of us being unmarried, you know. People might think things."

"Quite right of you, Abigail, dear, to advise caution," Mrs. Inkberry said with a nod to Mrs. Morris. "A young woman without family cannot be too careful in her relations with the male sex. She must have a care for her reputation."

"I know, Josephine," Mrs. Morris answered, "but I was in error. Mrs. Bartleby said in her column it was quite acceptable for Beatrice to walk with her young man."

"She did?" Mrs. Inkberry was clearly dumbfounded. She glanced around the room, and all five of the other women present nodded in the affirmative.

"She wasn't referring to me specifically, of course," Beatrice said and went on to explain the rule Emma had outlined six weeks earlier. "So you see, Mrs. Inkberry, it was quite all right. I've known Mr. Jones four years now. I mean, we see each other nearly every day, with me closing up the shop for Mrs. Wilson at six o'clock most evenings, and him always leaving the barrister's office at the same time, and us living two streets apart and always walking home the same way. As for his good character, Mr. Jones would have to have that, I should think, being a barrister's clerk. And sometimes when we're queued up at the costermonger's cart for lunch, I've seen him buy two pork pies just so he can give one to that poor indigent woman who's always rummaging in the alley rubbish heap. That says a great deal about a man, doesn't it?"

Emma was in complete agreement. The entire reason she'd written that particular column, which did bend the rules just a bit, was solely so poor Beatrice could walk home with her chivalrous young man. Mrs. Morris had a kind heart, but she was a rather silly woman, truth be told, and inclined to be overly punctilious about these things. Even Auntie, who'd been Mrs. Morris's friend for years, had always thought the other woman rather narrow.

"Well," Mrs. Inkberry said, "if Mrs. Bartleby said it was all right, Beatrice, then that settles the question once and for all."

"Reading that made me so happy," Beatrice said, "and it so relieved my mind. I told Mr. Jones straightaway. If Mrs. Bartleby says it's all right, I told him, then we can be sure it *is*. He and I have been walking home together every work day since, Mrs. Inkberry. Sunday afternoons, too, in the park. That's where he proposed, not more than an hour ago." She looked down at the ring on her finger and began tilting her hand this way and that so the silver would catch the afternoon sunlight through the windows. "We'll be married before Christmas."

Emma smiled to herself and took a sip of tea. Yes, she decided, her new life was a very satisfying one indeed.

She was still feeling quite happy with her new life Thursday afternoon when the delivery boy from the *Social Gazette* came to pick up her column, despite a four-day bout of what she believed was called "writer's block." Now, with young Mr. Hobbs knocking on her door, she typed the last paragraph with frantic fervor.

"Wait a bit, Hobbs," she called to the closed

door as she whipped the last page out of the typewriting machine. "I shall be with you in a moment."

She folded all the pages of her column and shoved the sheets into an envelope, then she sealed the edge, dribbling wax on her desk in her haste. She ran for the door, opened it, and presented the envelope to the boy with a heartfelt sigh of relief. "Here you are, Mr. Hobbs."

To her surprise, he did not take the envelope from her hand. Instead, he shook his head. "I's been told to tell you you're to bring your papers down to the *Gazette* yourself. I'm just here to fetch you."

"But—" Emma broke off, frowning in puzzlement. This was a very odd and unexpected development, but Hobbs appeared to know nothing more about the matter. She fetched her bonnet and put on her gloves, then tucked her column into the pocket of her skirt and accompanied the lad to the offices of the *Social Gazette* on Bouverie Street.

When they arrived, the boy was dismissed, and a clerk with a harried expression on his face ushered her up to Barringer's suite of offices. Emma's astonishment increased further when she found Mr. Ashe, the earl's secretary, engaged in the task of packing up his things.

"Good afternoon, Mr. Ashe," she greeted him. "What is it you do here?"

The secretary placed his silver inkstand in the wooden crate on his desk before replying. "Lord Barringer has sold the newspaper," he told her.

"I was offered a post as secretary to the new owner, but I have been with Lord Barringer for many years and have chosen to remain in his employ, so I am packing up my things, as you see."

"The *Social Gazette* has been sold? To whom?"

"To me, Miss Dove."

The voice that came from behind her was appallingly familiar. She closed her eyes for a moment, praying that she was mistaken, but when she opened her eyes again and turned around, she found there was no mistake. Standing in the doorway, one shoulder against the doorframe and his arms folded across his chest, was her former employer.

Emma stared at Marlowe, and a little knot of dismay formed in her tummy as she felt her wonderful new life crumbling into dust.

Chapter 7

It is perfectly possible to form a satisfactory, mutually agreeable alliance with a woman. But only if you are not in a church at the time.

Lord Marlowe
The Bachelor's Guide, 1893

"**L**ord Barringer has sold the *Gazette* to you? This is . . ." Emma paused, struggling to regain her poise. "This is most unexpected."

"Barringer and I have been discussing a possible sale for several months. We came to terms last week and signed the documents yesterday." He straightened in the doorway and gestured to the office behind him. "I should like to discuss the situation with you."

She preceded him into what had been Barringer's office. Though the furnishings were still intact, all personal traces of the former occupant had been removed. The bookshelf was empty, the elegant desk was bare, the paintings had been removed from the walls, no carpet covered the wooden floor.

Marlowe closed the door and moved to stand behind what was now his desk. He indicated the chair opposite his own. "Please sit down."

Emma didn't want to sit down. She wanted to get this over and depart. She pulled her latest column out of her skirt pocket. "For next week's edition."

She held out the envelope to him, though she fully expected him to refuse it. Her eyes met his across the desk, daring him to tell her that her silly little column was being dropped from the newspaper, and that she was now unemployed.

That would be quite all right with her. She wouldn't write for Marlowe now if he were the last publisher on earth. Besides, she had gained some measure of success during the past two months, and she could surely find another publisher to take her on.

Fortified by these internal reassurances, she was able to speak with a measure of good cheer. "You don't want it? Oh, but what am I thinking? Of course you don't. It's all about tableware. Runcible spoons and fish knives and that sort of thing. Dull as ashes. Who'd want to read that?

She started to put the envelope back in her pocket, but to her surprise, Marlowe held out his hand. She gave him the envelope and he set it to one side of his desk, then once again gestured to the chair. "Miss Dove, I'd like to be comfortable while we talk, but as a gentleman, I can't sit until you do. Etiquette, you know."

She lifted her brows in a skeptical sort of way that made short shrift of his expertise in that regard.

"I truly do have some knowledge of good manners." Laugh lines creased the corners of his deep blue eyes, and a rueful smile curved his mouth. "Although, as someone recently reminded me, I do not employ that knowledge as often as I should."

Emma reminded herself that self-deprecating charm was one of his greatest talents, one that had enabled him to get around her so many times over the years, and she did not smile back. Instead, she took a deep breath and decided she wasn't going to wait meekly for the ax to fall. She took the offered chair, then she took the initiative.

"My lord, I am aware of your feelings regarding what Barringer has chosen to publish in the past. You have already made them quite clear to me. In light of that, I'm sure you intend to take the *Social Gazette* in a new and different direction."

"That is true, but—"

"And," she went on in a rush, "it's obvious the silly, inconsequential stuff I write can have no place in your plans."

"On the con—"

"If you do intend to publish the column I just gave you, I would appreciate it if you would arrange for my compensation. Then you shall never have to see me again, read a single piece of my work, or endure any further lectures from me about your manners."

She started to rise, but his amused voice stopped her.

"Miss Dove, I've just admitted I don't always mind my manners, but I do know a few rules of decorum. For instance, I believe interrupting people is a violation of etiquette, isn't it?"

Emma felt the heat rush into her face, and she tried to muster her dignity. "I wasn't aware I was doing that," she said. "My . . . my apologies."

"Apology accepted." His voice was grave, but there was still a suspicious curve to one corner of his mouth that made her stiffen in her chair.

He must have seen it, for his amusement vanished at once. "I wasn't laughing at you. Well, perhaps I was," he amended, "a little. It's just that you always take these matters of etiquette so very seriously."

"And we both know you don't."

"The only thing I take seriously is business, and even that had best be fun or it's not worth doing." He pulled a copy of the *Social Gazette* out of a drawer and unfolded it on top of the desk. Opening it to page three, where her column was located, he went on, "I admire your perspicacity in understanding my intentions. I do intend to make changes here. Sweeping ones, in fact."

Emma wanted this business over. "If you are removing my column from the paper, just say so, please."

"I have no intention of removing it."

"You wish to keep it?" A lady was never supposed to betray surprise, but Emma couldn't hide her astonishment. Perhaps she hadn't heard him right. "But you hate my writing."

"*Hate* is perhaps too strong a word."

"You called it silly." Emma folded her arms and glared at him. "You said it wasn't any good."

"That is not precisely what I said."

"Let's not split hairs. It's what you believe."

He didn't argue. Instead he gave her a curious look. "Does it matter so much to you what I believe?"

"When I worked for you, it mattered. I respected your judgment. I trusted you with my writing, something very dear to me, hoping one day you would deem it worthy of publication. All the while, you couldn't be bothered even to read any of it, much less judge it fairly."

"I did read some of it, and I am not going to explain myself again on that point. Nor am I going to justify the opinion I formed." He paused and studied her face for a moment before he spoke again. "Miss Dove," he said and leaned forward in his chair, "I rejected your work because I honestly did not see its appeal to the public. But it's obvious I made an error of judgment. I was unable to look at your work objectively."

"Because you do not enjoy reading it, you could not understand that other people would."

"Just so. You called me closed-minded, and I

have come to realize that in regard to your work, at least, it was a fair accusation."

Emma was slightly mollified by that. "And now you want to publish it?"

"Yes." He held up his hands, palms toward her. "I freely admit I do not understand what is so fascinating about decorating a flat or planning menus for wedding breakfasts." He paused, lowered his hands, and leaned back in his chair. "But given your success, I would be a fool not to acknowledge that such fascination exists and find a way to take advantage of it. You uncovered a need, Miss Dove, a need I did not see. Wherever there is a need, there is also the potential to make money. I don't have to like your work in order to publish it."

"You mean, now that I have proven I can make money, you wish to profit from what you have rejected and ridiculed?" Emma stood up. "No. I shall take my column to another publisher, one who respects my work and appreciates it."

She expected him to laugh at that declaration, but he did not. "You are free to take your work elsewhere, of course," he said as he rose to his feet. "Should you make that choice, I cannot stop you. Pity, though," he added as she started to turn away. "If you leave, I won't be able to expand your column into an entire section of its own."

She froze, then slowly turned back around. "I beg your pardon?"

"I had thought to devote an entire section of the *Social Gazette* to matters of etiquette and style." He shook his head. "A great business opportunity lost. Such a shame."

She frowned, studying his face, searching for any sign he was being disingenuous, but she could find none. "Are you truly serious?"

"I told you, I am always serious about business."

Emma swallowed hard. She sat back down. "What, exactly, did you have in mind?"

"Whatever you like. Etiquette, shopping, recipes, clever ideas like pink flamingos and such. It would be your decision, for you would be in charge of all content. You could conduct interviews, dispense advice, answer questions from readers, share cookery recipes. Just keep the public's interest. That is all I ask."

Emma felt a rush of excitement so powerful she could scarcely breathe.

"I know that Barringer kept your identity a secret," he went on, "and although I hate to give the man credit for anything, in this case I must agree with him. Your credibility would be hurt if people knew your background. Besides, secrecy does add to your appeal."

Emma did not reply. Creative ideas were ricocheting around in her brain so fast, she couldn't think of anything of say.

"Before you decide, Miss Dove, it's only fair to warn you that I intend to be heavily involved in this project, as I am with all new ventures. Because I am changing other aspects of the *Social Gazette* in order to make its style more modern and fresh, and because I just paid Barringer an enormous amount of money for this paper, I shall oversee all aspects of it for the foreseeable future, including your section. You would report directly to me, and I would edit your writing myself."

Emma's excitement dimmed with those last few words, and she came to her senses. "It will never work," she said.

"Why not?"

"Because I don't like you." The moment she said it, Emma pressed her gloved fingers to her mouth, horrified by her lack of tact. Aunt Lydia would have been appalled.

But to her amazement, Marlowe began to laugh. "I shudder to think how little money I'd make if I only did business with people who liked me, Miss Dove."

She lowered her hand. "That was rude. Forgive me. I should not have said it."

"But you meant it." His amusement faded, and he tilted his head, studying her. His expression became thoughtful.

Under this scrutiny, Emma shifted in her chair. She didn't know what to say. She'd probably said quite enough already.

"Despite the recent friction between us, I always thought you and I rubbed along rather well," he murmured. "Was I wrong?"

She sighed, knowing the damage was done. "No," she answered. "But we got on so well because I never questioned you. I was your secretary, paid to follow your orders. My duties had nothing to do with my personal opinion of you or how you conduct your life. To have expressed my opinions would have been an unpardonable impertinence."

"You seem to have little trouble expressing them now." He laughed again, but this time his laughter had a hollow ring to it. "I know there are men with whom I've done business who have no fondness for me, but it never occurred to me that you had any dislike for me."

She hadn't known it, either, until the words had come bursting out of her mouth. "It isn't dislike, I suppose, but more of a lack of common ground," she began, trying to explain what she didn't quite understand herself.

"Don't qualify your honest opinion for the sake of politeness."

"I'm not. It's just that we are very different people, you and I, and we see things from a very different perspective. You think what I write is silly and pointless, but that is partly because you're a peer. Peers can be rude, and no one cares. Peers can bend the rules, sometimes even break them. People in my class of life don't dare behave that way. This is particularly true of women. When I was a girl, my father was very strict. He was a retired army sergeant and I had—" Emma stopped, feeling her throat start to close up.

"You had what?" he prompted when she paused.

It was hard to talk about personal matters with anyone, especially about her life with her father, but she owed Marlowe some sort of explanation for her opinion. It was only fair.

She forced herself to go on. "I had what you

would no doubt deem a rather . . . rigid child-hood. There was no teasing or any such nonsense in my father's household. So to me, you seem glib and brash and insincere. Everything seems like play to you, so it's hard for me to know when you are serious and when you are making fun. And I think you have very little consideration for oth-ers, not buying presents for people yourself, your lack of punctuality, that sort of thing. And your life, I cannot help but feel, is a terribly dissolute one—your disdain for marriage, your liaisons with cancan dancers and other women of low moral character."

He laughed again. "Well, a liaison with a woman of high moral character would hardly serve the intended purpose."

Emma supposed that was a joke.

His grin faded and he gave a little cough. "Yes, well, so you disapprove of me. In addi-tion to being manipulative and insincere, I am glib, brash, inconsiderate, unpunctual, and a rake. Did I leave anything out?"

Put that way, it sounded quite harsh. She hadn't meant it to be such a thorough condem-nation, but then, she wasn't accustomed to criti-cizing anyone. "It's not as if you have much regard for me, either," she hastened to say, ter-ribly uncomfortable. "I know you think I'm dry as dust and have no sense of humor."

"Well, you can't blame me for that. You never laugh at my jokes."

That did make her smile a little. "Perhaps be-cause they aren't amusing?"

"Yes, yes, all right. I did leave myself wide open for that, didn't I?"

She became serious again. "The point is that I cannot go back to the sort of . . . of unequal arrangement we had. For what you propose to work, I would have to feel free to express my strongest opinions as a writer and you would have to respect them." With every word, Emma's spirits sank a little more. "We would have to look at each other in a new way. Not as an employer and his secretary, not as a lord and an army sergeant's daughter, but instead as two people whose opinions and ideas are equal in importance and value. We should have to regard each other with mutual respect and consideration."

"You don't think that's possible?"

Emma thought of all the times he'd taken her for granted. All the times she'd been too intimidated to speak up. "No."

There was a long pause, then he nodded. "You're right, I suppose. You don't like me, and I don't really like what you write, so it does seem rather a hopeless business." He gestured to the door. "I'll walk you downstairs."

Neither of them spoke as he escorted her out of the office and down to the foyer. They paused by the front doors.

"I am going across the street to my offices," he said, "but I can arrange for a hansom to take you home."

"That isn't necessary. I am sure the *Social Gazette* will do very well under your leadership. I hope so," she added and meant it.

"Thank you. And I am confident you will easily find another publisher for your column." He opened one of the front doors and after she had walked through, he followed her outside. "I shall see that you are compensated for the column you gave me today. I wish you every success, Miss Dove." He bowed to her. "Good-bye."

Emma watched Marlowe's broad-shouldered back as he turned and walked away, and a heavy tightness pinched her chest. She told herself she had made a sensible decision. If she had agreed to write for him, allowed her work to be edited by him, it would have been a disaster, for they were like chalk and cheese. They should never agree on anything. She'd been very sensible to refuse.

There it was. That horrid word again. *Sensible.*

"Wait!" she cried and started after him.

He paused and turned at the corner, waiting as she approached and halted before him. "If we do this, what would be my compensation?"

This abrupt turnabout caused him to raise an eyebrow, but he didn't question her sanity. "You would receive ten percent of the net advertising revenue for your section," he answered.

She thought of all the times she'd negotiated merchants down to a reasonable price and decided this was no different. She decided she was going to ask for what she really deserved. "Fifty percent would be fair."

"Fair is not a consideration. I am taking all the risk."

"I've heard you say many times the higher the

risk, the higher the potential reward. And you love risk. You thrive on it. Besides, the *Gazette* has had a significant increase in popularity because of my writing, and I deserve to be rewarded for that."

"Believe me, I have already paid dearly for that popularity, which might not last. The public has taken a fancy to you, granted, but that could be a transient thing, here today and gone tomorrow. If that happens, I'm the one who loses thousands of pounds. I'll give you twenty percent."

"Forty," she countered. "I think I can keep the public's interest for a long time to come."

In for a penny, in for a pound, Emma.

"And since we are negotiating terms," she rushed on, "I want it understood that regardless of your station or mine, regardless of our history, you will treat me as if I were your equal from this point on. I won't make you coffee, and I won't buy gifts on your behalf, and I won't be responsible for whether or not you make meetings on time, ours or anyone else's. And when it comes to the editorial decisions, you will have to trust my instincts, not yours."

"I promise to keep an open mind, but if I feel you're rambling on too long about tableware or printing too many pieces about Afternoon-at-Homes, I will have no compunction about saying so. I've never really critiqued your work as an editor would, but from now on you'll receive detailed, honest criticism from me. I might seem glib to you, but I can be brutal when I need to be, so be prepared to take it on the chin, Miss Dove.

If you can do that, I'll give you twenty-five percent. Are we agreed?"

She looked down at the hand he held out to her, a big hand with long, strong fingers. She might not like him much or approve of the way he lived his life, and she thought half of what he said was utter nonsense, but she knew one thing. When Marlowe shook hands on something, he kept his word. She clasped his hand in hers, and in doing so, she grabbed on to a dream bigger than any she could have imagined for herself. "Agreed."

There was a reassuring strength in his grip, but she felt dizzy. This had happened so fast, she found it hard to take it all in.

He let go of her hand. "We'll continue to adhere to a Saturday publication date. I'll need four full pages of content from you each and every week. Can you do that?"

"I can do it." With those words, all the exhilaration she'd felt upon first hearing his plans came flooding back. "What I can't do is believe this is really happening."

"Believe it, Miss Dove. I want to put out the first issue of the new *Social Gazette* three weeks from Saturday. Since your last column's gone to press, and you just gave me one for the following week, I'll need one more ordinary column for the interim period." When she nodded, he went on, "I'll also need an outline of your proposed content for our first issue by Monday. Once I approve it, you'll have one week to give me the articles. I'll need two days to go over them, so we'll meet on Wednesday to discuss my edits. Get your revised content to my secretary by Thursday night. I'll approve it the following day before it goes to press. And bring me your outlines for the next issue the following Monday. Does all that make sense?"

She nodded.

"Good. From then on, we'll meet on Mondays so you can submit your work and outlines, and on Wednesdays to discuss revising them. I hope that suits you?" Without waiting for an answer, he continued, "We'll go over your first edits a week from Wednesday. I don't have any engagements or appointments scheduled for that day as yet." His brow creased with a frown. "At least, I don't think I do. With the secretary I have now, I can never be quite sure."

"What time shall we meet and where?"

"Nine o'clock in the morning. My office."

She laughed. "Don't be late."

"Without you, I'm late for everything nowadays." He glanced up and down the street, looking for a break in the heavy traffic so that he could cross. "But I shall do my best to be punctual, if only to improve your opinion of me."

She turned away, but she'd barely taken half a dozen steps along the sidewalk before his voice called to her.

"Miss Dove?"

She looked over her shoulder to find him smiling at her.

"If you had stuck to your guns," he said, "I'd have given you fifty percent."

"If you had stuck to *your* guns," she answered at once, "you'd only be paying ten."

Harry gave a shout of laughter. By God, Miss Dove had wit. Who'd ever have thought it? He watched her as she started down the sidewalk, and he realized that was another facet of her character he'd never seen until now.

She'd been spot on about his assessment of her. He *had* thought her dry as dust, but her words of a moment ago and the grin that had accompanied them told Harry he'd been wrong about that, too. And about the appeal of her writing. In fact, he'd been wrong about a lot of things.

He'd always thought her rather plain, at least until the day she'd resigned and he had discovered there were red glints in her hair and gold sparks in her eyes. He thought of how she'd looked moments ago, breathless and laughing as she'd told him not to be late, and he realized that he'd never seen her laugh before. A great pity, that, for when laughter lit up Miss Dove's face, she wasn't plain at all.

One thing was clear. She didn't like him. That took him back, rather. Women usually liked him. Without being unduly conceited, he knew that. On the other hand, Miss Dove was giving him cause to doubt a lot of the things he thought he knew.

It was obvious she had drawn some strong conclusions about his character over the years— his flaws, in particular, and he'd had no idea of it. She disapproved of him, yet she had worked for him for five years. Why?

Intrigued, Harry studied her slim, straight back as she walked away, and it occurred to him that in this new equal relationship they were supposed to have, he was at a distinct disadvantage. She had made a far greater study of him than he had of her.

It was clear he was going to have to even things up in that regard and do some studying of his own. His gaze lowered speculatively to the curve of her hips. All in the name of equality, of course.

Chapter 8

Chivalry is required of a gentleman. It also has some very pleasant rewards.

Lord Marlowe
The Bachelor's Guide, 1893

Miss Dove was always efficient, and Harry was not surprised when he received all her articles for their first issue three days early. After reading them, he realized two things. First, she truly could write. Second, no matter how excellent her descriptions, no matter how warm and friendly her narrative, he would never, ever understand why napkin rings made out of lavender fronds or what young ladies were allowed to eat at dinner parties made for interesting reading.

Still, because of her already-proven success, he

used as light a hand as possible in editing her work, and he tried to keep an open mind about the content, but he did have some definite criticisms for her that needed to be addressed, as well as some significant changes he wanted made, and he decided to return her work to her for revision as quickly as possible to give her more time. He could have accomplished this by messenger, but he decided it would be much better for their new spirit of cooperation if he explained his opinions and suggestions in person.

When he called at her flat Saturday afternoon, however, he found that a meeting to discuss her work might not be possible. She appeared to be in the midst of redecorating. The door leading into her flat was open, and the smell of fresh paint was in the air. When he paused in the doorway, he found that the walls were now a pale robin's-egg blue with cream-colored moldings, and a new carpet of gold, cream, aubergine, and teal had been laid over the center of the wooden floor. She had removed one of the settees and rearranged her furnishings in order to make room for a cherrywood desk and matching chair.

During this redecoration, however, she had not abandoned her flair for the exotic. A small teak table, its base carved in the shape of an elephant stood beside her desk, and on it reposed an enormous vase filled with peacock feathers.

As for Miss Dove herself, she was standing on a ladder before one of her front windows, hanging a length of heavy teal-blue silk onto a cherrywood rod. The other window along that wall was open and already boasted a similar drapery, which rustled in the warm June breeze.

She made a sound of vexation, and Harry watched her as she rose on her tiptoes and lifted her arms overhead. Curling one hand around the rod to keep herself steady, she used the other to tug at the drapery, which had caught somehow on the bracket. Her efforts, however, seemed to be in vain. Harry set down his dispatch case and started toward her, thinking to assist, but something stopped him halfway across the room.

Her position in the tall window, with her arms raised above her head and the late afternoon sun pouring in, made the silhouette of her upper body plainly visible through the white linen of her shirtwaist. He could see the lines of her torso tapering to her narrow waist. When she turned sideways on the ladder and stretched her arm toward the edge of the rod, he caught a glimpse of her body in profile, including the small, unmistakable swell of her breast.

Suddenly Harry couldn't move. He felt riveted to the floor, and he could only stare at her as the slow burn of arousal began spreading through his body. Before he knew what was happening, his mind was conjuring up images of Miss Dove that were far more specific than the silhouette framed in the window. He'd always preferred voluptuous women, but the modest curves Miss Dove possessed began to seem damned luscious in his imagination.

He tried to collect his wits. He reminded himself this was Miss Dove he was looking at. Miss Dove, who was straitlaced and buttoned-down and smothered in rules. Miss Dove, who didn't like him, who disapproved of him, who thought him dissolute. He couldn't refute that description at this moment, for some very dissolute thoughts were going through his mind.

His gaze skimmed down the length of her dark brown skirt, then traveled slowly back up. She had to have beautiful legs. If they were long enough to need that much fabric to cover them, they had to be quite fine. He'd speculated about her legs once or twice since she'd first come to work for him, but this time Harry allowed his thoughts to become much more detailed. He began to envision shapely thighs and pretty knees.

She shifted her weight on the ladder, her skirt swaying with her effort to free the drapery, and Harry took a step closer, giving her backside a most ungentlemanlike study. With all the froufrous women wore under their clothes, it was hard to be certain, but after due consideration, Harry decided the curve of Miss Dove's hips wasn't due to any sort of padding.

"Oh, hell and damnation!"

Her frustrated exclamation was so unexpected, it shattered the fantasies Harry's imagination had been conjuring, and it was so out of keeping with her strict notions of propriety that he laughed in surprise.

She turned sharply at the sound, the ladder rocked, and she almost fell off. "Careful, Miss

Dove," he admonished, and came to her side. He put a hand on the ladder to steady it.

"The curtain is stuck," she said and moved as if to have another go at loosening it.

"Don't," he ordered. "Come down from there, and let me do it."

Before she could descend on her own, he put his hands on her waist, thinking to be chivalrous and lift her down. But the moment he touched her, he forget that intent and his thoughts became much less noble. His forearms brushed the sides of her hips, and another wave of desire shimmered through his body. He'd been right. She was wearing a petticoat or two, maybe, and a corset, definitely, but no padding. He slid his hands down an inch or two, grasping her hips, and his thumbs brushed the base of her spine. There might not be much to Miss Dove, but what she had was genuine.

His hands tightened, and he leaned closer, breathing deeply of talcum powder and fresh cotton, pristine, maidenly scents he'd never dreamt could be erotic until now. If he moved one inch closer, he'd be kissing—

"My lord?"

Good God, what was he doing? Harry shoved lusty thoughts of kissing Miss Dove's backside out of his mind at once and reminded himself that he was a gentleman. He lifted her down from the ladder, set her on her feet, and then, reluctantly, he let her go.

She turned around, but she didn't look into his eyes. She stared straight ahead, looking at his chin. Her cheeks were pink, and she was frowning.

Probably because she wanted to slap his face for manhandling her as if she were a wench in an East End pub and he were a longshoreman. He'd deserve the reprimand, no doubt, but he couldn't regret the cause. Harry gave her another long study, from the coppery sun-glints in her brown hair all the way down to the toes of her hideous, high-button shoes, then back up again, ending his perusal at the tip of her freckle-dusted nose. No, he didn't regret it a jot. He wished he could manhandle her again. And that was stupid.

Five years of having a female secretary, and he'd always been able to shove away any lascivious thoughts about Miss Dove that had occasionally crossed his mind. He'd managed to do it, in fact, without any serious effort. But at this moment it was proving far more difficult. He couldn't explain it, but something had changed between them.

He knew he had to put aside these inexplicable new notions about Miss Dove and get his priorities back in order. She wasn't his secretary any longer, but they were about to engage in a venture that could be highly profitable, and he had no intention of messing that up. He took a deep breath and pointed to the ladder behind her. "If you move aside, I shall endeavor to solve your problem."

She finally looked into his eyes. "Hmm? What?"

Instead of repeating himself, he put his hands on her arms and gently moved her out of the way, then he ascended the ladder and freed the drapery ring from where it had gotten hung up on the bracket. When he came back down, she was still frowning, and he decided a bit of levity might not go amiss.

"Hell and damnation?" he teased, ducking his head to look into her face.

"I beg your pardon?"

"Hell and damnation. That's what you said."

She gave a huff of vexation, her frown deepening. She pulled at the cuffs of her shirtwaist rather in the manner of a disapproving nursery governess. "Don't be ridiculous. I didn't say any such thing."

"You did. I heard your words distinctly." He shook his head and made a sound of *tsk-tsk.* "Such language from London's greatest arbiter of proper decorum. What would people say?"

"Well, I didn't know you were standing there!"

"You only swear when you're alone, then?"

"I don't swear." The absurdity of that statement made him grin, and she went on, "Well, I don't! Not usually."

"Your secret is safe with me," he went on in breezy disregard of her denial. "I won't tell anyone you curse like a Blackpool sailor."

"It was just that the curtain wouldn't move, and I couldn't reach it where it was caught, and I was so frustrated and then . . . and then . . . Oh, dear." She pressed three fingers to her forehead, looking thoroughly unhappy with herself. "It was very wrong of me," she said on a sigh. "Very wrong."

Harry couldn't imagine what it would be like to be wound so tight that an occasional slip of the tongue could be cause for such self-reproach. "Enough of this, Miss Dove. You take things far too seriously, you know, and really need to laugh more. To advance that end, I could make jokes. Oh, but no, that won't do," he added, tongue in cheek. "My jokes are not amusing. At least, so I've been told."

She gave him a wry look, but there was a promising curve to one corner of her mouth. Encouraged, he went on, "Perhaps you should tell jokes to me." He leaned a bit closer to her, adopting a confidential air. "Know any naughty ones?"

She looked away, pressing the smile from her lips before she returned her gaze to his. "If you've teased me enough for one day," she said in the brisk, no-nonsense fashion he was used to, "perhaps you should tell me why you are here."

"I have finished reading your work, and I wanted to discuss it with you."

"Oh." She shifted her weight from one foot to the other, looking uncomfortable. "I thought our meeting for revision was to be on Wednesday. In your office."

"It is, but I was so overcome by curiosity, I couldn't wait."

"Curiosity?"

"Yes. I have to know why young ladies are only allowed to eat the wings of a chicken at dinner."

"At dinner parties," she corrected.

He pretended to be enlightened. "Ah, that explains it. Now I understand."

She bit her lip, studying him in obvious uncertainty. "Are you teasing me again?"

"I'm not, I assure you. I've been racking my brain trying to think of a reason for this custom, and I've given up in despair."

"You came all the way across town so that I could explain why young ladies eat chicken wings?"

"And because the revisions I am going to suggest are fairly extensive and might take some time. Not that I'm going to shred you to ribbons or anything," he added, noticing her expression of uncertainty deepening into worry. "But I did think you might be glad of some additional time to complete them."

"I see." She glanced past him, then walked to the door and closed it, reminding him of her nosy landlady.

"No one saw me come up," he said before she could ask.

"Good." She turned around, flattening back against the door. "This is a lodging house exclusively for women. You shouldn't really be up here." She gave an awkward half laugh. "People can be so silly, you know. Ladies, especially. They gossip, and think things. I should hate for anyone to see you and think . . . that you and I . . .

that we are . . ." She straightened away from the door and her chin came up. She met his gaze. "I should not wish anyone to believe I entertain men in my rooms. I am not that sort of woman."

At this moment, Harry rather wished she were just that sort of woman, but he didn't think it would be wise to say so. "Does it matter what other people think?"

"Of course it matters." She stared at him in disbelief. "Don't you think it matters?"

"No. Why should I? More to the point, why should you? You just said people are silly to be thinking things and gossiping about nothing. Why are you are wasting a moment caring about their opinions?"

"Because . . . well . . . because . . . oh, it just matters, that's all. They might think we're having a . . . an amour!"

She looked so appalled, Harry didn't have the heart to tell her that dozens of people in London had come to that conclusion long ago about Viscount Marlowe and his female secretary. "If that sort of gossip got to your landlady, would she toss you out?"

Miss Dove considered that for a moment. "No, but she would have a long, heart-to-heart talk with me."

"She takes quite a keen interest in your affairs."

"Mrs. Morris is a bit of a fussbudget, and overly protective, but she was a dear friend of my aunt, and she has known me for years. I have a care for her opinion."

"If she's known you for years, then she ought to be convinced of your good character by now. If she's not, the worst that happens is that you have to abandon a friendship with someone who clearly wasn't much of a friend to begin with. And find a new flat, too, of course."

"That's bad enough," she said with a touch of humor. "Do you know how difficult it is to obtain an affordable flat in London nowadays?"

"You and I are going to be making so much money, you won't care."

She tilted her head, giving him a thoughtful look. "What if we don't make any money?"

Harry dismissed that notion with a laugh. "We will make money. Trust me on that."

"How can you possess such confidence?" Before he could answer, she went on, "I've seen you lose money before."

"I'm not saying it never happens, but I don't think it will in this case."

"You never think it will. That's my point. And when it does, you always shrug it off as if it doesn't matter." She gestured to him with an up-and-down wave of her hand. "I've seen you lose thousands of pounds on a deal without letting it affect you. You always think you'll make it up somewhere else."

"I always do, don't I?"

"Yes, but that won't be of any use to me."

"You worry too much." He walked over to her and put his hands on her arms. "It never does any good to dwell on what could go wrong. There is risk in everything."

"Not all of us have your confidence. I don't."

"Don't be absurd, of course you have confidence. Yes, you do," he insisted when she shook her head. "You are the one who resigned her safe, secure post to go off and write for a living. If that's not confidence in one's abilities, I don't know what is."

Unexpectedly, she smiled, a winsome, wide curve of her lips. "That wasn't confidence at all. It was rage. I was furious with you because you didn't know who Mrs. Bartleby was."

He'd rarely seen her smile, and he liked it. "Now, that's a sight, by heaven," he murmured. "You must smile more often, Miss Dove, for I vow, you look very pretty when you do."

He was rewarded for this by seeing her smile vanish at once, and he remembered how she'd accused him of insincerity. He suddenly felt self-conscious, and he didn't like the feeling. He wasn't used to it. She had described him as glib, and he supposed he was, for he didn't often say the wrong thing, especially to women. But with this particular woman, it seemed he couldn't ever manage to say the right thing. She stirred in his hold, and he let his hands fall away.

"Don't stiffen up and get all starchy," he said. "I wasn't trying to pet you or soothe you or anything of that kind. I simply decided I like your smile, and I said so."

"I didn't mean to . . . to get all starchy, as you put it. It's just that . . ." She tugged at a loose tendril of her hair. "It's just that I'm not accustomed to receiving compliments. From you, I mean. I don't know quite how to react."

"I believe the established mode when given one is to say thank you."

That made her laugh. "I'll try to remember that. Thank you."

"You're welcome. And I cannot believe I am now dispensing advice on etiquette. Who'd have thought it?"

"My influence rubbing off on you, perhaps?"

"No doubt." He bent and picked up his dispatch case from the floor beside the door. "Next time I need to come here, I'll send my card up and you can receive me in that drawing room downstairs in the proper way. I hope that meets your notions of propriety."

"It does. And in light of our new spirit of co-operation, I shall endeavor to accept compliments more graciously."

"And you'll smile more often."

"Yes, yes, all right, that, too! Are you satisfied now?"

"Satisfied?" He lowered his gaze to her mouth and noticed for the first time that her lower lip was very full and looked very soft. "No, I'm not satisfied at all."

Innuendos such as that were clearly wasted on her, for her face took on a hint of bewilderment that told him she hadn't the first clue what he meant. That was probably for the best. Kissing her was a bad idea. Arousal stirred again inside him. A very bad idea.

"Did you want to go over those revisions now?" she asked.

"Revisions?"

She gestured to the dispatch case in his hand. "Isn't that why you came?"

"Of course. Yes." Harry struggled to remember the reason he was here. "Quite right."

"Very well, then. Go downstairs to the parlor, and I'll follow you directly."

"We could just stay up here," he suggested with a naughty grin, only half in jest. "Liven up the lives of your neighbors, you know, and give them something sensational to talk about."

She didn't seem to find that suggestion as intriguing as he did. "If they talk about something sensational, it isn't going to be me," she told him and opened the door. "Go," she urged in a whisper when he didn't move, "and make certain no one sees you."

He looked at her with mock sadness. "There is no sense of adventure in you, Miss Dove," he murmured, shaking his head as he started through the door. "None."

Harry went downstairs in a hole and corner manner, his efforts to avoid detection in a ladies' lodging house making him feel rather as if he were the dastardly villain in a comic play, but all his skulking proved unnecessary. He encountered no one on his way down to the parlor. The place was quiet as a tomb.

He sat down on a terribly uncomfortable horsehair settee in the parlor to wait, but he didn't have to wait long. Miss Dove entered the room only a few minutes later.

"What revisions did you have in mind?" she asked, sitting down beside him.

He handed her the typewritten sheets she'd sent him three days before, sheets now marked with his scribbled notes and comments. She began to look them over, but almost immediately glanced at him again. "You were serious," she said, pointing to his query in the margin of the first page. "You weren't teasing."

"Well, I admit I'm not quite up to snuff on what young ladies are allowed to eat, but why the wings? Why can't they eat other parts of the chicken?"

"Because the wings are the only pieces that have no human equivalent."

"What?" It took him a moment to appreciate what she meant. "Now you're teasing me, Miss Dove," he said. "A young lady can't eat a chicken thigh or breast because human beings have thighs and breasts?"

A blush tinted her cheeks at those words. "I know it seems a bit fastidious, but—"

"Fastidious?" He began to laugh. "It's absurd."

"No doubt you think so," she said, giving him a look of reproof. "But it's a matter of delicacy."

He gestured to the pages in her hand. "If that's so, then why can't young ladies eat quail? A quail's wing is delicate enough for any girl, I daresay, for it has just enough meat on it to feed two ants at a picnic."

"Exactly, which is why quails are served *whole*. Since young ladies can't eat the . . . umm . . ."

"Breasts," he supplied, vastly amused.

She folded her arms. "The point is that because quails are served whole, young ladies do not eat them at dinner parties."

"They don't eat much else either, from what I can see." He moved closer to her on the settee so that he could read from the top page of the sheaf in her hand. "No plovers, no pigeons, no snipe. No oysters, mussels, clams, or whole lobsters. No artichokes, no savories, no cheese." He paused for breath, then went on, "Nothing too rich, nothing too highly seasoned. And never more than one glass of wine. Did I miss any no-noes?"

She sighed. "When it comes to my work, I do wish you would be serious."

"I am serious," he assured her. "After reading this, I understand why women have such tiny waists and go about fainting all the time. I thought it was corsets, but no. You're all *hungry*."

Miss Dove pressed her lips together, but not before he saw the smile she was trying to hide. "I've never fainted in my life."

"Maybe not, but you must admit I have a valid point. Life is far too short to live half-starved."

"Hardly that. These rules are reserved for dinner parties, and are usually observed among only the young, unmarried ladies."

"Which explains why they all want to get married," he answered at once. "If I had to exist on a diet of plain puddings and chicken wings, even I might begin looking for a spouse."

That did the trick. She burst out laughing. "Really, my lord," she said, "I don't know why you are so surprised by all this. You've attended many dinner parties. Surely you know when carving that you always present the chicken wings to the young ladies."

"No one who knows me ever asks me to carve at table. I cut the beef too thick and saw at the chicken."

"You just want to give young ladies plenty of meat so they won't expire before dessert."

He straightened on the settee, staring at her. "Why, Miss Dove, you made a joke."

"Clearly, it wasn't a good one, or you would have laughed."

"It was dreadful," he agreed with her, "but it proves one thing. You were wrong, and I was right."

"What are you talking about?"

"You said the two of us could never work together as equals. That we wouldn't be able to get along. This conversation proves you were wrong. I think—" He paused and leaned closer to her, lowering his gaze to her mouth. "I think we're getting along splendidly, Miss Dove."

Her lips parted, her lashes lowered, and it crossed his mind that in one more moment they would be getting along as well as a man and a woman ever could. But then she scooted away from him on the settee, and his hope vanished into oblivion.

She rustled the papers in her hand and cleared her throat. "So, now that I've satisfied your curiosity about chicken wings, my lord, shall we go on?"

Harry forced himself back to the task at hand. He explained some of idiosyncracies he'd observed in her style of writing, especially her tendency to explain things in too much detail. He argued with her over particular paragraphs he'd crossed out or where he'd edited her too heavily for her liking.

Despite all that, she seemed to take his criticisms rather wall, perhaps because their talk of hungry young ladies and chicken wings had broken the ice. They finished on a note of agreement over his suggestion that she include at least one article for men in every issue, and she promised to have one written by the time they met again, on Wednesday, as they had originally planned. She then began sharing with him some of the ideas she had in mind for future issues.

Harry tried to give her work his full consideration, he truly did, but it wasn't long before he found his attention wandering to a far more intriguing topic than picnic luncheons and drawing room presentations. As she rambled on about various picnic viands, he stared at her mouth and started imagining again what it would be like to kiss her. By the time she stopped talking, he'd imagined it about twenty-seven different ways.

It was the silence that brought Harry out of his luscious contemplations with a guilty start, and he found her watching him expectantly as if waiting for his opinion.

"Absolutely sound," he said, even though he hadn't heard a single word she'd said during the past hour. "I agree."

She gave him a wide smile, so he assumed he'd said the right thing, but he knew he mustn't keep getting distracted this way. What was true when she was his secretary was equally true now. If they were going to work successfully together, he could not indulge in any more lusty imaginings about her. But as he remembered how she'd felt in his hands a short time ago, as he imagined the scents of talcum and cotton, he wondered why he'd never noticed before now what a pretty smile she had. He had the feeling that putting thoughts of kissing Miss Dove out of his mind was going to be like putting Pandora's gifts back in the box. Tricky, very tricky.

Emma thought their discussions that afternoon had gone very well. Surprising, after the way things had begun.

She lay in bed, staring up at the darkened ceiling of her room, scarcely hearing Mr. Pigeon's loud purr beside her pillow or the clatter of London traffic through her open window. Her thoughts were fully occupied with Lord Marlowe and what had happened that afternoon.

He'd touched her. Never before had he done such a thing. His intent had been a chivalrous one, to be sure, assisting her down from the ladder, but then he had not carried it through. Instead, he'd slid his palms down to her hips and held her there. In his hands.

Aunt Lydia's many warnings about gentlemen and the animalistic aspect of their nature came back to haunt her. Emma knew she should have slapped his hands away, told him in no uncertain terms what she thought of such ungentlemanlike behavior. But instead she'd stood there with his hands on her hips and his thumbs caressing her spine, too shocked to move, with a strange, hot sort of tension flowing through her, something she'd never felt before.

No man had ever touched her, at least not in the way Marlowe had done today.

She thought of Mr. Parker, the only man with whom she'd ever shared any sort of intimacy. Their friendly conversations in the drawing room of Auntie's genteel little house had been conducted in chairs spaced half a dozen feet apart. Their strolls around the park in Red Lion Square as he'd told her his plans to become a barrister had been side by side, without even a brush of hands. Their waltzes together had been beyond reproach, their bodies separated by the perfect distance. And always there had been Auntie hovering nearby, ever watchful of Emma's virtue and reputation, ever ready to intervene should young Mr. Parker make any untoward advance upon her young niece.

But he never had. A clasp of hands, a kiss on her knuckles, a hand on her waist during a waltz.

But nothing more than that. Not a single thing that was improper.

Not sliding his palms down her hips. Not caressing the small of her back with his thumbs in slow circles that made her burn and tingle in the strangest way. Nothing like that.

She closed her eyes, and put her hands where Marlowe had put his. Before she could stop herself, she slid her palms along her hips just as he had done, and felt again that hot tension in her body. She jerked her hands away.

What Marlowe had done was just the sort of thing Auntie had always warned her against, the sort of thing no gently bred woman should ever permit, the sort of thing that had always made her maintain a cool, impersonal distance toward her handsome male employer. Gentlemen being what they were, Aunt Lydia had often said, it was up to females to enforce the boundaries of propriety with the most scrupulous care.

But he touched me, Auntie. He touched me.

She'd been very wrong to allow it.

Emma sat up, wrapping her arms around her bent knees and curling her toes beneath the hem of her cotton nightgown. She rested her forehead against her knees, hot with guilt and shame, even as she felt an unmistakable thrill. Now she knew the effect a man's caress, however brief, however improper, could have on a woman.

She could not allow it to happen again.

Emma fell back into the pillows with a sigh. Perhaps she was fretting about nothing. With that thought, she tried to adopt an attitude of determined optimism. Perhaps Marlowe, like herself, had realized the impropriety of what had happened and would be sure to behave more appropriately in future. After all, once they had moved to the parlor downstairs, things had seemed to smooth out between them, and for the remainder of the afternoon, his demeanor had been quite gentlemanlike.

Despite his warnings, she had not found his critiques to be brutal. And he'd listened to her ideas with an assiduous attention she'd never seen him display before. She'd gone on far too long about the details of her picnic luncheon menus, but even then he hadn't expressed either boredom or impatience. And though he had occasionally offered a murmur of agreement or a nod of encouragement, he had kept mum for the most part and listened to her in a most polite fashion.

Perhaps she had judged Marlowe too harshly. Perhaps he wasn't as insincere and dissolute as she'd always thought him to be. Still, gentlemen being what they were, she knew it was up to her to be sure that episode on the ladder was never repeated.

Chapter 9

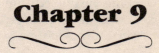

Pandora is a most uncooperative creature. Female, of course.

Lord Marlowe
The Bachelor's Guide, 1893

By the time of their meeting on Wednesday, Miss Dove had once again donned the aura of brisk, cool efficiency Harry was used to. That was very wise of her, no doubt, and a sensible course for both their sakes, but he couldn't help feeling a bit let down. He wanted to see more of the other Miss Dove, the one whose smile could light up a room. The one who cursed when she thought she was alone. The one who hadn't slapped him for caressing her hips.

Her revised work had been delivered to him

by messenger the afternoon before, and he approved all the changes she had made. The article for men she'd added at his request, however, had required some heavy editing, for it was clear Miss Dove had never needed to choose a valet, but she voiced no objections to the changes he'd made.

Though her manner today was very much that of the Miss Dove he had always known, there was something different about her these days. The woman who'd been his secretary wouldn't have lost her temper and tossed him out of her flat. She wouldn't have hurled criticisms at his head or bargained with him over the percentages of a business deal. Miss Dove had changed, and he didn't know quite how the change had taken place, but he did know that she was beginning to intrigue him in a way she never had before.

Perhaps her newfound success had given her a measure of quiet confidence in herself he'd never seen her display. Or perhaps it was because she now demanded a level of regard from him he'd never really accorded her before. His gaze lowered to the starched pin tuck front of her shirtwaist. Or perhaps, he added wryly to himself, it was just because he kept imagining her naked.

"I shall have these ready to be typeset by tomorrow," she promised, breaking into his speculations.

Curious, he asked, "How do you know so

much about these things? Crystal and napkin rings and what's proper? And where do you get all these creative ideas of yours?"

"My Aunt Lydia was a governess prior to her marriage, and she was very meticulous in matters of conduct. That's how I learned what's proper, as you put it. I lived with her from the time I was fifteen."

"What about your mother?"

"She died when I was only eight. I barely remember her." Miss Dove looked past his shoulder, staring thoughtfully into space. "She was always telling me not to play in the mud," she murmured. "I remember that."

"You weren't allowed to play in the mud? Why not, in heaven's name?"

"My father didn't like it if my clothes were stained or dirty. Being a military man, he was very precise, you know."

Harry did know. He was getting a fairly clear picture of Miss Dove's childhood, and it was too grim for words. "So, you went to your aunt when you were fifteen. Was she married?"

"She was a widow by then and lived in London, only a few blocks from here, in fact. When my father died, I came here to live with her."

"Your aunt did not make her home with you and your father before his death?" Harry asked in surprise.

The oddest expression stole across her face, a hard, frozen sort of look. Like a mask. Looking at her, he got an uneasy feeling he could not explain. "No," she answered his question after a moment. "My father did not . . . did not care for my aunt. She was my mother's sister."

The aunt didn't care much for the father, either, Harry guessed. There was something very wrong with all this. He could sense it, and he didn't like it. "But surely, with your mother gone, would it not have been best for you to have lived with your aunt anyway?"

"No. At least," she added with a smile that seemed forced and brittle, "my father did not think so. As I said, they did not get on. But to answer the rest of your question about crystal and napkin rings and the like . . ." She paused to consider the matter, then said, "I don't quite know where I get my ideas. They just come into my head. I read a great deal. I take long walks, observe what I see, and write about those things that interest me. I converse with many people—matrons, merchants, craftsmen. And, of course, I love to visit the shops. Today, for example, I intend to explore the area around Covent Garden Market. In fact," she added with a look at the watch pinned to her beige jacket, "if we are finished here, I should be on my way. It's nearly eleven o'clock." She put her papers for final revision in her dispatch case and stood up.

Harry rose as well. "I should like to accompany you," he found himself saying.

She paused and gave him a dubious look. "You want to go with me? You?"

He laughed. "I know it's a shock."

"To say the least. You loathe visiting shops."

"And you adore it. Which is precisely why I always fobbed off the buying of presents on you. You're far better at choosing gifts than I am. You have a talent for finding just the right thing for each person."

"Why, thank you, my lord. There's a great deal of pleasure in knowing you've chosen a gift the recipient will appreciate."

"If it's so much fun, why don't you take up that task on my behalf again?"

"Absolutely not," she said at once.

He sighed. "You have become so heartless. Think of my poor sisters."

That didn't seem to impress her.

"I'm no good at choosing gifts, Miss Dove," he said as he walked her to the door. "You have no idea how frustrating it is when it's two days until Christmas, and you can't think what to buy."

"Serves you right for waiting until two days beforehand."

"Perhaps, but I'm still dreading Christmas-time without you."

"There's no need. You just need to pay closer attention to what people say. And you'll have to go shopping, of course."

He groaned.

That made her laugh. "Think of our outing as a perfect way to practice."

"Oh, very well. I shall endeavor to hone my shopping skills by watching you."

With that, he and Miss Dove departed for Covent Garden Market, and during the next two hours, he came a bit closer to understanding her.

He discovered she was a good listener, and that gave her a natural ability to interview people and draw information out of them. A butcher's wife told her where she might purchase the finest mustards. The costermonger taught her how to make the best Cornish pasty. The policeman at the corner of Maiden Lane and Bedford Street informed her which side streets were safe and which were not. She was willing to be schooled by anyone on any subject, paying careful attention to what people told her and penciling notes about what she learned into a little notebook. No wonder she knew where to find the best boots and how to make paper animals. She took advantage of a basic truth about human nature. People loved to feel important by sharing what they knew.

He kept himself in the background, and there were times when she seemed to become so absorbed in her conversations with others that she forgot he was there. He enjoyed this opportunity to study her unobserved, but there was no possible way he was going to get another tantalizing peek at her silhouette in the sun. Not today anyway.

She was clad from head to foot in a beige linen walking suit, buttoned up tight to show only the high collar of her white shirtwaist and the narrow green ribbon tie around her neck. The enormous leg-of-mutton sleeves and peplum of her jacket exaggerated the width of her shoulders and hips all out of proportion to her slender shape, and a straw bonnet with heaps of green ribbons and cream-colored feathers prevented him from appreciating the red lights in her hair. Unless he ducked his head to look her full in the face, the wide brim of her hat concealed her eyes from his view.

Nonetheless, as they walked amid the fruits and vegetables of Covent Garden Market, he consoled himself with what he could see: the soft, pale skin of her ear and cheek, the delicate slope of her nose, and those pretty, golden freckles. He wondered how many freckles she possessed that he couldn't see. He wondered how long it would take to kiss them all.

Whenever he started thinking such things, Harry tried to steer his thoughts in a more impersonal direction, but just as he'd suspected the other day, it wasn't proving an easy thing to do. He kept remembering the sight of her on that ladder, the curve of her breast and the slender lines of her torso. He kept thinking of long, slim legs and imagining soft, hot kisses. Pandora's gifts, in other words, just weren't going back in the box.

He decided a bit of conversation was in order. "Miss Dove, I am beginning to appreciate how you have learned so many things," he told her as they strolled on opposite sides of a long wooden stand laden with bushel baskets of the first summer fruits. "You are a good listener, and people respond to that."

He was rewarded with a smile. "Thank you. Of course, it would be easier if I could tell people I am Mrs. Bartleby. People would be much more assiduous. But since we are keeping her identity a secret, I must be content to remain merely her secretary."

"Yes, as you were interviewing people, I noticed you introduced yourself in that capacity. I take it Mrs. Bartleby doesn't need to butter people up but her secretary does."

She made a face at him. "I do not butter people up."

"Oh, yes you do. You butter up everyone you meet. Well," he added wryly, "everyone but me."

To his surprise, she stopped walking, bringing him to a halt as well. "I am so sorry about what I said that day, truly," she said, turning to look at him over the top of the fruit stand. "I don't know what came over me to speak with such a lack of tact."

"You should be sorry," he told her with mock severity. "It was a most unflattering assessment. You are a difficult person to impress, Miss Dove."

"Am I?" She plucked a plum out of the basket in front of her. "Why do you care? You said it doesn't matter what others think of us," she reminded as she put the plum back and selected another, "so why should you care about impressing me?"

Startled by the question, he stared at her over the top of the fruit stand, and no quick, witty answer came to his lips.

"It's not so simple, is it, my lord?" she murmured, and a tiny smile curved her mouth as she lifted another plum out of the basket for inspection. "Sometimes, what others think of us does matter, even if it shouldn't. Which is why young ladies eat chicken wings and why I pay attention to the opinion of my landlady. Knowing proper conduct is important. That's why people read Mrs. Bartleby."

"How wicked you are to use my own words about impressing you against me."

She met his gaze over the plums. "The point is, we all care, to some degree, what others think of us."

"I don't," he told her. "Not about most people anyway. But you and I are . . . friends." A lie, that. He didn't want to be her friend. He wanted to kiss her, and that was the reason her good opinion mattered. It gave him better odds.

"So we are friends now, are we?" she asked, sounding amused.

"Except for the fact that you don't like me," he amended and watched her smile. "I am choosing to ignore that fact."

She laughed. "For the sake of our friendship?"

"Just so."

She put the plum back in the basket, picked up another, gave a vexed exclamation, and put it back. "These plums are dreadful, and at such a price, too!"

He glanced at the placard. "A dozen for sixpence seems reasonable to me."

"It's outrageous. In season, plums should be three for a penny."

"You are a miser, Miss Dove."

She didn't seem to like that description. She frowned at him. "I am frugal," she corrected.

"Whatever you say."

"And I don't much care for plums anyway. The skins have a rather sour taste. Oh, I do wish it were August! Then the peaches would be in. I adore peaches, don't you?" She lifted her face, closed her eyes, and licked her lips. "Ripe, sweet, juicy ones."

Erotic images flashed through his mind, images of peaches and a very naked Miss Dove. Lust flooded through his body, and before he could stop it, he was fully aroused.

"My lord, are you all right?"

"What?" Harry shook his head, striving to regain his equilibrium, as the object of these sensual imaginings looked at him with concern.

"You have such an odd look on your face. Are you ill?"

"Ill?" That was one way of putting it. "On the contrary," he lied. "I am well. I am perfectly well."

She nodded in acceptance of that statement and returned her attention to the fruit displayed before her. He jerked at his collar, exasperated with himself. What was wrong with him? He wasn't a lad of thirteen, for God's sake, unable to control his own arousal. And he certainly wasn't the sort of man who allowed a woman's opinion to bother him or erotic imaginings of her to interfere with matters of business, and he didn't like virtuous women any way. This sudden attraction to Miss Dove was inexplicable. And most inconvenient.

Though their situation had changed somewhat, she still worked for him. The circumstances that had always acted as a wall between them were still in place. He had to keep them there. He was a gentleman, and a gentleman did not take advantage of women in his employ, especially innocent virgin spinsters. He must stop thinking erotic things about Miss Dove. He simply must.

As she moved along the fruit stand, he lingered behind, striving to eliminate from his mind any fantasies of feeding fruit to her while both of them were naked. Once he felt his baser desires were firmly under control and he was again master of himself, he caught up to her where she was waiting for him at the end of the stand. "Are you finished here?"

She shook her head and held up a small wooden basket. "I thought to purchase some of these early strawberries."

Harry made a smothered sound and gave up the fight. After all, he reasoned, there was no harm in *thinking* luscious things about her. He just had to remember not to act on them.

Marlowe was behaving very strangely. Emma contemplated this fact as they sat across from each other on the grass in the Victoria Embankment Gardens and consumed an impromptu luncheon of cold tongue, bread and butter, and strawberries.

He'd remarked she was difficult to impress,

yet she had never known him to have any desire to impress her.

Still, there was no mistaking that he didn't seem quite himself today. There was that very odd look on his face when she'd mentioned peaches. A dazed, uncomprehending look, as if he'd just gone off into a world of his own. She couldn't account for it.

And then there was the way he kept staring at her mouth.

He was doing it now.

Emma paused, a strawberry poised halfway to her lips. "Why do you do keep doing that?"

"Doing what?"

"Staring at me. It is most disconcerting."

"Is it?" He didn't look away. Instead, he leaned back on his forearms and tilted his head to one side. He began to smile.

"It makes me feel as if I have something on my face," she told him. "And why are you smiling like that? Did I say something amusing?"

He lifted his gaze from her mouth to her eyes. "You don't have anything on your face, and I do not mean to stare. My apologies. I am simply trying to get to know you better by making a study of your person. In our new spirit of equality, you understand."

Though he was still smiling, he sounded sincere. Gratified, she decided a show of conciliation on her part was in order. They did have to work together. "Despite what you may think, there are things about you I do admire."

"Well, go on," he prompted when she paused.

"Don't stop now, in heaven's name. You must tell me what my admirable qualities are."

"You have very shrewd business instincts, for one thing."

He sat up, reached for a strawberry, and gave her a rueful look as he ate it. "Not so shrewd when it comes to a certain Mrs. Bartleby."

"Anyone can make an error of judgment. Besides, I have come to accept that what I write is not your cup of tea, so to speak. And you were right that my popularity could be a transient thing. You, on the other hand, have a history of success, and I cannot help but admire that. I respect your business acumen."

That said, she ate her strawberry and reached for another from the basket.

Marlowe, however, was looking at her askance. "Is that all?" he asked. "You respect my business acumen?"

Emma looked at him in bewilderment. "What were you expecting me to say?"

"Not that," he said with emphasis. "As gratifying as it is to know I have your respect, that's not a very flattering thing for a woman to say to a man."

She looked at him with doubt as she ate her strawberry, uncertain if he was teasing. "So it's flattery you want from me?"

He paused as if thinking it over, then gave a decided nod. "Yes, I do," he said and grinned. "After your litany of my faults, my masculine pride is wounded. I am in serious need of buttering up."

He could be so outrageous. "No," she said,

folding her arms and trying not to laugh. "Flattery will only make you conceited."

"Not with you to keep me on the straight, narrow, humble path." He stirred and edged closer to her on the grass. "I know you said you don't like me, but I refuse to believe you think me wholly bad. There must be something besides my business acumen that you like about me, Emmaline."

"I did not give you leave to use my Christian name! Besides," she added, making a face, "I hate Emmaline. Calling me that won't help you."

"All right, then. Shall I call you Emma instead? Is that what your friends call you?"

"Yes, if you must know. But I don't know why you keep referring to friendship. It is impossible for us to be friends."

"Why?"

She sniffed. "A gentleman, so my Aunt Lydia always said, is never a trustworthy friend to a woman."

He chuckled. "Shrewd woman, your aunt." He stretched out his long legs parallel to hers, so close they were nearly touching. It went beyond the bounds of propriety. She opened her mouth to point that out, but then his knee brushed hers, and she could not seem to speak.

"You still haven't told me what you like about me," he murmured and leaned forward, coming so close that she caught the masculine scent of sandalwood soap, so close that she could see the dark blue ring around the irises of his eyes. He eased his hand between her leg and his, flattening his palm on the ground between them and resting his weight on his arm. His wrist brushed the side of her thigh.

"C'mon, Emma," he coaxed. "Butter me up."

Warmth flooded through her, a tide of it that made her sure she was blushing all over. She feared she was the one being buttered up, for the way he looked at her made her feel as soft as butter in the sun. She stirred, flustered, restless, and acutely aware of his wrist against the side of her leg.

For some reason, his smile widened. He must have been able to perceive her agitation, but he did not move away from her, and she knew he was not going to do so until she gave him what he was waiting for.

Oh, how she envied him his glib tongue at this moment. Emma swallowed hard, and looked straight into his brilliant blue eyes. Her breath caught at his heart-stopping smile. Her pulses began to race, and she understood for the first time just why women made such fools of themselves over him. "You are a very handsome man."

He pulled back a bit and gave her a dubious look, then he glanced around as if uncertain she was speaking to him. Seeming to determine that he was, indeed, the recipient of this compliment, he returned his gaze to hers, yet his expression was still skeptical. "*You* think I'm handsome? You do?"

"Yes," she admitted. "And very charming when you wish to be."

He leaned forward again until his forehead was only inches from the brim of her hat. "I should very much like to kiss you." His lashes lowered. "By God, if we were in a more secluded spot, I'd do it, too."

Her heart slammed against her ribs. "What abominable conceit!" she said, ashamed that her voice came out breathless and rushed instead of properly remonstrative. "As if I would let you!"

He didn't look the least bit chastened by that, the wretched man. His smile came back, and this time it was downright wicked. "Is that a challenge, Emma? Are you daring me to kiss you?"

She felt a shiver of excitement at those bold words, and it took her a moment to gather her poise. "What nonsense you talk," she said, then picked up her dispatch case and rose to her feet. "Now that I've flattered you so lavishly, which cannot be a good thing for any man, we'd best be going back. I have writing to do for next week's issue."

She stepped away from him, putting a much more proper distance between them. But as she brushed bread crumbs from her skirt, she heard him murmur something under his breath. It sounded like, "Emma, I never refuse a dare."

She knew she ought to impress upon him that she hadn't dared him to kiss her, and that he was not, under any circumstances, permitted to do so. But as they left the Embankment, Emma didn't say anything about it. Aunt Lydia, she feared, would have been greatly disappointed in her.

Chapter 10

Because she has no chaperone to watch over her, the girl-bachelor must apply the most exacting standards of propriety to her own behavior, lest gentlemen make inappropriate advances upon her person.

Mrs. Bartleby
Advice to Girl-Bachelors, 1893

Emma's typewriting machine tapped out one word, then another, then two more. A vague feeling stirred within her that something was wrong, and she stopped typing. Staring at the sheet of paper before her, she read aloud the last few words she had written. "'Therefore, when a lady is in need of kisses—'"

With a groan, she leaned forward in her chair and rested her forehead on the typewriting machine, grinding her teeth in frustration. Kid

171

gloves, she'd meant to type, not kisses. This was the fifth time in a row she'd typed the wrong word. What on earth was the matter with her today?

Even as she asked herself that question, Emma knew the answer. She glanced sideways at the window, imagined again sitting on the grass in Victoria Embankment Gardens, looking into a pair of teasing blue eyes.

I should very much like to kiss you.

Thinking about that man had been distracting her from her work for two days. Try as she might, she couldn't stop thinking about him. It was exasperating.

Reminding herself that she had a stringent deadline to meet and no time for daydreaming, she sat up, pulled the sheet of paper out of the typewriting machine, and set it aside, along with several other error-filled pages. She started to reach for a fresh sheet of paper, then for no reason at all she plunked one elbow on the desk instead, rested her chin in her hand, and closed her eyes.

C'mon Emma. Butter me up.

That melting warmth washed over her again, as delicious today as it had been two days ago. In her mind's eye, she saw him sitting there with that look of mock skepticism on his face, acting as if he didn't believe her, acting as if her compliments were a complete surprise to him when he already knew full well the potent charm he possessed.

Really, how did he manage it? she wondered and

once again straightened in her chair. *How did he manage to make harmless words sound so iniquitous?* It was a talent she suspected could be very dangerous to any woman's notions of proper behavior. Especially hers.

Is that a challenge, Emma? Are you daring me to kiss you?

The man was so outrageous. Daring him to kiss her, indeed. She didn't even like him. After she had sternly reminded herself of all the reasons why, she pressed her fingers to her mouth and wondered how it would feel to have his mouth on hers.

The clock on her mantel chimed and Emma came out of her reverie with a guilty start. She glanced at the clock, dumbfounded by the fact that it was half-past two. Where had the day gone? She had to be at her appointment in half an hour's time.

Emma jumped to her feet and ran for her bedroom, stumbling over poor Mr. Pigeon and earning herself an indignant howl from him. "Sorry, Pigeon," she told him over her shoulder as she entered her room.

She hurriedly replaced her shirtwaist with a fresh one, but all her rushing proved wasted, for she had to rebutton the front twice to align it properly. After donning her green serge walking suit, she secured a simple straw boater on her head with a hat pin and stuffed her little notebook and pencil into her reticule. Hooking the reticule to her wrist by the braided handle, Emma ran for the door, pulling on her gloves as she went, buttoning them as she ran down the stairs.

Breathless, she emerged from her building and started down the sidewalk, moving at the quickest pace permissible to a lady. She hated being late.

"Emma?"

The sound of her name caused Emma to glance sideways toward the street. There, stepping down from his carriage with a newspaper in his hand, was the reason she was in such a rush, the very man who'd been tormenting her thoughts for two days. Knowing it was impossible to pretend she hadn't seen him, Emma stopped and waited as he approached, but the moment he halted beside her, she spoke. "Good afternoon, my lord. Forgive me, but I cannot tarry. I have an appointment in just a few minutes."

She resumed her rapid stride along the sidewalk.

"I brought you something." He fell in step beside her, keeping to her rapid pace with ease. As they walked, he held up the newspaper in his hand. "Tomorrow's edition."

Emma came to a halt, her appointment forgotten. "Already?"

"Ink's barely dry," he told her, "but here it is. First copy off the press. Want a peek?"

She took it from him, opened it to her section, and gave an exclamation of surprise at the sight of her pseudonym so prominently displayed. She began flipping pages, scanning the articles she had written. As she always did when her words appeared in print, she felt like a little girl at Christmas who'd gotten the perfect present. "It's wonderful!" she cried and couldn't help laughing with exultation. "Simply wonderful!"

"Emma, your column has been in this newspaper every week for over two months," he reminded her. "Do you get this excited every week?"

"Yes," she said and paused to look up at him, still laughing. "Yes, I do."

He grinned back at her. "If it makes you smile like that, I'll bring you a copy every Friday afternoon."

Before she could reply, a church clock began to chime the hour. She made a sound of vexation. "Oh, dear, is it three? Heavens, now I truly am late!"

"On another journalistic expedition, are you?"

"Yes." She folded the paper and held it out to him. "Thank you again for showing it to me."

He shook his head in refusal. "That's yours."

"But it's the first copy. Don't you want it?"

"No. I want Mrs. Bartleby to have it." He gestured over his shoulder to the open carriage at the curb. "I have my carriage. I can easily take you where you are going."

"Thank you, but it wouldn't be proper for me to ride in your carriage. And in any case, it isn't necessary. I'm only going to Au Chocolat," she added as they resumed walking, "and that establishment is on the next corner."

"You have an appointment with a confection-er's shop?"

"Yes. I am meeting with the owner, Henri Bourget. Of course, he thinks he is meeting with Mrs. Bartleby's secretary."

"Which reminds me of something I meant to ask you the other day. Isn't posing as someone you're not considered a lie?" he teased. "Or bad form, at least?"

"I'm not the one who insisted upon secrecy. Besides, it is a minor prevarication to preserve journalistic integrity," she said at once. "For purposes of research."

He laughed. "A confectioner's is research, is it?"

"It is! I am toying with a theme of sweets for our third issue. Desserts, comfits, that sort of thing. It was one of the ideas I told you about last Saturday. Don't you remember?"

"Um, of course. Have you a sweet tooth, Emma?"

"Oh, yes. I adore sweets. Particularly choco-late." She bit her lip and gave him a helpless look as they paused at the corner. "I fear you have learned my secret weakness. I would do anything for chocolate."

"Would you?" he murmured and paused to give her a searching glance. "Do you mind if I accompany you?" he asked after a moment. "I should like to purchase some chocolates for my sisters. As you so rightly pointed out, I need to begin selecting gifts myself, and chocolate is a gift I know would please all my sisters." He reached for the newspaper in her hand. "Allow me to carry that."

"Thank you. Do your sisters like chocolate, then?"

"They adore the stuff. Baffling to me, but there it is."

"You don't like chocolate?" When he shook his head, she stared at him and began to question his sanity. "How is that possible?"

"I've a preference for savories and salty things. I've a particular addiction to sardines."

That made her laugh. "Now you are joking."

"On the contrary, I am perfectly serious."

Her laughter subsided, and she once again studied him with doubt. Then she sighed. "I never can quite tell when you are teasing me."

"Yes, I know, and because of that, I am beginning to appreciate just how much fun teasing you can be. I intend to do a great deal of it from now on."

"Lovely," she said with a groan. Now she'd never get any work done. "That's just lovely."

When faced with a woman's confession that she would do anything for chocolate, a truly honorable man would have refused to speculate on what the word *anything* encompassed. But Harry had been deemed a dissolute fellow who lived an immoral life, and as the owner of Au Chocolat gave them a tour of the premises. Harry's thoughts were occupied with all sorts of wicked possibilities.

Their tour ended in a sort of reception room,

where a bottle of champagne in a bucket of ice awaited them, flanked by crystal flutes and a selection of chocolates on a silver tray. Also on the table was a paperboard box wrapped in pink tissue paper and white silk ribbon. Monsieur Bourget gestured to the table. "Perhaps your lordship and the secretary of Madame Bartleby would care to sample our truffles and have a glass of champagne?"

Emma looked at the selection of chocolates as if she'd just found heaven. "How thoughtful of you, monsieur."

The Frenchman indicated the pink-wrapped box on the table. "Please ask Mrs. Bartleby to accept this selection of truffles as our gift. We believe we make the finest liqueur chocolates in London, and we hope she will conclude the same in her column."

"I will be sure she receives them," Emma answered with a straight face, "but, of course, I cannot guarantee what her opinion will be. Alas, I am merely her secretary."

The Frenchman had no chance to reply, for at that moment another gentleman entered the room, a frown of concern on his face. He came to where they stood by the table and said something to Bourget in a low voice.

A brief exchange of words in French followed, only about half of which Harry understood, for they spoke rapidly and his French had always been awful, but there seemed to be a problem with the tempering of a particular batch of chocolate.

Bourget turned to his guests and spread his hands wide with a smile and a shrug. "Alas, they can do nothing without me. Miss Dove, Vicomte Marlowe, I fear I must leave you for a moment. If you will pardon me?"

When they nodded, he gestured to the table. "Enjoy the truffles. I shall return in a few moments." With a bow to them, he departed with the other Frenchman, leaving Harry and Emma alone in the room.

Harry turned toward her and set aside the newspaper he'd been carrying to reach for the bottle of champagne. "Shall we avail ourselves of Monsieur Bourget's hospitality?" he asked, pouring a glass for each of them.

Emma put her little notebook and pencil in her reticule, then set the ecru linen bag on the table. She unbuttoned her gloves, pulled them off, and laid them beside the reticule. Sipping champagne, she studied the selection of sweets for a moment, then she chose a truffle of dark chocolate with thin ribbons of pink icing on top.

Harry studied her as she daintily took half the truffle into her mouth, and he smiled at the expression of ecstasy that crossed her face, his imagination going wild. When he saw a drop of liqueur filling slide down her bottom lip and onto her chin, he was quick to take advantage of a heaven-sent opportunity.

Even as she set down her flute of champagne and started to reach for one of the folded linen serviettes on the table, Harry was lifting his hand to her face. He caught the droplet of liqueur on the pad of his thumb, then lifted his hand to his own mouth. Her eyes widened as she watched him suck at the tacky spot.

"Hazelnut," he murmured and glanced down. "It was delicious, but I didn't get any chocolate."

Before she could guess his intent and stop him with some ridiculous rule of etiquette, he grasped her wrist, lifted her hand, and opened his mouth. His lips closed around her fingers and the remaining half of the truffle.

She gasped, but though she tried to pull her hand away, he wouldn't let her. She glanced at the door, then back at him as he slowly pulled the candy from her fingers with his mouth.

He saw her lips quiver and heard her breathing quicken. He perceived the change in her body, a purely feminine reaction of passion tempered by modesty. By innocence. Harry's body began to burn.

Rosy color came up in her cheeks. She took another desperate glance around and tried again to pull her hand away, but he wouldn't let her.

"Not yet," he murmured around the chocolate in his mouth, still holding on to her wrist. "I missed a bit."

He swallowed the bite of truffle, then pulled the tip of her forefinger into his mouth. She made a startled sound, and he knew she was shocked by what he was doing and by her own body's response. He could feel her pulse racing against his thumb as he sucked the last vestiges of chocolate from her fingertip with slow, deliberate relish.

Her resistance began melting away as he licked chocolate off her fingers one by one. Her hand relaxed in his hold. Her gold-tipped lashes lowered, and she closed her eyes. When he turned her hand over and pressed a kiss to her palm, she made a soft little sigh. Her fingers curved around his face, the damp tips caressing his cheek, sending desire coursing through every nerve ending in his body.

He flicked his tongue over her palm, and he felt the shiver that ran through her. He lifted his head, watching her face as he lowered her hand and eased his body closer.

She sensed his intent, for she lifted her face without opening her eyes and parted her lips. Pure instinct, he judged, doubting she even realized what she was so prettily asking for. If she had, she would surely have called a halt, but all her senses were focused on only one thing: the awakening of her own desire.

It was one of the most erotic things Harry had ever seen in his life.

He didn't have much chance to enjoy it. The tap of footsteps in the corridor told him someone was coming, and after pressing a quick kiss to her knuckles, he let go of her hand. By the time Bourget reentered the room, Emma's dreamy expression was gone, and Harry was on the other side of the table, studying the truffles as if trying to make up his mind.

"Once again, forgive me," the Frenchman said, coming toward them.

"Pray do not distress yourself, monsieur," Harry replied and picked up a truffle. Looking at Emma, he added, "We have been thoroughly enjoying ourselves."

She made a choked sound, her cheeks scarlet.

He grinned at her and took a bite of truffle.

She flattened her palm on the table beside the tray and leaned toward him, her eyes narrowing as she watched him eat the candy. "I thought you did not care for chocolate."

Harry donned his best innocent air. "Why, Miss Dove, whatever gave you that idea?"

Chapter 11

It has been my duty, dearest Emma, to guide you into womanhood. To instruct you in proper conduct, to steer you through the difficult dilemmas of your youth, and to protect you from the evils of this world. I have tried to instill within you a true sense of what it means to be a lady, and when I look at you now, I know I have succeeded. I am proud of you, my dear. So very proud.

Mrs. Lydia Worthington's final words
to her niece, 1888

Emma suspected Auntie would not be so proud of her now. As she and Marlowe left Au Chocolat and started back toward Little Russell Street, neither of them spoke, and Emma was glad of it, for her feelings were in such disarray, mere conversation was beyond her.

She knew certain things were wrong. Everything in her upbringing told her that. Allowing a man to lick chocolate off her fingers was wrong. Allowing a man to sit so close to her at a picnic that his leg touched hers and his hand brushed against her thigh was wrong. Had Aunt Lydia been with them during either of those incidents, no such liberty would ever have been allowed. Had Auntie's mere presence not proved a sufficient deterrent, her pointed little cough or the delicate tap of her parasol would have done the trick.

Notwithstanding Beatrice and her most excellent Mr. Jones, for whom she had bent the rules a bit, Emma had advised young women to rigidly enforce the boundaries of propriety in her manuscripts. Were Mrs. Bartleby to find herself in such a predicament as Emma had been in this afternoon, that lady would have stopped Marlowe at once and slapped his face.

Emma feared she was not made of such stern stuff as her fictional creation.

When Marlowe had licked chocolate from her hand and sucked on her fingertips, she'd been so caught up in how it made her feel that stopping him and slapping his face had never occurred to her. The touch of his mouth on her skin had vanquished all her good sense and staunch principles in an instant. How mortifying to know her convictions were so shallow.

She cast a sideways glance at him as he walked beside her. He had never behaved this way toward her before. He had teased her sometimes, of course, and talked a bit of his nonsense now and then, but this was not the same. The way he teased her now was personal, intimate, flirtatious. No man had ever flirted with her before. No man had ever made improper advances upon her person, and Marlowe's sudden propensity to do so was baffling. He could behave this way with any number of women, and had surely done so many times. Why her? Why now?

I should very much like to kiss you.

In her youth, she had sometimes thought of Mr. Parker and dreamt of kisses. She'd put aside notions of that sort long ago, buried them deep down inside herself, along with her broken heart and her crushed hopes. But she could feel those secret, romantic dreams flaring back up, dreams of a different man's kisses—a man far less proper, far more presumptuous than Mr. Parker had ever been, a man who wanted to kiss her and made no secret of the fact, a man who made her wonder, just as she had done as a girl, what it would be like to be kissed.

Emma glanced at him again and felt an overpowering, giddying rush of excitement. She wanted his kiss. It was wrong, she reminded herself, for a man to kiss a woman to whom he was not married, or at the very least engaged, and Marlowe was the least likely man on earth to marry anyone. He was a corrupt, worldly man who had illicit liaisons with dancing girls. And it wasn't as if she wanted to marry him anyway.

They paused at the corner, and still watching him, Emma touched the fingers he had kissed to her lips.

He turned his head, looked at her, and smiled. Her breathing stopped, and her heart gave a leap of queer, painful pleasure within her breast.

It was too much, that feeling. She looked away and jerked her hand down. She was a steady person, she reminded herself as they crossed the street. She did not get stirred up or want what was forbidden. She was not giddy. She was *not* wanton.

"What's wrong, Emma?"

Marlowe's voice broke into her thoughts. "After what happened, I don't see how you can ask me such a question, my lord."

He laughed. "After what happened, I think you should call me Harry."

Emma made a sound of exasperation. "I daresay you do, *my lord*."

He shrugged, shifting tomorrow's edition of the *Social Gazette* and the boxes of chocolate he carried for his sisters to his other arm. "It was only a kiss on your hand."

"You make it sound so innocent!" She realized she had raised her voice, and she took a quick glance around as they walked to make sure no one was within earshot, but the London traffic was loud enough to prevent any other pedestrians from hearing their conversation.

"I may not be as . . . as knowledgeable as you in matters of this kind," she said, returning her gaze to his. "But even I know you were not merely kissing my hand! You were . . . you were . . ." Her hand began to tingle, her whole body grew warm, and words failed her.

She looked away, thrusting her gloved hands in the pockets of her skirt, and quickened her pace, but Marlowe kept up with her easily, his long strides much more relaxed than her jittery steps. "Emma," he said as they turned onto her street, "nothing happened." The very gentleness of his voice only made things worse. "It was harmless fun."

"It was not harmless. Anyone could have walked into that room and seen what you were doing!"

"No one did."

"But they could have! And it would have been my reputation that suffered for it, not yours."

For the first time, a shadow of guilt crossed his face. His gaze shifted away from hers. "You didn't stop me."

"You wouldn't let go of my hand."

"You weren't pulling very hard."

She could not argue with that, for it was true. "And it was very wrong of me! Oh, how could I have allowed you to do such a wicked thing?"

"You think what just happened was wicked? Emma, you're not going to go to hell for this, you know. No one's going to send you to bed without any supper or take away your Christmas presents."

That ignited her temper, adding to her already tempestuous emotions. "Don't make fun of me!" she flared, stopping in the middle of the sidewalk a few feet from her front door.

He sobered at once and also came to a halt. "I'm not. But it seems to me you are getting awfully worked up over a harmless flirtation, and I do not understand why."

Because of the way it made me feel.

She wanted to shout those words at him in the midst of the street. Instead, she took a deep breath and turned away. She walked to the door of her building. "Things like that are never harmless," she murmured over her shoulder, striving to remember Auntie's dire warnings from her girlhood. "Thinks like that can lead to—" She stopped, hand on the doorknob.

Behind her, he gave a low, throaty chuckle. "In a confectioner's shop? Believe me, if I'd intended what happened to lead anywhere, I'd have gotten you alone in a much more romantic place before I ever started kissing your hand."

"How very reassuring!" She started to open the door, but his palm flattened against it, preventing her from taking refuge inside.

"What is this really about?" he asked.

"Let me go." When he didn't comply, she turned around to face him and scowled. "I cannot imagine what people will think about a man accosting a woman at her door in this ungentlemanlike manner."

"What people? Your landlady? It occurs to me that you spend a great deal of time worrying about what other people think."

"It is always important to consider the opinions of others."

"No, it's not. If you're looking for what is right and wrong, you won't find it in other people's opinions. You won't find it in etiquette books.

There's only one way to figure out right and wrong." He leaned forward, and without warning, he touched her just beneath her breastbone.

She sucked in a sharp breath.

"Look here," he said, his palm flattening against her solar plexus, his fingertips resting between her breasts. "That's where you'll always find the truth."

Painfully conscious that she was in her own street, where her neighbors could see her, Emma glanced around, but thankfully it was the dinner hour, and no one seemed to be about. "You mean truth is in one's heart, I suppose?"

"No. What I mean is that you find the truth about everything in your guts. Your heart can lie to you. Your intuition, your instincts never do."

"And you always follow this guide yourself?"

"Usually." He paused and let his hand fall away. "Not always."

It was none of her business, but she had to ask. "When you listened to your heart instead of your instincts, what happened?"

"I got married."

"I see." She hesitated, but she had to ask. "And which organ was it—your heart or your guts—that led you to divorce your wife?"

He made a sound of derision. "I suppose like all of society, you condemn me for what I did. Despite the fact that I was the wronged party."

"I was brought up to believe that marriage is a sacred vow before God and not to be broken, if that's what you mean."

"How easy that is for someone like you to say."

"Just because I am a spinster, it does not mean I cannot form an opinion on the morality of divorce!" she countered, stung.

"Your opinion being that no matter what my wife did, I was wrong to divorce her?"

"It's not my place to say."

"Not your place?" He laughed, but it was a harsh sound. "Mrs. Bartleby spends a great deal of time advising people about the proprieties, so what's proper in a case such as mine?" His voice was low, vibrating with an anger she'd never heard him express before. "What decorum should a man adopt when his wife spends every day of her married life loathing her husband and pining for another man? Should he be civil and sporting about it all and pretend to her that it doesn't hurt? Should he be a saint or a martyr who never lashes back?"

He turned toward her, and in the twilight, something glittered in his eyes, something cold and icy blue. "When she runs off to America with her lover, publicly humiliating him and leaving his entire family open to scandal, should he have a stiff upper lip about it? Pretend it doesn't matter? Should he file for legal separation? Should he live celibate? Take a mistress?"

She was startled by the raw pain in his face. "You loved your wife," she said, appreciating that fact for the first time.

"Of course I did!" He looked away, drew a

deep breath. "I wouldn't have married her otherwise."

"I didn't understand that. I thought—" She paused, considering. "I suppose I always thought that if you loved her you would have gone after her."

"I should have followed her to New York, you mean? Dragged her from her lover's arms and resigned myself to spending my life in hell? Would that have been more proper than divorce?"

She looked at him helplessly, with no answer to offer. Divorce was an unthinkable thing to her, as alien a concept as going without a corset or not going to church. On the other hand, what did she understand about the private relations between men and women? Next to nothing.

"I fell in love with Consuelo the first moment I saw her," he said, turning to lean back against the brick wall of the building. "I knew nothing of her character, nothing of her mind, nothing of her temperament, but I didn't care. I fell in love with her the first moment I looked into her eyes. She had the biggest, darkest, saddest eyes I'd ever seen. I'd set myself on marrying her before the introductions were even finished. It happened that fast."

She stared at him, stunned, her mind flashing back to the day long ago in Auntie's drawing room when another man had confessed a similar experience.

"I was in love once, too," she blurted out.

"Were you?"

She nodded and leaned back against the door, staring across the street, her mind's eye seeing right past the tidy brick buildings in front of her to Red Lion Square six blocks away. "His name was Jonathan Parker, and he was a friend of my mother's family. I vaguely remember having met him once or twice when we were small children, but after my mother died, my father cut all ties with her family and acquaintances, and I didn't see him again until I moved to London to live with my aunt. Mr. Parker and I became friends. The best of friends."

"Sweethearts?"

Emma drew a deep breath. "I thought so."

"What happened?"

"He came to call at Auntie's house nearly every day. He dined with us two or three times a week. It was uncanny how much he and I had in common, how we thought the same way about everything. At parties, if there was dancing, we always paired up for the waltzes, for we danced together perfectly. We were seen together so often, it became a forgone conclusion we would marry one day. Everyone thought so."

"And?" he asked when she paused.

"And then, one night he went to a public ball. I was supposed to attend as well, but I developed a terrible cold and could not go. Auntie stayed home with me, but the next morning, I heard that Mr. Parker had danced all my waltzes with someone else, a very pretty girl with blond hair. Her name was Anne Moncreiffe and she was from Yorkshire."

As she spoke, Emma was relieved that talking about it brought no pain. "Three days later, when I had recovered from my cold, Mr. Parker came to tell me, his dear friend, the happy news. He had fallen in love with Anne. She was the most beautiful, the most vivacious, the most charming creature he'd ever met, and he was going to marry her." She paused, shaking her head, still baffled by it. "He'd only just met her, and already he had decided to marry her. The six years he and I had spent in such close company were obliterated by a mere three days with her."

"I'm sorry he broke your heart."

"It was not just my heart. I lost my dearest friend that day. Betrayal hurts, too."

"Yes," he agreed. "It does."

"How?" she asked, curious, hoping Marlowe could explain a phenomenon she had never understood. "How does something like that happen? How can anyone fall in love in an instant?"

"I don't know. Speaking from my own experience, I can only describe it as a sort of madness."

"And then one comes out of it?"

"Yes. If one is lucky, the madness passes before the wedding day. I wasn't so fortunate, but what of your Mr. Parker? Is he happy in his marriage?"

"The last I heard of him, he was happy. Of course," she added with rather uncharitable glee, "he lives in London and his wife lives in Yorkshire."

Marlowe gave a shout of laughter. "The recipe for true marital bliss, no doubt."

"No doubt," she agreed, laughing with him. She felt strangely light of heart all of a sudden, as if a weight had been lifted from her shoulders. She turned her head and looked at him. "It's odd, but you're the first person with whom I've ever spoken of it. Auntie knew what had happened, of course, and our friends, but no one talked about it, including me. Ladies, you see, don't break down in front of anyone, and they don't ask each other indiscreet questions. I never felt able to tell anyone how much it hurt."

"It always hurts to find one's love is not reciprocated."

"Your wife never loved you?"

"No. And the odd thing is, I knew it." He pressed a fist to his own abdomen in the same place where he had touched her moments before. "I knew it here, in my guts. But I didn't listen. I listened to my heart instead. Had I listened to my instincts, I would have saved both Consuelo and myself from years of misery."

Abruptly, he shook his head and moved as if to depart. "It's getting dark. I'd best be on my way."

"Yes, of course. Good night, my lord." She turned to open her front door, but his voice stopped her.

"Emma?"

She looked over her shoulder at him.

He was standing on the sidewalk, watching her. "If you really think what I did today was wrong, then why didn't you stop me?"

Without waiting for an answer, he turned

away and started toward his waiting carriage. It wasn't until he was in the vehicle and it was halfway to the corner before she admitted the truth. "Because even though I thought it was wrong, I felt it was right. And that terrifies me."

She watched as the carriage vanished around the corner. She knew the rules for nearly everything, and yet, she couldn't help wondering if those rules had anything to do with what was right and what was wrong. Worse, she was beginning to think that despite being a mature woman of thirty years, she knew nothing at all about life.

Chapter 12

Virtue may be its own reward, but to my mind, that's not much of an incentive.

Lord Marlowe
The Bachelor's Guide, 1893

As much as he hated to admit it, Harry knew that Emma was right. What he'd done at Au Chocolat would have hurt her reputation had anyone seen them. Despite his insistence to her that what he'd done had been harmless, he knew it wasn't. A woman's virtue could be so easily compromised. He didn't care what people thought, but he was a man, and he was fully aware that for a woman, the consequences of what had happened could have been far more serious.

He knew he had to put things with Emma

Dove back on the impersonal footing they'd had before. Instead of meeting with her, he used the excuse of other business obligations to avoid her. He sent her revisions to her by courier and communicated with her through Quinn.

Distance, however, did not prove the deterrent he'd hoped for. Time and again, he found his thoughts veering toward that afternoon at Au Chocolat, his imagination reliving that moment when he'd seen passion come alive in her face. He'd never seen anything like it before.

Until that moment, he'd never dreamt such a deep capacity for passion existed within the prim and proper Miss Dove. Now he knew the truth, but it did him little good. She was not the sort of woman to ever consider an illicit liaison, a fact he found so damned aggravating, his only choice was to redouble his efforts to stay away from her.

On a more positive note, his domestic life smoothed out a bit. Diana, it seemed, had finally accepted the fact that neither of the Dillmouth girls nor one of their Abernathy cousins was the special woman destined to capture his heart or get him to the altar. Their visit at an end, all four young ladies returned to Lord Dillmouth, much to Harry's relief, and life within the Marlowe household returned to normal, at least in most respects.

Breakfast, however, remained the place to discuss the wonderful Mrs. Bartleby. Now that he had acquired her, Harry might have found this sort of conversation much more acceptable than he had when she wrote for Barringer, except that the women of his household were determined to learn that lady's true identity. Having discovered that he had purchased the *Social Gazette*, and Mrs. Bartleby's column along with it, they made every possible attempt to wheedle her real name and family background out of him.

Harry, however, was no fool. Though his sisters could be trusted with the secret, he had doubts about the other two women in his family. Despite her pretense of dignified restraint, Grandmama was a terrible gossip. As for his mother, heaven bless her, she couldn't keep a secret if her life depended upon it. Harry was determined to keep mum.

"How can you be so tiresome?" Louisa looked at him with disappointment. "She writes for you now, doesn't she? I don't see why you don't just tell us who she is."

"It is vital to preserve her anonymity," he answered as he began spreading butter on his toast.

"Well, it isn't as if we'd go around telling everyone," his mother said with a sniff. "We can be discreet, I daresay."

"You are discretion itself, Mama," Harry answered, even managing to say it with a straight face. "But I must respect Mrs. Bartleby's privacy."

All the women of his household were forced to accept this, but Harry didn't like the thoughtful way Diana kept looking at him throughout the meal. When he departed from the table to have his carriage brought around, she followed him. Her pretext was asking for Jackson to fetch their second carriage so that she might go out, but Harry understood his sister well enough that he knew the second carriage was a pretext.

"Have you heard anything of Miss Dove?" Diana asked him as they waited together in the foyer. "Has she found other employment?"

He turned and gave her a sharp, searching glance, but Diana wasn't looking back at him. She seemed thoroughly absorbed in the task of putting on her gloves.

"I'm certain she has," he answered.

"Hmm, perhaps she's writing those etiquette books now?"

"Perhaps she is. I wouldn't know."

"Wouldn't you?" Diana turned, and there was an ironical little smile at the corners of her lips, but before he could answer, she spoke again. "I wonder if Miss Dove might give me some assistance with my wedding plans. She's so efficient, and I'm sure her advice would be impeccable. Even Mrs. Bartleby would no doubt approve of Miss Dove's knowledge in such matters, don't you think?"

"Diana—" he began, but she cut him off.

"Don't worry, Harry." Her smile widened into a grin. "I won't tell."

"How you guess these things is beyond my ken," he grumbled.

"Simple deduction, dear brother. Rather like Sherlock Holmes, you know." Her expression became serious. "But I do need help with the wedding, Harry, really I do, and I'd love some of Mrs. Bartleby's clever ideas. Would it be all right if I asked Miss Dove for her assistance?"

He gave her a rueful look. "Could I stop you?"

"Of course. If you ever said no to me, I would accept that. It's just that you never do say no. You spoil me. Spoil us all, really. In your eyes, nothing is too good for us."

He looked at his sister, and he wanted to tell her why. He wanted to say it was because he loved them all. Because he was head of the family and he had to take care of them and he would cut his heart out before he'd let anything happen to them. He wanted to say that nothing was too good for them because nothing he could give would ever make up for how they had staunchly stood by him through the five painful years it had taken him to obtain his divorce. They had been as disgraced in the eyes of society as he, but had never complained, had never questioned his decision, and he knew he could never do enough to make up for that.

Harry looked into his sister's eyes, and he wanted to say all those things. "Diana, I—" He stopped, the words stuck in his throat. What an irony. Glib as he was, he always found it so hard to say the serious things, the important things. He cleared his throat and looked away. "Yes, well, soon you'll be Rathbourne's problem," he said lightly. "Poor fellow. Good thing he's got pots of money. Spoiling you requires lots of it."

She jabbed him in the elbow for that comment.

"Your carriage, my lord," Jackson said, stepping away from the window to open the front door.

Harry started out to his carriage, but his sister's voice followed him. "Harry?"

He paused and looked over his shoulder. "Hmm?"

"We love you, too."

Harry jerked at his tie. A tight sweetness squeezed his chest. "Get all the clever Mrs. Bartleby ideas you like," he told her. "Just be discreet about it."

Diana understood at once. "Because Miss Dove hasn't the background and bona fides?" When he nodded, she went on, "People are so silly, aren't they?"

"They would be more than silly," he said and started out the door. "They would be cruel. So it's important to preserve the secret of Emma's identity. I don't want people ridiculing her."

Emma? Diana stared at the door in astonishment as Jackson closed it behind her brother. He'd called Miss Dove by her Christian name. As unconventional as Harry could be, some things were just pounded into one from birth, and referring to a woman by her Christian name was just not done. Unless . . .

"Good lord," Diana murmured, causing Jackson to give her an inquiring glance. She shook her head in reply, but did not speak, for she was trying to wrap her mind around the incredible thought that had come into her head. A man did not use a woman's Christian name unless she was an intimate acquaintance.

Diana cast her mind back to the one time she'd met Harry's former secretary, and she felt a mo-

mentary doubt. There had always been gossip
about Harry and Miss Dove, but Diana had always found it hard to take seriously. If memory
served, Miss Dove's hair was a nondescript sort
of brownish red. She wasn't plain, exactly, but
she was no exotic beauty. And she certainly did
not possess a volatile temperament. She was not
Harry's sort of woman at all, and Harry would
have been the first to say so.

Still, Diana had introduced her brother to any
number of dark-haired, hot-tempered beauties
during the five years since his divorce from Consuelo had become final, with little success. Perhaps
Harry's sort of woman wasn't what any of them
had thought her to be, including Harry himself.

Diana smiled. Enlisting the aid of Miss Dove
could prove fruitful in more ways than one.

Emma was determined to concentrate on her
work. She would not indulge in any more idle
daydreaming that put her behind schedule. She
would not be disappointed every time Marlowe
sent his revisions to her by courier instead of
meeting with her in person. She would not miss
his teasing and his laughter and his company.
And she most certainly would not imagine him
licking chocolate off her fingers.

She'd determined years ago that he was not
the sort of man any woman with sense would
want. A sensible woman would run as fast as
she could from a man who broke off romantic
liaisons by letter, who had the propensity to fall
in love instantly and often, who put a woman's

reputation at risk for a bit of fun, who was divorced and would never remarry. And despite all her own efforts to become more daring, Emma was at heart a woman of sense.

No, best all around if they kept their distance from one another as they had always done in the past. Marlowe was clearly of the same mind as herself. His avoidance of her these past two weeks proved that much.

Emma stared down at the blank page in the typewriting machine before her and wondered why she felt so dismal.

What was the matter with her, in heaven's name? She was living the dream she'd cherished for years and doing it quite well. The first two expanded Mrs. Bartleby issues had been a huge success. She had a nice, cozy home, a nice, cozy circle of friends, and a nice, cozy life. What more did she want?

A sharp rat-a-tat startled Emma out of her reverie, and she rose from her desk. She crossed the room and opened her door to find Mrs. Morris standing in the corridor with a card in her hand.

"Lady Eversleigh to see you, Emma," the landlady informed her, sounding quite impressed. Lady Eversleigh was Marlowe's sister, and despite the tarnished social standing of the Marlowe family among their own set, a peeress always impressed the middle class.

The landlady presented the card with a flourish. "She's waiting upon you in the parlor downstairs."

Emma stared down at the card in puzzlement.

She could not think of any reason why the baroness would pay a call upon her. "Please tell her I shall be down directly."

Mrs. Morris departed, and Emma gathered her unruly thoughts. Whatever the reason for the baroness's unexpected visit, it certainly wouldn't do to be daydreaming about kissing Lord Marlowe when his sister was sitting in front of her.

A few moments later, Emma went downstairs where she found the baroness engaged in a friendly tête-a-tête with Mrs. Morris on the settee.

Emma had met Marlowe's sister once, four years earlier, and the moment she saw the other woman again, she was struck anew by the baroness's resemblance to her brother. She had the same dark brown hair and striking blue eyes.

Lady Eversleigh came forward to meet Emma, her hands outstretched in greeting. "Miss Dove, how do you do? We met once several years ago, though I expect you do not remember the occasion."

"But I do. I had come to your brother's house in Hanover Square, delivering some contracts for him to sign. I was standing in the foyer, waiting, and you came walking through on your way out somewhere. You asked who I was, then you insisted I not stand in the foyer. You took me into the drawing room. How could you think I would not remember you after such a kind gesture?"

"Kind? Nonsense. It was simple politeness. That Jackson had left you standing in the foyer was unpardonable."

Emma knew that a mere secretary did not get shown into the drawing room of a lord. Marlowe's butler was well trained, for though she was not a tradesman to go down to the servants' entrance, nor was she an acquaintance paying a call. Lady Eversleigh was clearly as unconcerned with social conventions as her brother.

"Besides," the other woman went on as she resumed her seat, "if nothing else, I was prompted by a spirit of profound gratitude toward you."

"Gratitude?" Emma asked as she also sat down.

"Yes. It is thanks to you that Harry began remembering things like birthdays and social invitations." She glanced at Mrs. Morris. "For that alone, my entire family is indebted to your dear Miss Dove."

"Fancy that," the landlady murmured, seeming quite pleased.

The baroness returned her attention to Emma. A hint of mischief so like her brother came into her expression. "And I have to say that you always did choose the most wonderful presents for us. Heaven only knows what we shall get now that you are no longer Harry's secretary."

Emma smiled back at her. "You were never supposed to discover that little secret."

"Yes, well, as my brother will tell you, I love a mystery, and I've a knack for ferreting out secrets." She hesitated, then went on, "Secrets are, in fact, part of the reason I am here."

"Indeed?" Emma was growing more astonished by the moment.

"Yes." The baroness glanced at Mrs. Morris again. "I wished to speak with you about a most important and delicate matter . . ."

In the pause that followed, the landlady took the hint. "Heavens," she said and rose to her feet. "Here I am dawdling when there is so much work to be done. I shall leave the two of you to your little visit, dear Emma," she added, trying to conceal her disappointment at being left out of things. She departed, closing the door behind her and leaving the two women alone.

"In what was can I be of assistance to you, Lady Eversleigh?" Emma asked.

The other woman gave a grimace. "Oh, I do hate it so when people refer to me by my title. The name gives me . . ." She paused and gave a little shudder, closing her eyes for a moment. "It gives me painful memories." Opening her eyes, she leaned closer and added, "I wish we could all use Christian names. So much simpler. All this emphasis on titles and position and who's the right sort of people gets so tedious sometimes. You wouldn't agree, I know, being that you are the famous Mrs. Bartleby and the standard-bearer of proper decorum."

Emma couldn't hide her surprise at those words. "You know about me?"

"I told you I have a knack for finding things out. But I promised Harry faithfully I would not tell anyone about you, and he knows me well enough to trust me. The secret of Mrs. Bartleby's identity is safe with me. Now, as to the reason I've come to see you, you may have heard I am to be married in January to the Earl of Rathbourne.

"Yes, and please accept my congratulations on your engagement. But you make me curious, Baroness. How does your engagement bring you to me?"

"My sisters, my mother, my grandmother, and I have been reading your column faithfully every week. We adore Mrs. Bartleby."

Pleasure welled up inside Emma at those kind words. "I am so glad! I rather like her myself."

"You should. I am here because, having guessed your identity, I have come to enlist your aid. Cheeky of me, I know, but there it is. I need your help. You see—" The baroness paused, shifting on her seat as if suddenly uncomfortable. "You may know that my brother's divorce was a long, painful business. For Harry especially, but for the rest of us as well."

"Yes." Emma eyed her with understanding and compassion. "I know."

"Many of our acquaintance condemned my brother for his action. He—and we—were shredded to ribbons in the newspapers of Harry's competitors. The most terrible things were said. And of course, it didn't help matters when, shortly after Harry's decree was granted, the Queen issued a declaration condemning divorce and censuring those who break the marriage bond. It was issued in general terms, but everyone knew to whom that censure was addressed. Socially, it rather sealed our fate."

Emma bit her lip, rather ashamed of her own

rigid stance on the subject. She was also irritated suddenly by the strictures of society in a way she had never been before. "To my mind, it isn't right that your entire family should suffer for the action of one. And as for your brother's divorce, he and I spoke about it not long ago, and I now appreciate what a wrenching decision it was for him. He did not make it lightly, I know."

"Harry told you about his divorce?" The baroness stared at her. "He talked with you about it?"

"Yes, a little. You seem rather astonished, Baroness."

"So I am. Harry never talks about painful things. Never." She gave a little laugh. "Well, this is turning out to be quite a day for surprises."

"I am truly sorry that your social position has been so adversely affected. If you would like me to write a Mrs. Bartleby column about the absurdity of guilt by association, I would be willing to do so."

"No, no. That isn't why I've come to you. And in any case, Harry owns the *Social Gazette* now, and everyone would think he made you do it."

"True. I hadn't thought of that. Why then, do you need the aid of Mrs. Bartleby?"

"I want your help with my wedding."

"Your wedding?" Emma was astonished. "But surely your mother, grandmother, and sisters—"

"I love my mother dearly, Miss Dove, but she is, to put it bluntly, a featherbrain. My grandmother is very old-fashioned—she still believes in throwing rice and old shoes at weddings, for goodness' sake, and you and I both know that is never done nowadays. My sisters are helping as best they can, of course. Vivian is designing my gown herself—she loves to design clothing and such. She's quite good at it, really. And Phoebe is handling all the details of invitations, the seating arrangements, and that sort of thing. But the woman I really need is Mrs. Bartleby. I want to be sure everything is done impeccably. I've come to you not only for my sake and the sake of my family, but also for Edmund. My fiancé suffers the stigma of divorce as well. If our wedding is perfect, then society hasn't a shred of criticism to throw in our faces about it. Even more, I want this wedding to be the most stupendous social event of the year, and I need Mrs. Bartleby's clever ideas. I want your help with the flowers, the wedding breakfast, the decorations—oh, everything." She paused and flashed a charming smile that once again reminded Emma of her brother. "I told you I was being cheeky."

"Not at all! I am flattered that you should think of me, Baroness."

"I have to caution you that if you consent to help me and people find out, there are some among my set who might not look so favorably upon your advice."

Emma considered the matter. "Some people would look down their noses, I suppose, but as I said, I don't agree with this notion of guilt by association." She paused and took a deep breath, aware she was making a risky decision, but knowing her conscience could not let her do otherwise. "If people wish to condemn me just because I have assisted with your wedding plans, then let them."

"I think we can avoid that problem if we keep your involvement a secret. We can't tell my mother or grandmother, for they'd blurt it out to someone straightaway, but my sisters can be discreet."

"I shall be happy to assist you in any way I can."

The baroness clasped her hands together in gratitude. "Thank you, Miss Dove."

"I shall enjoy the project. Truly. When shall we meet to begin planning things?"

"Let me think. My family is going to Torquay for August."

Emma nodded. Everyone in society went sea bathing at Torquay in August.

"Harry only intends to come for a week, for he says he has too much work here in London," the baroness went on. "Work is all he ever seems to do. I grow quite concerned about him sometimes, the way he works so hard."

"It is his idea of fun," Emma said without thinking.

The other woman gave her a startled look. "Yes, you've the right of it there," she said slowly, studying Emma in a thoughtful sort of way. "Another reason for the snobs to condemn him, I fear. A gentleman, they say, shouldn't earn his living. They would deem it beneath them."

"No doubt most of those gentlemen are in debt."

Her dry response made the baroness laugh. "A wicked observation, Miss Dove, and so true. Anyway, when we return from Torquay, we are going straight on to my fiancé's estate in Derbyshire for several weeks. Then we journey to Berkshire at the end of September to spend the autumn at Marlowe Park. I propose you come to stay with us the first week of October. Though I must warn you that Mama and Grandmama will pester you endlessly to reveal the true identity of Mrs. Bartleby."

"I'm accustomed to that," she assured the baroness. "And I accept your invitation. We shall put our heads together, and between us, we shall make your wedding the most beautiful one of the year."

"Oh, I'm so glad I came to see you today!" She grasped Emma's hands in an impulsive gesture that was quite endearing. "Thank you for agreeing to help me."

After Lady Eversleigh had gone, Emma went back upstairs. She sat down at her desk, still feeling a bit stunned by what had just happened. To be asked to help a baroness with her wedding was a great honor. To be sure, there were those who would condemn Mrs. Bartleby and refuse to read her again if they knew what Emma had just agreed to do, but even if the baroness had not suggested they keep it a secret, Emma would have agreed to assist her anyway. For once, she didn't really care what other people thought, and that was probably the most astonishing thing of all.

Chapter 13

Some men are attracted to virtuous women. Should
any of you fall into such a predicament, my friends,
you have my utmost sympathy.

Lord Marlowe
The Bachelor's Guide, 1893

Harry had never been one for self-deceit.
The reason, of course, was that he paid
attention to his instincts, and they always told
him the truth, if he was listening. But lately, the
gut feelings upon which he had always relied
could not be trusted. Right now his business
instincts were shouting at him to stay away
from Emma Dove. His instincts as a man, however, were telling him something completely
different.

He wanted her, and avoiding her was not making him want her any less. That was the plain, unvarnished truth.

Harry leaned back against his desk and curled his fingers around the mahogany edge. Behind him, he could hear Quinn reading back dictation, but he paid no heed. Instead, he stared out the window of his office and stopped trying to push Emma out of his mind.

Emma. A sweet name. His thoughts about her of late were not sweet. In fact, they were quite torrid, and growing more so with each day he stayed away from her. He closed his eyes and formed a picture of her body in his mind, one conjured solely from fantasy, one of lithe, slim legs and small, round breasts, and a long mane of brown hair that turned red in the sunlight.

". . . and therefore I must decline your countering offer . . ." Quinn's voice floated past him.

Emma. A pretty name. He inhaled a deep breath, imagined the scents of fresh cotton, talcum powder, and her. For perhaps the hundredth time, he imagined kissing her mouth and all her other pretty parts as well. He imagined stripping her out of her plain white shirtwaist and doing things to her that were anything but proper.

". . . should you wish to reconsider accepting the original terms we discussed . . ."

Handsome, she'd called him that day in the Victoria Embankment Gardens, as serious as if she were reciting back catechism, her hazel eyes wide and utterly without flirtation or guile. Innocent eyes.

He didn't want her to be innocent.

Any man who was unmarried and wanted to stay that way steered clear of innocent virgins. He'd only had one in his entire life, on his wedding night, and his memory was perfectly clear on how that had turned out. It had been a disaster, and quite a fitting prelude to the rest of his married life.

His mind drifted back fourteen years. A lifetime ago, it seemed. The whole mess with Consuelo had begun when he'd gotten involved in several business ventures with her father, first in London, then in New York. When Mr. Estravados had invited him to spend a month with him and his family at their summer home in Newport, he'd been happy to accept. And so, on a hot, muggy August afternoon in Rhode Island when he was twenty-two, he'd looked across a tennis net into a pair of dark, haunted, *innocent* eyes, and his life had gone straight to hell.

He lowered his head, staring at the carpet, imagining Consuelo as he'd last seen her, on her knees with her hands clasped together, sobbing. Begging, for God's sake, begging him for a divorce.

Let me go, Harry. Please, just let me go.

". . . yours, sincerely, et cetera. Do you wish to make any corrections, sir?"

It was the silence that brought him out of the past. "Hmm? What?"

He glanced over his shoulder to find Quinn regarding him impassively. "Do you wish to make any corrections to this letter, my lord, or shall I send it?"

He hadn't heard one word of the letter. "Perfect," he answered. "Send it."

Quinn departed from his office, and Harry rubbed a hand over his face. Hell, if thinking of Consuelo wasn't enough to get his priorities in order, nothing would be. What was wrong with him? He couldn't seem to govern his thoughts about anything nowadays.

Perhaps he needed a new mistress. That would surely set him right again. Or perhaps he needed an even quicker form of relief. He grabbed his hat and left his office at a rapid stride. Passing by Quinn's desk, he said over his shoulder, "I'm leaving for the day."

"But, sir, I think . . . that is, I believe—"

Harry halted by the door. "Yes, yes," he said with impatience. "You believe what?"

His secretary looked at him with uncertainty. "I have a notation that you have an appointment here in your office only a few minutes from now." He glanced down at his desk, running his finger along a line written on his blotter. "Mr. William Sheffield, manager of production at the *Social Gazette*, two o'clock. I believe you intended to discuss improving production procedures? I could be wrong, of course." He looked up with that agonized expression Harry often found so irritating.

I think you have very little consideration for others . . . and your life, I cannot help but feel, is a terribly dissolute one—your disdain for marriage, your liaisons with women of low moral character . . .

Recalling those words, Harry's desire to invade a brothel and spend a few hours in the arms of a courtesan didn't seem quite so pleasurable a prospect after all. He ground the heel of his hand against his forehead with a sound of frustration. He was supposed to be putting Emma Dove out of his mind. Imagining her naked was bad enough. Did he have to hear her lectures in his head as well?

Harry looked up. "No, Mr. Quinn, you are not wrong." He pulled his watch out of his pocket, noting his appointment was in a quarter of an hour. "I shall go across the street and see Sheffield myself," he said, hoping the short walk would be enough to clear his head. He put his watch back in his pocket and started to depart, then stopped. "Quinn?"

"Yes, sir?"

"Thank you for reminding me of my responsibilities. It is part of your duties to make certain I get to appointments on time. Keep doing it."

Leaving an astonished Mr. Quinn staring after him, Harry departed. By the time he arrived at Sheffield's office a few minutes later, he had resolved to keep his mind on business matters, and for the next two hours, not a single thought of kissing a prim, innocent spinster entered his head. Not once did he have fantasies of unbuttoning her starched white shirtwaist or pulling up her plain wool skirt as he returned to his office. Not once did he imagine the scent of talcum powder or the feel of soft, white skin as he wrote his next editorial for *The Bachelor's Guide*. Not once.

Then she showed up and ruined everything.

He had already bid good day to Quinn and was on his way out when the woman he'd been trying so hard to forget cannoned right into him, bringing both of them to a halt in the corridor outside his offices. Involuntarily, his hands came up to grasp her arms and keep her from falling.

"Oh, I'm terribly sorry," she said and looked up from the papers in her hand.

The momentary collision of her body against his sent arousal coursing through him like a jolt of electricity, and her upturned face with its pretty golden freckles and soft pink mouth served to vanquish two hours of carefully cultivated resolve in an instant.

"Lord Marlowe," she said in surprise. "What are you doing here?"

Harry realized he still had hold of her arms. He let go of her, stepped back, and forced himself to say something. "Well, I do own this building, you know," he said, striving to sound offhand. "And this is my office. It's not unheard of for me to come by on occasion."

"Yes, of course," she said, laughing a little as she touched a hand to her forehead. "That was a rather inane question, wasn't it? It's only that I was just thinking of . . ." She paused, gave a little cough, and gestured to the papers in her other hand. "That is to say, I was reading, and was not paying any heed to where I was going. Are you all right? I didn't tread on your feet or anything?"

"No." Even as he answered her, he wanted to shout that damn it, no, he wasn't all right, not in the least, and it was all her fault. At this moment, his body was burning everywhere hers had touched him. Desperate, he tried to think of something ordinary to say. "So what are you reading that has you so preoccupied?"

She rustled the manuscript pages. "Outlines for our next issue. I thought I would bring them to your office, since I had to pass right by. I'm on my way to Inkberry's, you see."

Valiantly, he tried to carry on mundane conversation. "Inkberry's Bookshop?" When she nodded, he went on, "I thought we were doing an entire issue on the topic of sweets. Have you changed your mind?"

"No, no," she assured him. "I still intend the next issue to be all about sweets, as you'll see from my outline." She handed over the typewritten sheets to him. "I am going to Inkberry's because I want to see if Mr. Inkberry has any books on the history of the . . . of the . . ." She paused and cleared her throat. "The history of . . . the, umm . . . chocolate trade."

She thrust her gloved hand into her skirt pocket, the same hand he'd been kissing that day two weeks before, and a delicate flush came into her cheeks. Harry realized he wasn't the only one who'd been thinking about that day, and with what he'd been going through, he found that fact very gratifying.

"Your sister, Lady Eversleigh, paid a call on me this afternoon." She glanced around, then added in a whisper, "She guessed I was Mrs. Bartleby. She wanted help with her wedding plans."

"Yes, I know. Diana has a talent for discovering secrets. But I've sworn her to keep mum."

"Yes, she told me." There was a long moment of silence, then Emma shifted her weight and glanced at her brooch watch. "It's already past four o'clock. I should be going."

"Wait a moment, and I'll escort you down," he said, the words out of his mouth before he could stop them. But he couldn't take them back, and worse, he didn't want to. He went into his office, dropped the sheaf of papers she'd given him onto his desk, then he returned to the corridor. He gestured to the stairs, and both of them began walking in that direction. "Does Mrs. Bartleby believe Inkberry's is the finest bookshop in London?"

"Of course. Even if it weren't, I shouldn't dare say so," she added as they went down the stairs. "The Inkberrys would be quite hurt were I to be so disloyal as to recommend a rival establishment."

"You know the proprietors, I take it?"

"Oh, yes, I have been acquainted with Mr. and Mrs. Inkberry since I first came to London. Mrs. Inkberry was my Aunt Lydia's greatest friend." She smiled. "And Mr. Inkberry is such a dear. If any books on etiquette come in, he always sets them aside for me. I like to see what other etiquette writers are advising."

"Ah, keeping abreast of the competition, are you? That's very wise." He paused to open the front door for her. "And I understand it is a fine bookshop," he said, following her out to the sidewalk, "with a fine collection of old, rare volumes. Is that true?"

"Have you never been there?" she asked.

"No, I have not had that pleasure."

"Would you . . ." She paused and cleared her throat. "If you do not have another engagement, perhaps you would . . . that is, Inkberry's truly is the best bookshop in London. There are others which are more famous. Hatchards, for instance. But Inkberry's is superior in every way, at least, in my estimation. And . . . and besides, you ought to see it. I mean, being a publisher, and . . . and everything—" She broke off amid these ramblings and took a deep breath. "Would you care to accompany me?"

He shouldn't. But he was going to. He'd known that before she'd even asked, because he'd never been very good at doing what he should. "It would be my pleasure."

The bell jangled as Marlowe pushed open the door of Inkberry's. He followed Emma as she went inside. The elderly man behind the counter smiled at the sight of her. "Emma!" he greeted warmly and came around from behind the counter.

"Good day to you, Mr. Inkberry. Are you well?"

"Well enough." He wagged a finger at her. "Josephine has the opportunity to visit with you every Sunday afternoon at tea, but I am not so fortunate. It has been far too long since you've come to the shop, my dear."

"I know, and I am sorry for it. Truly. But I shall do better in the future, I promise. How is Mrs. Inkberry?"

"Very well. She's upstairs, so you must go up and have a visit before you leave. Take tea with us." He glanced at the man beside her.

"Oh, Mr. Inkberry, this is Viscount Marlowe. I worked for Marlowe Publishing at one time, you know. My lord, this is Mr. Inkberry."

"How do you do?" Marlowe bowed. "Your bookshop is the finest in London, I hear."

"And I've no doubt who told you that." Mr. Inkberry chuckled and gave Emma another fond glance. "I believe we've some new etiquette volumes in, and some cookery books, too." He gestured to the doorway that led to the bookshop's deeper interiors. "I've set them in the usual place for you."

Emma walked through the doorway, making her way toward the back of the shop. Marlowe remained behind, talking to Mr. Inkberry, and the voices of the two men faded as she wandered through the rooms to the back. The windows were high, enabling light to filter in over the tall, overstuffed bookshelves, but the interior was still rather dim, and the air felt cool after the summer heat outside. The distinct scent of book dust permeated the air.

Emma went to the very back wall where Mr. Inkberry set aside books for certain favored patrons. The crates containing these books were located under the stairs that led up to the Inkberrys' living quarters above the shop. She pulled the crate out into the light to have a look, but she found nothing of interest. A few of Mrs. Beeton's cookery books she'd already read and some of Mrs. Humphrey's etiquette volumes, which were nothing extraordinary. There was also a copy of *Everybody's Book Of Correct Conduct*, by M.C., and that most excellent standby, *Manners and Rules of Good Society*, by a Member of the Aristocracy.

Since she had read all of these, Emma pushed the crate back into place and decided to browse through the other books in this room, for this part of the shop was her favorite. It contained more exotic reading fare, travel guides from Baedeker and Cook's, history texts of many lands, and heaps of maps. Anything Mr. Inkberry had on the history of the chocolate trade was sure to be somewhere in this room.

She perused the nearby shelves, noting with pleasure some fine volumes of Arabian poetry. She scanned the titles, her gaze moving upward shelf by shelf until she reached the top. There, a matching set of books in red leather caught her eye.

She stood on tiptoe, squinting as she tried to

discern the titles high above her head. When she realized what she was looking at, Emma gave an exclamation of delighted surprise. Mr. Inkberry hadn't told her about *these*. Of course not. She began to count them, and her delight only increased when she had confirmed that it was a complete set, with all ten original volumes intact.

Not that it mattered, really, she thought, gazing at them with longing. She couldn't possibly buy them. Still, it wouldn't do any harm to have a look. She reached up, stretching, but even standing on the very tips of her toes with her arm extended as far as possible, the books remained beyond her grasp. She lowered her arm and dropped back onto her heels with an exasperated sigh.

"Allow me," a deep voice spoke from behind her.

Emma froze at the sound of Marlowe's voice right behind her. Startled by his closeness, she hadn't even heard him enter this room of the shop. As he lifted his arm overhead to remove one of the books for her, his chest brushed against the back of her shoulder, and she caught the scent of sandalwood.

He pulled the volume down, but when she turned to face him and held out her hand, he did not give the book to her. Instead, he paused to read the title, much to her dismay.

"*The Book of the Thousand Nights and a Night*," he read, "by Sir Richard Burton. *Volume Ten*." He looked at her in amusement. "And all this time you have been lecturing me on propriety?"

Caught, Emma lifted her chin to what she deemed a dignified angle. "I don't know what you mean."

He tapped the book against his palm. "I wonder," he murmured, "would Mrs. Bartleby deem this to be acceptable reading for a proper young woman such as yourself?"

It wasn't proper at all. It was Burton's unexpurgated version of the tales, and said to be downright salacious. Emma tried to divert the conversation. "I may be proper, my lord, but I am hardly young."

"No? You look about nineteen." He reached out with his free hand and touched his fingertips to her cheek. "Must be the freckles."

Emma's tummy dipped with a strange, weightless sensation as he traced his fingers lightly across her cheekbone. His hand fell away before she could even think of telling him not to touch her like that, and he stepped back, presenting the book to her with a bow.

She did not take it. There was no point. She could never buy it, and had only intended to have a quick peek. Now she couldn't even do that, not with him standing there, watching her, knowing what it was. She shook her head in refusal. "Put it back with the others, please."

Instead of complying, he opened the book to read the imprint, then he glanced at the other books above. "These are originals from the first printing in 1850," he said, returning his gaze to her face. "All ten volumes together, a rare find in these days. Do you not want them?"

She wanted them terribly. "No," she lied. "As you said, Burton's version is not appropriate reading for . . . for someone such as myself."

"So? Buy them anyway. I shan't tell anyone you read naughty books."

"They are not naughty," she protested.

"Read them already, have you?"

"Not Burton's version! But I have read Galland's." She swallowed hard. "I was looking at these because I . . . I wanted a . . . a comparison."

"For research purposes, no doubt." The amused curve of his lips told her he wasn't the least bit fooled by her explanation, but to her relief, he returned the book to its place without probing her motives any further. "So did you enjoy Galland's version of the tales?"

"Yes, I did. Though had I been in Scheherazade's position, I doubt I would have survived."

"Why do you say that?"

"I hardly think the sultan would have been so impressed with discussions of etiquette that he would have spared my life. To a man, tales of genies and flying carpets would be much more exciting than tableware."

"I am forced to agree with the sultan about etiquette and tableware, but as for your fate . . ." He paused, his gaze raking over her. "You underestimate your charms, Emma."

Pleasure flared up inside her at those words, but when his gaze paused at her mouth, the bookshop suddenly felt much too warm, and she turned her back. Facing the shelves, she ran her fingers along the spines of books as if perusing their titles, but her thoughts were not on volumes of Persian poetry.

I should very much like to kiss you.

She felt a dizzying throb of excitement. With Marlowe right behind her, she closed her eyes and once again imagined his mouth on hers. Oh, what would it be like to be kissed by him?

She heard a sound and opened her eyes. Glancing up over her shoulder, she realized he was still standing behind her and was scanning the shelves above her head. Emma gathered her thoughts and forced herself to make ordinary conversation. "What do you like to read, my lord?"

He pulled a book out, glanced at it, shoved it back. "I don't like to read at all, truth be told."

"You don't read? But you publish books."

"Exactly so. I enjoyed reading when I was a boy, but these days, I read all the time and it has rather taken the pleasure out of it for me. When I am at leisure, reading is the last thing I want to do."

"That makes sense, I suppose. But for me, reading is an adventure. It makes me an armchair traveler and takes me places I shall never be able to go."

"And if you could be more than an armchair traveler?" He leaned down close to her ear. "If you possessed a magical flying carpet, and you could journey to any place, where would you go?"

He was so near, she could feel the heat of his body behind her in the cool shadows of the bookshop. His arms came up on either side of her shoulders, trapping her without even touching her. She stirred, then stilled, staring at his hands and the strong fingers that gripped the shelf in front of her. Her breathing began to quicken.

"Where would you go?" he repeated, his warm breath brushing her ear, making her shiver. "The sultan's harem?"

"Certainly not," she said primly and pulled a book from the shelf, opened it, and pretended to read *The Rubaiyat*.

He was not deterred. Peering over her shoulder, he saw the title printed at the top of the page. "So the Persian garden of Omar Khayyám is your destination of choice, is it?" He laughed low in his throat. "I believe that beneath Miss Emmaline Dove's protective shield of propriety, there beats the heart of a hedonist."

"What?" She snapped the book shut, shoved it back into place, and turned, bristling at that description. "I am no such thing!" Realizing she had spoken too loudly, she cast a quick glance around, but much to her relief, they were alone in this part of the shop. "Please refrain from insulting me."

"I meant no insult. Quite the contrary. I find this hidden aspect of your character fascinating."

"How could such an egregious description of me be fascinating?"

"It is not egregious. And it is fascinating because I have known you five years and never dreamt this side of you existed. The more time I spend in your company, the more surprising you become."

He leaned toward her, and she pushed at his arm to extricate herself from what could only be described as an embrace, but he didn't move. Failing in her attempt to escape, she tilted her head back to look him in the eye and frowned at him. "You have no right to call me such things. Hedonist, indeed!"

"There is nothing wrong with enjoying the pleasures of life. God knows, there's enough pain. And I am basing my conclusion about your character upon what I have seen of your preferences."

"My preferences? I have no idea what you mean."

"Liqueur chocolates, ripe juicy peaches, tiny red strawberries. The tales of Scheherazade and the Persian poetry of Khayyám. It seems to me that you enjoy some very fleshly pleasures."

"I don't!" she denied in a fierce whisper. "You make a fondness for chocolate and fruit sound like decadence. Like . . . like carnality."

"Food can be very carnal, believe me." His lashes lowered. "Attribute that opinion to my dissolute nature."

He was doing it again. She lifted her fingers to

her lips, then stopped and pulled her hand down. He smiled at that, as if he knew what she was thinking. As if he'd been thinking it, too. As if, when he stared at her mouth, he was thinking about kissing her, and doing other things, too, carnal things. She had only the vaguest idea what those might be, but before she could stop it, Emma's whole body stirred with a delicious, answering thrill.

"By the way, Emma, I must contradict what you said earlier."

She tried to think, but his closeness and his words were making that impossible. "What I said?"

"If you had faced the sultan armed with a box of chocolates, you would most certainly have survived."

The reminder of what had happened two weeks before at Au Chocolat heightened her excitement even as it embarrassed her, and Emma turned her face away. Of course he thought her a hedonist. What else could a gentleman think of a woman when she allowed him to rub his leg against hers in a park? When she allowed him to suck chocolate off her fingers? When she allowed him to take the liberty of embracing her in a bookshop?

Emma's controlled, confined upbringing condemned these things, even as something else, something deep in her soul, cried out for them with a hunger that was frightening. Desperate, panicky, she met his gaze and fought back. "I am a virtuous woman, my lord," she informed him. "I am not in any way decadent or carnal! I am not . . . fleshly!"

"No?" He lifted his hand, and his knuckle brushed beneath her chin. He tilted her head back, then he shifted his hand so that his fingertips touched her mouth. She quivered inside, her fierceness and panic ebbing away along with any strength to fight him.

Don't. Oh, don't touch me. You mustn't do these things.

She opened her mouth, but somehow she could not make the words of protest come out. She could only stand there defenseless as he stared at her parted lips and traced their outline with his fingertips. Around and around, making the quiver inside her intensify until it felt like the fluttering wings of a thousand butterflies.

He slid his hand to her cheek, and she gave a gasp of shock. "What are you doing?" she whispered.

He bent his head and paused with his lips an inch from hers. "Committing a serious breach of etiquette," he murmured.

And then he kissed her.

The moment his mouth touched her own, Emma forgot where they were, forgot what was proper, forgot everything she had ever been taught about right and wrong. There, in the half-light and shadows of a dusty bookshop, she forgot that kissing was only for married people and that she was a spinster of thirty. With this man's warm palm cupping her face and his lips pressed to hers, joy unfurled inside her, beautiful, painful joy. It was like nothing she had ever felt before. It was like nothing she could ever have imagined.

It was like springtime.

She closed her eyes, and her other senses bloomed with a vivid clarity they had never possessed before. The masculine, earthy scent of him. The callus on his palm where his hand cupped her cheek. The taste of his mouth as he parted her lips with his. The sound of what could only be her own heart, beating like the rapid wings of a bird as it soared upward toward the heavens.

How sensitive her lips seemed, as if they were a conduit to every other nerve ending in her body. She tingled all over, vibrant, electrified. The skin around her mouth burned from the sandpapery texture of his, and she realized it was due to the hint of beard stubble on his face. How alien a man was, and yet how wonderful. So foreign, yet somehow so familiar.

She brought her hands between them to touch his chest. His silk waistcoat felt smooth against her palms. Beneath it, his muscles were hard and warm. Emma slid her palms across his chest beneath his jacket to his shoulders, savoring the strength of a man's body for the very first time, knowing somehow that for this moment, all that strength was hers to command. She wrapped her arms around his neck and pressed closer, wanting that strength to enfold her.

Her move seemed to ignite something inside

him. He made a rough sound against her mouth, and his free arm wrapped around her waist. He lifted her onto her toes, pulled her fully against him. His free hand curled around the back of her neck. He deepened the kiss, and his tongue entered her mouth. Emma made a wordless sound of shock, but then she touched her tongue to his, and waves of pleasure shimmered through her. For the first time, she understood what carnality truly was.

She clung to him, pressing her body to his with an immodesty that should have shocked her, but the feelings rushing through her were so powerful and so extraordinary, Emma could not care about modesty. She felt his body, so much larger than her own, hard and strong against hers, yet strangely, he did not seem close enough. She wanted him even closer, she wanted something more, something she could not name. She stirred, her hips moving against him. She moaned low in her throat.

And then it was over.

His hands gripped her arms, pushing her back, breaking the kiss. His breathing was harsh and rapid, mingling with hers in the space between them. His eyes were as deep and vividly blue as the sea.

His hands ran up her arms, cupped her face. "You've never been kissed before, have you?" he whispered.

Wordless, she shook her head.

He began to smile, and she stiffened. Was he laughing at her? Had she done it wrong somehow? All of a sudden she felt gawky and awkward and terribly afraid. "You shouldn't have done that," she whispered back.

"Probably not." He pulled her close and kissed her again, hard and quick. "But I don't often do what I should. I'm naughty that way."

With those words, he let her go, turned away, and disappeared around the other side of the bookshelf.

She heard his footsteps carry him out of the room, but she didn't follow. She couldn't, not yet. Instead, she just stood there, clothes rumpled and bonnet askew, in the back corner of a bookshop on Bouverie Street, too dazed to move.

She pressed her fingers to her lips. They were puffy, burning from the rasp of his unshaven face. Now she knew what it was to be kissed. Now she knew, and nothing would ever be the same.

Emma had the absurd desire to cry, but not with the guilt and remorse a proper woman would feel. That kiss was the most beautiful thing that had ever happened to her, and she wanted to weep with joy.

Chapter 14

A woman's virtue is a fragile thing, and it must be guarded with the utmost zeal. In this endeavor, my dears, look not to the gentlemen of your acquaintance for cooperation. Alas, they are often as concerned with depriving you of your virtue as you are with preserving it.

Mrs. Bartleby
Advice to Girl-Bachelors, 1893

It was the sound of a creaking stair tread that roused Emma from her euphoric trance. She glanced at the stairs and saw Mrs. Inkberry standing there, her small, round form illuminated by the shaft of sunlight pouring through the window on the landing.

She'd seen what happened.

Emma knew it at once. The frown on the older

woman's usually good-tempered face made that fact crystal clear. Emma's joy evaporated.

Mrs. Inkberry glanced in the direction of the doorway where Marlowe had gone, then back at her. Her frown deepened. "Come up, Emma, and have a dish of tea with me."

She did not wait for agreement, but instead turned and went up the stairs. It would have been unthinkable for Emma to refuse. Refusing dear Mrs. Inkberry would have been almost as grievous a discourtesy as refusing Aunt Lydia. With a growing sense of dismay, she followed the older woman upstairs, along a corridor, and into the drawing room.

Mrs. Inkberry rang the bell for tea, then sat down on the settee. She patted the seat beside her for Emma to sit down, but she did not speak again until the parlormaid arrived bearing a tea tray.

Annie dipped a curtsy and gave Emma a smile of greeting. "Good day, Miss Emma."

Emma's answering smile was perfunctory.

The tea things made a slight clatter as Annie set the tray on the table beside her mistress. "The master not coming up, ma'am?"

"Not yet. Annie, there will be a dark-haired gentleman somewhere about the shop, a prosperous-looking gentleman in a black frock coat and striped trousers. Find him, take him aside, and tell him it is my wish he leave the premises at once."

Emma's mortification increased with each word, and she ducked her head. Marlowe's kiss still burned against her mouth, and she felt it must be like a brand, obvious for anyone to see.

"Then," Mrs. Inkberry continued, "you may tell Mr. Inkberry his tea will be ready in half an hour. See that Cook has a fresh pot ready to serve at that time. Close the door behind you."

"Very good, ma'am."

The parlormaid's print dress and stiff white apron rustled as she departed. The click of the latch told Emma the door was closed, but she did not lift her head. She stared at her lap, waiting as the older woman mashed the tea and poured.

It wasn't until Mrs. Inkberry had handed her a cup of the fragrant beverage that she spoke. "Emma, dearest girl."

Just what Auntie might have said, affectionate words spoken in a tone of grave concern, with the barest sigh of disappointment at the end.

Of course Mrs. Inkberry was disappointed in her. Anyone who loved her and cared about her would be. She had allowed a man to commit an insult upon her person and had done nothing to stop him. Worse, all it had taken was one touch of his mouth for her to throw aside a lifetime of moral rectitude. She had done far more than acquiesce to his kiss. She had reveled in it.

Even now the memory of it was enough to tilt her from remorse to joy.

Mrs. Inkberry's next words tilted her back again. "Emma, your aunt brought you up with the strictest principles and a full awareness of right and wrong. But I can appreciate that without her guidance now, you may sometimes become . . ." There was a delicate pause. "Con-fused."

That described her topsy-turvy state of mind and her inexplicable actions of late rather well. She nodded in complete agreement.

"Now that Lydia is gone," the older woman went on, "there is no one to advise you. No one but myself, that is. I have known you since you were a girl of fifteen, and I should like to think that were you to wander from your genteel up-bringing, Lydia would have wished me to guide you back. I realize you are no longer a girl, but a mature woman. . . ."

If I'm a mature woman, then don't treat me like a child. Stop smothering me.

Those words flared up out of nowhere, re-sentful and defiant. Emma bit down on her lip and didn't say them.

"Being unmarried," Mrs. Inkberry went on, "you are still blissfully unaware of what men can be. How coarse their actions if they are not true gentlemen."

"Nothing like this has ever happened before!" she cried. "He has never—" She broke off, re-membering that day at Au Chocolat. She could not lie to Mrs. Inkberry. "He has never been coarse."

"I am glad to hear that what I witnessed was the only inappropriate thing he has done," Mrs. Inkberry said, making Emma wince. "Still, my dear, it is incumbent upon me to act in Lydia's stead and caution you. Men, however they may seem, can lead women to wrong."

How could anything as beautiful as that kiss be wrong? Defiance flared again, hotter and more fierce. "Is it so terrible a thing to be kissed by a man?"

"It can be, yes," the older woman answered in a gentle voice. "If that man is not your husband, or at the very least, your fiancé. Has this man offered you marriage?"

Emma stared at her gloved hands clenched in her lap. "No."

"Do you believe him capable of courting you in honorable fashion and marrying you?"

She thought of the parade of women she'd seen Marlowe set aside during the years she had worked for him. Women for whom he hadn't cared a whit, women for whom he'd never spared a thought once they were gone. "No."

"A man who accosts a lady in a bookshop and attempts to make love to her, yet who is not honorable enough to court her properly, become acquainted with her friends and family, and offer her marriage is not a gentleman. You know that as well as I do, Emma. You were brought up to know right from wrong."

"That kiss didn't feel wrong," she said stubbornly.

Mrs. Inkberry sighed. "Lydia always said you are very much like your mother."

Startled, she opened her eyes and turned to stare into the other woman's face, dismayed. "Auntie told you," she said with dawning awareness. "She told you about my parents?"

"That they had to marry, you mean? Yes, she did."

Something of her distress must have revealed itself on her face, for Mrs. Inkberry reached out and patted her arm in a reassuring way. "Now, now," she murmured. "Your father married your mother in the end and did right by her, so there's no shame in it now."

"But she told you my parents had to marry. If they hadn't, I would be . . . I would have been . . . illegitimate." She stirred, her dismay deepening. "Who else did Auntie tell about this? Does Mrs. Morris know?"

"No one else knows, Emma, not even Mr. Inkberry. I've kept Lydia's confidence many years now. And Lydia felt a great responsibility for you. It weighed heavy on her shoulders, and there were times when she felt a need to confide in me and seek advice. She and Mr. Worthington had no children, you know, and I'd raised four daughters of my own. Please do not be distressed that she told me."

Emma shook her head, far more concerned by her aunt's remark than Mrs. Inkberry's knowledge of the circumstances surrounding her birth. "Auntie always told me that it was up to women to enforce the boundaries of propriety because men will not. Do you believe that to be true?"

"Yes, of course, women must set the boundaries. Left to themselves, men cannot be counted upon to exercise restraint. They have certain . . . animal spirits we do not possess."

Emma was beginning to think herself an exception to that well-established dictum, now that her own restraint had been tested and found woefully lacking. While kissing Marlowe, enforcing boundaries had been the last thing on her mind. "My mother stepped out with my father before they married. And Auntie believed I am like her?"

Was that the reason she had to keep reminding herself that the things Marlowe had done were wrong? Because she was at heart an immoral woman only trying to be good? "I am not a hedonist!" she burst out. "I am not immoral. Did Auntie think I was?"

To her amazement, Mrs. Inkberry smiled at her. "I believe your aunt simply meant there is a strong desire for romance and adventure in you, and also an innate sense of curiosity. Given that you possess these qualities, it is only natural that from time to time you would rebel."

Emma's fingers slid to the tiny scar on her cheek. There were always consequences to rebellion, painful ones. She did not want to be a rebel. She lowered her hand and took a quick gulp of her tea.

"But Emma, because of her nature, your mother made a mistake, one that could have cost her dearly had your father not done the right thing in the end. I should hate to see you make the same mistake. Lydia, were she alive, would no doubt feel the same."

Emma took a deep breath and got a firm hold of her good sense. She looked into the compassionate brown eyes of the woman beside her. "I should not wish to dishonor my aunt's memory by any of my actions," she said and wondered why speaking those words made her feel as if there were a lead weight on her chest, pressing her down until she couldn't breathe.

Look there. That's where you'll find the truth.

The heaviness she felt was just where Marlowe had put his hand when he'd told her those words. She ignored it and forced herself to continue. "I should not wish to dishonor myself."

Mrs. Inkberry's kindly face beamed with approval and relief. "Very wise of you, Emma. Very wise and sensible."

"Yes," she said dully. "I know."

"There is a maneuver, dear, that a woman can use to defend herself if a man gets fresh with her. A well-placed blow with one's knee. I taught it to my daughters. Would you like me to show it to you as well?"

"Thank you, Mrs. Inkberry, but that won't be necessary," she said and gulped down the rest of her tea.

It wasn't necessary because she had no intention of allowing Marlowe to get fresh with her ever again. No matter how it made her feel when he did.

As his carriage rolled away, Harry stood on the sidewalk of Little Russell Street in the shadows of dusk, a paper-wrapped bundle of books tied with twine dangling from his fingers. He stared at Emma's building, but he didn't cross the street to go in. He could see by the light in the window that there were several ladies in the parlor, and though Emma was not among them, he could not enter the building without being seen. He glanced up at the lighted front windows of Emma's flat and saw her pass by one of them, then he looked again at the parlor, trying to figure out a way in.

Only a few months ago, if someone had told him he'd be skulking about outside Miss Emmaline Dove's rooms, aching with lust, he'd have called that person demented. But he hadn't known then how enticing a slender redhead with freckles could be. He hadn't known how much passion lurked beneath his former secretary's reserved, maidenly exterior and how intoxicating it was to bring it out. Now he knew, and it was torture. Sweet, painful torture.

He set the books he'd bought for her on the pavement and leaned back against the brick wall of the building opposite hers. For the hundredth time in the past few hours, he thought about that kiss. He remembered every detail of it: the soft, sweet yielding of her mouth, the feel of her arms around his neck pulling him closer, the heat of her body as she'd moved against him with the awkwardness of inexperience, making him realize she'd never been kissed before. But the thing he remembered most vividly was her face afterward. Though she hadn't been smiling, her face had shone with so much astonished pleasure it had taken his breath away. Never in his life had he seen a woman look so radiantly beautiful. It had taken every ounce of strength he possessed to let her go and walk away.

He'd waited for her to follow him out of that room, lingering amid volumes of Byron and Shelley and other dead poets, for what had seemed an eternity. Instead of Emma, however, a maid had appeared, informing him that the mistress of the house required him to leave. He'd known the reason at once, of course. They'd been seen, and from the maid's message, he could discern who had seen them.

He remembered what Emma had said, that Mrs. Inkberry had been her Aunt Lydia's friend, and he could well imagine what sort of shameful lectures she'd received after his departure. He glanced again at the window. Knowing Emma, she was probably filling herself with reproaches and recriminations at this very moment. He'd never known a woman more smothered in rules. He suspected her aunt and her father could take the credit for that.

He, of course, was no good at rules. He wanted to kiss her again, and again, and again. One taste of her mouth was acting upon him like an opiate, for now he craved her kisses like an addict. That was why he stood here, filled with thoroughly dishonorable intentions, trying to find a way to get up to her flat. He hoped that once he was there, she'd put all those rules aside and give him kisses and a great deal more.

Once he was in her rooms, he thought he had a fair chance of bringing her around to his way of thinking on the topic. Her propriety was a shell; underneath it, she was soft as butter. She wanted him, and he knew he could use that desire, use his experience against her innocence to pleasure them both. First he'd drug her with kisses as she had drugged him. Then he'd take her down on that exotic Turkish carpet she had, rid her of any nonsensical ideas in her head about what men and women were supposed to do, and show her what they really did.

Two grenadier matrons crossed his line of vision. They gave Harry and his expensive, finely tailored clothes a long, curious study as they passed by. He glanced around and saw that a group of boys playing marbles on the corner had stopped their game and were also staring at him with curiosity. He knew he couldn't stand here, in this enclave of bobbin lace curtains and working-class respectability, much longer without drawing even more attention.

Hell with it, he thought. *Who cares what anybody thinks?*

He straightened away from the wall, picked up the books, and started across to her front door, then stopped in the middle of the street for no reason whatsoever.

With an oath, he changed direction and walked to the group of boys playing marbles on the corner. A few minutes later, one of those boys was sixpence richer, Emma had the complete set of Burton's *The Book of the Thousand Nights and a Night*, and Harry was on his way home in a hansom cab, wondering if he was the one who was demented.

Chapter 15

Give me a kiss, and to that kiss a score; Then to that twenty, add a hundred more.

Robert Herrick, 1648

Aunt Lydia would have returned the books. Her father would have burned them. Emma kept them.

She didn't even waver over the decision to do so, a fact which rather surprised her. Even more surprising, she chose to display the salacious collection on the bookshelf in her parlor, where she had a perfect view of them from her desk. She could look at them to her heart's content while she attempted to write about proper decorum. Perhaps it was hypocrisy of a sort, but every time she looked up from her work and saw the bright red covers of those books, they made her smile, a secret delight she could hug to herself and savor whenever she wished.

She was a rebel, after all, it seemed. Like her inclination to curse when she was frustrated or her indulgence in too much chocolate when she was sad, those books were a tiny rebellion against the strict confines of her upbringing. Marlowe's kiss, however, was a different matter. Allowing it had been a far more dangerous form of rebellion than a few curse words or a set of notorious books.

Mrs. Inkberry had been right to remind her of the fragility of a woman's virtue, and the consequences a woman suffered if she lost it. Yet every time Emma thought of Marlowe and what had happened in the bookshop, a dark, hot longing stirred in her soul, another secret delight, but one she could not afford to savor. Whenever she felt it well up from deep within, Emma strove to suppress it, reminding herself that no good could come of romantic notions about a man who would never give a woman the honor of his name.

They had taken to corresponding about her work through couriers of late, but when she received a note from him requesting that they resume their meetings in person, she was certain sufficient time had passed for her resolve to once again be strong. Nearly two weeks had passed since he'd kissed her in Inkberry's bookshop, and that amount of time was surely long enough to regain one's self-possession and curb one's more wanton thoughts and impulses.

But late Wednesday afternoon when she walked into his office, she knew she had been utterly and completely wrong. As his secretary announced her, he turned from the window to look at her, and his smile pierced her heart, bringing back all the sweet, painful pleasure she'd felt the moment his lips had touched hers. When their gazes met, her dark, secret hunger was in his eyes, too, and she knew all her efforts had been for naught. That kiss had created an intimacy between them that would forever exist. Twenty years could pass, and it would not matter. The moment she saw him again, she would still feel this brief, heartrending pang of joy.

Her steps faltered, and she stopped still several feet from the chair opposite his desk, one hand tightly clenched around the handle of her sturdy leather dispatch case. She couldn't seem to move, couldn't seem to take another step. "Hullo," she said.

"Emma." His smile widened, and the pleasure inside her became unbearable. She lowered her gaze, but she found that did not help her, for peeking above the breast pocket of his dark blue jacket was the unmistakable pink edge of the thank-you note she'd sent him for the books. She bit her lip.

"Will that be all, sir?"

The sound of the secretary's voice, so ordinary, broke the spell. Marlowe looked past her. "Yes, thank you, Quinn."

The secretary departed, and Emma walked the few remaining feet to Marlowe's desk. She sat down, set her dispatch case by her feet, and tried to remember the real reason she was here. "Shall we go over revisions, my lord?" she asked, striving to sound brisk and businesslike, acutely aware of the open door into the outer office, knowing the man sitting at her former desk could hear their conversation. "Are they so very extensive?"

"No. Why do you ask?"

She didn't tell him it was because while writing them she'd spent far too much time staring at a shelf full of red leather books and trying to put him and his kiss out of her mind. "I thought that was why you wanted to meet in person."

He glanced at the open door behind her, then leaned forward and murmured in a low voice, "I wanted to meet in person because I wanted to see you."

Her pleasure welled up and spilled over into a smile. "Oh."

He pulled a sheaf of papers in front of him. "But since you asked, I do have a few things." He began flipping through the pages. "You tended to go on too long about blanc mange. Your piece on the history of chocolate sounds too much like a teacher's lesson. You need to spice it up more. If you need help with that, I'd be happy to assist."

Emma sucked in her breath, and he paused, looking up with an innocent air. "Something wrong?"

"No." She cleared her throat. "Not at all. What else?"

He returned his attention to sheets in front of him. "I think that's all. Except that in the instructions for how to make a caramel sauce, you forgot the sugar."

"I did?"

He nodded, smiling. "Had trouble concentrating, did you?"

Emma wasn't going to admit that for anything. She held out her hand. "Let me see."

He handed over her articles, and she saw that she had, indeed, forgotten the most important ingredient in her recipe for caramel sauce, and despite Marlowe's assurance that her revisions weren't too extensive, she discovered the error in the caramel sauce recipe was only one of many. The pages seemed covered with his corrections and comments.

Heavens, she thought with dismay, if she continued to be in this much of a muddle, her writing career was in serious jeopardy.

A slight cough sounded from behind her. She and Marlowe both glanced at the doorway and saw Quinn standing there.

"I have finished my duties for the day, sir, and it is now past six o'clock," the young man said. "Is there anything else you require before I depart?"

"No, Quinn, you may go."

"Very good, sir. If that is all, I shall bid you good evening." The secretary bowed and departed, and a few moments later, Emma heard the outer door to the suite close. She and Marlowe were alone.

"I'll start making these changes tonight," she said hastily, bending to shove the papers into her dispatch case. "Did you read through my outlines?"

"Yes." He reached for another sheaf of papers. "They seem quite acceptable, but there was one thing I wanted to ask you about." He began flipping through pages. "Give me a moment, and I'll find it."

She watched him from beneath the wide brim of her straw bonnet as he searched through the pages of her outline. A lock of his dark hair fell over his brow, and he absently shoved it back, only to have it fall again. She wanted to reach across and touch it, curl it in her fingers. She wanted to press her mouth to his mouth. She wanted—

"Here it is," he said, tapping his finger against a line of text. "What is fan language?"

She took a deep breath, shoving thoughts of kissing him firmly out of her mind. "Oh, it's something my aunt told me about when I was a girl. Since I decided to do a piece about fans, I thought it would be amusing to include it."

He looked up. "But what is it?"

"Supposedly, women in former days used fans to communicate covert messages to young men in whom they had romantic interest. A woman might wish for a particular man to ask her to dance, for example, or indicate that she desires to make his acquaintance, and she would use specific gestures with her fan to tell him so."

"Gestures? I don't know what you mean." He

stood up and came around to her side of the desk. "Show me."

"What, right this minute?"

"Yes. Have you a fan with you?"

"Of course." She reached into her pocket and pulled out her summer fan of ivory-and-willow-green-striped silk. "I always carry a fan in summer."

"Excellent." He gestured to her to stand up. "I don't understand this fan language business, and I want to see these gestures for myself."

Emma rose from her chair. After thinking for a moment, she gestured to the other side of the room. "Go over there and stand in the doorway," she told him. When he had complied, she went on, "Pretend we're at a ball and—"

"I can't do it," he interrupted her. "I can't pretend we're at a ball when you're wearing that monstrosity of a hat."

"It is not a monstrosity!" she shot back, then immediately touched a hand to her bonnet. "What's wrong with it?"

"Everything. Why women put all those feathers on their hats nowadays is incomprehensible to me. You look like you have an ostrich's backside on top of your head. Besides, the brim's so wide, unless you're looking up at me, I can't see your face, and I like looking at your face. Take it off."

This male criticism of her best bonnet, a bonnet that had required a shilling's worth of feathers to make it over in the current fashion, was completely forgiven with his admission about her face. Emma tucked the fan back in her pocket, and with both hands free, she pulled out her hat pin, took off her hat, and laid both accessories on the desk. Then she once again pulled out her fan. "Now, as I was saying, pretend we're at a ball. You've just come in, and though we've never met, I've seen you, and I like the look of you."

"We don't have to pretend that part," he said, slanting her a grin that was too self-satisfied for words. "You did call me handsome, remember?"

She gave him a frown of mock sternness in return. "Pay attention," she ordered and opened the fan wide. "You observe how I am holding it, in my left hand, in front of my face, looking at you over the top? That means I desire to make your acquaintance."

He tilted his head, studying her across the room. "If you were holding it in your right hand, it would mean something different?"

"Yes, that would mean I wanted you to follow me. At which point, I would exit the room, and you would come after me."

He gave her a dubious look. "People really did this? You're not making it up?"

Emma laughed. "I accused my aunt of that very thing. I told her that if you wanted to convey secret messages, a fan hardly served the purpose, since everyone else would see and understand what you were saying. But she was most insistent that she and her friends talked to men this way at balls and parties."

He shook his head. "I don't believe it. Men

would never go along with this sort of thing. It's too complicated, and too subtle. How would any man know you were communicating with him and not simply using the fan for its intended purpose? What you've shown me is too easy for a man to misunderstand. We prefer direct, specific communication."

"Yes, but women are not allowed to be direct. If I wanted to meet you, I couldn't just walk over to you and introduce myself."

"More's the pity. I can safely speak for men everywhere when I say we'd adore it if women would do that very thing."

"I daresay you would, but that's not the way it's done. You know that as well as I do. Of course, I could inquire of my friends if they knew you and could perform an introduction, but I might not wish to be even that obvious. Gossip does get about."

"God forbid society should ever allow a woman to do something in a straightforward fashion. All right, then, let's assume I've correctly interpreted your signal that you wish to meet me." He started across the room toward her. "And since I have a strong passion for women with red hair, I most definitely want to meet you."

Emma caught her breath in surprise, and her hand tightened around the fan in her grasp. "You prefer women with black hair."

He halted in front of her and lifted one hand to the side of her face. His eyes met hers as he began to twirl a loose tendril of her hair around his fingers. "I'm changing my mind."

His knuckles brushed against her cheek, and he tucked the strand of hair behind her ear. Her body began to tingle at the feather-light contact.

"Have you changed yours, Emma?"

He'd asked her something. She blinked. "What?"

"You said you didn't like me," he reminded her, his fingertips lightly tracing the curve of her ear, making her shiver. "You said I was dissolute."

"You are." Unfortunately, that fact didn't seem to have much effect on her dazed senses. She closed her eyes and tried to remind herself of her conversation with Mrs. Inkberry, but thinking about her virtue didn't help much, either.

His hand curved around the back of her neck. His palm was warm against her nape, his thumb caressed her jaw. "But do you still dislike me?"

"I never disliked you."

He made a sound of disbelief that caused her to open her eyes. "I know that's what I said, and when I said it I thought it to be true, but it wasn't. Not really. I disapproved of you, yes, and I resented you because I felt you didn't give my writing the chance it deserved. And there's no doubt you took me completely for granted when I was your secretary. I hated that, and it's something I won't ever let you do again. But as hard as I tried to dislike you, I never really could." She swallowed hard. "Every time I become thoroughly exasperated with you, you manage to get around me somehow. Soften me up or say just the right thing or make me laugh."

He smiled. "Perhaps that's because, despite my flaws, I'm a very likable fellow. Charming, witty, modest . . ."

She laughed. She couldn't help it. He *was* charming, and she had always been well aware of it, though she hadn't always appreciated it as she did now.

But none of that meant she could let him take advantage of her. When his hand tightened at her neck and he leaned toward her, she snapped the fan closed, bringing it between them, pressing it to her mouth before his lips could touch hers. He straightened and let her go. "Is that a signal of some sort?"

She nodded and lowered the fan so that she could reply. "It means I don't trust you."

"Emma!" He looked at her, obviously pretending to be offended. He put a hand on her waist. "You don't trust me?"

She shoved his hand away. "Not one little bit."

"You really do like to make my life difficult these days, don't you?"

Her smile widened. "It has a certain appeal, yes."

"Enjoy it now, for I will get my revenge. Now, where were we?" He frowned as if thinking about it. "Ah, yes, I've correctly interpreted your signal that you wanted to meet me. Let's suppose well-meaning friends have introduced us. So, the next step is clear." He bowed to her. "Miss Dove, may I have this dance?"

"We can't dance. There's no music."

"This is our enchanted moment. Don't spoil it

with trivialities." He took up her gloved hand in his bare one and put his other hand on her waist. "We can sing the music."

"I don't sing," she said even as she shoved her fan in her pocket and lifted her left hand to his shoulder in preparation for a dance. "When I was a little girl, I heard the vicar tell my father I couldn't carry a tune in a milk pail. My father told me to mouth the hymns in church silently from then on." She paused, surprised that the memory of that incident so long ago still had the power to sting. She tried to shrug it off with a smile. "The congregation was grateful, no doubt."

Marlowe didn't smile back at her, and oddly enough, his sudden gravity made him seem more handsome than ever before. "Sing as loud as you please, Emma. I don't give a damn if you sound like a corncrake."

That sting was suddenly in her eyes and she blinked rapidly, looking away. Tightness squeezed her chest. "Thank you, but I think it would be best if you did any singing required."

"Very well." He swayed back and forth, pulling her with him as he counted, "And two, and three, and four." With that, they started to dance and he began to sing one of Gilbert's nonsensical Bab Ballads in a rollicking baritone. "Strike the concertina's melancholy string; blow the spirit-stirring harp like anything—"

She burst into laughter, interrupting the song, but he didn't miss a step. *"The Story of Prince*

Agib?" she asked as he continued to lead her in a waltz about the room.

"Yes, well, given your love of the *Arabian Nights*, it seemed appropriate."

He hummed a few more bars as they danced, but then, for no reason she could identify, they both came to a stop. She stared up into his face, and in the sudden silence, everything else in the world seemed to fade away into insignificance. Everything but him.

He let go of her hand and once again curved his hand around the back of her neck. "I don't believe there's any such thing as fan language," he murmured. "It'd be too easy for a chap to misinterpret things. For instance, when you put that fan to your lips, you said it means you don't trust me, but I think it means something else."

"You do?"

He nodded and began rubbing the back of her neck just above the collar of her shirtwaist, his fingertips stirring her hair. "I think it means you want me to kiss you."

"That's not what it means!" She stirred in his hold, but she knew this attempt to escape was halfhearted at best. He seemed to know it, too, for he ignored it. His fingers caressed her nape in slow circles, and waves of warmth began flooding through her body, a feeling that compelled her to make some sort of protest. "I was not telling you to kiss me."

"How's a man to be sure? That's my point. You couldn't just take pity on the poor, muddled chap and say straight out, 'I want you to kiss me.' That wouldn't do." He stopped caressing her neck and slid his hand up to entwine his fingers in the knot of her hair. He tilted her head back, but instead of kissing her, he paused, his lips only a few inches from hers. "A lady would never say something like that, would she?"

"No." Emma licked her dry lips. "She wouldn't."

The palm of his other hand flattened against her back, pulling her fully against him, causing her to suck in a startled breath at the hard feel of his body pressed so intimately against hers. "I don't want to misunderstand things, Emma, because then you might slap my face and call me a cad. So, how does a lady use her fan to tell a man he can kiss her?"

"I don't know," she whispered. "My aunt didn't tell me that one."

"Damn." His lashes lowered, then lifted. "I suppose I shall just have to take my chances."

He kissed her then, and at the touch of his mouth, she felt any shred of resolve she had left crumbling into bits. Along with it went all of Mrs. Inkberry's well-intended caution, and her arms came up around his neck.

His tongue touched her lips, and she knew what he wanted. With a sound of accord, she opened her mouth, and he deepened the kiss at once, his tongue touching hers. The carnal ache she'd felt in the bookshop rose up again, quicker this time, hotter. When he pulled his tongue

back, she followed. It was a move of pure instinct, not conscious thought, and it amazed her
that within her was this bold, lascivious creature who put her tongue inside a man's mouth
and liked it.

He tasted warm and tangy, rather like the
strawberries they'd had in the Victoria Embankment Gardens, and she wondered if he'd eaten
strawberries at luncheon today. She pressed her
hands to the sides of his face, as if to hold him
there, and he went utterly still while she explored
this new, foreign territory. She touched her tongue
to his again, ran it over the straight, hard line of
his teeth, brushed it against the insides of each of
his cheeks. She paused only long enough for a
quick breath of air, then traced his lips with her
tongue. Above and below the edges of his mouth,
she felt the texture of his face, different this time,
and she realized he had shaved not long ago. She
took his lower lip between both of hers and
pulled, sucking gently.

He made a smothered sound against her
mouth and a shudder rocked his body. Emma
knew it was because of what she'd done. He was
feeling the same things she felt. Oh, the thrill of
that! To know that she, a plain spinster of thirty,
could make a man like him feel like this. It was
power, potent, quixotic, glorious power.

He didn't let her keep it, though. He captured
her mouth fully with his and turned them both,
using his body to push hers backward a step or
two. The backs of her thighs hit something hard,

and she realized it was his desk. He slid his hands down to cup her buttocks, and she jerked with a yelp of pure shock, opening her eyes.

His opened as well, and for one split second they stood there, gazes locked, rapid breaths mingling. Then she felt his hands tighten, and he lifted her onto the edge of the desk.

"You've been telling me all these rules," he said between ragged breaths, "but they're all women's rules." He pulled his hands from beneath her. Still looking into her eyes, he lifted his hands to the top button of her shirtwaist.

She stiffened and her hand closed over his wrist. He watched her, waiting, his eyes intensely blue, his mouth gravely beautiful, his fingers toying with the button and her virtue.

"What—" She broke off, excitement rising within her, even as instinctive feminine caution whispered a warning. But something else was driving her, a desperate, aching need for his touch. "What are men's rules?" she whispered.

"When you tell me to stop, I'll stop." He drew a deep breath. "I swear I'll stop."

It was the unsteadiness of his voice that disarmed her. She relaxed her hold on his wrist and gave a quick nod, as exhilarated by her capitulation as she was shamed by the ease of it.

She closed her eyes as he unfastened the first button of her shirtwaist, then the next, then the next, removing barriers one by one. He pushed back the linen edges and pressed his mouth to the exposed skin of her throat, licking her bare skin with his tongue. She arched against him with a moan and tilted her head back, wanting more of this sweet delight.

He blew warm breath against her skin as his fingers unfastened buttons and hooks, pulling back layers of linen, cambric, satin, and nainsook to expose the skin from her collarbone to just above her breasts. She stirred with agitation, her fingers tightening convulsively on his shoulders, as he kissed the top of one breast and worked his other hand beneath the fabrics where her undergarments were still fastened. She knew she should call a halt, but when his fingertips grazed her nipple, the sharp, piercing sweetness of it was so great, her whole body jerked with the sensation. She cried out, but she did not say stop.

He lifted his head and captured her mouth with his, smothering the echo of his name against her lips. His hand tightened at her breast, he groaned into her mouth, and he deepened the kiss. He touched her nipple again, sliding his fingers back and forth across it within the tight confines of her underclothes, and her body shuddered in response. She felt as if she had no ability to govern her own body, for his touch was causing her to move in the strangest way, arching into his hands in little twitches that she could not stop. She could hear herself making soft, queer noises against his mouth, smothered, primitive sounds, and she felt as if she were drowning in a sensuous haze. What he was doing was like nothing she'd ever felt before, and she wanted it to go on and on and on forever.

Suddenly, without warning, he broke the kiss, yanked his hand out of her bodice, and straightened away from her. Cursing under his breath, he began buttoning her back up.

Dazed, Emma tried to come to her senses. She opened her eyes and looked at him. He didn't look back at her, but kept his gaze on what he was doing. The late afternoon sunlight cast a soft glow over the room, but there was nothing soft in his face. It seemed ravaged.

"I didn't say stop," she mumbled, and her own lack of resolve frightened her.

"I know." He gave a short, harsh laugh. "God, I know."

His hands stilled, then tightened around fistfuls of fabric. Abruptly, he let go and turned away. "It's getting dark," he said over his shoulder. "I'd best escort you home. We'll ride in my carriage, and I don't give a damn if it's proper or not."

Emma didn't argue. Given what had just happened, talking about propriety seemed ludicrous now, especially when that dark, hot hunger was raging inside her, ready to flare up when he touched her again. And he would touch her again. She was only fooling herself to think she wouldn't let him.

Stop, she thought dismally. Such a simple word. And so hard to say.

Chapter 16

When one has interesting companions, there is nothing more enjoyable than social intercourse.

Mrs. Bartleby
The *Social Gazette*, 1893

Not making love to Emma was one of the hardest things Harry had ever done in his life. He was beginning to think it had also been one of the stupidest. He shifted on the carriage seat, trying to ease the stiff agony in his trousers, but it was useless, since the cause of all his discomfort was sitting right across from him, looking lusciously disheveled, her lips still puffy from his kisses.

She wasn't looking at him, thank God, but staring at that god-awful hat in her lap, plucking at the brim. Probably wondering if she was going to hell.

The carriage bumped. He grimaced and shifted on the seat again. He closed his eyes, rested his head against the back of the seat, and cursed virgins, proprieties, and the inexplicable notions of chivalry that were wont to come over him nowadays.

Tell me to stop and I'll stop.

What had he been thinking, to say something as idiotic as that? Worse, she hadn't even been the one to call a halt. He had. And why? He'd remembered where they were, that was why. He'd thought Emma's first time shouldn't happen on a desk.

Harry wanted to get out and let one of the horses give him a good, swift kick in the head. Then he wouldn't be capable of doing any more thinking.

The carriage jerked to a stop, and he drew a deep breath of relief. His driver had barely opened the door and rolled out the steps before Harry was out of the carriage and offering his hand to assist her down. He walked with her to the front steps of her building.

"Good night, Emma," he said with a bow and turned to depart.

"Would you—" She stopped and cleared her throat, gesturing to the door with her hat. "Would you like to come in?"

He felt a glimmer of hope, then snuffed it out, remembering who he was talking to.

"Why?" he asked bluntly. "Are you inviting me up to your rooms?"

She colored up at once. "No. Of course not. I just thought . . . perhaps some tea." She met his gaze. "In the parlor. Downstairs."

She wanted to have tea? He stared back at her in disbelief. "Tea?"

She nodded. "We could both do with a bit of refreshment, I daresay."

There were times when he wondered if she was real. Looking at her now, he began to think perhaps some moor spirit had taken over her body four months ago with the purpose of making his life hell. He'd probably forgotten to leave a pin in the caves at Torquay one summer, and in consequence, the pixies were after him, intent on revenge. "Maybe if you had whiskey and a siphon, I'd take you up on it. God knows, I could use a drink. Otherwise, no. I intend to go home."

If he had any sense, he'd go to a brothel.

"Mrs. Morris might have a bottle of whiskey about."

Harry studied her for a moment, and dissolute fellow that he was, he began to speculate about possibilities, reckon up the odds of getting into her flat. He could be a very persuasive fellow when he set his mind to it. After due consideration, he figured he stood a fair chance of getting up to her rooms, where he could make love to her in a bed. Making love on desks could come later. "Then I accept," he said and followed her inside.

The infamous nosy landlady, Mrs. Morris, was in the parlor, and proved delighted to meet Emma's former employer, though she was a bit flustered at the unexpected arrival of a peer of the realm. Emma should have warned her he would be accompanying her today. Though, of course, she was as accustomed as anyone to genteel company—Emma's own aunt, for example, had been a dear friend and a lady of the utmost respectability, having been married to the third son of a baronet. A cup of tea? Of course, Emma, a cup of tea for her guest was no trouble at all, unless his lordship would prefer a whiskey? And no, she insisted to his lordship, it was no bother to make a full tea with sandwiches. It was well known that gentlemen need sustenance. Of course, she would supervise the preparations herself, she assured him, and bustled out of the room to go belowstairs and see what repast could be got that was worthy of a viscount.

Emma sat down on a hideous horsehair settee and began pulling off her gloves. "Poor Mrs. Morris. A full tea, indeed. And at seven o'clock, too!"

"I'm hungry." He sat down beside her, leaned close, and pressed a kiss to one corner of her lips. "Very hungry."

"What a lot of bother you're being." The words were a criticism, but her voice had a breathless quality that caused his hopes to rise.

"That's one of privileges of being a peer. I'm allowed to be a bother." He tilted his head to kiss her mouth.

She leaned sideways, evading him. "I thought you wanted a drink."

He rested one arm along the carved wooden back of the settee behind her shoulders. "I changed my mind. If your landlady is below-stairs ensuring that her cook makes me the perfect tea, I have more time alone with you."

She glanced at the door, looking worried. "We're not alone. Someone else could come in the room at any time. Other tenants live here besides myself."

"Let's take a chance." This time he was successful in capturing her mouth for a quick kiss. "Be reckless."

"I don't take chances."

"Yes," he said ruefully. "I know."

He studied her profile, the delicate line of her jaw and chin. The room was dim in the growing twilight, but he was so close, he could see the gold tips of her lashes, the tiny star-shaped scar on her cheek, the round little mole just in front of her ear. He kissed it.

"Harry," she whispered, lifting her shoulder to nudge his chin, but he liked to think it was a halfhearted gesture.

"I'm keeping an eye on the door," he promised, his lips brushing her cheek. "I don't suppose I can close the blasted thing?"

"Heavens, no!"

She sounded so horrified, he would have laughed had the situation not been so damnable. "Since I can't close the door and ravish you as I'd like," he murmured, "I shall have to settle for conversation."

She leaned back, realized his arm was behind her, and hunched forward.

"Emma, relax," he said gently and removed

his arm from the back of the settee. "Lean back, close your eyes."

She complied, and he did the same. "So," he said, "what shall we talk about? The weather? The Queen's health? How you're driving me mad?"

"Why did you stop?" she whispered.

He turned his head, but she wasn't looking at him. She was staring up at the ceiling. He leaned closer and spoke in a low voice near her ear. "I had this idiotic idea that I probably shouldn't deflower a virgin on top of my desk."

Color flamed in her face, but she still didn't look at him. "I would not have been able to stop you. I would not have had the strength."

That took him back. "God, Emma, I would never force you."

"That isn't what I meant. I thought I should say stop, once, while you were . . . umm . . ." She paused and gave a little cough. "But then I couldn't say it." There was a note of surprise in her voice. "I just couldn't form the word."

"Because it felt so good?"

There was a long silence before she answered. "Yes."

He brushed his knuckles along her cheek. It was so soft, like velvet against the back of his hand. "So many ways I could make you feel good," he murmured, thinking out loud, desire rising within him. "It's become my favorite pastime of late, thinking about how I'd make love to you, Emma."

She pressed against the settee behind her,

sinking into the cushion at her back as if she wanted it to swallow her up.

Being an optimist, Harry took that as encouragement. After all, she was free to stand up and walk away, but she hadn't done so. "How I'd take down your hair first and let it slide through my hands. All that long, pretty red hair. How I'd unbutton your shirtwaist and slide it off your shoulders. How I'd take off your skirt." His throat went dry, and he had to stop a moment. "You see?" he said after a moment. "I've imagined it all, step by step."

She made a wordless sound of surprise, and he could tell she was unnerved by the knowledge that he'd been having fantasies about her.

"The corset cover and petticoat would be the next to go," he went on. "Which reminds me . . . from the brief, tantalizing glimpse I had earlier, I have to tell you that your underwear is much too plain, Emma. I'd like to see you in absurd little camisoles of silk with pearl buttons on them. That's pure selfishness on my part, though. I'm partial to pearl buttons because they come undone so easily. Next, I'd strip you out of your corset—"

"Stop talking about my undergarments," she whispered, the rosy blush in her face spreading down over her face and neck. "It isn't . . ." She wet her lips. "It isn't decorous."

"Decorous?" He laughed softly. "Emma, when he's taking off a woman's clothes, a man doesn't feel decorous. Neither does she if he's doing it right. Besides, we're just talking, making conversation." He nuzzled her ear. "Having social intercourse, you might say."

She made a choked sound.

"I'd be kissing you the entire time. Your lips, your throat, your bare shoulders—"

"Oh, stop!" Her voice was a soft wail, so low he barely heard her. "Please stop."

"Why?"

"It's embarrassing!"

"Is it?" He eased back and made an open-handed gesture to the doorway. "If you don't wish to hear it, then leave."

She didn't move. "Mrs. Morris has gone to a great deal of trouble. Leaving would be rude."

"It would also prevent you from hearing what I'd do next." He ran his finger along her jaw, watched it quiver. He touched her mouth. "You do want to know what's next, don't you?"

She made a tiny sound of denial against his finger, but she still didn't leave. Didn't even move to the chintz chair opposite. She pressed her lips together against his caress, and went still.

"I think now I'd have to stop undressing you for a bit and just touch you." He touched his hand to the nape of her neck, and she jumped as if shocked by a jolt of electricity. "I'd run my hands over your shoulders and down your bare arms," he told her, feeling lust overtaking him with each word. "I'd touch your breasts, your belly, your hips, through your chemise and drawers—"

She made an inarticulate sound of shock.

"Is that what you have on?" Harry brushed the

side of her neck with his lips. "Or a combination, perhaps? I've imagined stripping you out of both, of course, but which do you usually wear?"

She didn't answer, and he nipped the taut tendons of her neck, feeling her shiver in response. "Emma, Emma, tell me," he coaxed against her skin, "so I can imagine it when I'm not with you. A chemise and drawers?"

She didn't move.

"A combination, then?"

Her stiff little nod confirmed that, and he continued, "I'd leave that on for now."

"You would?" The moment the words were out of her mouth, she bit her lip, still not looking at him.

"I have to," he explained. "I can't get you out of it without taking off your shoes first."

"Oh." It was a hushed sound.

"Since you've got on a pair of plain walking shoes today, and not those ugly, high-button things you usually wear—"

She interrupted with a sound of indignation. "I don't wear ugly shoes!"

Since most of her shoes were hideous, he ignored that bit of nonsense. "Just now, I'm fully occupied with the luscious task of removing your garters, so we won't argue the point, but I'm going to buy you some pretty shoes, Miss Dove, at the first opportunity. Dozens of 'em, frivolous, frippery little slippers of velvet and brocade. Now, don't interrupt again, if you please. Interrupting is rude, you know. So, now that I've got your shoes off, I have to remove your stockings—"

It was not Emma who interrupted, but the sound of footsteps on the stairs. Harry groaned and pulled back, and the moment he did, Emma scooted sideways, as far from him as she could get without abandoning the settee altogether. Another hopeful sign. He drew several deep breaths, forcing down his arousal.

Mrs. Morris entered the room with the tea tray. A maid in print dress and cap followed with a second tray, this one laden with food.

"Put it there, Dorcas," the landlady ordered as she set her tray on the tea table opposite the settee and took one of the chintz chairs that flanked it. The maid deposited the tray of sandwiches and cakes on the table in front of Emma and Harry, gave a curtsy, and departed.

"I say," Harry said, leaning forward and trying to look properly grateful for food when he was ravaged with lust, "this is the prettiest tea I've seen in ages. And on the spur of the moment, too. Your tenants are so fortunate to have you."

Mrs. Morris simpered as she began to pour the tea. "Not all my tenants eat in, my lord, but for those who do, I flatter myself that I set a good table with proper food."

He glanced at Emma, but she was looking away, paying no attention to either of them. The blush had receded from her complexion, leaving her skin once again as pale as milk. "Does Miss Dove eat in?" he asked, returning his attention to the woman opposite.

"She didn't too often, sir, when she worked for you. She had some late hours, then, she did.

But now that she is the secretary to that wonderful Mrs. Bartleby, typing up her manuscripts for her, well, she eats most all her meals in."

Harry leaned forward and reached for a seedcake from the tray on the table and ate it as he tried to think of some excuse, any excuse, to get the woman out of the room.

"Sugar?" Mrs. Morris asked as she poured him a cup of tea. "Milk?"

"Neither, thank you, but perhaps . . ." He paused, frowning a little, scanning the tea tray as if searching for something.

"Yes, my lord?" The landlady leaned forward in her chair, terribly eager to please. "Was there something else you wanted?"

Harry gave her a deprecating little smile. "No, no, I don't wish you to go to any further trouble on my account."

"It would be no trouble," she assured him. "No trouble at all."

"I was hoping you might, perhaps, have some lemon?"

"Lemon?" She glanced at the tray, then back at him, giving an awkward laugh. "Why, how silly of Hoskins not to have provided it! I shall bring it at once."

"How kind you are." He gave her his very best smile. "And so thoughtful."

Beside him, Emma made a sound of exasperation.

Mrs. Morris didn't seem to notice. She fluttered like a debutante, fingers lightly touching her hair as she stood up. "I shall return in a moment," she said, and left the room, once again leaving them alone.

Harry slid to Emma's side of the settee. "Now, where were we?"

"She hasn't any lemons, or she'd have brought them out along with the tea. Now she'll have to send Hoskins to the costermonger on the corner."

"I hope she goes herself. It'll give me more time to get you naked." He silenced her protest with a kiss. "I believe I was removing your stockings. Since your legs are so long and lovely, I'd have to take heaps of time over this part. I'd slide them down one at a time, slowly, so very slowly. I'd pull them off your pretty feet, then I'd caress your ankles and your calves and the backs of your knees. God, how I'd love to caress the backs of your knees." Imagining it, he felt the thick heaviness of lust overtaking his body, and he knew he couldn't endure much more of this. He opened his eyes.

She was staring at him, her eyes round as saucers, her lips parted.

He decided he could endure a little more. He tilted his head to kiss the velvety skin of her ear. "I think it's time for me to take off that combination of yours," he murmured. "I want to see your breasts."

She made a squeak of protest. "You couldn't see my—" She stopped, then tried again to speak. "It would be dark!"

"Make love to you in the dark? That would be a sin, Emma. No, I'd have to have light so that I could see you." His words, whispered against her ear, were making her shiver. "So I could look at you while I touched you, so I could see my hands on you."

Tortuous as it was, his strategy was working, for he could hear her breath coming in quick little huffs. His own breathing was none too steady, either. "I've imagined your breasts in my mind a hundred times, Emma." He closed his eyes again, punctuating his words with kisses, his body on fire. "A thousand times." His voice cracked, and he could feel his control slipping irretrievably away.

He strove to retain it just a little longer. "I'd caress your breasts over and over, kiss them." He drew her earlobe into his mouth, scored her skin ever so lightly with his teeth. "Suckle them."

She inhaled a deep, shuddering gasp, shoved aside his hand before he could stop her, and bolted. But she didn't run for the door. Instead, she went to the window, flung up the sash, and began taking deep breaths of the sultry evening air.

He moved to rise and follow her, but just then he could hear Mrs. Morris's footsteps coming up the stairs for the second time. Damn, he'd forgotten all about the woman. He sank back down, his body in agony. Quick as lightning, he unbuttoned his jacket, jerked it off, draped in the most casual manner possible over his hips. He was just reaching for a bite of food from the tray as Mrs. Morris reentered the room.

"Here we are," she said brightly. "My apologies, your lordship, but it took my cook forever to find the lemons. In the very back of the larder, they were."

Her gaze skimmed past Harry, who was eating a cucumber sandwich and trying desperately to appear complacent, to where Emma was standing by the window, sucking in great gulps of air and cooling herself rapidly with the fan. "Emma, are you unwell?" she asked with a frown of concern.

"I'm perfectly well," Emma said in a strangled voice, fanning faster. "It's just . . . it's just so hot in this room."

"It is warm," the landlady agreed as she sat back down. "Quite sensible of you to open the window, dear." She set the plate of lemon wedges on the tray and looked at Harry, smiling. "Emma is always sensible. Such a sweet, steady young woman. Her Aunt Lydia was a dear friend of mine. . . ."

He'd wager Emma wasn't feeling either sweet or steady at the present moment. As for himself, Harry knew he was an unholy mess. Arousal was coursing through every cell of his body, his heart was thudding in his chest like a runaway train, and he was painfully aware—for the second time this evening—of having a full erection and no relief in sight.

He watched Mrs. Morris pour him a cup of tea, but for the life of him, he could not manage any more of the polite, inane conversation required.

"Mrs. Morris, forgive me," he interrupted her praises of that dear, departed paragon, Aunt Lydia, and glanced at Emma, who was still standing by the window, fanning herself. "I fear that Miss Dove is quite overheated. I can hardly think tea—being a hot beverage, you understand—is quite the thing for her. Perhaps a glass of water?"

"I don't need a glass of water," Emma said from the other side of the room.

"You do look a bit piqued, dear," Mrs. Morris said. "Perhaps water would be a good idea."

Harry gave an emphatic nod, and when the landlady walked to the door, he followed her. They paused in the doorway, Harry leaning close to whisper a few words. Her mouth opened in stupefaction, but she did as he bade, going out and closing the door behind her.

Emma frowned as Harry came to her side. She glanced past him to the closed door, then back to him again. "What did you say to her?" she demanded.

"I'm not a patient man, Emma, and any patience I do have is utterly gone. I told her I wanted a moment alone with you, and asked her to give us some privacy."

Emma groaned and put her face in her hands. "There's only one honorable reason an unmarried man asks to speak with an unmarried woman alone, and that's to propose," she mumbled. Lifting her head, she scowled at him. "And we both know," she added in a fierce whisper, "that any proposal made by you would be a thoroughly dishonorable one."

"We don't have much time." He pulled her into his arms and played his last card. "Take me upstairs to your rooms," he said, and began pressing kisses to her face. "Let's make love and end this torture."

"We can't!" she moaned. "Mrs. Morris would see. She would know."

"I'll send her on an errand. I'll climb your fire escape." He was running out of options; arousal and desperation were clawing at him. "I'll pay her to stay silent."

He knew those words were a mistake the moment they were out of his mouth.

"Money buys anything, does it?" She jerked out of his embrace. "Mrs. Morris is a kind, thoroughly respectable woman. She wouldn't take your money. She wouldn't give a wink and a nod, and look the other way. And even if she did, it wouldn't matter. I should still have to see her afterward."

"What of it? You wouldn't have a scarlet letter branded on your chest, if that's what you're afraid of!"

"Don't you understand? She was a friend of my aunt. She knows me. I would have to face her every day, and she and I would both know I was . . . w-w-was—" Her voice wobbled a little. "That I was unchaste."

"For God's sake, Emma, she isn't your friend. She was your aunt's friend. And you wouldn't have to face her if you didn't wish to. You can move. I'll get you a new flat. Better yet, I'll get you a house."

"Like Juliette Bordeaux?" She looked at him, her gaze becoming scornful. "Shall I get a topaz and diamond necklace, too, a few months from now, purchased by your secretary, along with a note of farewell delivered by your footman?"

He felt as if he'd been slapped. "It isn't the same thing."

"Isn't it? What makes it different?" She folded her arms. "I am not a cancan dancer in a music hall. I deserve to be courted in honorable fashion or not at all!"

He should have known this was coming. "You want me to marry you, is that it?"

She looked so appalled, he would have been insulted if he weren't so relieved.

"Marry you?" she cried. "Heavens, no!" Her gaze raked over him with a disapproval worthy of her sainted aunt. "No woman with sense would marry you. You're the poorest prospect for matrimony I've ever met."

"Quite so. I'm glad we've got that straight."

"And, damn it all, Harry, I don't wish to marry anyway. Why should I? I've quite a successful career. I'm Mrs. Bartleby."

"You're not Mrs. Bartleby," he shot back before he could stop himself. "Your Aunt Lydia is Mrs. Bartleby."

"That's not true! The ideas I put in my articles are mine."

"Some of the ideas are yours, I grant you, like that origami business and the napkin rings, but the *voice* isn't you. I've published enough writing in my life to know! You're not Mrs. Bartleby, fussing about rules like some middle-aged matron." He threw some of her own writings in her face to prove his point. "You don't really believe girls shouldn't eat any part of the chicken but the wing.

You don't really believe girls shouldn't eat quail or cheese and that they should only select the plainest dishes on the menu."

"Rules of conduct are important, for young ladies especially!"

"Not if the rules are silly, and making poor girls starve themselves on wings of chicken and plain pudding is silly! It defies common sense. Being a sensible person, Emma, you know that as well as I do. Why do you write about rules you don't really believe in?"

Her eyes narrowed, and he saw his chances of getting her into bed diminishing, but he was so frustrated, he almost didn't care. "You're not Mrs. Bartleby. You're not Aunt Lydia. You're Emma." He grabbed her shoulders and gave her a little shake, wishing he could shake some sense into her stubborn brain. "You swear and you read naughty books. You're passionate and warm and the sweetest thing I've ever tasted. And I don't think you really believe I was wrong to divorce my wife, and I don't think you disapprove of me nearly as much as you think you ought. If you did, you would never have agreed to come back and write for me. And I know damn well you don't believe kissing me is wrong."

"If two people are not married nor engaged to be married, it is wrong! It is!" She tried to jerk free, but he wouldn't let her go.

"Why? Because of what you've been told, but it's not what you *feel*. And I've known that since the day I kissed you in that bookshop, because I saw your face afterward. God, Emma, it was radiant, your face, all lit up from the inside like sunshine. It was the most beautiful thing I've ever seen. And tonight you didn't believe it was wrong when I touched you, or you would have stopped me. When I said those things earlier, you could have told me to leave. You could have slapped my face. You could have dressed me down in spades, but you didn't. You wanted me to say those things. You wanted to hear them. You did, Emma, you know you did."

"It was wrong of me to listen to any of this." She clamped her hands over her ears. "But I won't listen anymore."

"You will, by God." He grasped her wrists, pulled them down, held them in a hard grip. "The woman I kissed in that bookshop and in my office wasn't thinking about proprieties. She was just feeling it, taking it in like oxygen. That woman kissed me the way every woman ought to kiss a man."

"You've kissed enough women to know."

He ignored that. "Why can't you be honest about what you really think and how you really feel? Where is Emma? What happened to her? What happened to the little girl who liked rolling in the mud and singing off-key?"

Her face twisted, and she made a choked sound like a sob.

He knew he was hurting her, but he was driven to say these things, for he was at the end of his tether. "I'll tell you what happened to her. She's been stifled and smothered by people and their opinions her entire life."

"Who are you to criticize my family? You never met any of them, you don't know anything about them!"

"I know all I care to know, thank you. But they didn't succeed in snuffing Emma out completely, did they? There are times when she breaks through, and when she does, Lord, she's so lovely she makes me ache with wanting her."

She sagged and all the fight went out of her. "Go away," she said. "Please, just go away."

"You've called me insincere, Emma, but it's you who lies. You lie to yourself. You push aside what you want to do in favor of what you should do. You ignore what you really think-in favor of what you ought to think. You are dishonest in your own heart, and that's the worst dishonesty there is. You're so damned concerned about being a lady. Why can't you just allow yourself to be a woman?"

He freed her hands, but before she could turn away, he cupped her face in one hand, wrapped an arm around her waist, and kissed her.

She didn't respond, but stood limp in his embrace, not fighting, but not responding either. That did something to him, cracked him right through the center, and he felt himself coming apart. He kissed her harder, inflamed by lust and anger and complete frustration.

A tear rolled over his fingers. It burned like acid.

"Christ!" He shoved her back and let go of her, violence roiling within him. For weeks, he'd been panting over her like a puling adolescent, and for what? So that she could make him feel like a beggar or a brute? He had to get quit of her. Now. For good and all.

He raked his hands through his hair, straightened his clothes, tried to speak in a civilized fashion when he wanted to break something. "I won't touch you again," he said, crossing to the settee to retrieve his coat. "Ever. We'll put the wall of propriety back up between us and resume being indifferent acquaintances." Even as he said it, he knew what a joke that notion was. He took a deep breath.

"On second thought," he amended, "I think it would be best if we don't meet in person about your work anymore. We'll go back to conducting our discussions through written correspondence and couriers."

He turned and walked toward the door. "That way, your precious virtue remains intact," he fired over his shoulder, "and I'll regain my sanity."

He opened the door of the parlor, not surprised to find Mrs. Morris hovering on the other side. Red-faced, she straightened away from the keyhole. Harry bowed and walked past her without a word, wondering why Emma gave a damn about the opinion of a woman who eavesdropped on private conversations and spied through keyholes. In fact, there were a lot of things Emma gave a damn about that he didn't understand.

He walked out the front door and slammed it behind him hard enough to rattle the windowpanes. Women of virtue were a pain in the ass.

Chapter 17

Being good all the time is a very bad bargain.

Miss Emmaline Dove, 1893

It was starting to rain. From her position on the chair beside her desk, Emma stared through the open French window that gave onto her fire escape, watching the long curtains stir in the storm's breeze. She didn't know how long Harry had been gone, but to her, a lifetime had passed. Her lifetime. As the clock had ticked away the minutes and chimed the hours, remembrances had run through her mind one after another.

White dresses with mud on them, and Mama's placating voice making excuses to Papa about why Emma's best Sunday dress was muddy *again*.

Mouthing hymns in church, trying not to sing out loud and offend God's ears.

Having her hair cut . . . the scent of a burned book . . . Papa at the other end of the dinner table and a month of cold silence.

She touched her cheek, and felt her throat closing up until she couldn't breathe. By sheer will, she forced her father out of her mind and thought of Auntie instead. That was better. She began to breathe again. Auntie had been capable of showing affection. Auntie had never gone days without speaking to her. Auntie, she knew beyond doubt, had loved her.

But there were memories of sitting up straight, and reminders to wear gloves, and not to run, and not to become overwrought, and to always be nice. Waltzes are one foot apart. Dessert forks go above the dinner plate. Handkerchiefs are never starched. Gentlemen have animal spirits. People don't kiss unless they're married or engaged.

Harry's words came back to her, words that hurt because they were true. *Mrs. Bartleby isn't you. She's your Aunt Lydia. . . . Where is Emma? What happened to her? What happened to the little girl who liked rolling in the mud and singing off-key?*

She knew what had happened. In exchange for affection and approval, she had paid the price of losing herself, bit by bit, in thousands of tiny, imperceptible pieces taken out of her over many years, until she had become a woman half starved and half smothered and only half alive.

And then Harry had kissed her and everything had changed. She had come awake at that moment, as if after a long winter's sleep. Afraid, yes, but so awake and alive—in every fiber of her being and every cell of her brain and every whisper of her soul. Yet tonight she had thrown all of that aside and reached instead for the smothering safeness of what was familiar and approved.

She closed her eyes and breathed deep, thinking of the things he'd done to her in his office and the shocking things he'd said he wanted to do. Just thinking of it all made her whole body fiery with shame and excitement.

Take me upstairs.

She would have, God help her, a lifetime of virtue melted away in the scorching heat of a man's erotic, illicit promises, if she hadn't known her landlady was eavesdropping on the other side of the door, hoping against hope a proposal of marriage was in the offing for dear Lydia's niece.

Emma had a sudden, absurd desire to laugh. How shocked Mrs. Morris must have been to overhear the truth—that the viscount had been making a proposal of a very different sort, and how dismayed she must have been to learn that dear Lydia's niece was in truth a carnal, fleshly hedonist who had relished every word he'd said. Even the painful words that were brutal, blunt, and true.

Where's Emma? What happened to her?

A wave of resentment flared up within her against all the things she had been denied, resentment against all the people whose love she wanted or whose approval she craved. Resentment against herself for waiting so long to discover how rich life truly was, how exhilarating it was to take risks and how luscious a man's kisses and caresses could be. For throwing it all away out of fear.

Too late now. Emma turned her head and looked at the vase of peacock feathers by her desk, her birthday consolation prize. Once again, she had waited until it was too late.

Being good all the time was a bad bargain.

Emma jumped to her feet and caught up her reticule from the desk, pulling out her latchkey and verifying she had enough coins for a hansom. She blew out the lamp, but though she closed the French window, she deliberately left it unlocked. She went out the front door of her flat, locked the door behind her, and dropped her latchkey into her bag.

She ducked down the back stairs unseen, out to the alley, and into the pouring rain. In her haste, she'd forgotten to don a mackintosh, get an umbrella, or even put on a bonnet, but that couldn't be helped. She wasn't going back.

Emma ran out of the alley, pausing at the corner. She rubbed a hand over her wet face and glanced up and down the dark, empty, rain-drenched street. Not a cab in sight.

There were always hansom cabs by the Holborn Hotel, and she headed in that direction, her steps quickening to a run. Dodging traffic at the corners, she ran all five blocks without stopping, coming to a breathless halt beside the first available hansom. "Fourteen Hanover Square," she told the driver, her words coming in gasps. "And there's an extra half crown for you if we get there in a half hour or less."

She jumped inside, and the cab jerked into motion. Emma drummed her fingers against her knees, tapped her feet, and kept changing her position on the seat as the minutes clicked by. The hansom seemed to crawl toward Mayfair by inches, and just as she'd known would happen, caution and doubt had time to whisper to her.

She didn't even know if he was home. He was probably out. At his club. Or with some music hall dancer. What would his servants think when she came waltzing in asking to see him? What if he didn't want her anymore? What if she was making the biggest mistake of her life?

She shoved doubts and cautions aside. Tonight she intended to become an unchaste woman. Emma pressed a hand to what Harry called her guts. She didn't feel she was making a mistake. She didn't feel sinful. She felt . . . crazy, wild. She felt like herself for the very first time.

Her tummy was quivering with excitement and fear. Her body ached with longing. This cab ride was taking forever.

She opened the window and stuck her head out, blinking against the drops of rain that hit her face. They were nearly to Regent Street. Hanover Square wasn't far now.

Still, it seemed another eternity before the hansom turned into Hanover Square and stopped before number 14. She didn't verify the time, but gave the driver the extra half crown along with the fare just because she felt like it, then she jumped out of the hansom and raced for Harry's front door, praying that for once in her life, she wasn't too late. She grabbed the bellpull and gave it a hard yank.

Chimes sounded within, and moments later a footman opened the door. He stared at her in amazement. "Yes, miss?"

"I've come to see Marlowe," she said, walking right in as if she paid calls on the viscount's household every day of the week. "Is his lordship at home this evening?"

The servant looked her up and down, askance. "I . . . I am not certain, miss. I shall inquire. What name shall I say?"

"Tell him . . ." She thought a moment, wondering wildly what the etiquette was in these circumstances. Her own name was clearly out of the question, as was her pseudonym. "Tell him Scheherazade is here to see him."

The footman frowned as if not thinking her quite right in the head, but he departed, leaving her standing in the foyer.

There was a long mirror on the wall opposite, placed to reflect the light from the windows that flanked the front door, and Emma walked toward it, laughing under her breath.

Heavens, she looked a fright. Small wonder that footman had stared at her in such amazement. Her skirt clung to her hips, and the soaking wet linen of her shirtwaist clearly showed the layers of undergarments beneath. Her hair had come down, and her combs were long gone, lost in her race for the hansom, no doubt. She hadn't even noticed at the time. Tendrils of her loose hair were plastered to the sides of her face, while the rest hung in a sodden tangle down her back. She was dripping water all over the golden terrazzo floor.

Emma's lips curved in a rueful smile. Clearly she wasn't at all versed in seduction. Any woman who possessed such a skill would have taken more pains with her appearance before showing up at a man's door, especially when he'd vowed never to see her again. She toyed with her hair, combing it through her fingers, trying to put the tangled strands in some sort of order, but it was useless.

"Emma?"

At the sound of his voice, she met her own eyes in the mirror. *No going back now, Emma,* she thought, as she drew her shoulders back and turned toward the wide, curving staircase to her right.

He was standing on the bottom step, one hand on the elaborately carved wrought-iron railing, and the sight of him jangled her nerves even more, for she hadn't expected him to be in a partial state of undress. He was clad only in dark trousers and a claret-red dressing gown. He wasn't even wearing a shirt, and she could see the vee of his bare chest between the edges of his dressing gown. Her heart began to race.

He looked at her without expression, his lean,

handsome face giving nothing away. No easy smile, no teasing words. "I thought we agreed we weren't going to see each other again."

"There was no agreement. You decided. I decided . . . something different." She grasped handfuls of her sodden skirt and started toward him. "Harry, I have to talk to you."

He glanced up and down her body as she approached. "My God, you're soaked to the skin."

"I had to run five blocks to get a cab. After you left, I thought about what you said. All of it."

He turned his face away, looked at his hand, watched his own fist open and close over the black pineapple filial atop the newel post. Then he looked at her. "You shouldn't be here, Emma. My valet, a footman, and I are the only ones in the house. Most of the servants have gone to Marlowe Park. The rest have gone with my family to Torquay."

Now that she'd decided to give her chastity away, she wanted to get on with it, but she didn't quite know how to set about it. "Yes, I know, but this is important." She glanced at the footman who hovered nearby. "Is there somewhere we could speak privately?"

He rubbed a hand over his face. "Lord, we wouldn't want anything to be easy today, would we?" Heaving a sigh, he turned and gestured to the staircase. "Come on."

He led her up the stairs to the drawing room. Once they were inside, he reached for the bell-pull. "I'll have Garrett light a fire."

"No, no. I don't need a fire. I'm not cold. It's

August. And besides, after all those things you told me, how could I be cold? I feel as if I'm on fire."

He looked at her for a moment, then he closed the door, leaned back against it, and folded his arms over his chest. "What do you want to talk to me about? I thought we both said a great deal already this evening. What more is there to say?"

"I want to tell you a story."

He stirred against the door, clearly impatient with this. He unfolded his arms. "You came here at this hour in the pouring rain to tell me a story?"

She nodded and began to laugh. "Yes. Crazy, isn't it?"

"Emma—"

"It all started with this peacock fan. This big, extravagant peacock fan. It was so expensive, and so impractical, but it was gorgeous and exotic and I wanted it so very desperately. I dithered for days, going back to that shop several times, but I could never bring myself to buy it. It cost two guineas, Harry. Two! You know how I am."

That made him almost smile. Almost. "Miserly."

"Frugal."

"Whatever you say."

"Anyway, the day you told me you wouldn't publish my new manuscript was my birthday, and—"

"Your birthday? I didn't know. You should have told me."

"I never expected you to know my birthday. I

know how you are about things like that. And besides, no employer knows his secretary's birthday. Anyway, I was so angry with you because you didn't know who Mrs. Bartleby was, and I thought you hadn't read any of my work, and I was going to resign my post, but by the time I was halfway home, I had talked myself out of it. I do that, talk myself out of things I want because they are impractical or frivolous or improper."

"Yes, and unless I've gone completely off my onion, we had an argument on that very topic earlier this evening."

Emma persevered. "I decided to go and buy that fan as a birthday present to myself, so I went to that shop, but when I got there, another woman was buying it. She was just a girl, a young, pretty girl in her first season, and she was taking the fan to a ball. I had waited too long, you see, and lost my chance to buy it. And right there, in that shop, I suddenly saw the whole history of my life laid out, with me making the same choices over and over, choices that were good, safe, sensible, respectable. Waiting for Mr. Parker to propose, waiting to buy that fan, waiting for you to publish my writing, when I knew in my guts you'd keep rejecting it."

She took a step closer to him, then another. "The point is, all my life I've hung back, never going after what I really wanted, trying to be content with settling for less. Meanwhile, life went on all around me, but I was never really a part of it. That's what spurred me to resign my post."

She stopped in front of him. "You see, when I watched that girl walking out the door with my peacock fan, I thought to myself that was only right. After all, it was the springtime of her life, and my own springtime had passed me by years before. I let it happen. I let it slip away. I've let so many beautiful things slip through my fingers in my life because I've been afraid. I don't want this to be one of those times."

She touched him, cupped his face in her hands. "I want what I missed, Harry. I want my springtime."

He straightened and unfolded his arms. Grasping her wrists, he pulled her hands down, holding them in a hard grip. "Let's get this clear. What, exactly, are you trying to tell me?"

"I want you to make love to me. Is that clear enough?"

He didn't look happy about it. His mouth turned down with an almost sulky curve. "You know I'll never marry again."

"I didn't ask you to marry me."

"This means an illicit affair. Are you sure that's what you want?"

Emma took a deep breath and tossed aside thirty years of being a good girl. "Yes, Harry. That is what I want."

Chapter 18

Many people have called me crazy. There are times when I believe they're right.

Lord Marlowe
The Bachelor's Guide, 1893

Harry knew he'd finally gone mad. He knew this because Emma Dove was standing in his drawing room, propositioning him. A few hours ago, that had been about as likely a possibility as pigs flying and Liberals winning an election. He had to be having delusions.

Even so, he was seeing Emma standing in front of him in provocative disarray, her hair down and her wet clothing clinging to her body. He'd just heard her offer him an affair. It didn't really matter if this was all some crazy dream.

He was going to get her upstairs and naked before he woke up.

"Come on, then," he said and grabbed her hand. He picked up the nearest lamp, led her out of the drawing room and up to his bedchamber. Once inside, he closed the door and set the lamp on his dressing table, then he reached into a drawer of the table and pulled out the small red velvet envelope he kept there. He could feel Emma's gaze on him as he laid the envelope on his pillow. When he turned toward her, she was looking at the envelope with curiosity.

"What is that?" she asked.

Now was not the time to explain such precautions. "I'll explain later."

She nodded, an expression of such infinite trust on her sweet, freckled face, and he was seized with sudden, inexplicable doubt.

"You're sure about this?" he asked, cursing himself for this last pang of conscience. "You don't want to change your mind? Once it's done, it can't be undone, Emma."

"I know." She took his hands in hers. "Remember all those things you told me earlier you wanted to do to me?" When he nodded, she went on, "Good, because now I want you to do them, Harry. Every single one of them."

She lifted his hands, bringing them to her breasts, and with that, he was lost. He opened his palms, embracing the shape of her even through layers of fabric. Arousal began spreading through him like a slow, warm ache.

He pushed her wet hair back from her shoulders and began to unfasten her shirtwaist, just as he'd imagined doing so many times, but the reality was proving a different thing entirely from anything he'd conjured in his imagination, and Harry couldn't help a low chuckle.

"Why are you laughing?"

"All the times I'd imagined doing this, I never thought it was going to be hell to undo the buttons. They're cloth-covered and damp. Now I know I'm going to buy those pearl buttons for you."

She laughed, too, but it sounded nervous. "I can do this, if—"

"Not a chance of it. This is my fun, and you'll not deprive me of it. Just unfasten the cuffs."

She complied, and once both of them had completed their tasks, he was able to slip off her shirtwaist. Pulling it out of the waistband of her skirt, he tossed it onto the floor nearby, then reached for the first button of her corset cover and began the task all over again. When that was done and he was able to slide the second garment from her shoulders, he knew that even if he had to wade through a thousand more buttons, it would be worth it.

Her shoulders were dusted with plenty of golden freckles for him to kiss. They faded more and more as his gaze moved down, however, until by the edge of her corset, her skin was pure white. Harry traced his fingers across her bare shoulders, over her collarbone, and down her arms. The texture of her was like warm silk, and he wanted to linger, but arousal was already overtaking him, and he knew he'd have to come back for more of this sweetness later. He had more clothes to get rid of first.

He undid the buttons at the back of her skirt, and the heavy, sodden wool fell to the floor around her ankles in a heavy whoosh. "Step out of it," he told her, and she did, shoving it out from under her feet as he lifted his hands to the edge of her corset, finding the first hook amid the ruched tucks. He unfastened hooks one by one as he pressed kisses along her shoulder.

Strands of her hair tickled his cheek as he turned his head to kiss the base of her throat. Her pulse was hammering against his mouth. *Only a few more buttons to go,* he thought with relief as the corset fell away and he began to unfasten her combination. Soon he'd be touching nothing but her bare skin.

Emma, however, as she was wont to do nowadays, confounded him. She grasped his wrists and pulled his hands down, stopping him. He lifted his head and looked at her.

"This isn't fair," she told him. "I mean . . ." Her voice trailed away, and she frowned, looking down. "Don't I—" She stopped again.

Harry had a pretty clear notion of what she'd been about to ask, but he wanted her to say it. "Don't you what?" he prompted.

She fingered the sash. "Don't I get to undress you, too?" she whispered.

"Do you want to?"

She nodded, staring at his chest. "Yes. Yes, I do."

He spread his arms wide. "Go on, then. To-night's all about what you want." He grinned. "I'll teach you all the things I want some other time."

Emma untied the sash, then grasped the facings of his dressing gown. She slid the heavy silk back from his shoulders and it fell behind him to the floor. She stepped back a little and stared at his chest, but after a few moments he couldn't stand it. "Touch me, Emma," he said hoarsely. "Touch me."

She pressed her palms flat against his chest. "I've never seen a man's body before," she said and spread her hands over his pectorals. "Other than statues, I mean."

Harry inhaled a sharp breath and tilted his head back as she began to explore him. She ran her hands over his chest and across his shoulders, down his arms and back up again, over his ribs and down his abdomen. Her fingertips caressed his ribs and she leaned in, pressing a kiss to his collarbone. She laughed softly, blowing warm breath against his skin. "You're beautiful."

Something hot and tight twisted in his chest, something that had nothing to do with the lust in his body. Something in the naive wonder of her voice that hit him deep down and lifted him way up and made him feel as if he were king of the earth.

She rose on her toes and kissed him, her mouth soft and lush against his, and when she touched his tongue with her own as he had taught her, the contact sent shudders of pleasure through his body. Because of her inexperience, he'd taken the lead the other times they'd kissed, but she was taking it now, and Harry found this combination of her innocence and seduction incredibly erotic. Too erotic.

When she slid her hands inside the waistband of his trousers for more explorations, he knew he'd allowed her to take the lead long enough. If he let her go on, this would be over far too soon. Quick, hot copulation had its own rewards, but he'd introduce her to that delight some other time. He had no intention of letting it happen now. More than he'd ever wanted anything in his life, he wanted Emma's first time to be beautiful, as beautiful as he could make it.

"Enough," he said and grasped her wrists. He drew her hands away.

"But you said I could do what I wanted." She dropped back onto her heels, looking so vexed he wanted to laugh.

"Exactly." He let go of her hands and knelt down, then he lifted her foot to slide off her shoe. "You wanted me to do all those things I told you about, remember? I've got a few of them yet to do. Not to mention several other delicious things I didn't get around to telling you before. So, don't argue."

He tossed her shoe aside and removed the other one. Then he pulled off her garters and slid off her stockings, just as slowly as he'd promised her. She liked having the backs of her knees touched, he realized, for when he stroked her there, she stirred with a little moan and wobbled a bit on her feet. "Oh, Harry. Oh, my."

"One of these days," he murmured, "I'm going to kiss my way up the backs of your legs and over your bottom. But right now . . ." He paused and began to unfasten her last piece of clothing. "Right now I have something else in mind."

Still on his knees, he unfastened the buttons of her combination and slid the garment off her shoulders, baring her breasts. She lifted her arms as if to cover herself, but he couldn't let her do that. He let go of her combination, and the soft lawn fabric caught at the flare of her hips as he grasped her wrists. "I told you I want to see your breasts," he reminded. "Let me see."

"They are too small," she whispered as he spread her arms wide.

They were utterly lovely. He'd known they would be.

"Small? God, Emma, they're perfect. Small, yes, and round and sweet and white, with these gorgeous pink nipples—" His throat went dry, and he just couldn't say more.

He let go of her wrists and reached up to touch her breasts. He caressed them, shaped them. He toyed with her pretty nipples, brushing his thumbs back and forth across them and rolling them between his fingers. She began to moan soft and low, and he could feel the quivers run through her body. He leaned in, cupping one breast in his palm as he opened his mouth over the other.

She cried out, and her knees gave way. He

wrapped an arm around her hips and held her upright, his tongue licking her nipple. "Like that, do you?"

"Hum . . . h . . . hum . . ."

He laughed, nipping playfully at her breast. "Was that a yes?"

She nodded, making a strangled sound that was definitely affirmative. Her hands slid into his hair, pulling as if she could draw him closer than he already was. His arm tightened around her hips, and he suckled her, just as he'd told her he would.

Her fingers worked convulsively in his hair, and she began to whimper. Agitated, she stirred in his hold, her hips instinctively trying to move, but he kept his arm firmly around her, holding her against his body to keep her still, wanting to increase her tension.

"Harry," she moaned softly. "Oh, oh, oh."

He suckled her a moment longer, then he relented. Easing back, he yanked the combination down around her ankles. She stepped out of it, and he shoved it aside, then he grasped her hips in his hands and pushed her back toward the foot of the bed. "Grab the footboard behind you," he ordered, and she did, her fingers fumbling, then curling around the brass.

Pressing slow, hot kisses to her stomach, he touched the damp brown curls at the apex of her thighs. She sucked in a deep, strangled gasp of shock, and pressed her thighs tight together. She shook her head violently in refusal, but there was no way he was going to let her get away with depriving them both of this. Even though Emma Dove was the guiltiest damned woman he'd ever met, and even though his body was on fire and his cock was aching, and even though he was shaking with the effort of holding back, there was no way in hell he was going to skip this part. "Emma, I have to do this. I have to touch you here."

"Harry, even I don't touch me here!" she wailed, making him laugh even as he felt his control slipping. "Well, except to bathe! Oh, don't!"

She jerked as he blew soft, warm breath against her curls. "Let me do this. I want it, Emma. I want it badly. I want to touch you and kiss you here. Let me."

"All right," she whispered, so softly he almost missed it. Her legs parted a little, and he moved his hand between her thighs.

It was worth it all, just to touch her here. It was like touching heaven, and he groaned with the sheer pleasure of it. She was so soft and so slick, and the scent of her was driving him wild. He stroked the crease of her sex with his knuckle, and her body began to move in instinctive response. When he touched her clitoris with his tongue, she let out a shocked cry. Letting go of the footing she smothered the sound with her hands.

Reaching up, he pulled her hands away from her mouth and curled them back around the footboard, holding his own over them, refusing to let her smother the sounds of what she was feeling. If he taught her nothing else, he was bloody well going to teach her to enjoy being pleasured without letting any of that stupid respectability she'd been stuffed with get in the way.

"Emma, Emma, let it happen," he coaxed, his lips brushing her curls. "Just feel it and let it happen."

He kissed her and licked her, and after a moment or two, she gave a little sigh as something in her seemed to relax. She began to move her hips, and he took his cue from her, pleasuring her at the pace her body demanded, faster and faster, until she was trembling all over and arching into him, until she was moving with frantic little jerks and soft, primitive cries were coming from her throat. Until she made that sweet, long wail of feminine ecstasy and her body collapsed.

He rose, catching her before she could sink to the floor, and she clung to him, panting, her breaths hot against his chest. He lifted her into his arms and carried her to the side of the bed, then laid her on the mattress, and began to pull off his shoes.

She stared up at him, wordless. No one had ever told her anything about the relations between men and women, but she thought perhaps now she knew the reason for their reticence. How could anyone explain? No words in the world could describe what Harry had just done. That building sweetness, layer upon layer, higher and higher, and then an explosion of pure bliss and all that hot, dark hunger within her was assuaged.

That wasn't all there was to it, though, for Harry was watching her, his gaze hot and intense, pinning her to the mattress of his bed. He began to unbutton his trousers, and when he pulled them down, Emma lowered her gaze and stared in utter shock.

"Good Lord," she breathed and began to understand in a vague sort of way what was going to happen next. She felt a hint of panic. "Harry?"

He tossed his trousers aside and the mattress dipped with his weight as he joined her on the bed. He opened the envelope he'd placed on his pillow earlier and pulled something out, then he shoved the red velvet packet aside, and his body came over hers. She felt the hard shape of what she had seen, felt it pushing between her legs, and she swallowed down another gulp of panic. "Harry?" she said again, feeling a sudden frantic need for reassurance.

He rested his weight on one arm, suspended above her, and she felt his hand move between her thighs, along with that hard, extended part of himself. A lock of his hair had fallen over his forehead, and his mouth was grave. He looked like a sort of dark archangel. She didn't find that very reassuring.

He touched her where he had before, just a brief caress of his fingers within the folds of her most private place as he lowered himself onto her.

"Emma, listen to me."

His voice sounded strange, strangled and harsh somehow, his breathing heavy, and her panic rose another notch. But then his free hand touched her face, and her panic receded. She turned her head and kissed his palm.

"It's going to hurt, Emma." As he spoke, his hips began moving slowly against hers and his breathing quickened even more. "There's no way around that."

As he moved, she could feel the hard part of him rubbing the place where he had kissed her moments before, and that delicious pleasure washed over her again at this strange, extraordinary new caress. She arched into him as she had done before, and the pleasure grew stronger, hotter. She moaned.

"Emma, I can't wait," he said in a hoarse whisper. "I can't hold back any longer. I just can't." He shifted his body to rest his weight on his forearms, buried his face against the side of her neck, and flexed his hips against her. That hard part of him pressed deeper onto her. *Into* her.

She wriggled beneath him, not quite liking this. He made a rough sound deep in his throat and turned his head to capture her mouth with his. He kissed her hard, and without warning, he gave a powerful thrust of his hips against hers that brought that large, stiff, jutting part of him fully inside her body.

Even though he'd warned her, Emma was shocked by the pain when only moments before there had been such pleasure. She gave a high, thin cry against his mouth, her arms tightening around him, everything in her suspended by this frozen moment of violence.

Then he was kissing her—her hair, her throat, her cheek, her mouth. His breath was warm against her skin. "Emma, Emma, it'll be all right," he said, moving on her, pushing into her the same way she had arched against his mouth earlier. "I promise it will."

The pain was already receding. "I'm all right, Harry," she whispered, moving beneath him, trying to accustom herself to this very odd thing he was doing.

His movements were quickening, his thrusts against her stronger and deeper. He seemed to go into himself, almost as if he'd forgotten about her, his eyes closed and his lips parted. She watched his face, and it made her smile, for it was clear that she was pleasing him as he had pleased her. She pushed upward, and he groaned, his arms sliding beneath her as if to pull her closer, and she smiled again, liking this more now. The pain had eased to a sort of soreness deep inside, but it was nothing like before. She pushed again, matching the way he was thrusting into her as if they were dancing.

His breathing was harsh and ragged against her hair, his hips pressing hers into the mattress with quick, urgent force, and Emma began to feel it again, that wonderful thickening pleasure that he'd given her before, building, growing hotter, stronger.

Then, suddenly, shudders rocked him, and he

let out a hoarse cry. He thrust against her one last time and went still, his body covering hers, his face buried against her neck.

She stroked him, the hard, smooth muscles of his back and the thick, silky strands of his hair. When he kissed her hair and murmured her name, she felt an overpowering wave of tenderness for him like nothing she'd ever felt in her life before.

She was a fallen woman now, she realized, but she felt no regret, no shame. Just an incredible, overpowering happiness that opened and blossomed inside her like a flower turning upward toward the sun. This was what she'd hoped for, coming here tonight. It was the happiness of being alive, of feeling vibrant and beautiful. Yes, she was a fallen woman now. Emma began to laugh out loud. How wonderful.

Chapter 19

Romance is a giddy thing. It makes one want to laugh for no reason at all. To my mind, there is nothing wrong with that.

Mrs. Bartleby
The *Social Gazette*, 1893

"**E**mma?" Harry lifted his head, listening in amazement to the sound of her laughter, the last thing in the world he would have expected. As the waves of his orgasm had faded, reality had begun to intrude. Even with his body still on top of hers, he'd started to have apprehensions. Based on his only previous experience with a virgin, he'd expected tears, recriminations, at least regret. Her completely contrary reaction was quite a surprise. He raised himself on his elbows, looking into her flushed, glowing face. "Why are you laughing?"

"I don't know. I just feel happy."

She looked it, too, smiling up at him as if he'd just handed her heaven on a plate. Relief flooded through him, relief and an overwhelming satisfaction.

She laughed again. "You look like a pirate in some operetta," she told him. "As if you've just taken the ship, plundered it, and enjoyed the spoils of your villainy."

"How apt a description." He grinned, liking the comparison, loving the fact that she had been the one to make it. "How very apt."

He kissed her, then lifted his body.

"Oh!" she murmured, clearly startled as he slipped his penis free of her. As he rolled to his back, she sat up, and though he tried to remove the condom quickly, she caught a glimpse. "What is that?" she asked.

He wadded up the bit of vulcanized rubber in his hand, not thinking a used condom at all worth seeing, especially with a virgin's blood on it. But he appreciated her curiosity, and he reached over the side of the bed, feeling around on the floor for the red velvet packet. He handed it to her.

She opened it, pulled out one of the flattened rubber devices, and stared at it. "What is it for?"

"It's to prevent you from becoming pregnant. It's called a condom."

"Oh!" Then, with a dawning awareness, "Ohhh."

Color flooded her face, and she put the condom back in the packet. She handed it to him and ducked her head, plucking at the counterpane beneath them, frowning to herself.

He tossed the envelope back on the floor. "Your aunt never told you this is how babies are made, did she?"

When Emma shook her head, he felt a spark of anger. "God, why can't people just tell their children about these things?" he muttered, and fell back into the pillows to stare at the ceiling.

"Did your father tell you, then?" she asked. "Oh, but he must have done. On your wedding day."

"Wait 'til my wedding day? God, no! My father took me aside and told me the facts of life when I was eleven years old. Just the basic scientific facts, unfortunately. I wish he'd told me more about women."

"My aunt told me nothing at all. No doubt she felt such discussions far too indelicate. I suppose you think that's silly."

"It's more than silly. It's harmful. Ignorance of this can destroy people." He thought of Consuelo, remembering well her shock, her horror, her revulsion. He'd never forget that night. How could he? She'd lashed him with it often enough afterward.

"Harry, what's wrong?"

He shoved his former wife out of his mind. "Nothing. I just think people ought to be told these things, not stupid stories of cabbage leaves and storks and God only knows what else. It would save everyone a lot of grief if people were just told the truth."

"I agree with you."

That unexpected pronouncement had him looking at her. "You do?"

"Yes. I'd like to think Auntie would have told me before my wedding night if I had ever married," she said slowly. "But I'm not sure she would have, even then."

"I'm not sure of it, either. My wife's mother never told her. It made things very unpleasant for both of us." Abruptly, he rolled his legs off the bed and stood up. He crossed the bedroom and went into his dressing room. He wrapped the condom in paper and disposed of it in the wastepaper basket, then he poured water from the pitcher into the basin and washed his hands. He took up a fresh rag, wet it, rung it out, and took it into the bedroom.

Emma was still sitting up, her arms now wrapped around her knees. She looked at him as he came back to the side of the bed. He touched her, running a hand up and down her shin. "Lie back," he instructed her, "and stretch your legs out."

She complied, weight resting on her elbows. He nudged her thighs apart. There wasn't much blood, just a smear on each thigh, but enough to remind them both of the enormity of what had happened. He wiped the blood away, and as he did, he had to ask. "Did it hurt?"

"A little."

"I'm sorry about that." He paused and glanced

up from his task. "It won't hurt again, Emma," and he could hear the fierceness in his own voice. He tempered it. "If any of this ever hurts, you have to tell me straightaway. I wouldn't hurt you for anything."

"Of course you wouldn't, Harry."

Her conviction was rather shattering, especially in light of the fact that he had just done that very thing. Harry leaned down and pressed a kiss to her stomach, then straightened and took the rag to the dressing room.

When he returned, she glanced at his groin as he approached the bed, then she looked up into his face. "I've seen statues of men in museums," she said, "and I remember one very clearly. The fig leaf had been placed over the . . . the—" She broke off, waving a hand vaguely toward his anatomy.

"Penis," he supplied the required word as he stretched out beside her.

"Yes, thank you. The fig leaf had been placed over it, as I said, but they hadn't done a very good job, because from the side, I could actually see a portion of what was beneath, and I was terribly curious. Wondering what it was, knowing that if it was hidden, it had to be interesting, I tried to get a better look."

"And?"

"My aunt caught me," she told him, sounding quite put out. She swerved her head, her indignant gaze meeting Harry's amused one. "She bustled me away and I never got a really good look."

He grinned, clasping his hands behind his head. "Look your fill."

Emma rose up on her knees, swung her hair back over her shoulders, then she sat back on her heels, studying his naked body with a thoughtful face, seeming fascinated. She tilted her head this way and that, as if his cock were some sort of mystery to be figured out.

Striving for a straight face, he said, "It's not that complicated a device, Emma."

She reached out her hand, then drew back.

"Go ahead," he invited, and the moment she touched him, his desire began to stir. He closed his eyes, savoring it as she ran her fingers over him, her touch light and exploring. His penis began to stiffen, and she felt it, for she immediately started to withdraw her hand. He prevented her, wrapping her hand around his shaft, guiding her in how to caress him. "Don't stop."

He opened his eyes and watched her face as his penis hardened in her grasp; he saw her eyes widen.

"Seeing that statue when I was a girl, I never realized . . ." She drew her hand back and stared at his erection in amazement. "I never dreamt it stands up like that."

He gave a shout of laughter. "It salutes, too," he told her.

She nudged his hip playfully with her knee. "Oh, it does not!" Then she bit her lip and met his gaze, looking doubtful. "Does it?"

He laughed again. He couldn't help it, she was the sweetest thing. He pulled another condom out of the packet on the floor, then rolled to his side and turned her around, positioning her on her side as well, with his arm beneath her and her back against his chest. Keeping the condom in his hand, he eased his penis between her thighs without entering her and began moving his hips, sliding back and forth along her opening to make her ready for him. He kissed her ear and the side of her neck, which he knew she liked, and caressed her breast with his free hand. By the time he slid his hand down over her belly and between her thighs, her breathing was quick and shallow and her feminine opening was lusciously wet. He spread her moisture over her in light, slow circles, then he deepened the touch, stroking her back and forth with the tip of his finger as he slid the condom between their bodies with his other hand and sheathed himself.

He eased the head of his penis into her from behind, then pulled back. He repeated the move several times as he caressed her in front, teasing and tormenting them both until she was uttering a frantic moan with each breath and her hips were moving in quick jerks that told him she was close to orgasm. So very close.

He entered her fully then, pushing deep. At the same time, he touched her clitoris, and she came immediately, crying out his name, her body clenching around his cock in tight, quick convulsions that brought his climax as well.

Afterward, he felt lethargy overtaking him, and he wanted to fall asleep just like this, with himself inside her. But he could not give in to that desire, for they didn't have much time. He stirred and pulled free of her. Pressing a kiss to her cheek, he said, "Emma, we have to get up. I have to get you home before first light."

She nodded, and when he rose from the bed, so did she. They dressed in silence, but he knew there were things to be discussed before he deposited her at her door. It took him less time to dress than it did her, and while she finished, he went in search of his valet.

Cummings, being an experienced gentleman's gentleman as well as a man of tact and discretion, had appreciated his master's need for privacy this evening. He had foregone his usual sleeping space in the dressing room and gone belowstairs to sleep in one of the empty servant bedrooms. Harry went in search of him, and when he found the valet, he woke him, ordering him to locate a hansom cab.

Emma was dressed by the time Harry returned to his room. When he entered, she was sitting on the edge of the bed. She rose when he came in. "Is it time?"

"Almost."

He fetched one of his mackintoshes from his dressing room. "It's still raining," he explained, holding up the heavy oilskin garment.

"Are we taking your carriage back?"

"My valet's getting a hansom for us. I thought that would be better. I don't want anyone in your street to see the insignia on my carriage."

"Not a likely occurrence at this hour. It's three o'clock in the morning."

"I don't want to take the chance. I'm much more worried about how to get you back up into your flat without anyone knowing."

"There's no need—"

"Your front doors are locked, aren't they?"

"Yes. Mrs. Morris locks up at eleven o'clock, front and back, unless one of the tenants will be coming in late, from the theater or a revue. In that case, she leaves the door unlatched and has her maid wait up to lock it after the last person has come in. But—"

"You didn't do that before you came here, I suppose? Invent some excuse to be out late?"

"No, but Harry—"

"Well, there you are. We shall have to figure out a reason why you're caught out at this hour. Girl-bachelors might be allowed to walk with unmarried gentlemen on a public street at three o'clock in the afternoon, but somehow I don't think it would be considered acceptable for them to be out with said gentlemen at three o'clock in the morning."

"That is not a problem, as I've been taking pains to try and tell you, if you would just listen. I left my window unlocked. The *French* window, mind," she went on as he continued to look at her uncomprehendingly. "The window that leads onto the fire escape. Heavens," she added, shaking her head as she looked at him, "it's a good thing I'm a sensible person and able to think of these things, or we should be in dire difficulties indeed."

She pulled the oilskin from his hands and began to unfold it. "I believe I'm going to be rather good at this illicit love affair business, Harry. Don't you agree?"

Harry made all the arrangements. He found a cottage for them in Kent, a place only two hours from London by train, but one where she assured him she was not known. To keep away any village gossip they were to be known as Mr. and Mrs. Williams, a couple who highly valued their privacy.

They would journey there on Fridays and return on Mondays, he had explained during their most recent meeting at his office, a whispered conversation his secretary couldn't overhear through the respectably open door, their secret plans fitted between his comments on her writings and her outlines of future Mrs. Bartleby articles. They would come by separate trains, he'd whispered, and would leave the same way. He'd have the cottage provisioned prior to their arrival, and cleaned during the week while they were in London. No servants would stay with them, but he assumed from all her wonderful recipes that the great Mrs. Bartleby knew how to cook? If not, he could always toast them bread and cheese over a fire.

By the time all these clandestine arrangements were made, two weeks had passed. During that fortnight, Emma discovered a new delight: anticipation. By the time her train reached the small village of Cricket Somersby, she was in a state of such giddy excitement, she could hardly contain it.

He was there on the platform waiting for her, and the moment she saw his smile, Emma's heart gave a leap. She wanted to run to him right then, but even now, away from everyone they knew, they could not be so free. He took her portmanteau, and she followed him to a waiting carriage, where he gave her bag to the driver and assisted her into the vehicle. Once both of them were seated, the driver climbed up onto the box, and they were off.

Their cottage was a two-story, stone affair with a thatched roof, fat dormers, and a front door of bright red. It was surrounded by woodland, with a brook and pond nearby. There was a kitchen garden at the back, Harry told her as he carried her portmanteau inside, and it was comfortably furnished.

Emma paused in the small foyer, but she only had time to note that to her left was a parlor and to her right a dining room before she heard her bag hit the wooden floor with a thud. She turned around and looked at him as he shut the door, and her breath caught at the purposeful expression on his face. When Harry caught her up in his arms, bent her back, and kissed her, Emma pressed a hand to the top of her head to keep her straw boater in place and hoped those comfortable furnishings included a bed.

* * *

There was a bed, a big one, with an old-fashioned oak headboard. It had a thick, horsehair mattress with a chain-spring one beneath it, and it had been provisioned with sweet-smelling linens and pillows. Mrs. Bartleby, she assured Harry, would approve of such a bed, though not, she added somewhat ruefully, what went on in it.

That particular fact, however, was one she and Harry did not discuss further, and one upon which Emma did not dwell. Because of what Mrs. Morris had overheard that evening in the parlor, the landlady knew Emma was not Mrs. Bartleby's secretary, but was instead the famous author herself. Mrs. Morris also knew there had been no proposal of marriage in the offing for dear Lydia's niece. Though delighted by Emma's celebrity and pledged to keep that fact a secret, Emma felt sure the other woman suspected the real reason for her weekend trips to do "research." But to her great relief, Mrs. Morris asked no questions and gave no lectures, and Emma tried not to care about the expression of concern on the older woman's face whenever they chanced to meet in the corridors of the lodging house.

She had no regrets about the choice she had made, and little time for worry. There were plenty of other things to occupy her attention when she was with Harry and plenty to savor when they were apart. During the next four weeks, every moment with him at their cottage was filled with fascinating discoveries and joyous adventures.

She loved watching him shave. It confounded him, but observing him as he performed this daily ritual never ceased to fascinate her. "It's so . . . well, manly," she tried to explain, earning herself a shout of laughter for her trouble.

"I should hope so," he'd said severely, when he'd stopped laughing. "Shoot me with a pistol the day I do something girlish."

"I'm serious."

"So am I," he said with emphasis as he set aside the razor and picked up a towel.

"Watching you shave is . . ." She paused, leaning against the wall next to the washstand, studying him as he wiped away shaving soap. She ran her gaze over his bare torso, the powerful muscles of his arms and shoulders, trying to find the right word. "Arousing. It arouses me."

"It does?" He stopped and looked up from the mirror to meet her gaze, a hot, hungry look in his blue eyes with which she was becoming very familiar. She loved that look. They almost always made love after he shaved.

He taught her to fish, and she loved that, too—loved standing in the shallow brook in her bare feet with her skirt tucked up around her knees and feeling the excitement of patience rewarded when she flipped the evening's dinner onto the grassy bank. Harry studied her bare legs in the water and declared fishing to be his second favorite pastime. She already appreciated full well what the first one was.

He told her things no one had ever dared tell her before, such as the reason for her monthly and what certain intimate parts of the human body were actually called—hers and his. She learned how to spit—a disgusting habit—and how to make a decent bowline knot, and how caressing the underside of his penis just beneath the head drove him absolutely wild.

He introduced her to pleasures she'd never dreamed people did together: the cool delight of making love outside in the grass at night, the tender pleasure of letting him brush out her hair, the sweet intimacy of standing side by side at the washstand with toothbrushes and powder, the cooperation of cooking eggs and bacon in their tiny kitchen, the lovely relaxation of lying in a hammock together for an afternoon nap.

The hot days of August went by. They took long walks, exploring the countryside, and sometimes they encountered another couple who also seemed to enjoy walking. Though both of them looked at least seventy years of age, whenever Harry and Emma encountered them, they were always holding hands like sweethearts.

Harry took her punting on the stream. Emma couldn't swim, but he took her in the boat despite her misgivings, assuring her the water wasn't over her head, and vowing that one day he'd teach her to swim. She vowed that would never happen, and they argued about it. Her opinions mattered to him, and they argued passionately over other things, too. Things like politics, and manners, and the value of matrimony in society, and whether Blake was a better poet than Tennyson. He made her laugh at least a dozen times a day, and she discovered she could make him laugh, too, especially when she wasn't trying. But she didn't mind that. She liked the sound of his laugh.

He taught her to play poker, and Emma made another discovery about herself that amazed her: she liked gambling. Although, as she told Harry, she couldn't ever wager for real money, a statement which earned her another accusation of being miserly. But using matches as a substitute, one match being equal to one guinea, was exciting enough for her, because it was the challenge of competing against him that she liked. Adding to her excitement was that she had an incredible amount of beginner's luck.

"I've nothing left to wager," he told her when she raised him another ten matches and she'd already taken all his others.

"That's a shame." Emma grinned at him across the card table in the parlor, giving the lie to her words. "You have to fold, then, I imagine."

"Not necessarily, Emma." He paused. "There are things to wager other than money."

Something in his voice made her start tingling all over. She glanced at her four kings, then met his eyes across the table, hers wide with deliberate innocence. "Do you have something I want?"

"Heaps of things. The question is, which one do you want the most?"

Her heart began to race with excitement, but

she didn't show it. Instead, she tried to be very blasé. "Hmm, I seem to remember you said that one day you'd kiss your way up the backs of my legs and over my bottom."

"So I did. Is that what you want?"

"More than that, Harry. I want you to kiss me all over." She smiled. "For an hour."

"An hour?" He groaned. "I'll never be able to hold out that long."

"An hour, Harry. All over. Just kissing."

"Can I touch you all over, too?"

She tilted her head, pretending to think it over. "Yes, I'll allow that. But nothing else for an hour."

"All right, all right, if you're going to be stubborn about it." He laid down his two pair.

Emma got a full hour of the most blissful kissing and caressing she'd had yet, and though he grumbled that such a long prelude was pure torture for a man, they never wagered over matches again. Best of all, she realized, was the most valuable thing she'd learned in her first month of their affair: How to admit to herself what she wanted. And how to ask for it.

Chapter 20

I have come to have a true fondness for the country.

Lord Marlowe
The Bachelor's Guide, 1893

The following weekend, Harry finally got his way and taught Emma to swim. It took some doing, however. First he tried to persuade her by pointing out it was something everyone ought to know for reasons of safety. His concern didn't seem to impress her.

"That's sweet of you, Harry," she answered, shifting beside him in the hammock to settle her cheek in the dent of his shoulder, "but unnecessary, since I'm not going anyplace where the water is over my head."

He had no intention of giving up. "This isn't at all like you. You enjoy learning new things.

Besides, you're a sensible person and refusing to learn to swim just isn't sensible."

"Sensible." She lifted her head and made a face at him. "Horrid word."

"It isn't a horrid word." He kissed her nose. "I like my sensible Emma."

She still shook her head, and he frowned at her in puzzlement. "What is the real reason for this hesitancy? Tell me. Is it that you don't trust me to teach you?"

"Of course I trust you. I just . . ." She gave an aggravated sigh as he continued to look at her, waiting for an answer. "All right, if you must know, I just don't feel comfortable with taking off my clothes outside in broad daylight."

"Wear something, a combination or some other undergarment."

"Once you're wet, that's almost like being naked."

"Yes." He gave her a leer like some villain in a comic play. "Yes, it is."

"Harry, I'm serious."

He could tell that she was and sobered at once. "Shy, are you?"

"I've always been shy. Modest, I mean. You know that."

"God, Emma, you don't still feel that way with me, do you? I've seen you naked in daylight, and I thank heaven for it, too, by the way. Every time."

"I don't mind if you see me, but someone else might see me. I'd be mortified if that happened."

"That's why you won't learn to swim?" When

she nodded, he laughed and kissed her. "Woman, why didn't you just say so straightaway? I'll teach you at night." He kissed her again. "Naked. Damn, that is such a ripping idea, I'm amazed I didn't think of it to begin with."

That night, Harry got his wish, Emma got her first swimming lesson, and when he had her floating on her back in the water, moonlight washing over her bare skin, with her lips curved in a relaxed half smile and her eyes looking up into his with absolute trust, he was heartily glad no one else had ever taught Emma Dove how to swim.

"Dogs are better."

"Are not." Emma took a blackberry out of the fruit basket that sat between them on the blanket, and popped it into her mouth.

"Are, too." Harry reached into the picnic basket, pulled out a loaf of bread, and tore off a chunk. "Dogs are friendly and loyal."

"So are cats."

He made a sound of derision as he slathered butter on bread for both of them.

"Mr. Pigeon was very friendly to you," she reminded him. "And how can you say he's not loyal? He brings me birds."

"Dead ones."

"It's the truest sign of cat loyalty."

"Emma, he coughs up balls of hair. It's disgusting. How can you possibly love any creature that coughs up hair?"

"How can you love any creature that drools?" she countered and began to eat her bread and butter. "I think I'll bring Pigeon next time so you can get to know him better."

"Absolutely not."

"He adores you already, remember?"

"For your sake, my sweet, I'd like to say the feeling is mutual, but it's not. Nothing against Mr. Pigeon, but I loathe cats."

Emma didn't respond to that, for her attention had been caught by something in the distance. "There they are again," she murmured and gestured to an elderly couple, the same pair they saw at least once every weekend. Hand in hand, they were crossing the meadow about fifty yards away. "They always walk holding hands."

"Do they?" Harry pulled a hunk of cheese and a pot of mustard out of the picnic basket. "I hadn't noticed."

"It's very romantic." She paused, struck by a thought. "We walk all the time, Harry, and we never hold hands."

"Don't we?" His voice was light. "How very British of us."

What she'd said bothered him. She could tell, though she couldn't fathom why. She thought about pushing the subject, asking him why he never held her hand, but something in his face made her decide against it. Instead, she ate the last of her bread, took another blackberry out of the fruit basket, and rolled over onto her back to stare at the clouds and sky overhead.

"Consuelo and I used to walk holding hands. It was the only remotely romantic thing we were allowed to do."

Emma froze, the blackberry poised halfway to her lips. This was only the second time in all the years she'd known him that he had ever mentioned his former wife. She ate the berry, waiting for him to say more, but he did not, and after a few moments she spoke. "How odd," she said in the most neutral tone she could manage. She rolled back onto her stomach. "Americans are usually much freer about the proprieties of courtship than we are."

"Consuelo's father was half Cuban. He was also one of those very strict, old-fashioned types, and her mother was that way, too." Harry began to pare slices of cheese off the wedge in front of him without looking at her. "We were never allowed to be alone. All our conversations were in front of others, unless we were dancing. All so respectable, so proper. The only time I was allowed to speak privately with her before we became engaged was when I asked her to marry me. And even then, her mother was right outside the door, listening at the keyhole, I'm sure."

Emma heard the contempt in his voice, and she didn't know what to say.

"After we became engaged," he continued, "we were allowed to hold hands, and we could walk ahead of the others in our party if we wished to converse privately. But how private can a conversation be when a couple is surrounded by people barely out of earshot who can see everything you're doing? And as for anything like kissing, it simply wasn't possible."

He paused and looked up. "The first time I was able to kiss Consuelo was on our wedding day."

He gave a humorless laugh. "Is it any wonder our marriage was doomed? I was passionately, madly in love with a woman—girl—I knew nothing about, and I had no chance of getting to know her. Had I had that chance, I might have seen past my own infatuation and figured out the truth. But I was so young then, so stupid. I felt something was wrong, but I was only twenty-two, in a foreign country. I didn't want to mess things up by offending her or her family. It didn't help that we were constantly swarmed by the American press. They followed us everywhere, and most of them thought I was marrying her for her money and she was marrying me because I had a title and social position. They got it half right, didn't they?"

His hands stilled. The wedge of cheese was in shreds. He looked up. "Consuelo never loved me. She was a seventeen-year-old girl who had been forced—bullied, coerced, whatever you want to call it—into marrying me by her parents. I think Estravados had me in mind for a son-in-law from the moment he met me. You see, unbeknownst to me, Consuelo was already in love with someone else, a man her family considered completely unsuitable."

Emma nodded. "Yes. Mr. Rutherford Mills. I know."

"She tried unsuccessfully to elope with him, and that was part of the reason they watched over her so carefully. They thought she'd run off with the fellow again. I wasn't worth much more than Mills at the time, but Estravados liked me. More important, I had a title and an estate, and some powerful connections, and he wanted to do business in Britain. To him, I was a far better choice for his daughter than Rutherford Mills, who had nothing to offer her."

Harry poured himself a glass of wine and downed it in one draught. "So, after a quick but carefully supervised courtship, an even quicker engagement, and a hasty society wedding, there you are with a viscount in the family, social entre in Britain, no unsuitable suitor hovering by to steal away your daughter, and everybody's happy. Everybody except Consuelo, who proceeded to spend the next four years in abject misery, blaming herself when she wasn't blaming me. I tried to make her happy. God, I tried—"

He broke off abruptly and stood up. He walked a few feet away, leaned his shoulder against a tree, and stared across the meadow, his profile to her. "But you can't make someone happy. You can't make someone love you. Frustration sets in, resentment, too. And pain, discovering that your feelings aren't reciprocated, being made to feel like a cad for wanting to make love to your own wife, realizing you've been lied to." He rubbed his hands over his face. "Consuelo and I spent four years making each other thoroughly miserable. Acting pitiful and laying blame became her weapons of choice. Avoidance, deflection, and biting wit became mine. It reached the point where we could no longer speak a civil word to each other. She kept shutting her bedroom door, and truth be told, I reached the point where I lost any desire to open it. It was hell."

"I see," Emma murmured, appreciating how lonely he must have felt in such a marriage. Loneliness was something she understood very well, and her heart ached for him.

"I didn't know she'd begun to secretly correspond with Mills. Heaps of letters, pouring out stories of woe about what a nightmare it was living in England with me, assuring him that she'd always loved him, begging him to come and save her, take her away." He paused. "Begging was one of Consuelo's favorite tactics. She begged me for a divorce. I refused."

Emma nodded with understanding. "Because of your sisters."

"Even now, ten years after I first petitioned the courts, they still suffer society's disparagement. My sisters, my mother, even my grandmother, are snubbed by many in society to this day, and it hurts them." He looked at her with a flash of defiance. "Is it any wonder I have no patience with society's rules? That I think them silly and pointless?"

She shook her head. "It's perfectly understandable."

He shrugged, his flash of anger dying as quickly as it had come. "The rest, as they say, is history. She ran off with Mills to America, and did it as publicly as possible, to give me ample grounds to divorce Consuelo for adultery and name him as co-respondent. Estravados disowned her, she and Mills went off together. Last I heard, they were in the Argentine."

"Why on earth didn't she just tell you the truth before you married?" Emma asked, baffled. "Surely there must have been some opportunity. Why did she lie and say she loved you if she didn't?"

"It's clear you never met her parents. Estravados was a formidable man, and his wife equally so. Consuelo was no match for them. She just caved in under the pressure and did what was expected of her so she wouldn't disappoint her family."

Harry met her gaze, and there was something in his eyes that hurt her, bruised her deep down. "She was trying to be a good girl, to win her family's approval. So she lied to me, and she lied to herself."

Emma sucked in her breath. That hurt, to be compared to his former wife, especially in light of all the times in her life when she'd been dishonest with herself. She got up, walked over to him, and put her arms around his waist. "I have never lied to you, Harry, and I never will," she told him. "And I'll never lie to myself again, not even to be a good girl."

"Promise?"

"I promise."

"I'm hopeless at this," Harry warned her and picked up the carving knife and fork. "I told you I always saw at the chicken," he added, eying the bird before him with doubt.

Emma moved to his side of the worktable. She pointed to the place where he should cut away the leg. "If you angle the knife this way," she added, gesturing with her hand, "you sever the joint cleanly and avoid sawing at the bone."

Harry followed her instructions. "You see," Emma said as the knife went straight between the bones with ease. "Carving's easy. You just need to know where to place the knife when you cut."

"Perhaps I have mastered this part, but what about the wings? I have to learn how to carve those." He grinned at her. "After all, that's the only part you're allowed to eat."

"I have come around to your way of thinking about chicken."

"Have you?"

"Yes. Just eating the wing for the sake of delicacy *is* silly. Besides, I like the dark meat best."

"It's a thigh, Emma," he said, laughing. "You still can't say it, can you?"

"Thigh," she said, laughing with him. "I like thighs."

"Really?" He returned his attention to his task. "I'm partial to breasts myself."

Even a month after beginning this affair, she didn't always know when he was teasing, but she did know when he was making a wicked innuendo. A different inflection came into his voice, something sultry and provocative. She leaned closer, deliberately brushing her breast against his arm. "You think breasts are the sweetest meat, do you?" she murmured, becoming aroused.

"Why, Emma Dove," he murmured and set aside the knife and fork, "are you trying to seduce me?" When he glanced at her, that special look was in his eyes, and her body began to burn in response.

"Yes." She reached for him, fingers toying with the buttons of his shirt. "Let's make love."

"Excellent notion." He kissed her. "We'll eat afterward."

She glanced at the food on the worktable, then back at him, struck by a sudden idea. "Why not do both at the same time?"

He gave a low, throaty chuckle. "Emma, Emma, how terribly dissolute you've become."

"I blame it on your influence." She reached for a grape from the fruit bowl and pressed it to his mouth. "You're the one who said food was carnal."

"So I did." He took the grape into his mouth and ate it.

She began to unbutton his shirt, but to her surprise, he stopped her. "Go up and get the packet."

She glanced around the kitchen. "You don't want to take the food upstairs?"

"Too messy. And I don't want to have to run upstairs and fetch the packet later. It would spoil the mood. Besides, once we get started, I might lose my head and forget."

A vague uneasiness rippled through her at those words, and she couldn't define why. The

precautions they took were wise, the consequences dire if they forgot to exercise them. She
went upstairs and retrieved the red velvet envelope from the bedroom, shoving the odd, uneasy feeling out of her mind.

When she reentered the kitchen, she saw that
Harry had stripped down to just his trousers
and was assembling several of the foods they'd
intended to have for dinner on a tray. She
watched as he placed bite-size chunks of bread,
chicken and cheese on the plate, along with
grapes, peach slices, and two small pots, one of
mustard and one of honey.

"Honey?" she asked dubiously.

"Honey, Emma." He gave her a wicked smile,
and pulled the spoon up out of the honey pot.
Emma stared at it, watching honey fall from the
spoon, a stream of liquid gold in the late afternoon sunlight.

"Harry," she breathed, realizing what he intended. She was so shocked, so excited, she
could hardly breathe. She licked her lips. "You
can't possibly mean to—"

"Better get undressed," he advised as he repeated the gesture with the spoon.

She watched his hand, mesmerized, lust
pouring over her, lust that was as warm and
sweet as the honey falling from the spoon. "But
honey will . . . make me all sticky," she pointed
out even as she began to unbutton her shirtwaist.

He chuckled. "Getting sticky is the whole
point, my darling. That's why, when it comes to

this sort of thing, it's best if you're already naked before you start."

She was down to nothing but her combination before she realized he was making no move to take off his trousers. Instead, he was still playing with the honey, but he was watching her. "Aren't you supposed to be naked, too?" she asked as she unfastened the buttons of her last undergarment.

"It helps a man prolong things if he keeps his trousers on, and I want this to be a long meal. I'll finish undressing a bit later."

"Oh, no, you won't." She tossed her combination on the floor with the rest of her clothes and took the spoon out of his hand. "Strip off those trousers, Harry," she ordered. "Now."

"Getting awfully bossy, aren't you?"

"Yes." She laughed, rather amazed at that discovery. Amazed at herself for standing brazenly naked in a kitchen with her lover, amazed that she was thinking up wicked things to do to him with a pot of honey and a plate of food. "I like ordering you around."

"Now I've done it," he said as he unbuttoned his trousers. "I've let you see that I'm just putty in your hands. We'll never do anything my way again."

"Hurry up." She leaned one hip against the table and lifted the spoon to her lips. "I'm starving."

She licked the honey from the spoon with a lascivious boldness that she'd never displayed during their lovemaking before, and it seemed to amaze him as much as it did her, for she saw his eyes widen. She heard him catch his breath. She began to suck on the spoon.

He groaned and slid the trousers off his hips. "I wanted this to be a seven course meal for you, but there's not a chance of it now."

"As long as I can have dessert. You know my sweet tooth." She set aside the spoon and lifted the tray of food from the table.

Naked, they both sank to their knees. Emma placed the tray on the wooden floor beside them, but she wasn't quite certain what to do next.

He showed her. Taking a chunk of bread from the tray, he dipped it in the honey and brought it to her lips. She ate it. And then, remembering what he'd done that day at Au Chocolat, she licked the honey off his fingers.

"What happened to shy, modest Emma?" he asked, pulling his fingers back and reaching for a peach slice from the tray. He dunked it in the honey.

"I told you, I don't feel shy with you. Not anymore."

He brought the fruit to her mouth, rubbed the honey across her lips. "How do you feel?"

"Beautiful." She started to eat the peach slice, but he pulled it back and kissed her mouth, sucking on her lower lip as if it were a comfit. She flattened her hands against his chest, savoring the hard muscles beneath her palms. She loved the strength in him.

Once again, he pulled back. "Lie down."

When she did, he followed, leaning over her.

He slid the fruit slowly down the column of her throat, and the feel of it on her skin sent that warm, sweet honey-lust coursing through her body. She stirred, and the feel of the smooth wooden planks against her bottom was erotic, too.

"Do you remember that day when I went with you to Covent Garden Market?" he asked.

She closed her eyes. "I remember."

"We were at the fruit stands, and you said you loved peaches. Ripe, sweet, juicy ones." He touched the peach to the tip of her breast, making her suck in a sharp breath. "You said I had an odd look on my face. Do you remember that, Emma?"

"Yes," she gasped as he began to circle her nipple with the honey-coated fruit. "Yes, I remember."

"I was imagining this."

Stunned, she opened her eyes and looked into his. "You were thinking of doing this? With me?"

He nodded and fed her the peach slice, then he reached for another, dunked it in honey, and resumed his task, rubbing the fruit round and round her nipple. The stickiness of the honey pulled at her, puckering her nipple in a way that was so unbelievably erotic, she could hardly breathe. Emma stirred again, her lust growing deeper, hotter. When he let go of the fruit and bent his head to suck it from her breast into his mouth, she jerked, her body arching into that carnal kiss. "Harry," she groaned. "Oh, God, this is so wicked."

He laughed and ate the fruit, then lifted his head. He started to reach again toward the tray, but she seized his wrist. "No, no. I told you, I'm hungry, too."

She sat up, pressing her hand against his shoulder to roll him onto his back. Then she reached to the tray. "Like salty things, do you?" she said and picked up a chunk of cheese. She dipped it in mustard and fed it to him, then followed it with a bite of chicken. After coating a peach slice with honey, she put it between her teeth, then leaned down, using her mouth to feed that to him as well.

"Mmm," he murmured, gently biting the fruit in half and taking his portion into his mouth. "I think you're good at this."

She swallowed her half of the peach slice, pretending to be doubtful. "I don't know about that, Harry. I think I need more practice."

She took another peach slice, coated it with honey, and mirrored what he had done to her, rubbing the fruit around the flat nipple of his chest. He groaned out her name, and she smiled, loving the sound of her name when he said it this way. She dropped the peach onto his chest and sucked it off as she reached down to take his penis in her hand.

She began to caress his hard shaft the way he'd taught her. His breath began coming faster, harsher, and she knew the rest of their meal was going to have to wait. With her free hand, she gently cupped his testes.

His hips jerked, and his hand tangled in the knot of her hair. "Take me inside you."

She was savoring the pleasure she was giving

him at this moment, enjoying it too much to move on. She rubbed the underside of his penis with her thumb. "But I'm still hungry."

"You're killing me," he panted, his hand tightening convulsively in her hair. "Killing me."

Never had she felt bolder, more confident than she did right now. "Do you really want to be inside me?"

"God, yes. Come on, Emma. Come on."

She didn't comply, but continued to stroke and caress him, her own excitement rising.

"Emma, for God's sake—"

"When you want something," she murmured, savoring her power, "it's polite to say please."

"Please," he said at once. "Damn it, please."

She laughed. Straddling him, she eased his penis into her, savoring the feel of him, hot and thick inside her. Tilting her head back, she began to move above him. Her hair, already loosened by his hands, tumbled free of its combs. She moved in a slow, rocking motion, teasing him.

But she wasn't the only one who could tease. She felt his hand on her tummy, and then he touched her in the sweetest place of all. She moaned.

"Like that, do you?" he asked, brushing the pad of his thumb back and forth over her clitoris. "Do you?"

"Yes," she gasped, shivering. "Yes."

As he stroked her, she could feel the rising, thickening pleasure, and she began to move faster.

"Told you this was going to be a short meal,"

he panted, thrusting up hard to meet her as his thumb caressed her.

Beyond words now, she could only nod, frantic. She pumped her hips even faster, and he matched her pace, until they both reached the peak. She came first, crying out his name as she surrendered to the pure, white-hot bliss. He followed, climaxing inside her with one last, hard thrust.

She collapsed on top of him with a groan of utter satisfaction. She felt him kiss her hair, and she smiled. He always did that afterward.

They laid there several minutes, with him still inside her, and her cheek against his shoulder. She loved the aftermath almost as much as the lovemaking. Sometimes she loved it more, for there was a special sweetness to it, something poignant and precious. Something fleeting.

She shivered suddenly, as if a cool autumn wind had just swirled through the room.

Harry wrapped his arms around her. "Cold?" he asked, his palms rubbing her back, stirring her hair.

"No." She sat up. Still straddling him, she caressed his face and smiled. "You were right, you know."

He kissed her palm. "About the short meal?"

"That, yes, but you were right about something else, too." Emma leaned down again, her hair falling all around their faces. She kissed him, tasting the lingering, sticky sweetness of peaches and honey on his mouth. "I *am* a hedonist."

Chapter 21

Holy Matrimony . . . is an honorable estate, insti-
tuted by God . . . ordained for the blessing of chil-
dren . . . as a remedy against sin, and to avoid
fornication . . . for the mutual society, help, and
comfort that the one ought to have for the other . . .

Solemnization of Matrimony
The Book of Common Prayer, 1689

The hot days of August melded into the
cooler ones of September, and Emma's affair with Harry settled both their lives into a
new routine. They had their weekly meeting every Wednesday, left London for Cricket Somersby on Friday afternoons, and returned on
Monday mornings. The frenetic, euphoric bliss
of the first month eased into something different
between them. In the second month it became

something more comfortable, something that for Emma, felt deeper and richer.

During the week, when she stayed at her flat, even falling asleep to the steady purr of her beloved cat could not ease the emptiness she felt at not having Harry sleeping beside her. In fact, her flat didn't even seem like her home anymore. It was alien to her. The cottage was her home now.

She took pains to avoid Mrs. Morris as much as possible, for every time she saw her landlady, she had the feeling the other woman knew the dishonorable things she was up to. To her credit, Mrs. Morris asked no questions, but for Emma, the secrecy became harder to bear with each passing day.

Things only got worse when she stopped by Inkberry's Bookshop one afternoon in mid-September. She'd gone there with the intention of looking for books that might spark her imagination about weddings, for she was supposed to meet with Lady Eversleigh in less than a fortnight, and she hadn't come up with a single idea she liked. Mr. Inkberry had chided her for never coming to visit anymore, and he insisted she stay and have a cup of tea with them. "Josephine would be furious with me, my dear, if I let you get away," he told her as he locked the door and turned the sign in the window to show the establishment was closed.

So she sat in the Inkberrys' parlor, just as she had done dozens of times before, but this time everything was different. She was different.

"I hope you are enjoying your new situation, Emma, dear."

She gave a start at those words. She turned her head to stare at Mrs. Inkberry and felt a blush creeping into her cheeks. "Situation?"

"Working for Mrs. Bartleby." She paused and gave Emma a pointed stare. "So much better than working for that divorced, disreputable scapegrace, Viscount Marlowe."

Emma glanced at Mr. Inkberry, remembering she had introduced him to Marlowe. He must have told his wife the name of Emma's friend. Given Marlowe's views and reputation, and the fact that he'd kissed her, and in a public place, too, it was no wonder Mrs. Inkberry was looking at her with such severity. If only she knew how many kisses there had been since then.

Emma's blush deepened, but she struggled to maintain her poise. "Yes, I am enjoying my new situation very much. My, it's awfully warm for September, isn't it?"

Her situation was that she was living a lie. More than one lie, actually. Not only was she an unmarried woman having an illicit love affair, she was not secretary to the famous Mrs. Bartleby, and she was still working for Viscount Marlowe.

A sudden wave of melancholy washed over her, and as Emma sat in the parlor of Mr. and Mrs. Inkberry, sipping tea and evading questions, she realized that there was no aspect of her life now that she could discuss with the people she had always considered her friends.

Webs of deceit were not only tangled, they were also very lonely.

At Cricket Somersby, Harry was waiting for her on the platform as usual that Friday, for he always took the earlier train so they wouldn't be seen together at Victoria Station. He took her bag and they had just turned and started for the waiting carriage when a hearty male voice called out to Harry.

"Marlowe, by all that's wonderful!"

Both of them paused, and Emma glanced over her shoulder to find a blond-haired man of about Harry's age crossing the platform toward them, smiling in greeting.

"Wait here," Harry told her in a low voice, then set down her bag and began walking toward the other man. "Weston, wonderful to see you. What on earth are you doing in this isolated little place? Did you just get off the train?"

Emma watched out of the corner of her eye, and it did not escape her notice that Harry steered the man called Weston away from her, no doubt to avoid performing an introduction. She also saw the man give her a quick, assessing glance over his shoulder.

She turned her back at once and pretended an enormous fascination with the surrounding countryside, trying not to wonder what questions Harry's friend might be asking about her. It seemed an eternity before Harry rejoined her.

He picked up her portmanteau. "Shall we go?"

She didn't look back to see if the man was watching her, but instead walked beside Harry to their hired carriage without a backward glance. "Who was that man?"

"Baron Weston. We've known each other since Harrow." He handed her bag to the driver, assisted her into the open carriage, then stepped up to sit beside her.

"Is he a close friend of yours?" Emma asked. When Harry nodded, she went on in a low voice so the driver on the box couldn't overhear, "Close enough to know I'm not one of your sisters or a cousin?"

"Yes." He glanced up as the driver mounted the box. "Walk on," he instructed.

"Did he want to know who I was?"

"No, Emma." Noting her skeptical look, he went on, "He didn't ask me a thing about you. Men have a certain code about matters of this kind."

"Don't ask and don't tell?"

"Quite so."

That seemed to be the end of it, but Emma knew what sort of woman Baron Weston took her to be, and she knew she didn't like it.

All evening she couldn't help thinking about Baron Weston, and about Mrs. Morris, and the Inkberrys, and the secretive, oppressive realities of an illicit love affair. It left her feeling rather dismal.

"You're awfully quiet tonight," he said as they washed their dinner dishes. "Are you brooding about Weston?"

"I'm not brooding," she answered as she handed him a clean, dripping-wet plate.

"Emma, he doesn't know you," Harry said as he began to dry dishes. "He doesn't know your name or anything about you. He's only down here because a horse of his is racing in the Kent Field Derby. It isn't as if he has relatives in the neighborhood. We shall probably never see him again."

"No doubt he thinks I'm some cancan dancer or actress, or some other woman of low moral character."

"Well, if that's what he thinks, he's wrong, isn't he? My feminine companionship is much more high-minded nowadays." Harry tossed aside the dish towel and stepped behind her to slide his arms around her waist. "It isn't as if Weston is going to hurt your reputation. As I said, he doesn't know you. And even if he did, I already explained that men exercise discretion in these situations. So what does it matter what he thinks?"

"It matters to me, Harry. I'm not like you, you know. I can't just shrug off other people's opinions the way you do."

She stopped washing dishes and looked up, staring out the window at the countryside, and she couldn't help thinking how limited the horizons of her life had become. She could see the future, and it hurt to know that secret weekends in the country was the most she could ever have with him.

She thought of the old couple who always

walked holding hands, and knew she'd never have that with Harry. There would be no growing old together. She thought of the red velvet packet. There would be no children with him either. Her heart suddenly felt like lead, because she knew that one day, this affair would be over, and memories of him would be all she had.

Harry's arms tightened around her waist. "There's no sense in fretting about what Weston thinks," he said and pressed a kiss to her temple, "since we can't do a thing about it anyway."

You could marry me.

The moment that thought came into her head, Emma tried to shove it out again. She'd always known Harry would never marry her or any other woman. In embarking on this affair, she'd made a fully informed choice, and in their two months together, she had never regretted it. She was happy.

Blissfully happy, she repeated to herself with firmness. She dried her hands, put her arms over his at her waist, and leaned back against the strong, reassuring wall of his chest. Happier than she'd ever been in her whole life, she thought. That was the most dismal part of it all.

Emma's mood did not lighten the following day. She had never been a talkative person by nature, but she seemed especially distracted this weekend, and Harry knew she was still upset about what had happened the afternoon before. He wouldn't change a hair on her head or a freckle on her face, but sometimes he wished she could stop being so damnably concerned about the opinions of other people.

He looked up from the contracts he was reading to glance at her sitting in bed beside him, and he noticed that although she had her lap desk across her thighs and a quill in her hand, she wasn't writing anything. Instead, she was staring off into space.

He leaned over and noticed that with the exception of a few doodles and an ink blot or two, the page was blank. "It's coming along nicely, I see."

"Hmm? What?"

"Your list of ideas for Diana. Isn't that what you were supposed to be doing tonight? Coming up with ideas for her wedding to Rathbourne?"

"Yes."

He leaned over to take another look. "Ah," he said with a nod, trying to sound enlightened. "Blank pages quite fashionable this year, are they?"

She gave a little laugh. "Goodness, I haven't written a thing."

"So I noticed. What's wrong, Emma? Are you still dwelling on that business with Weston?"

She shook her head. "No, I was just wondering about that couple."

"Which couple?"

"You know, the old man and woman we sometimes see when we're out walking."

"We didn't see them today. What's put them in your head?"

"Your sister's wedding. I was sitting here, just trying to let ideas flit through my head, and I started wondering if your sister and Rathbourne would be like that old couple years from now, if they'd walk down country lanes holding hands. And I started to imagine what those two old people were like, and if they were married. Or maybe, I thought, they're like us, living in sin on weekends in some love nest. Maybe they are the local village scandal. Maybe—"

"Listen to you," he said with a chuckle, trying to lighten her mood. "Wondering about those people, inventing things about them. You should write a novel."

"Me, write a novel?"

"Why not? You're a good writer. You could do it."

"This from the man who said when I'm writing Mrs. Bartleby, I'm writing with Aunt Lydia's voice," she reminded him ruefully.

"I was in a state of acute male frustration when I said that. I'm sorry if I hurt your feelings."

She stopped doodling on the page. "Truth usually does hurt."

"Emma—"

"I'm not hurt anymore," she assured him. "You did warn me I'd need to learn to take it on the chin. Besides, you were right. When I write Mrs. Bartleby, I do hear Auntie in my head. It's not really a problem, since I'm writing factual sorts of things. But I couldn't write fiction. I don't have my own voice."

"Yes, you do. You just have to find it, and that

takes practice. I think you should try your hand at a novel. Or short stories, if you think that would be a less overwhelming way to start."

Emma put her quill back in the inkstand and turned to set her lap desk on the floor by her bed. She blew out the candle on her bedside table. "I'm no storyteller, Harry," she said and slid down under the sheet.

"Stuff," he contradicted and put his own work aside. "Tell me a story."

She turned her head and looked at him. "What, right now?"

"Right now." He leaned back against the pillows. "Give it a go, Scheherazade."

"And if you don't like it, do I get executed at dawn?" she asked, smiling.

"The worst punishment you'd get from me is a critique, but I won't even do that, I promise. I'll just listen. In fact, I'll even help you out and start it for you. Once upon a time . . ."

She groaned. "That's so clichéd."

"Well, this is a rough draft. C'mon, now. Stop stalling. Just tell me a story."

"Oh, all right." She laid there a few moments, thinking. "Once upon a time, there was a young girl who wanted a diary."

"Good," he encouraged. "Very good. Keep going."

Emma sat up. "She was lonely, you see, and she had no one to talk to. Her mother had died five years before and she was very shy and didn't have many friends. She was thirteen years old and girls are so terribly muddled at that age. She was frightened, too, because she was bleeding every month, and didn't know why. She thought perhaps she might be dying. No one had ever told her anything."

Harry began to feel a tight, painful pinch in his chest. She wasn't making this up. He leaned back against the headboard and watched as she curled into a ball, hugging her knees to her chest.

"There was no one she could ask about things. She wasn't allowed to write to her aunt, who didn't get along with her papa. And the maid who came every day to do for them was this stout German lady, much too formidable for a painfully shy girl to talk to."

"Perfectly understandable of her to want a diary."

"Her father wouldn't give her the money for a diary—they were very poor, and he couldn't afford something frivolous like that, he said. But she wanted one so badly, she went to a barber in the village where they lived and had her hair cut short. She sold her hair, and bought herself a diary. When she got home, her papa was already gone to the pub."

The tightness in Harry's chest began to burn into rage. He couldn't afford to buy his daughter a diary, but he could go to the pub? Bastard.

"She stayed up very late that night, writing and writing and writing. Boys and pretty gowns and what her wedding would be like, all those other things girls dream about. Being a man, you probably don't know much about that."

"Ah, but I do know. I have three sisters."

"Then you understand, a little, how she felt." Emma turned her head, rested her cheek on her knee, and smiled at him. "It was wonderful for that girl. It was such a relief, to pour out all these things, all the things she thought and felt and wanted to know about life. Then her father came home and saw what she'd done. At the time, she'd known he'd be angry, but she did it anyway. After all, hair grows back, she thought, and no harm done. Her father didn't . . . quite see it that way."

Harry closed his eyes for a moment. He did not want to know where this was going. He did not want to hear it. He set his jaw and opened his eyes. "Go on."

Emma lifted her head, hand at her throat, eyes staring past him into space. "Her father had this ring," she said. "Silver, with a star design."

Harry began to feel sick. "And when he saw what she'd done, what did her father do?"

There was a long pause.

"He called her a whore for cutting off her hair, backhanded her across the face, and burned her diary. He didn't speak to her again for a month." She hugged her knees tight. "That little girl never kept a diary after that."

Harry's rage deepened and spread until it was choking him. His chest hurt. He tried to think of something to say, but not a single word could leave his lips. He was so good at nonsense talk, but no good at emotional conversations like this. And besides, God, what could a man say?

But Emma was sitting there, huddled up on

the bed in a ball, just as that young girl with the cut on her face might have done, staring at the wall behind his head and reliving what had happened to her. Harry knew he had to say something, and it had to be the right thing.

He drew a profound, shaky breath and reached out, cupping her cheek in his hand. He turned her face so that she would see him, not the past. "Emma, Emma," he chided softly, his voice as gentle as he could make it. "You say you're not a storyteller?"

She looked into his eyes, and her lower lip trembled. "I didn't make that up, Harry," she whispered.

His thumb caressed the star-shaped scar on her cheekbone. "I know."

"Then what do you mean?"

He leaned closer and kissed the tiny star. "Because if you've suffered through something like that, you have the stuff of great stories inside you, Scheherazade."

She started to cry.

"Emma, no." Harry wrapped his arms around her and pulled her down into the mattress. He caressed her hair, kissed away the tears on her cheeks, and held her in his arms until she fell asleep.

Harry blew out the candle by his bed, but he didn't sleep. He laid there in the dark, thinking two things. On the one hand, he was glad her father was dead. But on the other, he wished the bastard were still alive so he could kill him.

Chapter 22

Dearest readers, it is my sincere hope that the information I have shared with you these past six months has been both useful and entertaining to you, but alas, it is time for me to bid all of you a fond farewell.

Mrs. Bartleby
The Social Gazette, 1893

Emma sat at her desk, looking at yet another blank page, this one in her typewriting machine. Only a few more days, and she was to journey to Marlowe Park, yet she had no ideas for Lady Eversleigh. Linen napkins folded into swans for the wedding breakfast was as inspired as she had managed to be.

Mr. Pigeon was curled up in her lap, purring in his sleep. She suspected he always missed her terribly when she left him behind for the weekends, because he followed her around like a love-sick schoolboy whenever she returned. Harry was crazy. Cats were ever so much better than dogs.

She turned her attention to the stack of typed manuscript pages by the side of her machine. Her articles for the next issue were finished, but only because she had taken the subject matter from old manuscripts. That seemed to be the state of her writing nowadays. Uninspired. Harry had been right that she was giving voice to Aunt Lydia, not herself, and every day since, it had become harder and harder to care about which shop carried the best ready-made plum pudding and where one could find velvet at a reasonable price and whether or not it was *comme il faut* to shake hands at breakfast.

Harry had told her she should try her hand at a novel. Maybe she should. A hint of excitement stirred. Maybe she would do that one day. But first she had to finish this project for Harry's sister. By the time she arrived at Marlowe Park, she had to have some ideas to give the other woman for her wedding. She had made a promise, and good girls always kept their promises. Despite all the liberating exhilaration of these past two months, despite all the wild lovely joy of being naughty, Emma knew at heart she would always be a good girl.

It seemed she'd come full circle, in a way.

Emma lifted Pigeon off her lap and set him gently in the nearest chair. She walked to the window and stepped out onto the fire escape, smiling as she remembered how she'd climbed up here after that first blissful night with Harry. There had been so many other blissful days and nights since then.

She gripped the wrought-iron rail and stared down at the alley four stories below. Melancholy came over her suddenly, a feeling that seemed to plague her quite often these days. Ever since that afternoon on the train platform at Cricket Somersby when Harry couldn't introduce her to his friend.

A knock sounded on her door, and Emma stepped back inside her flat. She walked to the door and found a young boy with a package wrapped in brown paper. "Miss Emma Dove?"

"Yes."

"Delivery for you, miss."

Emma accepted the box, tipped the boy a ha'penny, and closed the door. Her heart gave a little leap at the writing on the outside. Her name and address in Harry's handwriting. She began ripping away the paper, wondering what on earth it could be.

Other than the set of Burton's *Thousand Nights and a Night*, Harry had never given her a gift before. She'd never expected any. He wasn't that sort, and besides, she'd made it clear she didn't want the sort of things he'd give some cancan dancer. Books and flowers, she'd told him once, were the only acceptable gifts a man could give a lady not his wife. Jewels, perfumes, and pretty satin slippers were not. So, when Emma pulled back the wrappings and saw the blue leather of a book cover, she wasn't surprised. But when she pulled out the book and realized what it was, her heart broke into a thousand pieces.

It was a diary.

Emma waited until half past six o'clock before going to Marlowe Publishing for her Monday meeting with Harry. By the time she arrived, Quinn had already left, she noted with relief as she came in and closed the door. She and Harry would have complete privacy, and that was necessary for what she needed to do.

Harry must have heard her close the door to the corridor, for he appeared in the doorway of his office before she had even passed Quinn's desk.

"You're late. I was worried."

She looked at him, and her heart twisted with pain. He was devastatingly handsome, as always, but it was the look of concern on his face that tore at her and made her almost change her mind. Almost. He cared for her, she knew that. But she loved him, and that shade of difference was everything.

She'd known all along, really, that this would happen. Inevitable, she supposed, that a shy spinster of thirty should fall in love with her handsome employer, that a woman who'd never been kissed in her life before would fall in love with the man whose kisses would open up her heart and feed her starved soul. It was so predictable that it was almost a cliché, and it had all been so beautiful that just thinking about it made her want to weep and laugh all at once. It also made her yearn for more. But there wasn't any more. She'd known that all along, too.

She tightened her hand around the handle of her dispatch case and walked past him into his office. "I have my Mrs. Bartleby articles for this week's issue."

He followed her, but instead of going around to his side of his desk, he stopped beside her. "What's wrong?"

She set her dispatch case on his desk and pulled out a sheaf of papers. "I don't have an outline for the following Saturday, though," she said as she put them on his desk. "I haven't had time."

A lie, when she swore she'd never lie to him.

He put his hands on her shoulders, turned her to face him, but she couldn't look at him. Not yet. "Emma, did you get the package I sent over?"

"Yes, Harry. I got it. Thank you." She tried to smile at him without meeting his eyes. "You always said you're no good at choosing presents, but that's not true. You pick wonderful presents. Don't ever let Quinn choose them for you."

"I won't, but—" His hands tightened on her shoulders. "What is this strange mood you're in? You are truly beginning to worry me. Won't you tell me what's wrong?"

She gestured to the sheaf of papers on his desk. "Those Mrs. Bartleby articles are going to be the last ones I write for you."

"What? But why?"

"I'm going to write a novel."

"Excellent! I told you that you should. But

why not continue with Mrs. Bartleby? Do you think you won't have time to do both?"

She shook her head and gently pulled herself out of his grasp, taking a few steps back. "No, that's not the reason. You were right when you said Mrs. Bartleby isn't really me. She *is* Aunt Lydia, and I'm not the same woman I was six months ago who believed everything Auntie said was the utter truth and who wanted to share that truth with everybody else. I'm different now. Because of you."

He smiled at that. "Think girls ought to be allowed to eat quail and have a second glass of wine with dinner, do you?"

"Yes, I do. I know this leaves you in a bit of a lurch, being without Mrs. Bartleby. She's so popular now. I hope it won't hurt the *Gazette* too badly."

"I don't care about that. I mean, it always hurts me to lose money, you know that. But I want you to do what you want, whatever will make you happy. I'm glad you're going to try your hand at novels, truly. I promise I won't shred you to ribbons when I edit it."

She took a deep breath. "I'm not going to write it for you, Harry."

He stared at her, uncomprehending, a frown creasing his brow. He started to say something, but she managed to speak before he could.

"I can't write for you anymore because it would hurt too much. You see, I'm in love with you."

She managed to smile at the utter astonishment on his face. "Is it really so amazing that I would fall in love with you?" she asked tenderly. "It seemed inevitable to me. Even at the very beginning, when I first came to work for you, I thought . . ." She paused and pressed a hand to her midsection. "I felt it would happen. You mentioned to me once that when I was your secretary, there was a wall between us, and you were right. I'm the one who put it there, a wall of propriety and disapproval and distance because I knew if that wall wasn't there, I'd fall in love with you and you'd break my heart. Every time a new woman came in or out of your life, every time I read one of your editorials condemning marriage, I reminded myself of all the reasons no woman with sense would ever fall for you."

"Emma, I've told you, you're not like one of those woman to me—"

"Please, Harry, don't interrupt. The truth is hard enough to say as it is, and I have to tell you the truth because it's what you taught me. To say what I really think, do what I really want, understand how I really feel. That is the greatest gift anyone has ever given me. I told you, you're better at gifts than you think." She could hear her voice starting to shake, and she knew she had to finish this quickly before she humiliated herself by falling apart in front of him. "And that's why I have to end it between us."

"End it?" He took a step toward her. "What the hell are you talking about?"

"I have to end our affair, Harry. I can't live my life this way, lying to my friends, watching your friends look at me and smirk."

"Weston never smirked at you, Emma, and you know it."

"But others will, and there will be others. You know it as well as I do. And then there's your family. I can't go to your family home this weekend, and make plans with your sister for her wedding, and face your mother and grandmother across a dinner table, all the while knowing I'm your illicit lover and we are living in sin on weekends."

"There is nothing sinful about what's between us, Emma! And I don't give a damn what the world thinks of it."

"But I do," she said gently, and when he flinched, it hurt her, too. "And that is the difference between us. Our affair has been beautiful and wonderful and I'll treasure it forever. I have no regrets, and I have no shame. But I have to end it now, while it's still beautiful, before I start making demands for more of your time, and having expectations that you'll marry me. That's when they all drive you away, you know, all those women, when they start to cling to you. I won't be one of them."

She couldn't read anything in his face because he was blurring before her eyes, and she had to leave. Now. She turned away.

"Emma, wait." He wrapped his arms around her waist, hauled her back against him. "Don't do this," he said. "Don't do this to us."

She closed her eyes, fighting back the pain. "There is no 'us,'" she said, her voice catching on a sob. "And there never can be. Not without lawful marriage."

She fought hard to hang on to her composure, knowing it just had to be long enough to get out of his arms, out the door, and out of his life. She pulled against his embrace, but he did not release her, and panic began to claw at her. "Let me go, Harry!" she cried, twisting desperately to free herself. "For pity's sake, let me go!"

Those words seemed to do the trick. With an oath, he freed her, and she ran for the door without a backward glance. He didn't try to follow her, and as she raced down the stairs, it was humiliating to realize that in coming here she had hoped he would—that in some secret part of her soul she had harbored a tiny glimmer of hope that when she ended it, he wouldn't accept her decision, that he would magically realize marriage was wonderful and right, that he would drop down on one knee, declare he loved her, too, and propose. Lord, she should write novels, she certainly had the imagination for it.

Smothering her sobs with one hand, she jumped into the hansom cab she'd kept waiting at the curb. It wasn't until the cab was out of sight of Harry's office window that she broke down. She cried, but not because she had just ended the most beautiful thing that had ever happened to her. No, she cried because he had let her do it.

Let me go, Harry.

Her words went through his mind over and over. When she'd first said them, they'd felt like a kick in the groin. Or a stab in the heart.

Now they were like the lash of a whip, flaying

him with the rhythm of the train engine through the Kent countryside. He'd gone to her flat first, thinking to find her there, but she hadn't been home, and her damned landlady had insisted she'd gone away, taking her cat with her.

He'd cabled Diana, though he'd known she hadn't gone to Marlowe Park, and his sister's answering cable had confirmed it. She wasn't in Berkshire. Hoping against hope, he went to the cottage.

She wasn't there when he arrived, and the place was like a hollow shell without her. Thinking perhaps she would come on the next day's train, he stayed the night, and her words whispered to him with each creak of the bed and each sway of the hammock, making him unable to sleep in either place. Both were so empty without her.

I'm in love with you.

He stared at the pond where he'd taught her to swim and thought of her face, so luminous in the moonlight. He stood on the bank of the stream and imagined her standing in the water with her skirts tucked up around those long, beautiful legs. He saw her naked on the kitchen floor eating peaches, and by the washstand while he shaved, and beside him while he brushed his teeth. "I love you, too," he whispered to the mirror where he saw the ghost of her reflection, hating himself because he hadn't said it sooner. Because he hadn't said it to her. Hadn't even said it to himself. Because he hadn't realized it until she was gone.

Bereft, he walked the lane, wishing he'd held

her hand when they had walked together. He ought to have done that.

I want my springtime.

Harry stopped and looked around him. Springtime had gone, and summer, too. It was autumn now, and the leaves were starting to turn. He thought of autumn days toasting bread and cheese by a fire with her. That wasn't going to happen now.

This was stupid. She wasn't coming down here. Why should she? He started to turn and go back to the cottage to pack up what little he'd brought with him, but then he stopped. Coming toward him along the lane was that elderly couple that had so captured Emma's imagination. He remained where he was, watching as they walked toward him, hand in hand as always. He nodded a greeting and so did they as they went by.

Harry looked over his shoulder. "Pardon me," he called to them.

They stopped and turned around, looking at him in inquiry.

He gave an awkward half laugh and gestured to their joined hands. "Forgive me if I'm being impertinent, but are you two married?"

They laughed and looked at each other, but it was the woman who answered. "Of course," she said. "You're married, too, Mr. . . . ahem . . . Williams." She looked at him with knowing eyes, and she gave him a wise, gentle smile. "You just haven't realized it yet."

He stared after them in astonishment as they went on their way, and just before they turned and disappeared amid the trees, he heard the man say, "They always seem so happy, those two. I hope he makes an honest woman of her soon."

Harry stood there, feeling as if the earth were shifting beneath his feet, as if everything in his world were settling into place and becoming right for the very first time.

He started walking back toward the cottage, then he broke into a run. He only had twenty minutes to catch the train back to London.

It was Sunday, and tea time in Little Russell Street. Emma sat in the parlor with Mrs. Morris, Mrs. Inkberry, and her fellow girl-bachelors and conversed on all the proper subjects. The weather, always dubious. The health of the dear, dear Queen, always a concern. Fashion, always fickle.

Gossip was exchanged, jobs of work were bemoaned, and a good quantity of crumpets were consumed, except by Emma, who didn't like gossip, who no longer had a job, and who, in the throes of heartbreak and depression, had eaten nearly a pound of chocolates the night before. Just looking at the tea tray laden with sweets made her feel a bit queasy.

They talked about dear Beatrice's upcoming wedding. Beatrice glowed with happiness, and Emma tried very hard not to feel sorry for herself. Another subject discussed was, of course, Mrs. Bartleby's public farewell, printed the day before. Everyone wanted details from Emma, but when she refused to discuss it, they thankfully dropped the subject.

She'd done the right thing, and she knew it, but that knowledge brought little comfort. She ached with missing him. The past week had been nearly unbearable, but today was the worst. It was Sunday afternoon, and she wasn't lying in a hammock with Harry taking a nap. Now, she was back to sitting in Mrs. Morris's parlor taking tea on Sunday afternoons.

She stared across the tea table to the settee, where Prudence and Maria were sitting, remembering the night Harry had whispered naughty, naughty things to her, remembering all those times at their cottage when he'd done them.

Emma averted her eyes, staring down at her teacup. She was no longer Mrs. Bartleby. She was no longer Scheherazade. She was no longer a man's lover. She was back to being ordinary Emma Dove, halfway from thirty to thirty-one, and destined for terminal spinsterhood.

She attempted to be cheerful. She had started her novel, had seven pages, in fact. But she already feared it was going to be a romantic novel, and that thought made her depressed all over again. If she were not a person of character, she thought gloomily, it might behoove her to take up strong drink as other novelists were wont to do. She stared down at her cup with distaste. Gin, she thought, seemed much more appealing than tea.

She heard the front door open, felt the sharp gust of an autumn wind at her back, but she continued to stare into her teacup, uninterested in the new arrival.

And then, she felt it. An undefinable change in the room, a stirring, feminine flutter of interest in the air. Then she heard it, a sudden silence, except for the rustling of moreen petticoats and several tiny but unmistakable sighs. Then she saw it. Across from her, Prudence Bosworth and Maria Martingale simultaneously patted their hair.

Emma turned her head and looked over her shoulder. Unbelievable as it seemed, Harry was standing in the doorway of Mrs. Morris's parlor, and at the sight of him, her heart turned over in her breast with that sweet, painful joy, then crashing pain.

She tore her gaze away, feeling a wild need to bolt from the room. She might have done it, too, if his tall, broad-shouldered frame wasn't taking up the entire damned doorway.

"Good afternoon, ladies," he said behind her, earning himself another round of fluttering feminine appreciation. "Mrs. Morris, so delightful to see you again. How well you're looking. Tea? I say, that's kind of you. I'd love a cup."

Why, oh, why has he come here? she wondered in despair and desperation as introductions began all around her.

"Miss Bosworth. Miss Martingale. Miss Cole. A pleasure to meet you. Mrs. Inkberry, how do you do? Your husband's bookshop is the finest in London."

Emma closed her eyes. He was here to try and charm her back. Dread settled into her like a knot in her tummy, for she feared if he got her alone and started talking about taking off her stockings again, she'd be lost forever.

How fragile her convictions were, for one touch, one kiss, and any pride and self-respect she possessed would be gone. She would once again be his lover, and a willing one, too, enjoying those sweet, carnal pleasures with him. In secret. Until it was over and she got a necklace and a note.

Emma felt tea splash on her fingers, and she realized her hand was shaking. She clenched it tight around her teacup, so tight it was a wonder the delicate porcelain didn't shatter.

His hands appeared in her line of vision. "You've spilled your tea, Miss Dove," he said, his voice so gentle she couldn't bear it. She watched one of his hands open over the rim of her cup, while the other closed around the edge of her saucer. He pulled at the dishes as if to take them from her, and she forced herself to relax her grip. The tea things and his hands vanished from her view.

"Ladies, as a mere man, I confess that I am not up to snuff in matters of etiquette." He put aside her cup and saucer, then his hands reappeared in her line of vision, along with a handkerchief. He bent over her chair again, and to her utter astonishment, he took one of her hands in his. There was a collective intake of shocked feminine breath as he began to blot the spilled tea from her fingers with the square of white cambric.

"In light of my ignorance on the topic, it is providential that so many members of the fair sex are present," he went on in the most ordinary tone imaginable, as if he were discussing the weather, as if touching her naked hands in this way were a perfectly acceptable thing for a man to be doing.

"My lord," she whispered and cast a wild glance around the room, dismayed at their shocked faces. "Harry, stop it!"

His voice overrode her frantic whispering. "Ladies, I beg you will clarify for me one point in particular." He tightened his grip on her fingers as she attempted to jerk free. "When a gentleman wishes to offer a lady his hand in marriage, does he go down on his knee?"

Without waiting for an answer, he sank down in front of her chair. Emma stared into those eyes as beautiful and blue as the ocean, so terribly afraid she hadn't heard him right. But there was no teasing in his face. No devastating smile. He looked gravely beautiful.

"Advise me, Emma." He lifted her hand and kissed it. "How does a man go about proposing to the woman he loves?"

There were several dreamy sighs, and one most unladylike sound halfway between a sob and a snort. The latter, Emma greatly feared, had come from herself.

All of a sudden the ladies rose in unison as if jerked by invisible strings. Amid stifled giggles and whispers, they moved toward the door of the parlor and filed out. He glanced up, waiting until they had gone, waiting until the door had closed behind them, then he looked at her again. "I want to get everything right this time around, start off on the right foot, and all that, so I've got to do this proposing business in the proper way."

She stared at him, dumbfounded. Her wits felt thick like tar. "But you aren't ever going to marry again. You've told me so. You've told everyone so. You even write editorials about it."

"I'll have to eat my words now, won't I? Serves me right for being such a cynical fellow all these years." He tilted his head to one side. "Tell me, at this point is it acceptable for the woman to dither in this fashion? Isn't she supposed to just end the poor fellow's suspense and say yes so he knows he hasn't made a thorough idiot of himself?"

"No," she choked. "He deserves to suffer until she's convinced of the depth and sincerity of his affections."

"Would a ring help?" He began patting his pockets.

"You brought an engagement ring?"

"Was I not supposed to? I hope the devil it fits," he added, still searching. "Mrs. Morris told me your ring size, but—"

"Mrs. Morris knew about this?" Emma stared at him in amazement. "She knew you were going to propose?"

He stopped searching his pockets and studied her with pity, shaking his head as if he thought her a hopeless business. "How else was I going to ascertain your ring size? You wouldn't believe the trouble she's had sneaking into your rooms to steal one of your rings for comparison. You've been moping in your flat for days, I understand."

"I have not been moping! I've been writing my novel."

"My mistake. That's what I get for listening to gossip." He resumed his search. "All I can say is it's a good thing you went out and bought chocolates yesterday. They must have been for Mr. Pigeon, though, since you're not moping. Ah!"

With a cry of triumph, he pulled out a stunning band of platinum set with emeralds. "I hope you like it. Mrs. Morris wasn't able to ring me up until yesterday to give me your ring size, but she said emeralds were your favorite. And then I had to go running up and down Bond Street all afternoon, visiting jewelers, trying to choose an emerald engagement ring." He picked up her hand and slid the ring onto her finger. "It was torture, Emma. How you can find shopping an enjoyable activity baffles me." He leaned closer, inspecting her hand. "Does it fit?"

It fit perfectly, but though she opened her mouth to tell him so, she couldn't seem to speak. She closed her mouth again, staring stupidly at the beautiful band on her finger, watching it begin to blur before her eyes. Harry wanted to marry her? She still couldn't quite take it in, couldn't quite believe it.

He heaved a sigh. "I suppose if the lady is still not persuaded, some heroic gesture on the gentleman's part is required?"

She swallowed hard and looked up, forcing herself to say something. "That would be nice," she managed, "since I never got a proper courtship in honorable fashion."

"Cruel, Emma. Very cruel." He frowned, thinking a moment, then his brow cleared. "All right. To show you how much I love you, I'll make the supreme sacrifice and let the Pigeon live with us. He can stalk the birds at Marlowe Park to his heart's content. He doesn't sleep with us, though. I will not wake up with cat hair in my mouth."

She didn't laugh. "Harry, do be serious for once."

"I do talk a lot of nonsense, I know. You were right to say I'm a glib fellow. But the thing is—" He paused and took her hands in his. He took a deep breath. "I love you. I should have said it ages ago, I know, but it's so damned hard to say the things that really matter, and falling in love with you was so gradual and so natural that I didn't really even think about it. I mean, it wasn't as if I just woke up one day and realized it. And when you told me you were ending things with us, I should have said it right then, but I was so stunned. I couldn't believe it, you see. I couldn't believe you were leaving me when I'd been thinking everything was perfect. It rattled me, Emma. It rattled me so badly, I couldn't say anything, and then you were gone."

"But do you really want to marry me? Are you sure?"

"Emma." He let go of her hands and cupped her face. He kissed her mouth. "Dearest, sweetest Emma, when you walked out of my life, did you really think I could bear to let you go?"

"Oh, Harry!" Convinced beyond doubt, she

tore her hands out of his and wrapped her arms around his neck. "I love you so!"

"And I love you." He stood up, pulling her with him, and slid his arms around her waist. "So, even though I'm dissolute and inconsiderate and I'll probably be late for the wedding, you are going to marry me?"

"Yes." She began to laugh, her joy spilling over. "Yes. I will marry you."

"Not that it really matters." He pulled back and looked into her face, brushing his knuckles along her cheek. "We're already married, you know. We just have to say the vows in church so all our friends know it, too."

"Already married? What do you mean?" She frowned at him, puzzled. "Are you teasing me again?"

He laughed. "I'll explain it to you later. Right now, I have something more important to do." He lifted her face and bent his head.

And then he kissed her.

Emma tightened her arms around his neck and returned his kiss with passionate enthusiasm. After all, it was quite proper for a man to kiss a woman once they were engaged. Everybody knew that. Even Harry.

AVON TRADE *Paperbacks*

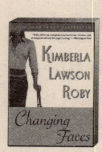